The Way Back

RLC

BALBOA.
PRESS

A DIVISION OF HAY HOUSE

Balboa Press books may be ordered through booksellers or by contacting:

Balboa Press
A Division of Hay House
1663 Liberty Drive
Bloomington, IN 47403
www.balboapress.com
1 (877) 407-4847

Print information available on the last page.

ISBN: 978-1-9822-0798-4 (sc)
ISBN: 978-1-9822-0796-0 (hc)
ISBN: 978-1-9822-0797-7 (e)

Library of Congress Control Number: 2018908088

Balboa Press rev. date: 07/06/2018

Imagine, if you will, your day starting out like any other. You know how that goes. Rushing here, rushing there, doing this, doing that. For all intents and purposes, pretty much the same as the day before and the same as the day before that for that matter. Without warning, you find yourself magically transported into the middle of a forest, instantaneously beamed there like a character from *Star Trek*. No one for hundreds of miles around. No signs or paths to lead you out of the woods. The first thing you notice is the sunlight, the glorious sunlight, announcing itself as if you had willed it there; small rays of illumination that trickle through the dense foliage and, like many voices, conspire to speak as one. You hear the beauty of the chirping birds and see the verdant hues of green and amber as this sunlight passes through the trees. You notice you are in a very old and lovely glen. The trees are ancient and massive. There's a bit of brush on the forest floor but nothing that would be difficult to move around in. A small stream cuts through the clearing. Listless tree limbs draw dancing shadows on its surface; the branches disappear over the vibrant, crystal-clear water, incorporating themselves into the infinite wilderness. Skirting the clearing in which you stand are two boulders blanketed with olive-green moss.

This is the unbelievable and utterly unthinkable situation in which I now stand.

PART I

CHAPTER 1

When I come to my senses, I realize that I'm wearing a backpack. Upon further inspection, it has enough food and water to last for a few days. But no compass. I have matches to light a fire, a flashlight, a rather big knife, and what appears to be a raincoat. I don't know how, but I'm dressed in the best outdoor clothes that exist on the planet: a wide-brimmed hat, brush pants, a wool shirt, and leather hiking boots. The only sounds I hear are the chirping of sparrows, the melodious song of a blue jay, and the chuckling of a pileated woodpecker that immediately reminds me of the *Woody Woodpecker* cartoons I watched as a child. Somehow, I feel he's laughing at me.

The sun is either rising or setting. I'm not sure how to look at it. But I'm optimistic. My mind wakes up again and begins to ask questions.

Where am I?

How the hell did I get here?

What the hell do I do now?

I look down at my feet and wonder if they still work. I have been standing in the same place since I arrived. I get an idea. Perhaps if I click my heels together and say, "There's no place like home," three times, I will be magically transported back to my home. Back to the last place I was before I found myself in this predicament. Maybe I'll wake up in bed and this will all have been a dream. And a strange dream at that! I latch onto this thought. Wouldn't that be nice? What the heck? I close my eyes and click the heels of my leather hiking boots together. *There's no place like home. There's no place like home. There's no place like home.* My eyes open slowly—first the left and then the right. But it's no use. I'm standing in the same place I was before. Overhead, I hear the laughter of the woodpecker. "Well, it worked for Dorothy, didn't it?" I shout up to Woody.

If nothing else, my feet have begun to work again. I step out of the spot where I've been trapped and explore my surroundings a bit. I've been in the woods before, but these woods are unfamiliar. Mysterious. My mind starts to race, and I become apprehensive. No. Frankly, I'm downright scared. It reminds me of a time when I was hunting pheasant and found myself turned around in the woods. I had no idea which direction to go to get back to my truck. At that point, I remembered a story I had read in an outdoor magazine about a fellow who had been lost in the woods for days. Finally, he climbed a tree until he spotted a road and made his way to it. Once on the road, he was rescued by a passing car. Wasting no time, I climbed the nearest tree and spotted my truck about a half mile away. Though I was saved, I never quite forgot that feeling of being lost and alone in the woods.

The feeling now is ten times worse. I am not only lost in the woods alone, but I have no recollection of how I got here. Why not find a tree and try that solution again?

I scout for a tree that is big enough to give me a good view of my surroundings and easy enough to climb. I don't want to fall and break my neck. I finally find a big ash tree that will serve my purpose nicely. It has branches low to the ground that ascend in perfect increments. I start to scale the ash carefully, one branch at a time. God knows I am not partial to heights. It was all I could do to climb a ladder at my house when I was painting the second floor; I remember going up the ladder as fast as I could and then painting for five minutes before the height got to me and forced me to scramble back down as fast as I could. To this day, the second floor remains unpainted. Nevertheless, climbing this ash as high as I must makes the second story of my house look like sea level.

As I climb branch by branch, my mind tries to make sense of this whole thing. I repeat to myself the questions of the day. *What's happening? What am I doing here? How did I get here? Where am I? Is this all a dream?*

At long last, I reach the top. Well, not really the top. Just as far as I am willing to go. Just high enough that if I stand up really tall, I can see just over the treetops and have a view in every direction. Hanging onto the treetop with the death grip I perfected while painting, I look out.

To the right, I see nothing. To the left, nothing. There is nothing behind and nothing in front. Nothing but trees and hills and brush. Only forest for miles and miles. I decide to become very still. Maybe I might hear something: a car driving down a road, church bells—you know, something.

Anything. I stand there holding on for dear life for quite some time and hear nothing. Not a sound. Not even the chirping of birds that I heard when I was standing on the ground. Just thinking of the ground causes me to look down, and the elevation sucks the breath from my lungs. My grip tightens as I realize that my search for help has brought me three stories up a tree. And the ground is looking up at me.

It brings me back to a class field trip I took to New York City as a ten-year-old. We were going to the top of the RCA building, whether I wanted to go or not. My classmates and I were whisked up in an elevator to the observation deck hundreds of stories above the street. As soon as the door opened, all the other kids ran to the side of the building to gaze out over the city. I meagerly ventured over to look out, and the view of the streets from that lofty perch caused me to collapse to the ground. I crawled back to the elevator as my classmates laughed and the elevator door closed.

I have that same sinking feeling now. The tremendous height that I'm at has jumped up, grabbed my ankles, and started pulling me down. I feel the urge to crawl. The same urge I felt when I was ten. But there is nowhere to crawl.

As if on cue, I hear the first sound I have heard since I left the ground. It is the cackling of that damned woodpecker piercing the forest. He's laughing at me again. I take a deep breath to get some air back into my lungs. My legs are still wobbly, and the urge to crawl creeps up my spine. My mind pleads with my eyes, *Don't look down! Don't look down!*

Where am I supposed to look, smartass? I reply to myself.

Look up! my mind urges, hoping my instinctual self takes over. This should be his area of expertise anyway. Unfortunately, I know he's as overburdened with fear as I am. The instinctual fight-or-flight response is in full gear. I try to obey my mind's wishes to look up. I do look up.

Right there, hovering above me about thirty yards from where my head emerges from the treetops, is a hawk. He hangs in the air, drifting on the thermal updrafts like the hang gliders I've seen along the rocky coast of Rhode Island, catching the updrafts and suspending himself in the wind. He looks down at me as if wondering, *What the hell is this guy doing up here?*

At that moment, my focus is on the hawk. He is magnificent. He is a red-tailed hawk, his fiery red tail illuminated even further by the sunlight. From where I am, I can see his eyes, which are bright and strong with a hint of yellow where his eyebrows would be. He is looking right at me. In fact, his gaze seems to be holding me up in the tree. As my attention on the hawk becomes more and more intense, my legs stop wobbling and an unusual calm overtakes me. My jumbled mind becomes suddenly clear as it instructs the parts of my body, what they should do and how they should do it. At the same time, all the destructive thoughts I have in my mind (like falling from the tree and breaking every bone in my body) drift out of my head. A calm—a calm I have never felt before—comes over me. My mind, now silenced, allows me to move freely. I relax the death grip on the tree. My body takes over, and I move with an unimpeded flow. I now possess the stealth of the acrobats I recall from the only circus of my childhood. (My fear of clowns, of course, ended that. But that's another story altogether.)

Well, if this is only a dream and I fall from the tree, I will surely wake up before I hit the ground. Isn't that how dreams work?

As this thought quiets, it seems as if I watch my body descend the tree, as if the tree is guiding me down. Each branch invites itself to me, and as I step on or grab each one, I feel a warmth unlike anything I have ever known before. Has the tree become a part of me? I cannot explain the feeling. It is like the tree is letting me down ever so gently.

As my feet finally hit the ground, my mind starts to cloud up again. The thought of it all comes rushing back into my mind again. I return to the realization that I am alone in the middle of god-knows-where, and I have less of an idea where I am supposed to go than before I climbed the ash. This is when the whole situation really hits home. I now feel the fear creeping up my spine. I'm breathing as if I've just run a marathon. My knees feel like Jell-O. The hair is standing up on the back of my neck. I'm paralyzed, yet my mind is moving a mile a minute, scrambling every which way. *What's happening to me? How did I get here in the first place?*

CHAPTER 2

I flashback to the last thing I remember doing. I'm working at the tennis club where I'm the head tennis pro. It's a lovely June afternoon around two. I'm out on my teaching court as I've been a thousand times before. I'm teaching Mrs. Hamshire, whose hour-long lessons always feel like six hours to me. She's a plump woman who's not very athletic, can't move well, and frankly can't play a lick. I haven't been able to figure out for the life of me why she continues to play tennis at all. I conclude that it's because her whole family does. Her husband is in the same boat, but their children are actually quite good. Their two sons are good players, and their daughter is exceptional. I've watched them all grow up and foresee a Division II scholarship in their daughter's future. Mrs. Hamshire wants to be involved in the family's activities, so I'm stuck with her as my Tuesday-afternoon lesson.

"Take the racket back! Take the racket back!" I bellow incessantly, trying to get her prepared to hit the ball well before it bounces back across the court in her general direction. Most of my time with her is spent on autopilot as I hit ball after ball to her and watch her flail helplessly at each one. My mind takes time off during lessons like this. Essentially, I'm elsewhere.

What will I do after the lesson? "Take the racket back," I suggest by rote.

What did I do yesterday? "Good," I encourage hollowly.

Shit! Did I leave the coffee pot on? "Okay, okay. Not bad," I say mechanically. A ball machine and a recorded message would have sufficed for these lessons. But, hell, I'm getting paid rather well to be there. At least physically.

At one point, the club actually did pay for a ball machine for anyone who wanted to practice. I sent away for the best machine money could buy. But on the day it arrived, one of my students canceled a lesson with me and opted for the ball machine instead. Right then and there, I decided that this machine was not going to cut in on my business. As soon as the client was done with it, I took the ball machine around the back of the club and shot it. When someone asked to use the machine a couple weeks later, I told them that I had sent it out to be repaired. I lied.

The night I shot it, I went out and had a few beers. I returned to the club around two in the morning and tossed the machine in the back of my truck. I drove for miles until I was far outside of town. I tossed it into the woods where it would never be seen or heard from again. After all, if someone wanted a ball machine, they could rent me. I'm as good as any machine; I actually speak.

So, from that trancelike state at the tennis club, hitting balls to Mrs. Hamshire, to this clearing, in this forest, in the middle of god-knows-where. I don't remember leaving the club or going to sleep. It's all a dream, isn't it? I'll soon wake up, safe and sound back in my wonderful life. Well, wonderful might be a stretch, but it's definitely better than *this*. Right now, I'd love to wake up back at the tennis club with fat, little Mrs. Hamshire wildly swinging at shot after shot. I suppose I could have been drinking and just made it home and passed out. But I've never blacked out from alcohol like that. That's what women do: "I'm so drunk I don't remember going to bed with you." Yeah, I've heard that one a few times.

"Okay, Rich, get a hold of yourself. Get it together," I hear a voice say. "If this is only a dream, you're going to wake up soon, so you might as well make the most of it." I look around and see no one. Again I hear a voice: "Pull yourself together. If this is a dream, then you are in control." Again I look around, and to my shock—there's no mistaking it—it's me talking to me, trying to rally the troops.

You know, that voice is always there, speaking to you. But more often than not, your mind is off somewhere in the outer limits, focusing on the past or the future. You don't even hear it. It's the voice of the unconscious mind and comes booming out loudly, particularly when you're tasked with saving your ass. The unconscious mind is the source of all your intuition. It is said to be the most creative aspect of the mind and is most aware of your psyche. If we could live in our subconscious minds at all times, we would have amazing intuition—intuition bordering on clairvoyance.

At this moment, perhaps more than I ever have, I need intuition. I need some direction before I go completely mad. Mad? This situation is outrageously insane, and at this point in the proceedings, who wouldn't be a little bit insane?

With the thoughts of insanity ringing between my ears, I hear a familiar voice. "Wait a minute! Wait a minute! Let's take a look at the facts." I know this voice very well. It belongs to my analytical mind, the "I" that tries to see everything through the scope of facts and figures and underlying meaning. He goes on: "Okay, okay, at this moment, we can't speak to what has happened and why you are in this place. Let's instead review what we do know." He loves to talk in this cut and dry way, and I'm used to listening to his advice, even if it is a bit mechanical. Since I'm not too familiar with the "I" in me that they call the unconscious I, I'm going to let this I have a shot. *Please continue.*

"First, we know that we are in this clearing and it's a beautiful spot. Second, we know from climbing that tree that there is nobody around for miles. At least nobody we can discern. Third, we have a backpack full of very useful stuff." I begin to feel the fear that reduced me to a deer in headlights start to wane. The serenity I felt descending the ash is slowly returning, and as a result, I'm once again able to move. "Let's check out the provisions in the backpack," I hear him say as I come to realize that he is me. I take the backpack, flip it over, and let the contents spill to the ground.

A bunch of cans, a few apples, some bananas, a bandana, a small bag of potato chips, some biscuits wrapped in a cloth napkin, what appears to be dried meat, and six hard-boiled eggs in a plastic bag all tumble to the ground. I discover a knife and fork wrapped in a bandana. Upon further inspection, I observe a book of matches that look as though they can light on the roughest of surfaces, a large knife reminiscent of the one Crocodile Dundee carries, a neatly folded poncho, and one of those cups that fold up. Strapped to the backpack is a canteen brimming with water. I reach down and pick up one of the cans. It's beans, Boston baked beans in fact. All of the cans are beans. I hear a voice say, "Who the hell packed for this trip?"

"Trip? There wasn't supposed to be any trip. Well at least none that I knew of," I answer.

"Me either," chimes Analytical I.

"I'm not too fond of baked beans or dried meat," opines another voice I've heard quite frequently. He's Wise Guy I. "And remember, we stopped eating potato chips because they have too much salt. The guy who packed this bag is a real asshole."

"Hold on. We should really be thanking the person that put this bag together for us. Without it, we would die of starvation." The voice of Grateful I is taking a stab at getting Wise Guy I under control.

It's starting to occur to me that I have a multitude of voices talking in my head. And they are all mine. You can call it multiple personalities. Or multiple parts of my personality. So much of personality is an act we put on in response to different events or to different people. You know, it's the little roles we play to project the type of person we think they might favor. Personality is very much a product of our environment. And I'm coming to realize that the voices in my mind, which I call the I's, combine to form this personality. It's not the real you but an altogether different you that rises to the forefront and speaks up at any given moment. It's all the different voices that spring up so you can play all the different roles you have to in your life. If you think of the I's as the actors in the play, the real you serves as the director, if you're lucky. Unfortunately, the I's, like spoiled prima donnas, are able to influence the judgment of the director. With all these I's speaking at once, things can become muddled up quickly, a cacophony of disparate voices. Too many cooks spoil the broth.

Here's the funny thing: when we say "I," this "I" is whichever one takes charge at that particular moment. We give them the power to affect our words or actions, and even we take them to be ourselves. It's a wonder that we can accomplish anything in life with all these voices in our heads at one time.

Just then, I hear a loud, powerful, booming voice.

"Wait a minute. I know what I'm doing. I've spent loads of time in the woods, and I'm going to get us out of here." I know this voice all too well. It's Ego I, and mine is gigantic. "Stop all this trying to figure out what's gone on," he continues. "That'll get us nowhere. It's time for action. That's right, action. Pick up all those supplies off the ground and put them back in the bag. We're walking out of here now. And tell all those other idiot I's to shut up. I'm in charge now, and we're moving out."

I've always had a hard time disregarding Ego I, even though he has been wrong on numerous occasions and caused me a lot of trouble. He seems to hypnotize me, and I have trouble resisting his advice, no matter the consequences. So why should this time be any different? I bend over and pick up everything, stuffing it back into the knapsack. I throw the pack over my shoulder and look around.

"Okay, move out," I hear.

"Move out where?" I ask out loud like somebody is actually talking to me.

"Come on. I hear you're a hunter and a woodsman. Use your skills."

"My skills?" I say. "My wilderness experience is limited to a little hunting and fishing in areas so close to civilization that I stop for lunch on the way and eat at the diner in town on my way home. I've only camped a few times up in the Catskills, and even that was just a few miles outside of the town of Roscoe." So much for my purported woodsman skills. But with no other choice, I give in.

"Okay, okay, I'm going," I say begrudgingly. But in what direction, I do not know.

"Let's figure this out before we make a commitment to any one direction," I hear Analytical I say.

"All right, what would you suggest?"

"Let's see. What side of the tree does moss grow on?"

"How the hell should I know?" I answer.

"What do you think, he's Daniel Boone or something?" Wise Guy I jumps in. He can't help himself.

"All right," I say, "the sun rises in the east and sets in the west."

"Wonderful!" interjects Wise Guy I. "That's only true in North

America *and* on planet Earth. You don't know if you're on either. Dumbass!"

"No need to start calling names, Wise Guy," scolds Ego I.

"Arguing isn't going to get us anywhere. We need to work together. All for one and one for all," sings Cooperation I in a sweet and calm voice.

Boom! Ego I comes in again. "Listen, everyone! Shut up! Does it really matter what direction we go? Any one is as good as the next, so let's get going."

I take a long look at the clearing. "Maybe we should just stay here and wait for help. We don't know what's lurking out there in this jungle," remarks Paranoid I. He has no confidence in new situations. In fact, he has no confidence in any situation.

"Don't worry. We can find our way out of anything, even when we're asleep and dreaming. Maybe that's all this is. A dream," says Ego I, unwilling to surrender an inch. "Besides, this is no jungle. It's a forest. There's no threat of lions and tigers."

"Ah, but there could be bears," Paranoid I says, seizing the opportunity to speak. "If we can agree on anything, I think we can agree that we're all afraid of bears. Remember all those dreams we've had from time to time about grizzly bears chasing us all around? In those dreams, they're everywhere, and we can't seem to get away from them. Only in the dreams that end well do we shoot them with a shotgun to save our life. We don't have a shotgun right now, do we?"

"Rich, where did you get this I?" says Ego I. "He's talking about dreams, and we don't even know if this is, in fact, a dream. He's just trying to confuse matters. This I, if I remember correctly, is the same I that tried to talk you out of playing football and kissing girls and drinking beer and smoking pot and a hundred other things that actually worked out quite nicely for you, now didn't they? I say get rid of him now."

I have to cut this out. There are just way too many me's. I'll never get anywhere with all these voices cluttering my mind. Which one is correct? Which one is the real me? Or is there even a real me? Maybe all I am is a multitude of I's, all trying to be heard, all vying for control and speaking for me at any given moment. Ahhhhhh!

CHAPTER 3

Without a thought, if that's indeed possible, I start moving forward, out of the clearing and into the woods straight ahead. I travel about two hundred yards very easily, as the forest floor is fairly clear, with only a few instances of easily avoidable brush. The trees rise up and tower over me, obscuring the sky and the sun, rendering all that talk about the sun rising in the east and setting in the west moot for the time being. I feel better walking around anyway, even if I have no idea where I'm going. The ground is flat in all directions, with many kinds of trees and shrubs. I can only name a few with certainty. I once bought a book on all the trees and shrubs in the Northeast and tried to learn the different species, but I never got too proficient at it. Lord knows even if I can figure out which tree is which, I would never be able to tell the difference between all the different bushes.

After traveling a mile or so, the terrain is now a bit more challenging. There are downed trees and bramble bushes with thorns the size of my thumb. I am bobbing and weaving my way through the forest at a much slower pace now. Occasionally, I get a glimpse of the sky, which is a bright blue like I've never seen before. There isn't a cloud to be found. I'm walking toward the sun, or at least I think I am. I have no idea for sure with all the backtracking I have to do to move through the underbrush, but at least I'm going somewhere. I think. At one point, after walking for an indiscriminate amount of time—whoever packed for me forgot to pack a watch—I pass an outcropping of some very large boulders that have an evergreen tree growing out of the middle of them. I find it odd at first glance. The tree trunk sits right on top of the rocks while its exposed roots run down along both sides of the boulders. All this room here with rich, dark soil, and this pine has decided to sprout up between a rock and a hard place. Pardon the pun.

After walking for some time, I come upon a similar sight: another pine growing between two boulders. Maybe pines like to grow around the rocks, or maybe those rocks attract this type of pine. I can't be certain. Very strange is all. The next thing I know, I burst out of the woods and into a clearing.

Wait. Is this the same clearing I started from? Is that why this pine looks so familiar? Because it is the very same one? I just spent who knows how long wandering around in circles. Am I certain that this is the same clearing where I began this whole mess? At this point, I can't be certain of anything. I look around and see the two huge rocks I sat on, the stream, and, if I'm not mistaken, the tree I climbed to see … well … nothing at all, actually. Yes, this is the same spot. "When the hell am I going to wake up?" I scream at the top of my lungs. My mind is unusually quiet, not a peep from the I's who are usually so willing to comment unmercifully whenever I make a mistake or do something dumb.

I walk over to the smaller rock and sit down on top of it. I reach around and pull the backpack off my shoulders, grab the canteen, and take a long pull off it. I push the hat back on my head a little and lean back against the bigger rock behind me. As I close my eyes, I hear Cautious I warn with a whisper, "Take it easy on the water. It may have to last you a long time." Yeah, he's right. Who knows how long I'll be stuck in this place, and the water has to last as long as I can make it.

I just sit there in a kind of daze for some time. I have heard about these kinds of things before. I must be in some sort of spell or trance or something. Well I'm going to get out of it. That's right, I'm going to get myself out of this. Who would do such a thing to me? Who that I know is magical enough to come up with a spell this good? Huh. I don't know. Magic seems like a bit of a stretch in the twenty-first century, if that's where I still am. I can't think of anyone who would want to curse me like this. *Wait a minute, wait a minute. What about that lady that lived across from you on Croton Street? You remember—the house across the street from you when you were a kid.*

The house looked more like a barn, and all the neighborhood kids avoided it like the plague. The lady was extremely scary at the time, though we were all of ten years old. She did have all those cats though, some of which were black, and the scuttlebutt among my crew of kids was that she was, in fact, a witch. Paranoid I conjures up this whole memory for me now. "Hold on," I say. "That was twenty years ago, and she was old then. That lady has to be dead and buried by now."

"Well," Paranoid I goes on, "my understanding is there is no shelf life as far as spells are concerned. I think once someone puts a curse on you, it's there for life. And if you remember correctly, you did kick her cat once when you tried to pet it and it scratched you. Remember? She saw you kick the cat in the ass and yelled at you with that high-pitched voice that scared the crap out of you for days. Didn't she say she was going to get you?"

"Yeah, that's right, she did say that."

"Well, there you go."

"But she did get me back."

And she had. One day, the Good Humor man came through, and all the neighborhood kids came clamoring out into the street for ice cream. I was with my brother, Mark. Neither of us had any money, and our parents weren't home. So all we could do was sit on the curb and watch all the neighborhood kids eat their ice cream. Suddenly, out of the house came the cat lady, as we called her, and Mark and I watched as she walked across the street toward us. All the kids scattered when they saw her coming, and she called out to my brother.

"Mark, come over here to the ice-cream truck," she said. She had this funny look on her face. But, come to think of it, she always had a funny look on her face. "Mark. Mark. Come here."

Mark, my younger brother, looked at me as if to say, "What in the world does she want with me?" He didn't move a muscle and continued to stare at me. He was pleading, "Save me," with his eyes.

"Mark, go see what she wants," I said.

Mark looked at her and then back at me. "You're my older brother. You're supposed to be looking out for me."

"Don't be such a weenie," I replied. "What could she possibly do? The whole neighborhood is standing around. Go ahead, get up."

Mark stood up slowly, never taking his eyes off me, and sheepishly walked over to where the cat lady was standing, though not too close to her, mind you. I heard her ask Mark what kind of ice cream he wanted, and he nervously whispered, "Strawberry shortcake."

With that, she turned to the Good Humor man, Frank, and said, "One strawberry shortcake pop, please." She handed Frank the money, took the pop, and handed it to Mark. With that, she turned toward me and, with a weird look in her eye, said in a loud, screechy voice, "Cat kickers don't get none!" She turned to cross the street, again sending all the kids scrambling out of her way, and I sat there envious and dumbfounded. All her cats had come out onto the porch to watch, and they followed her back into the house. I dare say that jaws dropped a little that day because, in the fifty years she had lived on that street, almost no one had ever heard her speak.

There was nothing I could say. I just shrugged my shoulders and mimicked her in a cackling voice, "Cat kickers get none!" No one said a word, until my brother laughed nervously and the rest of the neighborhood did the same. Now that should have been adequate punishment for a little cat-kicking, no? Oh, no, no, no—hold on. I'm actually entertaining thoughts from Paranoid I. Cat kicking and curses? He tends to take such trivial things and blow them out of proportion. It's bad enough that I'm even allowing him the floor. This has to stop. You have no idea where it can go from here, and I definitely don't want to hear any of it.

CHAPTER 4

Two squirrels, one black and one gray, run across the clearing chasing one another. A blue jay lands on a tree branch right in front of me and warbles out the coolest melody. I've heard this before walking in the woods, but I never knew it was the tune of the blue jay. "Huh," I wonder, "maybe I never knew this was the blue jay's call because I never truly paid attention to it before." Perhaps my head was not truly there when I was walking in the woods, or I would have realized it. At this moment, my mind becomes quiet, and the clearing comes alive. I hear other birds singing and see chipmunks scampering across the forest floor before disappearing up a tree. Bees are buzzing as they extract nectar from flowers. A cardinal swoops across and lands in the brush on the other side of the clearing. I can hear the babbling of the stream running on the outskirts of the clearing, its murmurs vanishing into the forest.

I hear a racket from above. Looking up, I see crows circling among the treetops. They seem agitated. I have learned from my hunting days that they serve as the alarm mechanism for the forest by signaling the arrival of an intruder. "Oh no!" I say to myself. "Is there a bear, a wolf, a mountain lion, or god-knows-what lurking?" I can feel fear rearing its ugly head again. I get up off the rock and look around for anything ominous. The crows are screaming now. My heart races, and my palms sweat. I take a few steps away from the rock and scan the periphery of the clearing. Everything seems to be just as it was before I heard the crows.

I look up and once again see the hawk, though from a new vantage point. The crows begin to dive-bomb him. They don't want him in their territory. The hawk is competition for their food source, and they are trying to chase him away. He just sits there, looking down at me, ignoring the crows as they fly around him and dive at him. The crows appear leery of the hawk and keep their distance somewhat. The hawk doesn't move. He behaves as if the crows pose no threat to him. I get a good look at him. He's a brilliant bird with bright red feathers underneath. His presence has the same calming effect it had on me when I tried to climb down the tree. As I continue to stare up at the hawk, I become aware of something much more portentous than all the lions and tigers and bears. Darkness is falling fast and starting to overtake the forest. I watch the sun slinking over the horizon.

The fear factor is flying on high-test jet fuel. *Man, I better wake up now!* All the I's in my mind are screaming. I have never been in the woods all night by myself. *Alone. Nope. Never.* Optimistic I has this crazy idea that maybe the darkness is just a passing cloud blanketing the sun.

Wise Guy I says, "Are you for real? Where did we get this guy from anyway? It *is* getting dark, you jerk!"

"Don't worry. We can handle this." Ego I has just stepped into the conversation.

"Okay, let's look at this situation from a factual point of view." Analytical I is back and assessing the situation. And at this point, I'm thinking he's the man for the job.

"Well, what do you think?" Wise Guy I wonders. Even he is so scared at this point that he doesn't have any wisecracks left. The sun is now hanging so low in the sky that it begins to disappear behind the trees, shooting specks of golden light across the clearing. I look and see that the hawk is still there, but all the crows have grown weary of the fuss and gone to roost.

"I can't believe this, I *really* can't believe this," I hear a voice in my head say. This must be Disbelief I. Man, how many of these I's do I have wandering around in there? "You don't really want to know!" comes an answer from inside my head.

"Everyone, shut up in there! I mean it!" I shout. "All right, what should I do now, Analytical I? You've got the floor."

"Select a spot not too close to the brook to dig a hole," comes the response.

"A hole? What do I need a hole for? Don't you dare get the idea I'm going to sleep in a hole!"

"Not to sleep in. To build a fire pit."

"Ah, yeah. A fire sounds good to me. How deep? And don't say six feet," Paranoid I says.

"Shut him up! We can't afford his input at this time. Besides, he'll have all the time in the world after it gets dark and he's scared out of his wits," comes a voice.

"That's a good point," I agree. "Hey, by the way, we don't have a shovel now, do we?"

"No one packed one, did they?" Wise Guy I snaps back.

"Find a stick or something," offers Analytical I.

I scurry around the clearing, looking for a stick that is sturdy enough to do the job. Finally, I find one that is about four feet long. I look around for the ideal spot to dig the pit. I decide to dig near the rocks I was sitting on. That way I can sit with my back against them and still be near the fire. I begin to dig but am chagrined to learn that the ground is extremely firm and the stick barely makes a dent. I labor for the next few minutes but am getting nowhere fast. The ground is nearly impenetrable.

I stop, frustrated. "Shit! Why isn't this working?"

"No, I guess it's not, Analytical genius. Don't you have a very big knife in your bag, dummy?" Wise Guy I chuckles.

"He's right, you know," Analytical I concedes. "Go get the knife."

I dart over to the rocks where I left the backpack and swiftly spill the contents to the ground. Grabbing Crocodile Dundee, I rush back to the spot where I was going to dig the pit and quickly have a hole in the ground. A rather nice one too, if I do say so myself. The hole is about two feet deep, a yard long, and a yard wide. It is just feet from the rocks. Now what?

"Find some good-sized rocks and place them around the pit," comes a voice.

"Rocks? Where am I going to find rocks out here?" I muse.

"There's rocks all over the place. This is the woods, is it not?"

"Yeah, I suppose it is," I answer.

As the darkness begins to fall, I start searching for rocks of the perfect size to border the fire pit. But to my disappointment, all I discover are rocks that are more appropriate for children to throw at each other in a rock fight—the size that would hurt someone but not inflict any real damage unless you hit them in the head. Too small for my purpose. My mind flashes back to my childhood and the neighborhood rock fights on Croton Street.

CHAPTER 5

As a boy, I lived on a street called Croton Street, just across from the cat woman. Most of the street's residents were of Italian descent. At the end of the Croton Street sat a vacant lot where a lot of families planted vegetable gardens, my grandmother included. There were three nice-sized gardens, but the lot was large enough that it left a big area overgrown with tall weeds and brush. Running north and south and parallel to Croton Street was a street called Broadway, and a couple of houses on Broadway shared backyards with the lot. The kids that lived on Broadway were of French descent and spoke with French accents. Of course, the Croton Street gang insisted that the lot belonged to them. We were very protective of it. To complicate matters, the ringleader of the Broadway gang had a backyard that bordered the lot. And my grandmother's house bordered the lot on the Croton Street side, which put me in the role of overlord, or at least sentry. Whenever I saw any of the kids from Broadway sneaking around the lot, I sent word out to all those on Croton Street that had sworn to protect and defend the lot to death. Because of their accents, we called the kids Frenchies, and the name just stuck. When I spotted them in the lot, the alarm went out, and everyone gathered in my backyard to strategize. In the winter, snowballs were the weapon of choice. In the summer, it was crab apples. In the spring and fall, we were left only with rocks. Garbage can lids doubled as shields. We even constructed rudimentary bows and arrows; the arrows had no tip and were merely small branches we took from the maple trees that lined the lot. But clearly, the bloodiest battles and cruelest casualties came as a result of the rock fights.

We finally reached a truce one day after some heavy rock fighting in the lot led to a barrage of rocks and found each side decimated by injury. "We want a parlay," said one of the Frenchies, and being the merciful overlord that I was, I agreed. After much debate, we came upon a solution to narrow the casualty problem. We concluded that snowballs and crab apples were acceptable forms of ammunition. The arrows were okay as well; they didn't really hurt too badly. But the rocks! Something had to be done about the rocks! And being the spring, this was rock season. There wasn't much other ammo available, so we signed a weapons pact limiting the size and shape of the rocks. We agreed that many lives would be spared. The rocks were to be no bigger than a quarter. They couldn't weigh much (though weight was difficult to measure). Perhaps most importantly, the rocks had to be smooth, without any jagged edges. These rocks were hard to find in the lot. The search for legal ammo led the Croton Street gang four blocks away to a stream we called Kill Brook. There we found an unlimited supply of smooth, small rocks.

That's the size of rock I'm finding on the forest floor all around the clearing. Not big enough to surround the fire pit but big enough for use in the Croton-Frenchy wars. Nevertheless, recalling Kill Brook led my mind to wander. Kill Brook started as a small stream up in the hills, ran the length of the town, and emptied itself into the Hudson River at a place we called Red Barn. We named it that because an old abandoned factory sat where the stream met the Hudson, and the factory had been painted red, reminding us of a barn. We never knew what function the factory served. Nevertheless, it was a great spot to fish for stripers. Baitfish, attracted by the running water and abundance of insect life, would fill the mouth of the brook. And, as any fisherman knows, find the bait, and you'll find the bass.

I learned that Kill Brook had been used by the local Indians for many different reasons. For one, it served as a boundary that separated native tribes. Kill Brook's constantly flowing water had sent all the silt out into the mighty Hudson, leaving only rocks at its bottom. Centuries of running water had molded these rocks until they were smooth and round—essentially the perfect ammunition in the Croton-Frenchy war. I credit one of our troops, Georgie, with the discovery. He was fishing at Red Barn at low tide, and before long, we had a full armory. The rocks at the bottom of Kill Brook were all different sizes, so we just selected those quarter-sized ones that had been agreed upon.

And suddenly I realize the brook that runs through the clearing is nearly the same size as Kill Brook.

I run over to the stream to look. Sure enough, it is teeming with smooth, round rocks of various sizes. I hadn't looked at the stream since my first arrival. This is largely due to the confusion as to where I was. But as a fisherman, in different circumstances, this would have been the first place I would have investigated. The stream is the width of a good-sized road. It has a good flow of water, with ripples on one side, that runs into a pool roughly three and a half feet deep. From there, it bends gently before it disappears into the forest. In the day's dying light, I spy flashes in the pool. Trout, alarmed by my presence, are scurrying to hide. No time to check the fish now, though. I'm on a mission. I carefully select the appropriate size stones, and after a few trips, I have the pit surrounded.

CHAPTER 6

Wood! That's what I need, I think. There isn't much lying around on the clearing floor, but I notice fifty yards away, just a little deeper into the forest, there are all sorts of tree limbs that likely fell in storms or what have you. Now, I know a little bit about building fires. I have a fireplace at home, and I'm always in charge of making the fire. First, I need to find small, dry branches without any leaves. I make my way out into the forest and find one of the fallen trees. Pulling off all the branches that had been on top of the tree, I now have enough kindling for my fire. After bringing them back to the clearing, I set my sights on some larger pieces of wood. I find plenty of logs lying on the forest floor that are just the right size. I don't have an ax with me, after all. I come back with my arms full and soon have a pretty-good-sized pile stacked up in the clearing.

I go over to the backpack and spill its contents on the ground. I find the matches and return everything else to the pack. As I pick them up, I realize that something is missing. "Paper," I say. I always rolled paper up into a ball and placed it underneath the kindling. The heat from the paper would ignite the smaller twigs, which in turn would light the larger logs. I don't have any paper out here, and I don't think I'll find any newspaper no matter how hard I search. My first thought is to use leaves, but this is still the green time of year, and they won't burn well enough. The kind of fallen dried leaves I need are nowhere to be found on the forest floor.

"Think," I hear Analytical I say.

"Aren't you supposed to be in charge of that?" I ask.

Wait, wait. I remember back home I used to go down the street while walking my dog, Ozzie. At the end of the street, there is a grove of pine trees. One day, I decided, I don't know why, to pick up some pine cones off the ground, take them home, and toss them into the fire to see what would happen. The fire had almost burned out by the time I got home. I tossed in the pine cones, and the fire flared up. I'm not sure what it is; something makes them flammable.

"That's it! Pine cones," I say to myself. I remember the pine tree that I saw earlier during my walk around the forest, the one growing out from between the two rocks. It isn't far from the clearing, and I try to remember the way. The pine tree was the last thing I remembered seeing before I reentered the clearing. So, in the faint lingering of the day's light, I look around and try to figure out where earlier I emerged back into the clearing. That way, I can backtrack to the pine. I remember the rocks were on my left, and I use that as a guide. But how am I going to find the pine in the dark?

"Use that flashlight, knucklehead," remarks Wise Guy I.

First, I go over to the backpack and return the matches for safekeeping. I pull out the flashlight and switch it on, and the light beams out like a bolt of lightning. The flashlight is a good size and has a bit of weight to it. If nothing else, I can use it to beat the hell out of whatever attacks me. There goes Paranoid I again. I walk over to the other side of the clearing and stand with the rocks to my left and slowly make my way out toward the forest. Everything looks so different in the dark. My steps are slow and careful. After a short distance, my light hits upon the pine. There it is, sitting on top of the rocks, and I notice it looks different from what I remember. The roots are literally rising up and wrapping around the rocks.

I again wonder why the pine has chosen such an obviously challenging spot to grow, particularly with all the good soil around it. But I now realize that, of course, it has no choice in the matter; the seeds fell where they fell, and the pine is merely making the best of the hand it was dealt. The pine and I have much in common. I guess we're both stuck between a rock and a hard place.

I shine the light on the forest floor, and pine cones are everywhere. I take as many as I can carry and head back the way I came, careful not to get turned around and lost in the woods. I emerge back into the clearing a bit to the right of where I entered the forest but safe and sound nonetheless. The sunlight has dissipated, so I must rely on the flashlight to find the big rocks and the fire pit. I toss the pine cones into the middle of the pit. Next, I take the smaller branches and break them up into even smaller pieces before laying them on top of the pine cones. I go over to the backpack and pull out the box of matches.

This is one of those large boxes of matches, not the cardboard books you often see. They remind me of the kind you see in cowboy movies. They have white tips and a strip on the side of the box, though they can be ignited on any rough surface. I remember, from the movies, cowboys lighting them on the soles of their boots. Particularly, I remember John Wayne holding a match in his hand, putting his thumbnail on its white head and scraping his thumb against it. The match head flared up violently and then calmed to a gentle flicker. It looked really cool, and I decide to try it that way. I take a match from the box. I hold it in my right hand, put my thumb on top just like the Duke, and push down hard. The match snaps in two. "Shit! Guess they just don't make 'em like they used to." I grab a second match, determined to give it another try. If John Wayne can do it, so can I. The second attempt yields pretty much the same result as the first; only this time the match lights before it falls apart. "Damn," I say.

I go back for another match, and this time I hear Cautious I say, "Be careful. You don't want to run out of matches before you get the fire lit."

I push him out of my head, saying, "Leave me alone. I know what I'm doing."

I put my thumb right in the middle this time and scrape the match with my nail down. To my surprise, the match lights with a small explosion. "There it is!" I say. Looking at the pit, I hold the match for a while until it produces a good, steady flame, then toss it into the pit on top of the pine cones. I'm expecting them to flare up like the day I threw them into the fireplace at home, but instead the match just sits there and finally burns out.

"What!" I yell. "Oh, come on! This has to work!" Not only is it extremely dark, but it is starting to get chilly. The night air is crisp and clear. It reminds me of a time when I was up in the mountains in Vermont. Even though it was fifty-five or sixty degrees earlier that day, I know it will get much colder now that the sun has gone down. I must be in the mountains somewhere, I surmise.

I pick up the box of matches again and take another one out when I hear Analytical I say, "Wait, you need something to start the pine cones with. Look around for some dried leaves or small amounts of dried grass or brush."

Thinking, *I already tried that,* I indulge him anyway and pick up the flashlight. Lo and behold, along the brook, I spot a patch with some brown grass and dried-up leaves. Undoubtedly, they had been pushed there during a storm. The creek would have swelled and left them to dry when it receded back to its normal size. I go over and collect handfuls of dry debris. Removing the pine cones and small branches, I line the bottom of the pit with the dried materials. Next, I place the pine cones and twigs on top. Reaching into my pocket, I pull another match, put my thumb in the middle of the white top and flick my thumb. I watch the flame grow stronger. I feel confident that I've now mastered the art of the John Wayne method of lighting a match. I carefully place the match at the bottom of the pit, and the dried leaves flame up. It's a small flame at first, and I pray that it catches the pine cones and small branches. "Please let this work. I really need this fire, and I'm pretty much out of ideas on to how to start the damn thing!"

I watch in suspense. The fire grows a little over time, and as it does, it ignites the pine cones one after another. This in turn lights the layer of twigs and brush I placed on top. I go over to the pile of larger logs I gathered earlier and select some of the smaller pieces. These will catch first, and then I can add progressively larger pieces. After adding larger and larger logs, I eventually have a fairly good-size fire going. Then I hear Paranoid I speak up.

"Animals, big animals won't come near a fire. You know, like bears." That was all he had to say. I start frantically tossing wood onto the fire like it's my job, everything I can get my hands on. You know my relationship with bears. The fire grows into a bonfire and begins to spill out over the rock border I constructed for just that reason. At this point, I don't care; I am under the influence of Paranoid I, and he knows it. Thoughts flood my mind; visions of mountain lions, wolves, killer raccoons, packs of wild dogs, bears, and, yes, even bigfoots are flying around my mind.

Now all those thoughts of wild animal attacks and limbs being torn from my body—as I fight in vain—are racing through my mind again. All courtesy of Paranoid I. Just two minutes ago, I was fine, no crazy thoughts of bigfoot attacks, and now I'm reduced to a raving lunatic. This is how Paranoid I works. He creeps up on you when you least expect it, and then wham! Fear has you out of control! And speaking of out of control, the fire has now almost reached that point. The inferno has flames nearly as tall as some of the smaller trees bordering the clearing. Nevertheless, I feel a little better about my chances of not being attacked and decide to sit down on the big rock.

I walk over to the large rocks where I sat before constructing the fire pit. I remove my backpack and sit with my back up against the biggest rock, to protect myself from any attack that might come from that direction. Yup, Paranoid I is still hanging in there. I feel the heat on my back as the fire, almost twelve feet away, has grown so big it nearly touches the rocks where I'm sitting. I feel a bit more secure now, knowing that I have the rocks protecting my stern and the large waves of the fire at my bow.

The wood crackles under the heat of the fire, and I watch the flames shoot up, etching shadows at the clearing's edge. Though bright enough to read a book at any place in clearing—if I actually had a book—I'm a bit troubled that I can't see out into the forest. Oh well. What self-respecting bigfoot in his right mind would brave this towering inferno?

"Of course, that assumes the bigfoots—or is it bigfeet?—in this area are in their right mind, now doesn't it? Big assumption," Paranoid I again steps in, his voice wavering.

"Don't start with me now," I protest. "I've had a long day today, don't you think? I don't need any more of your crap. Don't you guys ever take a break?"

"No, we don't," they answer together, one of the few times they speak in concert. "If we did, you might realize that you don't really need us. And then where would you be?"

I sit with my back against the rock, looking out into the fire, and a warm glow comes over me. And not because of the fire.

For the first time, stretched out and comfortable and feeling a bit tranquil, I realize that I'm hungry. I haven't eaten anything since I first arrived in this strange clearing. I pull the backpack onto my legs, reach in, and rip all the contents out at once. Let's see: bananas, potato chips, no, too much salt, hard-boiled eggs, some kind of handmade biscuits, a kind of dried meat, like jerky, always gives me gas, three cans of beans, Boston baked beans while we're on the subject of gas, three apples, a pack of sweet mint gum, and best of all, two hand-rolled cigars that look to have a really good wrapper. Just the kind I like: dark and spicy but not quite maduro. Next comes the Crocodile Dundee knife in its sheath, which I put down next to me, and the large box of matches, which I know better than to put down too close to fire. I leave the raincoat and flashlight in the bag. It isn't raining, and my focus is on supper.

CHAPTER 7

"What would you like?" I ask myself as if I'm in a Park Avenue restaurant. "Salmon sounds good, over linguine with some shrimp sauce." Well, beans it is. You can eat these beans right out of the can, and while they might not taste good, you can live off them. Plus, it's a hot meal. All I need now is something to open the can.

"Three cans of beans and whoever packed this bag didn't provide a can opener!" Wise Guy I is back.

"I don't know," I say. "I didn't pack it. Wait!" I exclaim, indulging this conversation with Wise Guy I. "I can use the big knife to open the top of the can, no problem." With that, I put tonight's dinner down in front of me. I kneel down over the can and place the tip of the knife around the edge of the round top. Taking the handle of the knife in my left hand and striking the top of the handle with the right, the knife goes through the aluminum top like butter. I continue around the top until I can pry it off—and voila! The world-famous Boston baked beans about to be baked, or at least as close to baked as I can manage. I move closer to the fire and place the can on top of one of the flatter stones I used as the fire pit's border. The heat from the rocks and fire, which has settled down a bit now, should be more than ample to quickly heat the beans.

Next, I return to the bag and fish out the biscuits that were wrapped in a napkin. I set the napkin down on the ground in front of me and place the fork and knife on it. I produce the foldable tin cup, unfold it, and fill it with water from the canteen. Small eddies of steam rise from the inside of the bean can.

"Dinner is served!" I say.

The can, being so close to the fire, requires me to find some tool to remove it from the rock. I find two small sticks that I use as chopsticks and set the can on the bare ground to cool for a couple of minutes. Biscuits, beans, and water. Who has it better than me? I begin to eat the fine cuisine as prepared by World-Class Chef I. Again, my mind begins to drift.

One minute I'm giving Mrs. Hamshire her tennis lesson as I daydream away, and the next I'm here in this mysterious clearing. Who provided this lovely meal for me? Where the hell am I? Is it truly a dream? Or have I been transported to another dimension or another space and time? Time. What time is it anyway? What is the year?

The can of beans does not last long, and the biscuit is gone in no time. With all that's happening, I was hungrier than I thought. I get up and look around again. I'm still unnerved by the fact that I can't see past where the light fades into the forest. I move out into the clearing to collect more wood for the fire. Suddenly, I hear a rustling in the bushes that stops me dead in my tracks. I stand very still, trying to hear whatever I can. I look out into the forest but still can't see past the clearing. I hear the rustling again. The hair stands up on the back of my neck, my heart races, and my palms sweat as I stand motionless and apprehensive. The bushes tremble in the darkness. I drop what little wood I collected, keeping my eyes trained on the spot where the bushes moved.

After another rustling, I see a pair of eyes ignite in the unlit brush. They glare out at me. I feel the breath escape my lungs, and my body freezes. My eyes must have grown three sizes from fear. My mind's eye spies images of all sorts of adversaries: wolves, bears, bigfeet, and yes, even aliens. Reaching down, I grab one of the sticks I meant for firewood. It's solid and sturdy, like a small baseball bat. While I return the stare, out of the corner of my eye, I see yet another pair of eyes looking at me through the darkened brush. Another one! I swallow hard and know I need to grab the knife. As I turn to grab it, yet a third set of eyes peers out from the darkness. They have me surrounded! I back up slowly, cautiously, all the while returning the gaze of whatever is out there. Distracted as I am, I almost step into the fire pit on my way back to the rocks to retrieve the knife. With knife and bat in hand, I squat down and prepare to make my last stand there and then against whatever predators have come to kill me.

"Put up a good fight. Go out with your boots on," I hear a voice in my head say.

"What?" I reply.

"You heard me. Put up a good fight," says Heroic I.

"Not now," I say. "I'm much too busy having the shit scared out of me. Uh … let's talk later."

I sit there for what feels like an eternity with my eyes looking at those eyes that are looking at me. Nothing is moving. The only sounds are the crackling fire and the violent cadence of my heart. This is it. The end of me. The end of me in this dream at any rate. When the hell am I going to wake up? This would be as good a time as any. Just like dreaming you've fallen off a cliff and waking just before you hit the ground. Surely we're are at that point in this dream. The bushes shake one more time, and I await the monsters about emerge.

CHAPTER

To my surprise, a deer and two fawns casually stroll into the light of the clearing. I do a double take, and sure enough, it's just a doe and her two babies walking around the clearing as if they own it. Hey, perhaps they do. I drop out of my catcher's stance (Heroic I prefers "ninja crouch"), my ass hitting the ground with a thud. The deer proceed to move around the clearing, keeping one eye on me. I slump back against the rock, the blood draining from my head and my adrenalin pumping the brakes.

Woooooof! It's only a mama deer and her babies. It must be safe here, or else they would have run from the clearing at first sight of me. I watch them browse for their own dinner, munching on the low-lying leaves. Without a care in the world, they make their way back to the stream and disappear into the delicate, dark forest. After they're gone, I feel a bit lonely. I wish they'd stayed. At the very least, they would have been a great alarm if any real danger were to approach. I finally put the knife down, keeping it very close, and return to the task I was performing before the excitement. Before long, I once again have a nice high fire going. Hey, who knows? Maybe somebody will see it from miles away and come rescue me.

"Yeah, like a rescue party. That's right, a rescue party with helicopters and planes and bloodhounds and … who knows … the National Guard! Yeah, maybe they'll all come. You read about people who go hiking in the mountains and end up missing. They send out search parties and vehicles and find them." Optimistic I is outdoing himself. He goes on reminding me of all the movies we've seen where people find themselves lost in the jungle, or a swamp, or in the mountains and are rescued by a St. Bernard or something.

"Wait a minute. Hold on there. Nobody even knows I'm missing," I say. "Why would anybody send out a search party for someone they don't even know is missing?"

"That's right, no one is looking for you, and no one is going to find you out here. Well … that's not entirely true. Bears'll find you. If—and that's a big *if*—anybody comes looking for you, there'll be nothing left but bones," Pessimistic I chimes in. "He's no good, I tell you. Get rid of Optimistic I. He can't be trusted. Bad things happen in this world all the time."

"Well, it's a lot better than the dark picture you're always painting now, isn't it," quips Optimistic I.

"You two guys can never get along."

I stand up, thinking my mind is my worst enemy. I walk over to where the firewood is and chuck a few more logs on the fire. It's really going now. I walk back over to my spot and sit down against the rock. Reaching in the bag, I pull out the potato chips.

"I thought we were trying to eat less salt."

"Oh shut up!" I say. "Why should I be worried about my salt intake when I don't even know where I am and will probably be killed by the end of the night? I'm going to enjoy a few potato chips while I still can."

The night is so peaceful that a wonderful calm comes over me. In the darkness just past the clearing, phosphorescent fireflies flicker. I look up, and through the gap in the forest's canopy, I see thousands of stars burning. The night air is cool but not cold, and I again wonder if I might be up in the mountains somewhere. But who knows where I am? I could be anywhere—or nowhere—for all I know.

I reach over, pick up the canteen, and pour myself a small cup, mindful that I have to conserve water. Perhaps eating those salty potato chips wasn't the best idea after all. In my relaxed state, I think it might be a good time to get some sleep. Again, I wonder what time it is. I look down at my watch before I remember that I don't have one. How the hell do I know if it's time for sleep?

"Go to sleep? How can you sleep, knowing you're alone in a forest full of dangerous animals?" Paranoid I says. I find it funny that for an I so skittish, he isn't shy about speaking up. I wish he were. "You know predators are prowling around out there just waiting for you to let your guard down and fall asleep."

"Why don't you man up?" I hear the voice of Courageous I step in. "Don't listen to this wimp. He's never steered you in the right direction anyway, and now he's trying to scare the hell out of you so you won't get any rest. How the hell are you going to get out of here tomorrow if you're too tired to walk?"

"Oh boy, here they go again." I recognize the voice of Reasonable I. "Look, we've got the fire going strong, and you know wild animals are afraid of fire. You've got that bat and Crocodile Dundee. You just saw the deer acting like there was no danger. Why not take a little nap, whether it's bedtime or not?"

Man, there sure are a lot of I's running around in there, I think. How in the world did I ever get anything done back in the real world with all this chatter going on in my head? And, for that matter, is *this* the real world? From all that's happened to me today, maybe I should get some rest. Maybe I'll even wake up back in my own bed.

I get up and throw a bit more wood on the fire, just in case, return to my spot by the rocks, sit down, and close my eyes. I lie there relaxed and peaceful when I hear Paranoid I say, "You better sleep with one eye open. That way, if anything happens, you'll see it coming." I think to myself that that might be a good idea.

CHAPTER 9

The thought of sleeping with one eye open reminds me of a fishing trip I once took with my best friend and fishing companion, Tony. We drove from New York to Maine, and Tony insisted on driving the whole way back. With one eye open. On the last day of the trip, we decided to take a break around noon and pack up around two so that we would be well rested for the ride back. But as it always happens when Tony and I go fishing, the last day of the trip is always a spectacular marathon. It had been a five-day affair, and we'd caught next to nothing. But as luck would have it, on that fifth day, the salmon were literally jumping out of the water. We fished until dark, when we frankly got tired of landing them. Since both of us had to be back at work the next morning, we had no choice but to drive back that night. Now, Tony had been in the navy and served in Vietnam. He often told stories of how he had stayed up for three or four straight days manning the forward fifty-caliber machine gun on trips up the Dong Nai River. I had heard all the stories countless times and had to admit that most were pretty funny.

We started back in his Dodge; he drove, and I sat in the passenger seat. I told him that if he wanted to get some rest, I'd be more than happy to do my share of the driving. He just turned slightly toward me and reminded me of his days manning the old fifty-caliber. I'd heard the story many times and knew once he started, there was no stopping him. When he finished, he told me that I just had to serve as the navigator, same as I did on the ride up—tell him where and when to turn. That was all. I told him that was fine, but if he did need a break, I was more than happy to drive for a bit. About two hours into the trip, I was falling asleep at different intervals, my head bobbing back and forth. At one point, I woke up wondering how Tony was doing.

"Are you all right?" I asked.

I looked over, and he was still chain-smoking Marlboros, as he had been the whole ride, but now he was driving with only one eye open.

"Wake up!" I yelled.

Without taking his eye off the road, he asked, "What are you yelling about? I got my good eye on the road. And besides, we're making great time." Good time was always important to Tony. We had made such good time on the way up that we had arrived two hours earlier than expected. That despite a speeding ticket on the Mass Turnpike for doing ninety miles an hour. He thanked the officer, told him the Red Sox sucked, and we were back on our way.

"What was that about?" I asked him.

"Well, the Red Sox do suck," he said. Sure enough, it was 1986, and they would lose the World Series to our Mets that October. Thanks to Tony's remarks, we received a police escort to the Maine border, the disgruntled officer hoping he could bang us with another violation … or two.

Tony drove the whole way home from that Maine trip with one eye open. And indeed, we did make good time, despite getting lost a couple of times when the navigator fell asleep.

If Tony could drive ten hours with one eye, certainly I can sleep against this rock here, keeping vigilant with just one eye open.

I make myself comfortable, sit back against the rock, and employ the one-eye technique. I try to close my left eye and keep the right open, but I realize I'm not particularly focused at all. *How the hell did Tony drive like this the whole way?* I wonder. I start to feel a little chilly and elect to use the poncho as a blanket. If only I could send a message out to someone and let them know I'm here. I take the poncho out of the backpack, grabbing it by the hood and rolling it out. Something falls out and hits the ground with a thud. I look down and see that my prayers have been answered: a cell phone!

"Yes!" I scream. "Yes!" I begin to survey the phone. It certainly isn't my phone; it is in fact an old phone, the kind that flips open to reveal a simple screen and keypad. It's not the kind that can send and receive text and email. Just your basic phone. But surely that's all I need! I can call for help! The phone will not light up, so I move closer to the fire to see the screen and the keypad. This still does not help. I grab the flashlight from the bag, locate the on/off button, and begin to think of who I should call for help. Tony? He always helps me when I'm in a bind. But I have his number programmed into my phone, and I can't remember it by heart. I could call 911 and have the police search for me. I look down at the phone. Nothing is happening. The lights will not turn on, the phone will not make a sound, nothing.

"Come on, you stupid machine. I need a break," I say and try the button again. Still nothing. I bet the battery's dead. Whoever packed this bag remembered batteries for the flashlight but couldn't take the time to charge the phone. Shit! Still in disbelief, I return to my spot by the rocks and sit down. Tempted as I am to throw the phone as far as I can into the woods, I hear a voice in my head.

"Put the phone back in the bag," it says.

CHAPTER 10

The early-morning sun illuminates the clearing with golden light in all directions. I find myself slumped over in my spot. I open my left eye first, still groggy in that twilight between sleep and waking when your body is still a little numb. This phenomenon dissipates quickly as I open my right eye and look out into the clearing. I keep rubbing my eyes, hoping that this is still a dream that I have not woken up from yet. I push back the poncho, which at this point is only barely covering my legs, and stand up. I'm still in this strange clearing, still a captive of this dream, if that's indeed what it is. I discover that my back hurts from the awkward position I slept in. The last thing I remember running through my mind before falling asleep was the notion that this was all a dream and I was sure to wake up back in my own bed. That was what kept me sane and calmed me to the point where I could fall asleep. No such luck.

I stagger over to the creek, kneel down, and splash water on my face with both hands. The water is cold, and its bite startles me at first. I repeat the process again, take a deep breath, and use my sleeve to wipe the water. Still unsure what the hell I'm supposed to do, I return to my spot and plop down. I smell the smoldering ashes from the fire that burned out overnight as I slept.

I sit there reflecting on my situation. I'm still in this godforsaken place. Apparently, the I's are now awake too, and they're doing a little reflecting of their own.

"Well, now," Wise Guy I says. "You're still stuck in this place, huh? As brilliant as *you* think you *are*, you don't have a clue what to do, do you?"

"We're going to die out here!" laments Paranoid I.

Optimistic I adds his two cents: "Oh, don't worry. He'll think of something."

"He can't think of everything. He's just not that smart," Wise Guy I mocks in his usual fashion.

My mind is all scrambled up, and I don't know what to do. Having all these I's battling each other isn't making it any easier. But then again, this isn't your everyday, rational situation, now is it? My mind is always confused when confronting these difficult situations. It has been that way all my life. Why should things be any different now?

"Stop! Stop! Let the man think! Get out of his head and give him some air," Analytical I shouts.

I stand up and walk to the middle of the clearing past the fire pit. I stretch out a bit, hoping to walk away from the conflicting I's. They follow me.

"What are we going to do now, smart-ass? You don't know where anyone or, for that matter, anything is?" Wise Guy is still at it. He just can't help himself. This is the kind of scenario that he loves.

"Shut up! Shut up!" I hear Reasonable I step in. "How's he supposed to come up with a rational solution when he has all you I's shouting at him? And we'll all be stuck here too. Give him a chance."

I look up through the only gap in the canopy of branches above my head. There's the hawk sitting on the same branch he was on the night before. Has he been there all night keeping an eye on me? I allow myself to believe this. I need all the friends I can get. He was there through the night keeping me safe. I'm sure of it. I don't care if the notion is crazy. What isn't crazy about this anyway?

Suddenly, the crows return and begin their ritualistic screeching and dive-bombing of the hawk again. The hawk merely looks down at me from his perch, leans away, and glides off into the wind. There goes my only friend and my protector. Once again, I am truly alone.

At that moment, my stomach awakens, and I find myself thinking about breakfast. It is now and truly has always been my favorite meal of the day. I usually eat breakfast out because I'm always running to work or someplace or another. Two eggs, home-fried potatoes, and toast is my favorite. Sometimes it's oatmeal with bananas and honey if I'm trying to eat healthy. Or Belgian waffles topped with honey when I'm not. That's what I'm talking about. But I don't see any diners in the proximity, so I have to resign myself to whatever I can find in the backpack. Let's see: there are eggs here, hard-boiled but eggs nonetheless, and biscuits. I take an egg out of the plastic baggy and carefully tap it against the side of a rock so I can peel the shell. I unwrap the biscuits and take a bite from one. While enjoying my breakfast, the thought comes to me, likely from Contented I, that it is a lovely morning and I should try to enjoy myself.

I look out into the clearing and see various species of birds looking for their breakfasts: grubs, seeds, or whatever else they can dig up. They seem to be in pleasant moods, singing and chattering as they go about their morning business. The golden light makes me, an amateur photographer, yearn for a camera to hold the pastoral beauty prisoner. Again I hear Woody Woodpecker wailing on the side of what must be a decaying tree. Rat-tat-tat. With the relative serenity of the morning, Woody's work has an almost urban appeal— the jackhammer of the forest. All things considered, this is a magical place. After breakfast, I get up, stretch again, and find myself over by the brook. The sun has risen a bit more, and as my eyes adjust, I can see right through to the bottom of the stream bed.

As I look over near a big rock in the pool, I see a little movement. My fly-fishing instincts take over, and I stand motionless. Trout. Nature has made trout difficult to spot. In fact, their scales can take on all the colors of the surrounding stream bed. But if you look carefully, you can see the small movements of water on the surface as the trout expel it over their gills. Also, when they're feeding, a trained observer can see their mouths opening and closing as they are different colors than their bodies. I stand there patiently, waiting for the trout to move and reveal himself. He finally makes his move, leaving the shadow of the rock and heading upward to snatch a mayfly off the surface of the water. The trout gracefully glides back down to his hiding place among the rocks. I can tell by the big red dots and brownish-golden color that this is a brown trout. Had he been a rainbow, he would have been silver in color with a distinct rainbow stripe down his back. If I only had my rod and reel. This is a trophy fish if I have ever seen one. Of course, I'd let him go. I always practice catch and release. I become aware of how quiet my mind has been since I first spotted the trout. As soon as I became aware of the fish and went into fly-fishing mode, my mind became as still and clear as the water that rests in that pool. For as long as it took me to see what the fish was up to, I became one with my surroundings. I trained my mind to be devoid of thought and focus on observation. Since I have no rod or reel, there will be no fishing. If I had, I would have instinctually, unconsciously selected the appropriate flies to catch this fish.

Without any fishing to be done, I see for the first time what it is like to be thought-free, to just be. To be observing yet also part of the scene. I like the experience and find it eye-opening. It is refreshing, and I feel truly alive. Any time in my life in which I can be free from my mind is quality time as far as I'm concerned. It comes to me that this is the same feeling I have during a tennis match. There is no time to think. If you're thinking, you're most likely losing. You have to get out of your mind's way and react. With the ball speeding along at often incredible speeds, you have no time to think. This is precisely what I would try to teach my up-and-coming players to do. It is also the hardest concept for a young player to grasp. In the present situation, I see that it is also possible to remain still, have control over your mind, and just be. To be the observer of the situation as it presents itself. I am not reacting to anything moving or flying around. I am merely watching the trout do what trout do, and in so doing, I become a part of my surroundings.

Now as pure observer, I turn back to the clearing and see it for the first time without interference from my mind. It is stunningly beautiful: the birds bobbing and skipping in the gentle breeze, the sunlight dancing on each leaf, and the smoke from the smoldering fire spiraling into the air. I notice that I am much lighter physically and feel more relaxed than I have since I arrived here. I am in this particular spot on earth for the first time and part of it all, one with the birds and the trees. I am out of my mind, literally, and it feels wonderful. I don't want to move because I don't want to lose this feeling.

Suddenly I hear, "Well, what are you going to do now, big man?" Wise Guy I is back, and with him all the other I's return. All my problems snap back like a bad dream.

"Quiet. Let me be a bit," I say. "It was so nice to have you out of my mind for a couple of minutes."

"Well we're back, and we're back for good. So let's do something."

"All right, all right," I say, "just give me a chance to think."

I glance back out on the clearing and immediately notice it's lost some of its shine. It is obvious to me that my mind has returned and my innocent perception of it is gone. I go over to the rocks and sit back down. I have a flashback of my high school football days.

I am playing quarterback for the Ossining Indians football team, where I have played for three years. I'm under center as the play unfolds. I drop back and throw a pass to the split end that goes for a sixty-nine-yard touchdown. But what is clear to me is that I hadn't been thinking at all as the play developed. As if in a trance, I see myself and the end, watch him as he catches the ball and streaks the remaining distance into the end zone. At that point, the noise of the crowd awakens me. My mind flashes again, and I see myself in a baseball uniform playing second base. I am in my stance between first and second, chattering away at the pitcher. I watch a grounder roll toward me. I move silently, thoughtlessly, toward the ball, glove it, and fire to first. Next, I'm in my basketball uniform in the high school gym, at the top of the key. I watch the ball come to me, and I, as if it is instinctual, shoot it right through the hoop. I see myself on a knoll covered with green grass talking to a boy about seventeen years old. There are two small white balls lying on the grass, one ten yards in front of me and the other one a little further down and off to the right. We stop at the closer one, and I notice we have two different-colored team golf shirts on. I look up ahead and see the green about 150 yards away with the flagstick sticking out from the back right portion of the green. I watch as I pull out the proper club from my bag and set the bag back down on the stand, all the while talking to my competitor. I love tournament golf, but I don't quite know why at that moment in time. I stand there, looking at where I want to put the ball on the green. All the talking has stopped now, and I go into my pre-shot routine. I move toward the ball, take one practice shot, and then strike it. The ball flies toward the pin and lands eight feet away. "Good shot," remarks my opponent, and the chatter begins again.

My mind now returns to the clearing, and I have a sudden epiphany. Perhaps that's why we play sports. I previously thought it was merely because they were good for you. They are great exercise, build character, and so on. But like looking at the trout in the stream, we find in sports that moment that we are all searching for. The moment when our minds drop out and we just are. In sports, we are searching for that ever-short moment in time that we crave: the ability to escape our minds. I now see that that is how we are intended to be. Only life gets in the way.

Across the clearing, the three deer from the previous night emerge from the brush and again nibble on the leaves that hang from the lower branches of the trees. I notice a lovely rust-red color in their summer coats. They don't seem to notice me, and if they do, they don't seem to care. As I watch them, I start to wonder again: *Where am I? What am I going to do?* I face the very real fact that I am running out of food and water and don't know what to do about it. Deep down, I'm still rooting for the outside chance that I'll wake up at any moment.

I hear a screech high up in the trees, and I move into the middle of the clearing. Circling above me is my old friend, the hawk. Well, he's back, and I feel safe again. I look back toward the deer, who are disinterested that I'm now up and moving around and continue to enjoy their breakfast.

"Well, the way things are going, you are going to be out of food shortly," I hear Analytical I say.

"You know, he's right. Time for action." I hear Courageous I add.

"And just what would you have me do?" I ask out loud as if he were standing right next to me.

"Break camp and go in search of some people who can help you."

"Where might they be?" I muse. "Maybe there is no one else in this dream or whatever this is. I could be the only one stuck here."

"Steady, steady now. You know you can get out of this," Optimistic I interrupts. "You can do this. You can find someone. Maybe there's a town … or a ranger station …"

"Or be killed trying."

"How come every time I hear from Optimistic I, you have to step in and ruin the moment, Pessimistic I?"

"Just trying to keep it real," he retorts.

"That's ridiculous," I say. "Don't tell me anything negative. I don't want to hear that dumb shit. Now, all of you, out of my head!"

I turn abruptly and walk back over to the rocks to gather my things. I don't know. I guess some of them might be right. I hope Pessimistic I is as wrong as he has ever been. I pick the backpack up, and the cell phone falls to the ground again. I bend down, pick it up, and flip the cover over to look at the face.

"No charge! Dead battery! Who packs a useless cell phone anyway?" I mutter. I turn the pack right side up and notice a small pocket on that side that I didn't see before. I stuff the phone in the pocket, again resisting the urge to hurl it into the woods. I fold up the poncho and slide it into the bottom of the backpack. Next, I put in the flashlight, followed by the matches and all the remaining food I have. I pick up the knife in its sheath and slide it under my belt behind my back. Just like Crocodile Dundee. Lastly, I strap the canteen to the side of the pack. Well I'm ready. For what I don't know. As on cue, I hear Courageous I say, "Okay, we're walking out of here, men. We're making the move. Nothing's going to stop us now."

"Did I not hear this yesterday?" I say. "And do you not remember how that ended up? I walked around in circles all afternoon and ended up back here because I was listening to all of you."

"Maybe we should just sit down and wait for help?" says Pessimistic I. "You have no idea what might be out there watching you and waiting for a chance to jump all over you."

"Don't listen to that wimp," Courageous I says. "We need to make something happen, and sitting around here isn't going to cut it. Besides, didn't that pain in the ass, Analytical I, already point out that no one knows we're out here and there won't be any search parties out looking for someone they don't even know is missing? How do you know you're even lost? You have no idea what's even happening. I say it's time for action."

"I hate to say this, but you're right," I agree. "We have to do something before the food and water run out."

"Well then make a move," I hear.

"Just, all of you, stop giving orders! Let me figure out where I'm going."

I move out into the middle of the clearing from the spot by the rocks where I spent the night. I decide to go in the opposite direction than I went the day before. I hear a screech from my hawk and, looking up, see that he's returned to his spot in the tree. He looks down on me and screeches as if to send me on my way or say goodbye, I'm not sure which. I look across the clearing and start in my chosen direction.

"Finally. We're moving," cracks Wise Guy I.

"Listen. It's a beautiful day, and I'm not going to listen to you and the rest of you. So sit back and enjoy the ride everybody."

Wouldn't it be nice to be able to clear your mind? But all day, you have to listen to them, twenty-four seven. Maybe the best remedy is to pay no attention. Sometimes, albeit briefly, they do go away.

CHAPTER 11

The morning is indeed spectacular. There is just enough of a chill in the air left over from the night before, and once my feet hit the ground, the going is easy. There are downed trees and small bushes interspersed on the forest floor but not so much that my progress is impeded. In fact, just the act of walking feels great. As far as I can tell, I'm walking in the opposite direction from yesterday. At least I don't see anything that I recognize. After about two and a half miles, the ground falls away, and I'm walking down into a ravine. Yesterday's attempt was all flat ground. The brush starts to become thicker, and there are patches of thorny bushes and fruit trees, apple and peach if I'm not mistaken, that have no fruit but beautiful flowers sending a sweet scent through the air.

As I continue walking, I think this would be a great spot to hunt grouse. I've spent many winters hunting grouse in the woods behind a small cabin I rented. The back of the house opened up on a swamp that bordered a large hill. The hill had once been the site of a peach and apple orchard. Though overgrown for years, the orchard still had enough fruit trees and dogwood buds to support a large number of grouse. Now the grouse is a bird indigenous to North America. It's a much bigger bird than the quail but a bit smaller than the pheasant. Though they spend most of their time on the ground, they can take off flying quickly; it can scare the hell out of you if you're not expecting it. They can also run quickly, and because they are weary and never expose themselves, they can be difficult to spot. They've learned their art of survival by creeping around the forest floor, hiding under bramble bushes and the like. With the fruit trees here to nourish them and the bramble bushes to hide under, this is indeed a great spot for the grouse. Now of course, I don't have my shotgun with me (I prefer twenty-gauge for this), so I have to imagine myself in grouse-hunting mode.

After hunting grouse without the aid of a dog to help me find them, I developed my own system. I approach the hunting area as quietly as possible, moving with short steps, vigilantly listening for the slight crunching of dry leaves that might signify a nearby grouse. Weaving across the forest, I stop frequently and listen. I know full well that the grouse will be nervous with all the stopping, and the next step or two will often flush them out and into the air. Hitting them as fast as they are when they take to the air is another matter altogether.

Though without a gun, I instinctually start my grouse-hunting procedure. I weave back and forth from thorn bush to thorn bush, stopping frequently to listen. At one point, as I pause, I realize that, again, my mind is devoid of all conscious thought. My head is clear and focused on any indication that a grouse might be roaming nearby. As with the trout, I have become one with the scene. As I slink down and circle around a pear tree and stop, I hear a faint crinkling. With my next step, a grouse shoots up in the air, its fiercely flapping wings producing a sound reminiscent of a helicopter lifting off. Without thinking, I raise my arms and fire an imaginary round into the air. I watch the grouse ascend over the trees, reach the apex of its flight, and gently glide back to the ground as it disappears into the forest. It was a big one.

And there's that pleasant feeling of vacuousness in my mind again. The feeling that I got from sports, fishing, and hunting in which I transcend myself and am utterly and completely in the moment. It seems to me now that I spent so much time performing these activities just trying to find that feeling.

"What are you standing around for? I thought we were trying to find a way out of this mess?" I hear Impatient I say.

"Man, I can't have any fun."

"You would have missed him anyhow," Wise Guy I quips.

"Nah, I'd've got 'im," I mutter under my breath.

"Don't kid yourself. I've seen you shoot," he replies.

"All right. All right. I'm going."

I start walking at a good pace again and come to a small creek. It is much smaller than the one back at the clearing. I wonder if this creek runs into that stream back there. I look for a spot where it narrows so I can cross without getting my hiking boots wet. About fifty yards downstream, I see a very narrow portion that is only about a foot deep and three feet wide, and I head in that direction. I put my right foot in the water and jump to the other bank. My left foot disappears into the mud on the other side as my right carries over onto firmer ground.

"Ahhhhh!" I groan as I pull my stuck foot from the mud and leave a bunch of tracks all over the bank. I continue on my way. After about a hundred yards, the forest opens up to a field of tall grass. I stop at the edge of the forest among a group of white birch trees and survey. The field looks to be about five acres square and is covered with grass that is hip high. I hesitate before crossing the field. The fact that I can't see my feet or legs in the grass leaves me feeling uneasy. Who knows what might be lurking? I decide to skirt the field to avoid having to walk through the tall grass. This is one of the few times I've been in the wilderness alone without a shotgun. I'd feel much safer with one. Then again, maybe there's nothing out there. Maybe I'm just being ridiculous.

"It's not ridiculous at all," I hear Pessimistic I say.

"Hey, you don't know what's out there in that grass, do you?" agrees Paranoid I.

"That's right," I say. I look out across the field and see a little bit of woods, then a small hill with an outcropping of rocks. Maybe I'll see a farm or a house from there. Perhaps even a town.

"Well, you should cross the field, get up on the hill, and see what you can see," says Analytical I.

"Or I could walk the entire edge of the field, backtrack a bit, and then climb the hill."

"Stop it. You chicken?" says Courageous I. "What is wrong with you? You scared?"

"Well, I don't know," I say.

"Get going. Be a man. Off you go," he replies.

I step out into the grass and make it twenty yards before something moves sharply about ten yards ahead of me. *What the hell is that?* I move forward a little, and again there is a burst of speed ten yards in front of me. I stop again, straining to get a look. The expression "snake in the grass" keeps coming to mind. And I hate snakes. But wait a second. If this is a snake, it's the fastest snake known to man. I reach behind me, pull the knife from its case, and hold it in front of me, the sun gleaming off its blade. When I move a couple of steps forward, it runs again. I jump back, looking as hard as I can, but I still can't see a thing. No, it ain't no snake, that's for sure; it's moving way too damn fast. The picture of a wolf pops into my head, and I turn around and think about retreating. But it can't be a wolf; they're huge, and they'd be taller than the grass. A bear? *No, a bear would be way bigger than a wolf, you idiot.* So, what is this? A fox? What would a fox be doing out here during the day? They hunt at night.

I move forward again. This time, nothing stirs. I continue to inch forward cautiously, at a snail's pace, until I find myself in the very spot where the creature last moved. Suddenly, the grass trembles again, and, with knife in hand, I peer out into a sparser section and spy a fluffy white tail. I exhale all the air from my lungs as I realize that my nemesis has been a harmless rabbit this whole time. A larger rabbit, don't get me wrong, but a rabbit nonetheless. You see how your mind can play tricks on you?

"You see?" I say. "Damn rabbit, and I had snakes, wolves, and bears all prowling around in my mind." At that point, I believe I truly do have shit for brains. With much more confidence than before, I continue to cross through the tall grass. I turn around and notice that I made a narrow path where I crossed the field. I see a big pine tree that has fallen, probably from a wind storm, and make my way toward it. As I get closer, I observe the large ball of roots still affixed to the tree and the hole in the ground that they left when the tree toppled. The small portion of forest before the hill is sparse, and the ground climbs at a gradual grade at the foot of the hill. I stop there and look up at the sun. It hangs straight up in the sky without a cloud in sight. I wonder what time it is. With the position of the sun and the growling of my stomach, I suppose it must be close to noon. At any rate, it's lunchtime, and I walk over to the pine and have a seat. I pull the backpack off my back and undo the top flap, fishing for something to eat. I pull out a can of beans but decide against it because I don't want to take the time to build a fire and can't stand the thought of trying to eat them cold. I return the beans to the bag and pull out the dried meat. It's some kind of jerky, which, as I've said, I'm not a huge fan of, but I'm hungry, and it requires no preparation whatsoever. I open the pouch, pull out a piece, and take a bite. It's salty as hell and has a smoky flavor, but all in all, as hungry as I am, I quickly eat about half the jerky that's been provided for me.

I realize that the jerky's saltiness has made me thirsty. Perhaps this wasn't the best choice for lunch since I have limited water left. After a big pull from the canteen, I screw the top off and realize that I only have about half the water I started with. I need to be very careful going forward. Returning the jerky to the bag, I feel an apple in my hand. I forgot all about them. I pull it out and take a bite, the sweet juice neutralizing the salt that lingered in my mouth.

While I'm enjoying the apple, I look down and study the ball of roots and the hole they left when they were ripped from the ground. Next to the hole, I see what appears to be a burrow. The opening is fairly large, though not enough so to alarm me. Maybe a skunk or a woodchuck. Or perhaps a fox. As I saw making my way across the field, there are probably a good number of rabbits for the fox to hunt. I toss the apple core into the middle of the field and see the grass move rapidly in the opposite direction from where it lands. "Yep. A lot of rabbits," I say as I fasten the canteen to the side of the bag.

I throw the pack around my shoulder and onto my back, jump down off the trunk of the pine, and turn to face the hill. It is a short walk through what was left of the wooded area to the base of the hill. I start up the incline. There are some shrubs and a few small pines, which would have made excellent Christmas trees. All in all, the going up the hill is easy at the start. Once I get three-quarters or so to the top, the slope gets much steeper. Moving up in a direct route is difficult, and I have to meander a little along the ridge to get to the top. Once over the ridge, the land flattens out for fifty yards or so. After that, the rock outcropping I saw from the field is on top of yet another steep ridge.

I stand there catching my breath, thankful that I've played as much tennis as I have, or else the climb would have been really tough. I look up at the rock formation. Some very impressive rocks all right. Two of them sit side by side and must be at least three stories high. I can see from where I am that the rocks are set in the hillside, the ground rising up behind them. I think I can walk around behind the rocks and get on top of them that way. From there, I ought to be able to see the whole valley below. I walk toward the twin boulders, across the flat ground, to where the steep incline begins. Along the way, I pick up a branch to serve as a walking stick to help me on my way. As I get closer, I notice a cave set back about fifty yards between two of the rocks. Some sunlight breeches the opening of the cave and illuminates it nicely. Beyond that is darkness. I stand there and look at the mouth of the cave as a feeling of familiarity descends over me. I feel as if I've been here before. But how can this be? I have no idea where I am and how I got here.

As I stand here contemplating, I see a shadow run across the face of the rocks. A bald eagle with a beautiful white head and a tail bursting in the sunlight flies to the top of the highest rock and lands. I look up at him, and he returns my gaze. He's a large, mature bird, and I'm thinking he may make his nest up there in those old rocks. I've seen many eagles during the winter while fishing in the Croton River, just a couple of miles from where I live. They move down from upstate because the Croton does not freeze over, and they can still fish there in the bitter cold of winter. Seeing them always makes me feel good, and this is no exception. His presence both relaxes and excites me.

In my mind, I hear Courageous I. "Well, a chance to explore a bit. We should have a look inside the cave and see if it leads anywhere helpful."

"What could be helpful inside a mountain?" Wise Guy I says.

"Oh, come on. Where is your curiosity? And besides, this could be a tunnel to the other side of the mountain," says Analytical I.

"I agree with him. There could be something in there that is helpful in the future. Let's have a look," says Courageous I.

"Don't go in there. You don't know what you'll find," chimes in Paranoid I.

"Here we go again. He's only trying to scare you out of looking,"

Courageous I replies. "Besides, I heard Analytical I say there may be some signs of human life in there, and you haven't seen or heard any people since you've been here. You haven't even seen or heard a plane. You haven't seen anything in this forest to suggest that there is human life at all. This cave could very well have been a mine, or perhaps someone lived inside of it many years ago."

Just then, I hear a rustling above me. I look up and see the eagle flapping his wings. Somehow I get the impression that he wants me to enter the cave. As I watch him looking down at me, he leans forward and lifts into the air, circling around the entrance. One of his tail feathers floats down and lands next to me. I pick it up. *Wow, I think, I always wanted a real eagle feather, but I've never found one out in the woods before. This must be some sort of sign. There must be something inside this cave that I need to see.*

"That's right," Courageous I says. "Let's have a look."

I know in that moment that I have to enter.

CHAPTER 12

I start down the alleyway between the two rocks, looking at the entrance to the cave about fifty yards away. The sides of the rocks create walls on both sides reminiscent of buildings in New York City. The closer I get to the cave, the more I feel fear overtaking me. By the time I reach the entrance, I can hardly breathe; the muscles in my legs have gotten tight, and a fire burns in the pit of my stomach. I stop and peer into the darkness. It looks as though it goes back quite a way. It's tall enough to stand up in without having to hunch over. I sling the pack off my back and open the flap, producing the flashlight from inside. For good luck, I slide the eagle feather under the band on my hat. I feel like an Indian brave now. Well, maybe not *that* brave.

I turn on my flashlight and point it into the deep darkness in front of me. The cave does indeed go back a way before turning to the left.

"Well, go ahead, jackass. Go on in," Wise Guy I says.

"Get out of my head. I don't really need any of this right now," I say. My legs feel like Jell-O, I'm breathing hard as I look into the cave, and I can't see anything. *Shit!* Bats can be in there. Or, even worse, snakes. But somehow, I know I have to go in there no matter what. It's as if I've come here to do just that. I take a deep breath, swallow hard, and take a slow and cautious step forward.

As I deliberately walk into the cave, shining the light everywhere at once, I'm overcome by a strange feeling. It's as if I'm entering not a cave but my own mind. The deeper I progress, the more I feel I am going inside myself. I keep looking at the walls to see if there is anything leaning against them or on them that someone may have left for me. Some sign of human life, ancient or otherwise. The further I go, the more the fear wells up inside me. All kinds of images continue to pop up in my head; everything I've been afraid of my whole life flashes before my eyes. Everything from falling off that building in New York City to flying in an airplane. All my childhood fears resurface as well: monsters under my bed and aliens outside my window coming to take me away. Nevertheless, I keep moving forward, slowly but surely. I reach the area where the cave twists slightly to the left. I am roughly twenty yards into the mountain now. There are still no signs that anyone has ever been here before, no evidence of people at all. At this point, I'm starting to wonder if this is an exercise in futility. Why am I listening to Courageous I anyway? And what does an eagle know anyhow? Just then, my light illuminates an image on the right side of the cave wall. Someone sketched the figure of an eagle. It looks a bit like a special I saw on TV about prehistoric cave paintings in France. It's amazing. Well, it looks like at one time there were people here, though unfortunately, it must have been long ago. I shine the light on the wall, hoping to find more of this artwork, and there, on the left, further down into the cave, is the drawing of a bear. I walk toward the image and notice that it is quite elaborate. I shine the light past the bear drawing and see what I think may be graffiti etched on the wall. After further investigation, it is one word: "Run."

Just then, I hear a wheezing sound echoing from deep within the bowels of the cave. I can't quite place the noise. As I approach it, I hear more clearly. It's definitely the sound of someone snoring. Don't tell me it's the cave artist back there snoring away? I shine my light back and see that the cave winds again, this time sharply to the left; the racket is coming from just around the corner. I reach up and rub the eagle feather for good luck.

Suddenly, without any indication why, all the fear leaves me. I become lighter and approach the snoring without any conscious thoughts in my mind. A musty odor like the smell of ten wet dogs now fills the air as I come upon the bend. I stop at the corner. The snoring is now unbelievably loud, and I can tell that whoever is sleeping is just around the bend. I really want to see this guy; hey, it's someone at last. I take a quick step out and around the corner and shine the light on the ground in front of me. And there, lying on the ground is not a man at all but my worst nightmare. The single thing that I have been most afraid of my entire life. The creature that haunts my dreams and has scared the living crap out of me more nights than I can remember.

CHAPTER 13

A bear! And it is not just your garden-variety black bear (though that would be bad enough). I can tell from the enormous hump on his back and the brown color of his fur that this is a grizzly bear. I freeze as my old friend fear retakes me. My legs won't move, the hair on the back of my neck stands at attention, my heart ascends into my throat, and, I'm not ashamed to say, I may wet my pants a little bit. Due to the fear, my hands are inoperative as the light from the flashlight shines down directly on top of the bear's head. I can see from where I'm rooted to the ground that his eyes are still closed, and in fact he has a rather pleasant expression on his huge bear face. Right here and now, it occurs to me that if I can somehow shake this fear-induced paralysis, I can creep back out of the cave without waking him and get the hell out of here. But fear is having none of that, and I am affixed to the floor of the cave, petrified. As I continue looking on at my dreaded opponent, I see his nose start to twitch. I remember my springer spaniel Ozzie would do the same when I put a dog biscuit in front of his nose while he was sleeping. He would smell the biscuit and ultimately wake up. At this is moment, it seems, I am the goddamn biscuit.

Suddenly, his eyes blink rapidly and slowly open. I can't help but think that he looks a bit like me when I wake up—you know, a little groggy at first. I always have to sit up on the edge of the bed and shake my head a little to get the cobwebs of sleep out of there. He is lying about ten yards in front of me and stands up in one quick motion. He still looks a little sleepy, though the flashlight is now shining directly on his front paws. In the faint light, I see his eyes come to life. My I's do as well.

Still frozen to the ground, I hear Analytical I say in a low tone, "Lie down and play dead."

Lie down? I think. *I can't even move.* This is what I always feared most; you can't escape a bear. They are fast and can swim and climb trees. Plus, they have noses like hunting dogs, which puts hiding out of the question. His eyes freeze on me, and his nose shoots up in the air like a hunting dog trying to get the scent of a grouse in the tall grass. He lets out a ferocious roar that nearly takes my hat off. He swats at me with a monstrous paw, though I'm too far for him to make contact. I drop the makeshift walking stick, and the light from the flashlight I'm still holding shakes something awful. "Lie down and play dead," I hear again.

That's when I hear a voice come from deep down inside of me, a voice I that I don't recognize as any of the other I's. A deep-down-inside voice. "Run! Run your ass off!"

Without another thought, I turn and take off, flying. I see the light at the end of the tunnel burning as brightly as the sun, and I'm running faster than I've ever run before. I don't think my feet are touching the ground. At first, I think he may not even have bothered to chase me. No such luck, however, as I hear him barreling toward me through the cave like a freight train. I think I must have pissed him off.

Now, in high school, I was one of the fastest guys on the track team, and I once ran the forty-yard dash in 4.3 seconds, which is world-class speed. However, whenever I ran the hundred-yard dash, I would beat everyone for the first forty yards and get passed over the course of the next sixty. I hope the bear doesn't know this. I reach the light and am out of the cave and sprinting through the alleyway between the two rocks. The bear has reached the mouth of the cave, and he's still coming fast. Out in the light of day, I can see him clearly. Man, is he enormous! I put my head down and push hard. I dash across the level ground, but when I reach the ledge, I fall and roll head over heels down the steep incline. The bear was right on my ass, but the fall propels me a little ways ahead of him once again. I hit the bottom and, uninjured, jump to my feet and take off again. Looking back, I can see my pursuer struggling to move down the hill.

"That's right!" I scream. "Bears don't run well downhill!" At this point, I'm now running across the level part that stretches fifty yards before the smaller hill dotted with brush and Christmas trees. The bear hits the level ground and is closing fast. *Ahhhhh! What the hell am I going to do?* I keep seeing the image of the clearing where I stayed last night and can't shake the thought that that's where I'm supposed to go. If I can just get to this next hill before he catches me, I can once again gain a small advantage, as I'll get faster and he'll get slower. Just as I reach the hill, I hear that bear howl again, and I know he's right on my ass. I leap, getting good air, and find myself about twenty yards further down the hill. The bear is now a full thirty yards away and is once again having trouble negotiating the hill. I lean forward and try to open up a bigger lead before we reach the field below.

By the time I make it to the field, I estimate that I'm now a full sixty yards ahead. I look for the pine tree where I ate lunch earlier and head toward it. The bear is not giving up, and as he finally reaches the bottom of the hill, he stops to see and smell the air to locate me. He stands on his hind legs, and I judge that he must be ten feet tall and mad as hell that I've interrupted his nap. I reach the pine and jump into the hole to catch my breath. I pop my head out to see where he is now, and he obviously can see or smell me, as he's running in my direction, roaring. I jump out of the hole and locate the trail I made in the grass when I crossed the field. I retrace my tracks as fast as I can go. The canteen that is strapped to the backpack smacks my face, the eagle feather flies in the wind (though still safely tucked into the hat), and the cans of beans clang together as I run across the open field. Rabbits burst out in front of me in all directions. I hear a thud and see that the bear was moving so fast that he hit the pine tree and fell into the hole. Either that or he thinks I may still be hiding in there. I'm hoping that the fall has put him off and he will abandon the chase. But not this bear. He is too pissed off. I see his head emerge from the hole, and he looks madder than he did before. He pulls himself out and into the field.

"Shit!" I yell. I'm easily seventy yards out in front of him, but a bear can run thirty miles per hour on flat ground, and that beats a 4.3 forty any time. I make it to the edge of the field and look for the spot where I crossed the stream earlier. I spot my muddy footprints and run to the spot. The bear is now halfway across the field and plowing through my trail like a bloodhound. I jump across the stream and up the embankment, making my way back toward the clearing. I still don't know what I plan to do once I reach it. Die, I guess. I have no plan, but I've had the clearing in my mind through this whole chase. Maybe once I return there, I will awaken from this dream-turned-nightmare. It's a recurring nightmare that I've been having since childhood actually, being chased by a bear. I'm now living it. Or am I?

The bear is now at the stream, and he continues in what seems like my exact footprints. I stagger into the clearing and head to my spot by the rocks. I reach down and drop the flashlight that I somehow managed to hold onto throughout and pick up the piece of wood that looks like a baseball bat. I also reach around and pull out the knife from behind my back. I can't run anymore; I'm exhausted. I sit down with my back to the rocks and wait to make my last stand against the mammoth, ten-foot grizzly. I can hear him coming, crashing through the woods, bulldozing anything in his path.

"What am I going to do? What am I going to do? Well … answer me!" But I hear nothing. "Where are all you I's now that I really need you? Where?" Nothing. Only the sound of the bear thundering through the woods and getting closer and closer.

Again, from deep down inside me, I hear that unfamiliar voice that told me to run when I was back in the cave. Only this time it says, "Put up a fight." I hear it again. "Put up a good fight."

The bear is there now, on the edge of the clearing where I saw the deer the night before. He rises on his hind legs and lets loose that godawful roar. He looks right at me. I stand up and look straight back at him. I'm now madder than hell myself. This is it, my nightmare complete, and I roar back at the bear as I slash my knife in the air and wave my bat.

"Come on! Come on!" I yell. "If you want me, come and get me! But if I'm going to die, you're going to know I was here. You're going to remember me!" The bear doesn't move. It is as if he can't or won't enter the clearing.

As I stand there, ready to fight to the death, and it would have surely been my death, I spot my friend, the hawk. He dive-bombs the bear, just as the crows did to him yesterday, though the hawk only dives once, letting out a screech as he passes over. That's it. I'm not the only one fighting this thing. I now have air support. After this, the bear's demeanor seems to change. He stops roaring and growling. Dropping back onto his front paws, he sniffs the air with his big old nose. In an almost leisurely fashion, as if he has lost interest in me, he turns and walks back into the forest from which he came. I drop to me knees, still feeling the effects of the adrenalin rush. I look up at the hawk, who is now circling higher, watching the bear's retreat. The last thing I remember is thinking, *Yes!* After that, I collapse.

CHAPTER
14

As I come to, my eyes open abruptly, the image of the bear still in my head. I jump to my feet and look over where I last saw him. Nothing. I scan the perimeter, and still no bear. I let out a sigh of relief, clearing all the stress I felt in his presence. The deer are back and once again browsing the low-lying branches and small shrubs. Seeing them relaxes me even more. If that big old bear is still lurking, they would be long gone. I look up and see the hawk back in his tree. I can't remember if it was him and him alone that saved me from being dead meat. I stand there dazed, looking up at the hawk, when I notice the sun is starting to set. I am not sure how long I've been out for, but it must have been awhile. The hawk glows in the waning sunlight, bathing in the brilliant pink light of the late-afternoon sky.

"Thank you for saving my life," I say to my hero. "You are a true friend, and if I can ever return the favor, I certainly will."

It is then that I hear that same voice from deep inside, the I that I can't identify. The one that told me to run when I was in the cave and to put up a fight. "*You* did it. *You* saved yourself."

"I did?" I say halfheartedly.

"Yes, you. You faced him down. You faced down your fears, and you stopped the bear from coming into the clearing. The hawk only reminded you that you could do it."

"But how?" I ask.

"All the answers will come in good time." And with that, the voice vanishes.

Turning around, I discover my hat with the eagle feather still stuck in the side. I pick it up, brush it off, and put it back on my head. Having been in a panic the night before, I gathered enough firewood to last for several nights. Making another fire won't be too much of a bother; all I have to do is gather some smaller branches and leaves to get it started, as I learned last night. First, still in a bit of a daze, I walk over to the stream, peel off my clothes, and jump into the pool where I saw the trout earlier. The water is cold and refreshing, particularly after all the running I did this afternoon. I just sit there and let it flow over me, rejuvenating my body and my mind.

As I come out of my dazed state, I feel a slight stinging sensation in both my legs and a little pain in my right knee. I wade a little bit back out of the water and examine my legs. Both are scraped up a bit, mostly from the fall I took down the hill. The pain I feel in my right knee reminds me of pain I've felt in the past after long tennis matches. It's hurt since my last year playing football; nothing too serious, but it always seems to recur after I push myself. Hey, not too bad considering a close encounter with a bear. It could have been worse. Much worse. Not only did I survive, but I'm left with just a couple of aches and scratches.

I lounge around the stream for some time as my energy and wits return. It's getting darker. The sun has almost completely sunk below the horizon, and I'm famished. I decide to get out of the water and get myself some dinner. I leap up onto the bank dripping wet. No towel. Off in the distance, I hear the woodpecker laughing.

"I'm starving," I hear Wise Guy I say. "How about something to eat?"

"Yeah, I'm getting hungry too. I'll take care of it. Just relax," I yell back at him.

"No towel either, dummy."

I consider using my shirt to dry myself off but quickly abandon the idea when I realize I'd have to sleep in a wet shirt all night. There is a cool breeze in the air, so I put my hiking boots back on without the socks. I certainly don't want wet socks either. "I'll air-dry," I proclaim. I pick up my pants, shirt, hat, and socks and carry them over to my spot next to the rocks. I definitely feel a bit funny walking around naked, with just my boots on, but also freer at the same time. Hey, there's nobody around to see me out here anyway. I'm getting increasingly sure of that.

I pick up the backpack and open the top flap. When I reach inside, I pull out a handful of goo. Well, looks like the bananas didn't make it. I scoop out the mess and hurl it into the woods. I then walk back over to my spot and take out a can of beans, place them on one of the rocks, and search for more kindling to start another fire. The deer are now sitting in the clearing with funny expressions on their faces, as if to say, "Get a load of this guy." I bet they have never seen anything like this before: a naked, confused human being hanging out in the breeze. I gather up some leaves and small branches that are lying on the forest floor and arrange them in the fire pit. As I did before, I select some small logs and place them on top, stacking them neatly in a square like Lincoln Logs, and fill the middle in with the kindling. I return to the pack, pull out the matches, and light one carefully. In no time at all, the fire begins to burn. When the heat has dried me off sufficiently, I put my clothes back on.

I grab the knife and the baseball bat and go back over to the rocks, sitting down with my back against them. It's dark now, and the fire is burning well; seeing is no longer a problem. To my surprise, the deer have not moved; rather, they elect to linger in the light of the fire. I hope they will stay the night. Not only do they seem to be good company, but they would, like a good dog, serve as a first-rate alarm if a bear or other man-eater comes a-calling. I take the knife, fork, and the napkin that the biscuits are wrapped in. Unwrapping the biscuits, I notice that only a few are left, and I decide to wrap them back up and save them for breakfast. As the beans heat up and the deer bed down, a calm comes over me. It is a feeling that all is right in the world, that everything will be okay. I look around for the sticks I used to pick up the bean can from the hot rocks the night before. I find a couple on the ground, and, holding them together, I lift the can off the rocks and place it on the ground. I pick up the fork and begin to eat. The beans are going quickly. Soon there's another can heating up on the rocks.

While this second can is warming, I venture over to the woodpile to select some more logs for the fire. Looking up, I spot the great white chest of the hawk in the fire's dancing light. I throw a few more logs on the fire, sit back down in my spot, and pick up the beans off the rock in the same manner as before. My eyes are fixed on the flames in a trancelike state as I sit and eat. My mind is going over all that has happened since I found myself in this strange situation.

Just then, Analytical I says, "This would be a good time for a conference. Let's get everyone together and try to figure out what's going on here."

"Get everyone together?" I burst out. "There's only me here, you jackass. Oh yeah, and by the way, where were all you guys when the bear was chasing me and I was running my ass off? I don't remember anyone helping out during that little affair."

"We were all behind you. And besides, you were doing great. We were all scared speechless," Wise Guy I says.

"By the way, if you keep eating like this, we're going to run out of food and die of starvation," Pessimistic I says.

"Aw, don't worry. We'll hunt our food. Live off the land," Ego I jumps in. "There's plenty of rabbits down in the field. All we have to do is go down there and catch 'em."

"Catch them?"

"That's right—catch them, cook them, and eat them," he continues.

Now, my ego is out of control, and I will be the first one to tell you that I've eaten rabbit a few times, and while it was delicious, I didn't cook it, and Lord knows I didn't catch it either. "Look," I say, "I don't have a shotgun, and even if I did, I don't know how to skin a rabbit anyway. So you can forget that."

"Come on. You can do it. You can do anything," Ego I states emphatically.

"Thanks, those are kind words there, Ego! Never a truer word spoken," I say, "but let's face it. We've got to get the hell out of here, wherever *here* is."

"That's what I'm talking about," Analytical I chimes in. "Let's bring all the I's together and have a powwow. I'm sure we can come up with a solution. There has to be some way out of this dream or whatever."

"Dammit!" I yell. "You don't feel pain in a dream. How do you explain my knee killing me and my legs all scraped up? No, I've never experienced pain in a dream. Not physical pain anyway. Besides, as far as a conference goes, I can't take all of you in my head speaking at once. I'll go mad."

"Well, you are a bit crazy, after all," Wise Guy I says. "You're sitting out in the forest with your back against a rock, eating all the food we have left, and depending on a knife, a stick, and a fire to keep you safe. Not to mention, you're talking to yourself."

"You see, this is why I don't want a conference. Shut up and leave me alone. I need to think."

"It's time for action, not words," says Courageous I.

"There, that's what has gotten us in trouble every time. Every time I listen to you, there's hell to pay. While we are on the subject, who was that I that spoke up in the cave, the one that told me to run? He was there again when we got back to the clearing. Where did he go? I never heard his voice before, but he's the one I want to listen to."

"Who? What voice? We're the only ones here. Must be a figment of your imagination."

"No, Wise Guy, not at all. I heard him loud and clear. What happened to him? And who is he anyway? Get *him*! I want to speak to *him*."

"You really are out of your mind. There's no one here but us. Don't you ever forget that," Wise Guy adds.

"Let me think for myself."

"Think for yourself. That's a good one. You'd be lost without us."

"I can't deal with this any longer. I'm going to get some sleep, and I think all of you should do the same."

With that, I get up, pick up the backpack, and pull out the poncho to use as a blanket, just as I did last night. I move over to the woodpile and throw more wood on the fire, observing that the deer have moved from their spot. I go back over to the rocks. This time, I empty everything in the backpack so I can use it as a pillow. I discover that I've forgotten about the two cigars wrapped up in the bandana. *Oh, man,* I think, *I'd love a cigar. I think a little celebration is in order after my harrowing escape today.*

I pick up the bandana gingerly and begin to untie it in the hopes that the cigars have not gone the way of the bananas. Upon closer inspection, I see that they, like me, have survived the chase and returned to the clearing in one piece.

I love cigars and have for some time. While these cigars have no bands and I have no idea exactly what kind they are, they smell wonderful. They are my favorite size: robusto. The size of the cigar of course refers to both the length and girth of the cigar. The size has a distinct effect on the taste when smoked. So, rolling cigars with the same tobacco but of different sizes results in slightly different tastes. Of course, it would take a real aficionado to discern the difference, much like a wine connoisseur distinguishing different vintages. I happen to be a cigar aficionado.

"Wow, what a wonderful job they did, whoever packed this bag for us."

"Who said that?" I wonder.

"Me," Grateful I says.

"Guess his taste in cigars is better than his taste in food, huh?" Wise Guy I adds.

"Leave the man alone," I say. "Whoever packed this bag made sure to pack these fantastic cigars, and I'd like to compliment him on being a man of excellent taste."

I pick up all the food and place it on top of the rocks. I take out a match and place the box up on the rocks next to the food. Biting off the end of the cigar, I strike the match against the rocks. I twirl the cigar around the flame of the match and take several puffs, lighting it perfectly. *Man, is this good*, I think. I haven't had a cigar in a couple of days, since I arrived here. The sweet aroma and incredible taste are relaxing indeed.

CHAPTER **15**

As I sit here enjoying myself, I begin to think. How did this all come about, and why am I here in this place all alone? One minute I'm at the club giving a tennis lesson. The next thing I know, I'm here with no idea what happened and what this is all about. I wonder, as I puff away on the cigar, smoke billowing around my head, if there are any people in this strange land I have found myself in. The only signs of human life I've seen are the drawings of the bear and the eagle feather in the cave. The bear lives there now, and undoubtedly, he's the only tenant. There hasn't been a plane in the sky, nor have there been any sounds or other indications of human existence. No car noises. No voices. Nothing. The nights are pitch black here, and it's not like I've seen any lights off in the distance—though I never did get to have a look from the top of the hill like I intended to do earlier in the day. And both days, I went off to find help and ended up back here where I originally started. It seems I have just been going around in circles. The first day, I got turned around in the woods and found myself back here. Today, when I decided to walk out again and encountered the bear, all I could think about was running back here. I guess deep down I believed that I would be magically saved from the bear and swept back home if I returned.

I'm conscious of the fact that I'm running out of food and there's precious little water left in the canteen. If I don't do something fast,

I'm probably going to die out here. Let's see, how long can you survive without food? Maybe a week. But I seem to remember you can only go a couple of days without water.

Maybe that's what I'm here for after all. To die. Or maybe I'm already dead, and this is where you go after you die. Well, if that's the case, it certainly doesn't look like hell. That being said, I hope this isn't heaven. I have a much better idea of what heaven should be all about. Besides, where are all the other dead people? Wouldn't there be a hell of a lot more dead people if this is where you go when you die? I'm sure of that. So, we'll go with that. I'm not dead yet, and I'm trying to stay alive. I take a long pull from the cigar and send the smoke floating up into the sky. Okay, that sounds like a much better perspective. What do I need most urgently in order to survive? Most likely water. And wouldn't you know it, there's a fresh creek over there, the one I just climbed out of. There's plenty of cool mountain water just a few feet away. I can drink the water from the creek ...

Parasites! Don't you remember that you had to get a shot for your hunting dog, Oliver, before you took him out in field in case he drank from any of the streams around? The shot was to protect him from parasites that live in creeks and streams just like this one. They're hiding there no matter how clean you think the water might be.

"That's right, we were told that he could contract any one of several diseases and die. And so can you. The creek is out as a water source," Analytical I says.

"I thought you guys were asleep."

"No, we were all just sitting around the fire listening to you go on about this, that, and the other thing," answers Wise Guy.

"Man, it was so peaceful without having to listen to all of you," I reply.

My mind flashes to a movie I saw about two guys that are shipwrecked on an island with nothing to drink but ocean water. I know you can't drink salt water or you'll die from it. I don't know why, but if you drink enough, you will. They solve their problem by boiling the saltwater and are then able to drink it. *That's it!* I think. *I'll boil the water from the creek, and then it'll be safe to drink.* Tomorrow, the first order of business is to boil water and fill up the canteen. I can use the cans the beans came in to do just that. Problem solved.

"I knew you could do it," Ego I declares emphatically. "Now what about the food?"

"I really don't know. I still have some food left, so I'll figure that one out tomorrow." My attention shifts back to my predicament. I feel like if I just had some direction, some kind of sign, I'd be able to get out of this. Something, anything, a path, a signal.

I flick what is left of the cigar butt into the fire and notice that the air is becoming a bit colder. I pull the poncho over my body, up to my neck, lie back, and fall into a deep sleep.

CHAPTER 16

The next morning, I'm awakened by deep snoring. This time it's only me. I look out into the clearing and spot twenty or thirty turkeys. I sit up and watch them strut around. I've seen turkeys in the wild before, but these look huge. I sit there for a minute, still groggy, trying to shake the cobwebs of sleep from my head and take in the show. Most of the turkeys are hens and jakes, but there are a few toms. The air is much colder than it has been since my arrival here. With the chill in the air and the knowledge that turkeys usually flock together at the end of the year, I suspect that it is probably somewhere between early fall and early winter.

Suddenly, I hear a racket behind me. I turn around and look up at the top of the rock where I put all the food the night before. There, on top of the rocks, is the murder of crows I saw attacking the hawk earlier. And it looks to me like they are rummaging through what is left of my food. I jump up furiously, throw off the poncho, and start waving my arms and yelling. The crows take off for the treetops. Looking over my shoulder, I see that all the turkey heads are up and turned in my direction. They look a little startled. And I too am a bit startled by the realization that the crows may have made off with the last of my food.

Well, it's a Mexican standoff. For quite some time, none of the turkeys move, and neither do I. They can't decide whether they should go back to foraging, and I can't decide whether I should try to salvage the rest of my food. Finally, I figure, what the hell? I start grabbing the food and putting it back in the backpack just in case the crows should decide to return. The turkeys follow suit and resume their hunt for breakfast. I put the knapsack back on the ground, pick up the bean cans that I have saved, and walk over to the stream to get some water. I look back at the fire and see that is out now, only smoldering bit. A patch of fog hangs over the water, and more fog has moved off the stream and into the forest. I think it may be colder than I originally thought. I dip both empty cans in the water and fill them to the top. I turn and walk back over, placing the cans on the ground near the fire pit, and search through the bag for the matches. The skittish turkeys have seen enough and disperse into the woods as I walk over to the woodpile. I pick up some small branches and dried leaves and heave them into what is left of the fire. This only produces a plume of smoke, so I strike a match and toss it into the pit. It's aflame in no time, and I add some small logs to the fire just for good measure. I place the bean cans full of water on the rocks along the fire pit, just as I did when heating the beans. Hopefully this will get the water in the cans to boil and I'll be able to refill the canteen.

While the water is coming to a boil, I decide to go over to the stream to wash my face and hands. No doubt, a watched can never boils. I walk over to the water, kneel down on a big rock, and, cupping my hands, splash water on my face. The water is extremely cold this morning and stings my face as it washes away any remnants of sleep from the night before. Suddenly I hear a sound! It's the unmistakable ringing of a phone! I stand up, water still dripping from my face, and turn in the direction of the sound. After wiping the water from my face, I take a look. I can only shake my head in disbelief. Sure enough, it is the sound of a phone ringing, just like the old-time phones you would hear ringing in someone's house before the dawn of cell phones. I look around and realize that it's coming from inside the backpack. I remember that I put the cell phone back in there. I can't believe it. Who would be calling me out here? I jump and concede that I don't care who's calling. Maybe I can finally get some answers! I turn and dash to the knapsack, pick it up, and scramble to pull the phone from the small side pocket. I toss the backpack on the ground and flip the phone open to answer, but just as I do so, the ringing stops. *Crap!* I think. *I missed it!* I look at the phone, and the power indicator still registers that there is no power to the phone. *Wise Guy must have been right,* I think. *I really must be losing my mind out here. I'm hearing things!* The forest is silent now. That is, except for the laugher of the woodpecker.

"Go ahead and laugh," I cry out. "I could swear that phone was ringing. You know what, I've had just about enough of you." The bird's taunting is relentless; he just keeps on laughing. "I don't know for sure if I'm losing my mind or not, but I know I heard that phone ring. Don't try to tell me you didn't hear it too." I look back at the phone. There is definitely no power. So how is it possible that it rang? It's nothing but an old piece of junk anyway. I should throw it in the woods or into the stream and let the current carry it away. It's good for nothing.

"What happened? Miss your call?" I hear Wise Guy I say.

"Don't start with me now. I'm not in the mood. Did you hear the phone ring? Did any of you hear it?"

"We all heard it," Analytical I confirms.

"You did, didn't you?"

"I would say that it was a phone," he replies.

"How could that be though? There's no power."

"Hey, stranger things have been happening around here, now haven't they?" offers Analytical I.

"Yeah, I guess you're right. Look at me. I must be losing my mind. I'm hearing dead phones ring, and I'm standing in the middle of the woods arguing with myself. I'm beginning to think there's too many of me …"

Just then, the phone rings again. I look at it in my hand and see that it's somehow lit up. I can't believe it! I just keep looking at it.

CHAPTER 17

"Answer the phone," Analytical I says.

"Oh yeah."

I flip the phone open and, after a brief pause, say, "Hello?"

The voice on the other end sounds oddly familiar. "Good morning. I hope I haven't woken you up."

"Woke me up? Woke me up? Who is this?"

"No one of any consequence." The voice starts to snicker.

"Where are you?" I ask.

"I'm right here. Right here on the phone talking to you."

"Where am I then?"

"You're right there. Why are you shouting?"

"Sorry, didn't realize I was doing that. This is beginning to sound like Abbot and Costello's 'Who's on First?' routine."

"Well, you're asking all these questions."

"I'm asking all these questions because I'm out here in the woods and I have no idea how I got here, I have no idea what's going on, and I have no idea where this is." I pause. "I have no idea who I'm talking to."

"Well, it's time to stop asking questions and listen. I know where you are, and I've been there too. I'm going to tell you how you can go about getting out of there."

"Getting out of here?" I ask. "And go where? Is there anyone around here? I haven't seen or heard or found any signs of human life in two days."

"There you go with the questions again," he says. "Can't you just listen for a change?"

"Perhaps you ought to listen to the man," Analytical I chimes in.

"Okay, okay, I'm listening. Tell me what to do and where to go."

"I'm going to tell you how to get to me, but what you do with that knowledge is up to you."

"Get to you? Where are you? Can't you come to me? I mean, if you know where I am and all."

"Questions again. I think you're not listening. And no, I cannot come to you. It doesn't work that way."

"Doesn't work like that!" I yell. "I'm stuck out here in the middle of nowhere in a dream or whatever this is for the last two days. I'm running out of food. I have no idea where anyone is or where I am for that matter. And you want me to just listen? Listen—you call the police and tell them to organize a search party and send helicopters and bloodhounds. Hell, have them get the National Guard on the hunt if they have to … hello? Hello? Hello?" I pull the phone away from my ear and look down at it. There is no light on the phone any longer. He's gone. Just like that.

"What! What? Come back, dammit. Hello?" Nothing. Ahhhh! Where did he go? I can't believe it. Maybe he's taking my advice to call the police.

"One can only hope," Analytical I says.

"Don't you know how to listen?" Wise Guy I pipes up. "The man says listen, but no, no, you couldn't."

"Shut up," I say.

"Well, you had your chance and blew it," continues Wise Guy.

"Don't start with me now. I don't want to hear any of it."

I sit down, bewildered, and put the phone on the ground. How could the phone ring without power? Who was that guy on the other end? Why did he hang up? What's going on? All these thoughts flash through my mind.

"That was your last chance. He'll never call back," Pessimistic I says.

"Maybe all of you are right. I should have just kept my mouth shut. Guess I panicked."

"That's our boy," mutters Wise Guy I.

"Don't worry. We don't need that guy. We can get out of here on our own," pronounces Ego I.

I pick my head up and look around. There is now a fog over the entire clearing and surrounding the woods. I laugh as I think it's like the fog that's overwhelming my mind. I can't help but think the voice on the other end of the phone sounded familiar, like an old friend I haven't seen in years. Suddenly the phone rings again. I reach down and answer in one fell swoop. "Hello! Hello?" I say, trying to sound calmer with the second hello.

"Well, are you ready to listen? No more hysterics?"

"No, no more hysterics. No questions. Say whatever you have to say. I'm listening."

"I know where you are. I've been there before. In fact, we've all been there before, and it's time for you to find a way out. I'm going to show you the path. If you follow it, you'll find me."

"Okay, okay, tell me," I plead, but ever so calmly to hide my excitement.

"You're on the upper stretches of the Soul River. The stream behind you is a spring creek that originates from water that bubbles up from the ground in a swamp about fifteen miles away. The Indians have a different name for this stream. In their language, it means one soul. Your journey begins here. Follow the creek downstream. Make sure you follow it. Never lose sight of it. The creek is small where you are, but it will get larger as it winds through the countryside and picks up many feeder streams. It actually becomes quite large until it crashes down a waterfall and into the Lake of Wholeness. Once you reach the waterfall, you'll find me on the other side of the lake. At no time should you attempt to cross the stream. Always remain on your side."

I stand there listening attentively to his directions, afraid to ask any questions. When he's finished with his instructions, I hear a pause on the other end of the phone. It isn't the longest pause, but it's long enough to make me worry that I've lost him. "Are you still there?" I ask.

"Yes, I'm still here with you."

"Is it all right if I ask you a few questions?" I inquire. "Now seems like as good a time as any. How far away are you?"

"If you put the phone down now and push hard, you should reach me by nightfall."

"Nightfall? What time is it now?"

"Time?" He seems to ponder the word. "I think it's time for you to get going. You don't want to be out there searching for me in the dark, now do you?"

"No, no, no. I don't do well in the dark."

"I know. You've been in the dark most of your life," he replies. What the hell is that supposed to mean?

"Another question: what about the bears?"

"Bears? What are you talking about?"

"Grizzly bears," I reply.

"Grizzly bears." He chuckles. "There haven't been any black bears in these hills for forty years, let alone grizzlies."

"No bears? A grizzly chased me five miles yesterday. I was damn lucky to escape with my life."

"Grizzly bears," he repeats again. "You have any whiskey in that pack of yours? Have you been smoking weed?"

"No, no whiskey, no weed," I say. "Just a real, live grizzly bear. And I'm kind of afraid to leave the clearing. He might come after me again."

He starts to laugh. It reminds me of the woodpecker. "Listen," he goes on, "I have lived here for quite some time, and I can assure you there are no bears. No black bears, no grizzly bears."

"If that's the case, what was chasing me?"

He roars with laughter. "I don't know. Must have been a figment of your imagination."

"Yeah, I guess my imagination is out of control." I don't want to argue with him.

"Listen," he says, "you have a lot of ground to cover. Let's get busy breaking camp. Remember to push hard and stay on your side of the river. Oh yeah, make sure you put all that water in the canteen. You're going to need it. Have a little breakfast, whatever you have left, and leave the place as you found it. Make sure the fire's out and you spread it around good."

"Listen, before you go, I have a lot more questions."

"No, no time for questions now. That will all come later," he replies.

"Just one more thing. What if I get lost?"

"Just follow the river. Besides, the hawk knows the way."

"The hawk?" I ask.

"Yes. You know, your hawk. Keep an eye on him and stay on your side of the river. Oh yeah, and we'll smoke that last cigar when you get here." With that, he was gone.

I take the phone away from my ear and look at it. The light has gone off, and once again there's no power. I sit back up against the rock in a kind of daze. I listened to all his directions. They seem simple, yet I'm still a little spooked about leaving the clearing. But it seems to be the only way out, and I know I have to take this opportunity, no matter what the cost. I can't help but wonder who I was talking to on the other end of the phone. Such a familiar voice. Still, I cannot place it.

I get up and go over to the canteen. Picking up the cans of water that have thoroughly cooled by now, I carefully pour them into the canteen and am surprised to notice that they fill it completely. I screw the cap back on the canteen very securely and stand up. I grab the backpack and take out all its contents. There's a little bit of dried meat left and one hard-boiled egg. The biscuits are still wrapped up in the napkin, but they've been thoroughly shredded by the crows. There is also a half-eaten apple that has likely met the same fate as the biscuits at the hands—or rather beaks—of the crows. I unwrap one of the less shredded biscuits from the napkin and take the hard-boiled egg out of the container and begin to eat. *He's talking about a journey now?* I think. *Seems like this journey started a couple of days ago, when I found myself here. And what did he say? No bears around here? What the hell was that yesterday?*

I finish my egg and biscuit and stand up. I walk over to the creek and fill the empty bean cans with water to use to put out the fire. It's then that I notice that there is no pain in my right knee. I know from experiences with tennis that the pain usually lasts a few days, and it seems strange to be so quickly pain-free. The rest of my legs don't feel sore either. I drop my pants and notice that all the scrapes have magically disappeared. "What the hell!?" I say. "How the hell can this be? Just yesterday, I was all cut up, hobbling around on a bad right knee, and today I'm completely healed."

I pull my pants back up, fasten my belt, walk over to the fire, and pour a little water over it. The fire makes a hissing sound, and smoke billows up from the pit. I pack up the two bean cans, the dried meat, the flashlight, the poncho, and the box of matches. I very, very gingerly return the last remaining cigar to the backpack. Next, I go over to a tree and rip off a branch that still has a few leaves attached. I take the branch over to the fire pit and, using it much like a broom, spread the ashes all around, taking care to leave the clearing like I found it. I pick up the backpack, fasten the canteen to the strap, and throw it over my shoulders. The knife goes back into my belt.

Walking out into the middle of the clearing, I look up to find the hawk. There he is, sitting up in a tree and taking in the day. I'm feeling a little apprehensive about leaving. My last two attempts to walk out of the clearing didn't exactly go according to plan, and both times I found myself back where I started. In fact, I have to admit I'm feeling a little afraid. As I stand here, looking up at the hawk, I really don't want to leave, but I know I can't stay either. I begin to wonder what's wrong me. Finally, some direction, and I'm reluctant to take it. It's no surprise that Analytical I steps in: "Okay, well, let's get going. This is the big chance we've been waiting for. We finally have a course of action. Let's go!"

"Okay, okay," I answer, "just give me a minute."

"You heard what he said. You need to push hard to get there before nightfall. What are you just standing around for?"

"He's scared. He's worried about bears and everything else chasing him through the woods," Wise Guy I jumps in.

"Don't listen to that guy. You can do it. All you have to do is follow the river, and you'll be out of here and back on the court in no time," Ego I encourages. "Beats the hell out of staying in this clearing and dying."

"It seems to me that once you find this guy, he can tell you where you are and how to get back to your life," supposes Analytical I.

"Yeah, that's what he wants, but he doesn't want to die trying." Pessimistic I is back.

"Here we go again. You guys never let me make up my mind on my own."

"Make up your mind once without us, and you'd be lost," says one of the I's. It could be any of them.

"That's ridiculous," I say. "I'm a mess! Besides, the whole forest seems to be foggy, and without the sun coming out to burn it off, it's likely to stay that way. It's going to be awfully hard for me to find my way."

"All you have to do is follow the river. How hard can that be? And don't forget, the hawk knows the way. Take him with you," suggests Analytical I.

"Take the hawk with me? What makes you think he'll come along?"

"Didn't the guy on the phone say the hawk knows the way? Sort of implies he'll lead the way."

"Yeah, that was some guy on the phone, a phone that had no power, and I don't even who or where he is. That could have all just been a hallucination. How do I know I can trust that guy … or a hawk … or even my own senses anymore?"

Courageous I speaks up: "I don't really think we have any choice. You've been offered a way out, and you're going to have to stop acting like a little girl. Get moving!"

Oh no. Every time I listen to Courageous I, I end up in trouble. "All right, everybody, shut up and let me think," I say. At that moment, I look up and see the hawk lean off his branch, swoop down, and fly right over the creek in the direction I'm supposed to go. I stand there with my mouth open as the bird flies out of sight.

"I guess the hawk kind of made up your mind for you," Wise Guy I says.

"You're right." I say, one of the few times I actually agree with Wise Guy I. "Just don't get a big head about it." I reach down, tie my hiking boots up tight, and look around for a good walking stick. I pull a branch off a sycamore tree and use my knife to shave off all the little branches. Now I have a wonderful walking stick. I take off my hat to make sure the eagle feather is safely secured for good luck. I walk over to the creek and take one last look at the clearing before I head downstream.

CHAPTER 18

I remember someone once saying that a journey of a thousand miles starts with one step. I put the phone in my pocket and ceremoniously take that first step. The fog that surrounds the stream is pretty intense, and I've already lost sight of the hawk. But I know I only have to follow the stream, and hopefully I'll catch up to him. The first 150 yards is rough. I'm battling through dense, low brush and thickets. Bobbing and weaving through the forest, I sometimes have to go as many as fifty yards out of my way before working back toward the stream. There is a chilly silence in the air. Seems I have forgotten just how quiet the woods can be when you're all alone. The stream is still the same size as it was when I left the clearing: about ten to twelve yards wide and slow-moving. Although fog engulfs most of the woods, it's much thicker over the stream bed. The fog in my mind is thicker still. Thoughts of what I might find when I reach my destination course through my brain. Who was that guy on the phone? Are there other people around? Will I be able to get the help I need to return to my life? I have so many questions. They'll be answered in time. Or so he said.

Time? What time is it anyway? Oh yeah, and where am I? Am I still in the United States? Am I still on planet Earth? I continue to slog through the thicket, and after about three miles, the stream becomes a bog. It's a large area of swampland, and here the fog has become pervasive. I stop, unstrap my canteen, and take a large sip while I try to figure out how to get around the swamp. It looks completely unbounded; the stream unfolds itself. Going around the bog will take too much time—time that I do not have if I'm going to make it to my destination by dark. From hunting duck in marshes, I remember learning that you can cross terrain like this by hopping on grassy clumps that rise up out of the mud. And there are many clumps like that here.

I begin to hop from one clump to the next, all the while trying to stay on what I believe is my side of the stream. This is quite a workout. I jump from one to the next to the next, all the while trying to figure out which direction the water is flowing. This goes on for quite some time until I finally plop down on solid ground. I was so focused on the physical (the jumping) and mental (where I should jump next) aspects of this task that I didn't realize there are now two streams that emerge from the bog. Somehow, I've ended up right smack in the middle.

As I stand there trying to choose, all I can remember is the voice on the phone repeatedly telling me to stay on my side of the stream. I was on the left side of the stream when I left the clearing. Now I'm standing at a fork in the middle. Uh, I don't know. If I skirted the swamp on the left, that would mean I should be on the left side of the stream on the left? The thought of backtracking and going around the swamp comes into my mind, but I quickly dismiss it. I'm here now, and that would take too much time. But now to continue down the left side ... I stand looking at the streams and realize I'm going to have to make a decision. I know I need to be on the left side. But the left of which?

I start to think about the many times in life we need to decide which way to proceed. Not just an actual, physical direction but a psychological direction as well. If our thoughts dictate our actions and our actions dictate the course of our life, then our decision at any (and every) crossroads determines our life's direction. Suddenly, the decision I am faced with, which stream to take, has a greater meaning. If I have to continue down the left side of the left stream, I have to cross it. And I'm not supposed to do that. Then again, if I follow the stream on the right and stay on its left side, who the hell knows where I'll end up? With the fog and the thick forest ahead, I can't see where either leads. Like it matters. I don't know where I am anyhow. But at every crossroads, I'm always trying to see where I'll end up based on the path I choose. Damn. I thought this was going to be easy. I stand there contemplating my options and wondering how the hell I've managed to mess this one up. Just then, the hawk flies by me very low to the ground and straight over the left stream. He veers off to the left about fifty yards away and lands in a tree. I can just barely make him out through the fog.

Analytical I speaks up: "Follow the hawk. That's what the man said."

"You know that means crossing over the stream," I say. "He told me not to cross."

"Well, dumbass, you're on the wrong side."

"Thanks, Wise Guy. What do you mean I'm on the wrong side? I just went through a swamp. There were no sides."

"Find yourself a place to cross, and you'll be on the right side again," Analytical I offers.

"This ain't brain surgery."

"Taking after Wise Guy?" I ask sarcastically.

Maybe that's what it takes. Maybe I'm at a crossroads, and it just takes someone, in this case a mystical hawk, to point me in the right direction. I'd never been conscious of this before, but from now on, I'll look for signs to help me find my way.

CHAPTER 19

I start walking down the muddy bank until I come to a shallow part of the stream with several rocks protruding from the water. Skipping rock to rock, I manage to cross and get back to the path I need to be on. When I reach the hawk, he takes off flying down the middle of the stream again. Well, I must be on the right track if he's going that way. I'm now on much firmer ground, and the foliage becomes more forgiving the farther I travel. I notice the stream is widening, and after a mile or so, it joins with another stream from the right. It is now a full-blown river. I wonder if that is the other stream that flows out of the swamp. In that case, arriving here would have been inevitable no matter which path I chose. Well, I guess I'll never know.

At this point, I step out of the woods and into a glen. Here there is high grass, and bulrushes dot the stream, or should I say river. It now resembles the Beaverkill River I remember from New York where I've done so much trout fishing. The fog has lifted, and I can see that the river is roughly forty feet wide as it meanders through tall grass. On both sides of the glen, the land rises. As I walk along, I see the same hill where I was yesterday. I see the bear come out from his cave between the two rocks. It's as if I'm in a movie. He gets up on his hind legs and sniffs the air. I'm a good mile and a half or two miles away, so I don't feel like I'm in any immediate danger. Man,

I wish I had a camera. I'd take a picture and show the guy on the phone that he has no idea what he's talking about. No bears here? Ha! If there are no bears here, then what the hell do you call that?

I stay motionless in the grass, hoping the bear hasn't caught sight of me. Just then, I notice that the blades of grass are all blowing in his direction. The wind is at my back—which means my scent is, no doubt, in his face. For a while, the bear stands on his hind legs with his nose in the air. *Please don't come down here*, I think. *Whatever you do, just stay up there.* That familiar feeling of fear is bubbling up in me, the same as it did yesterday. It creeps up my back, and my heart begins to race. All the little I's start to scream in my head. Everything from "Oh no, we're going to die" to "You can take him."

"Be quiet," I whisper. "You don't want him to hear you, do you?" I must be losing it. As I watch the bear, frozen to my spot, I hear very clearly the voice that was with me in the cave and at the clearing when it looked as though there was no hope.

"Steady. Steady," he says. "You faced the bear down yesterday, and he no longer has any power over you. Just ask him to go back into his cave."

"How do I do that?" I ask.

"Clear your mind."

"Not an easy chore with all those I's running around in there."

"You're bigger than all those I's. They will listen to you."

And indeed, with that, all the commotion in my head vanishes. I look up at the bear, and inside my head, I command, "Go back into the cave. Go back. I'm not afraid of you anymore." To my surprise, the bear takes a swat at the air in front of him with his huge right paw as if to swat my attention away. Or maybe he's just had enough of me. Who knows how the minds of bears work? He drops down on all fours and retreats into the cave.

I sit down. My mind is reeling. I still feel the fear in my legs, and my heart hasn't slowed any. I return my glance to the hill where I saw the bear. I'm in disbelief. I was so certain he would pick up my scent and come running down after me. The voice, the calming voice that told me to will the bear away, has left.

"Okay, we're all right. The bear's gone. I don't know how, but he just went away," Calming I says.

"Where have *you* been, Calming I? I could have really used you the last couple of days."

"Well, you see, I got pushed back. All you seemed to be listening to was Paranoid I. He really had you going."

"Yeah, I know. He and I are done now."

Just then, I hear Analytical I. "Let's get out of here. That bear might decide to come back."

CHAPTER 20

Had it come from Paranoid I, I might have tried to ignore it. But from the Analytical one? All I know is that I want to get as far away from that bear as possible. I come out of the tall grass running like a bat out of hell. I follow the river downhill, both the river and I picking up speed. Ripples of white water give its surface texture. I make my way to the rocky shore, probably running three miles or more, and I'm out of breath. The rocks here make it hard to walk. On occasion, I direct my gaze upward, but there is still no sign of the hawk. I'm hoping he's out in front, waiting for me to catch up.

I find myself off the rocks and back in the woods. To my left, a feeder stream flows into the river. There's no way around it. I look for a spot to cross. *I'm just crossing the steam, not the river,* I think. *I'm not disobeying the guy on the phone.* Fortunately, the feeder stream is shallow and easy to cross. I continue through the woods for another hour and a half. Here the river slows, and ahead of me there is a huge pool. When I arrive, I spook some ducks into the air, and noise scares the crap out of me. I'm not usually this on edge in the woods. The sight of the bear has me flustered.

The land starts to incline, and I can see up ahead that the river runs through a gorge with solid rock cliffs on both sides. The water runs right up against the cliffs, and I can't follow along the banks as I have been. I'm going to have to go out of my way a bit, work my way up a hill, and do some backtracking. I move to my left away from the river's flow and find a deer path that winds its way up the mountain. When I reach the top, I see the hawk sitting in a tree.

"Well, I think you have more sense than I do," I say. "'It's time for a rest. Besides, I'm hungry."

There's a big, flat rock at the apex of the hill. I climb on top of it and look over the side. From my perch, I can see the river hastening through the gorge, crashing against the high rocks on both sides. There's nothing but whitewater. I do not know how far I've come or how far I have left to go. All I know is I'm hungry and it's time for rest. I pull the backpack off my shoulders, open the top, and pull out a can of beans. Not in the mood to eat them cold, I return them to the bag and find instead the bag of dried meat I ate for lunch yesterday. There isn't much left, so I take a couple of bite-size pieces out and nibble on them. I look up at the hawk and see he looks a little hungry too. I put the rest of the dried meat down a few feet from where I'm sitting on the rock. Looking up at the hawk, I say, "There you go. Lunch." He just looks down from his perch. "Come on. It's yours. Come and get it." I'm about to use an empty can of beans and the knife as a makeshift dinner bell, but I think the wiser of it. I don't want to frighten my guide. Instead, I pull out the knife and a full can of beans, open it, and begin to eat them cold. "I hear cold beans are delicacies. Isn't that right, Mr. Hawk?"

I try my best to stomach the beans and continue to look down on the gorge. Turning to my left, I see the hawk has landed on the rock next to the dried meat. He's just perched there staring at me. "Go ahead. Enjoy. You might find it tasty. I, of course, don't care for it much at all." He's a little bit hesitant at first, looking down at the food, back up at me, down at the food and back up at me. "Hey, you take care of me, and I'll take care of you." He takes a peck at it and looks at me again. "Go ahead. I'm honored to have lunch with you." I go back to my beans and look back over the gorge again. When I turn back to him, I can see that he obviously trusted me; he is gobbling up the meat, and from the look on his face, I think he's enjoying it. I only saw the hawk from a distance before, but now that he's right next to me, I can see how big he truly is. He's spectacular. His tail is bright red, his talons and wings powerful, and his eyes, I can somehow tell, are full of awareness. He stands there looking at me as I look at him, and I wonder what he's thinking about. In a soft voice, I apologize. "Sorry, buddy, there isn't anymore." He sits there for a moment longer as if sizing me up. He then turns away and, spreading his broad wings, gracefully flies back up into the tree he came from.

I remember once going to a Renaissance fair where they had a demonstration on falconry. All the birds of prey sat on their perches in a field. There were a few hawks, a falcon, and a bald eagle, and before the show started, the audience was allowed to walk up close and have a look at each. I remember being struck by the size of the hawks and the eagle. The falcon was much smaller by comparison. The hawk that just sat next to me was much larger than any of the hawks in the show.

When the show began, the crowd all found seats in the bleachers to watch the falconer fly each bird. I learned that hawks and eagles must catch their prey on the ground, while the falcon is able to intercept another flying bird in midair. Falcons were used in the early days for pheasant hunting. It was considered the sport of kings. After demonstrating both the hawks' and eagle's ability to capture birds on the ground, the falconer swung a rubber ball on a leather string around his head to simulate a flying bird. The idea was that the falcon, once released, would fly up in the air, dive back down, and pluck the ball off the string. Unfortunately for the falconer, I don't think the falcon had that same idea. We were told that the falcon was a young bird and had not been trained much up to that point. When he was released, the falcon flew up to a tremendous height, soared off to his left, and took off, leaving the frustrated falconer twirling the ball around his head alone. The crowd sat in suspense for the next fifteen minutes as the falconer called after and whistled for the bird. We never saw him again. I'm not too sure the falconer ever did either.

I look up at the hawk in the tree and hope that he doesn't go the way of the falcon and abandon me. I really need him to help me find the way. I stand up and walk to the downstream side of the hill and into a stand of white birch trees. From there, I can see the valley stretch out in front of me. It is an enchanting place. I watch the river weave through the valley, and on the horizon, the sun glimmers off a large body of water. Hopefully that's the lake where I'm supposed to meet the fellow I spoke to on the phone. From where I stand, it looks like quite a distance to the lake. The sun is still high in the sky, and I think if I get myself going, I just might make it before dark. I walk back over to the ledge and look down at the river three stories below me rushing through the narrow gorge. I tilt my head up and look at the hawk. "Okay, my friend, we better get going. Show me the way." He turns his head toward the valley and then looks back down at me. With that, he leans off the branch and takes off gliding in the direction he just indicated. I pick up my backpack and return to the stand of birch trees where I watch the hawk dive down and land in a tree a little way ahead.

CHAPTER

21

It's time to get myself off this mountain and get going. Looking ahead, the hill has a rocky decline leading back to the river. I carefully climb down the rocks until I reach flat ground. Here the river slows and hooks sharply to the left. I'm now standing in an area of low brush and small pine trees. Suddenly, this piece of the woods comes alive. There are birds singing and chipmunks and squirrels running about. I see a flock of Canadian geese flying along the riverbank in the same formation that I've seen for years. After I travel a few more miles, the brush and evergreens give way to hardwoods again. The large trees form an umbrella that blocks almost all the sunlight from reaching the forest floor, and this prevents the growth of any brush or thickets on the ground. At this point, I realize I'm making good time. Tony would be proud.

I keep my eyes on the river. It speeds and slows as it winds through the valley. After some time, I stop where a beaver dam has caused the water to pool up. The dam is enormous and quite impressive. As I unstrap the canteen and take a long drink, I notice two beavers swimming through the water, their heads protruding just above the surface. No doubt this pool must hold some considerable-sized trout. I walk over to the riverbank, take the bandana out of the pack, and soak it in water to wash the sweat from my face. While doing so, I lose sight of the beavers.

Suddenly, I hear a tremendous splash about five feet in front of me. I nearly jump out of my skin. This is followed by another prodigious splash. It's as if someone were jumping off a diving board doing a cannonball. Startled, I jump back and look out across the pool to see what's happening in front of me. I see a beaver come up out of the water and turn to his side. He splashes the pool with his tail, causing an explosion of water that shoots up in the air. All in all, this goes on for a little while. Each time, I jump back, trying to avoid the geyser of water, and the beaver dives down below the surface. It comes to my attention that he is trying to chase me away from their lodge. Though it scares the hell out of me, it's kind of cool. I guess it would scare anybody who tried to intrude on their territory. I laugh a little after the show has concluded, bid the beavers goodbye, and sling the backpack over my shoulder. Off I go down the stream.

The day has been long, and I don't know how far I've come. I'm hoping against hope that the lake I saw from the top of the hill is the lake I am seeking. Though it's still not in sight, I have a feeling that I'm getting closer. As I come around a bend in the river, I see my old friend, the hawk, waiting up for me on a sycamore branch. I stop under the tree and look up at him. "How much farther, Mr. Hawk?" He replies by turning his head and looking downstream. "Okay, off you go. Show me the way. God, I hope we're getting close. I'm awfully tired." With that, the hawk flies out of the tree and down the middle of the river, around the bend and out of sight again. At this point, I'm dragging. I've been walking all day, since early this morning. I decide to sit down on a rock. Light passes through the treetops as the sun's alchemy turns everything golden and gleaming. It's the kind of light I recognize from the late afternoon in the fall. It must be around four o'clock. But who knows? I haven't seen a clock since I got here. I remember that I have a half-eaten apple thanks to my unwanted dinner guests: the crows. I pull it out and start to munch on it as I make my way downriver.

I walk on for another hour before I start to hear water crashing over the rocks. That's got to be the waterfall the guy on the phone spoke of. My pace quickens in anticipation of finally seeing another human being. The last person I saw face-to-face was Mrs. Hamshire at the tennis club. It feels like I've been here for three days, but who really knows how long it's been? It already seems like a lifetime ago. And yet, if this is a dream, it could have only been a matter of minutes. That's how time works in the sleeping mind.

As I begin to move more quickly toward the sound of what I hope to be the cascading waterfall, I begin to think. *I hope this guy isn't a total jackass. He did sound a little tough on the phone. He didn't want to answer any of my questions, and man do I have a lot of those. I hope he can straighten me out and get me the hell out of here.*

Now the sound of the water is very close, and there is no mistaking that it's the sound of a waterfall. I walk out on a flat rock and watch the river crash down over the sides of the bank, landing on another flat rock. From there, it falls another thirty yards and then runs fifty yards into a beautiful lake. This is some waterfall. It has to be a good seventy feet tall, all in all. I love waterfalls. We have one in the town where I'm from. It's a reservoir dam that crashes down into a river, and it's less than a mile from my house. I spend a lot of time there; it has some sort of magical allure to it. Oh yeah, and I love to fish in the river underneath it as well. The water crashing down from the dam oxygenates the river, and the trout love it. It's a great place to fish.

From my vantage point at the top of this waterfall, I can see the whole lake. It seems to stretch out about a mile to the left and about two miles to the right, with high, four-story rock cliffs rising from the banks on the right. These rock cliffs go on for about two-thirds of the lake. On my side, the left-hand side, there is a gradual incline down to the water line. There I see a section of bulrushes and a small beach with a few spots of overhanging trees and some rock formations in the water. As the sun sets, its casts a brilliant gold and pink shine on the face of the lake. I stand there and take in the sight. I can see the far side of the lake, but a thick phalanx of trees prevents me from seeing any farther.

I wonder how I'm supposed to find this guy. He said he would be on the other side of the lake, so I keep a sharp eye trained there. Suddenly, the hawk takes off and circles above my head before flying the length of the lake and disappearing on the far side. Before I lose sight of him, he lets out a screech, and I take that as an invitation to follow. The color on the lake has changed from pink to purple, and from the new angle the sun hits the water, all the colors reflect on the high cliffs on the right side of the lake. I've never seen anything like it.

As I look for a way to get down off the rocks, something catches my eye in the distance. Smoke. On the other side of the lake, back about one or two hundred yards, I see smoke rising through the trees from what looks as though it might be a chimney. "There," I say, like there's somebody with me. "Smoke. There must be a fireplace over there. *He* must be over there." Jumping down from the rock, I discover a path off to my left and start walking. As I'm hiking along, it becomes apparent that this path has not been made by deer. It is undoubtedly man-made. I become a little apprehensive. Who am I about to meet? What am I going to find out about my situation? I'm happy in one sense because I'm going to have someone to talk to, hopefully someone who can help. On the other hand, I have no idea what I'll find. Examining the path more thoroughly, I notice it has been dug up by hoof prints, obviously made by horses. The path widens more and more as I approach the other side of the lake. I realize that my pace is irregular. I have been walking quickly and then slowing down in alternating intervals, my pace coinciding with my thoughts. When I excitedly think of my salvation, I walk briskly. Then my anxiety kicks in, and I slow down as if I never want to reach the other side. My strides seem to move in tandem with my mind as these feelings of euphoria and fear supplant each other over and over again. This goes on for a while. Although the walk takes a short time, it seems like hours to me.

When I reach the others side, I notice two canoes and a kayak on the shoreline. They look like they have been handmade from tree bark. There is nothing modern about them. The trail now leads me back into the woods, and it has become very wide, the size of a modern road. It is dotted and dug up by horse prints. I cautiously proceed down the path a good 150 yards from the shore. There the woods open up into a large clearing, and on the right-hand side I see a very old-looking cabin.

CHAPTER 22

The cabin looks to be at least a hundred years old with a big porch running the entire length of the front of the building. The roof is made of tree bark, and from where I stand, I can see the chimney on the left side of the house billowing smoke up into the air. Across from the house is a pen with three good-looking horses. Farther down from the pen, I see what appears to be a barn. Just outside the barn is a corral that contains two cows. Chickens run wildly all over the property. A smaller building and a shed sit behind the house, all built in the same style as the cabin. All in all, it's pretty rustic. I look around and can't see anybody, but hey, someone obviously lives here, and that's good news as far as I'm concerned. I walk slowly up the path and step on the porch. There's a note attached to door. "Gone off hunting for dinner. Go inside and make yourself comfortable. My home is your home."

Well, this must be the guy on the phone. I turn the note over and over in my hands. I am kind of hesitant about going inside. Instead, I take a closer look at the building. Looking up and down both sides of the cabin, I notice that it has been built in a very old style. Logs are placed on top of each other and secured with square notches on each end. Dried mud has been placed in between the logs to cement each together and fill in the cracks. The roof is made of bark from different trees, mostly sycamore, that have been cut into shingles.

It's quite big as far as cabins go. Upon further inspection, it looks as though it isn't all the original building, as if it has been added on to at some point. From where I stand on the porch, I can see two windows on either side of the door. They have shutters that can completely close the windows off. The shutters have slits in the middle that look like gun turrets—like in cowboy movies. You can close the shutters and still fire out through slots in the window, all the while protected from enemy fire. There are two rocking chairs on the porch made out of wood. On the corner of the building sits a big rain barrel. Copper gutters run along the front and back of the building. The gutters look as if they were added after the cabin was built; they don't appear to be as old as the building itself. I turn to my left and walk the length on the porch. On the side of the house, I spot a vegetable garden with corn, potatoes, carrots, beans, and pumpkins. The pumpkins are quite large, and this all but confirms my suspicion that we are coming into autumn. I walk back toward the door and feel that the air is getting chilly and I am losing sunlight rapidly. Just to make sure there's nobody home, I stand in front of the door and knock. "Hello? Hello? Anybody home? Anybody home?" No answer.

As I reach for the knob, I notice a gun turret in the door as well. I try to peek through it but can't see anything. There must be a trapdoor behind it that can be closed for privacy. The door handle is white with an unusual maroon color. It is attached to a square box that houses the keyhole. This is cool. It looks to me like the key would have to be the size of keys you see in old Westerns used to unlock jail cells. After admiring the handle, I reach down, turn it, and slowly push open the creaking door. The room is dimly lit with just enough light coming through the windows for me to see. I move a little closer and peek in. There is one big room with a kitchen to the right, and on the left is a partition that adds another room. Through a door on the left side, I spy a ladder that goes up through the ceiling. A table sits in the middle of the room, large enough to accommodate six chairs, all handmade. In the middle of the room, up against the far wall is a large fireplace made of flagstone. Arranged on top of the mantel are five or six duck decoys, mostly mallards but one male wooden duck. I take a step into the room and see that the fire is still going, though it is small, and tiny puffs of smoke draft up the chimney. This must be the smoke I saw from the other side of the lake.

I take another step inside and notice a gun case on the wall next to the door. There are four Browning shotguns side by side and a thirty-odd six-rifle bolt action. Hanging above the fireplace, I see a cane fly rod. I walk into the kitchen and see an assortment of pots and pans that appear to be made of wrought iron. Some are white and badly faded from constant use. In the right corner of the cabin, a piece of string stretches from one corner to the other. What looks like tobacco leaves dangle from it. There is a mirror on the far side of the room hanging on the wall.

Moving a little farther into the room, I notice a big, ancient couch facing the fireplace, with a round, woolen rug on the floor. Covering the couch are two Indian style blankets. It looks as though the rug and the couch have been there as long as the house. I walk closer to the kitchen and see a wood-burning stove used for cooking. Pots and pans hang from the ceiling. There is a bushel of apples in the left corner of the room.

I walk over to the mirror, and I confess I am a little bit afraid to look into it. I've been out in the woods for some time, and I don't know what my face will look like. I hesitate for a moment while getting up the courage to have a look. To my surprise, my face is clean shaven. Not a hair on it. I reach up and run my hand along my cheeks and find that they are smooth as a baby's behind. I think this is strange. I should have a good-sized beard growing by now.

I poke my head through the door of the small room on the left. There I see a big bed with some clothes hanging on a line stretched across the room. The clothes look freshly washed and must have been set there to dry. The bed has been made and covered with several quilts and two big pillows at the end against a big headboard. A heavy Indian blanket sits on the floor to serve as a rug. I walk back into the middle of the room and see that there is an ashtray with a pipe on it sitting on a table. Looking back toward the door, opposite the gun rack, there is a bow and a quiver of arrows. Separating the windows that look out onto the porch is a shelf with several bottles of whiskey. Above the door, I see four eagle feathers tied together with a piece of rawhide and a large red bead hanging from them.

I notice there are no windows in the back or on the sides of the house, only the ones facing the front. Actually, it's kind of nice. It reminds me of a hunting lodge I used to have in Vermont. Of course, this one is much more primitive. There seems to be no electricity or electronic devices. No TV or radio, no electric lights and, what's more curious, no phone. I see several oil lamps and figure this must be the only way to light up the house at night. Although I don't feel particularly comfortable, I must admit it's a hell of a lot better than being out in the woods. I walk back out onto the porch. The crisp air hits my face, as the sunlight has now dissipated. I sit in one of the rocking chairs. I can just make out the silhouette of the hawk sitting on top of the barn. "What is this place, Mr. Hawk?" I ask. "Wouldn't you have to say this must be the right place? It's on the other side of the lake, past the waterfall. And, if I'm not mistaken, this is where I saw the smoke coming from." He just looks down at me, but I feel assured that I've reached my destination.

"Well, this is it, huh? This is what you call being saved," Wise Guy I says.

"Hey," I respond, "I have been walking around for two days and haven't seen any sign of civilization. My god, there weren't even any old stone walls like the ones I saw in the woods in New York, built hundreds of years ago. Nothing. Not a hint of anyone. So, I would think this is a major improvement. Wouldn't you say?" I hear him laughing.

"Don't listen to him. This is great. Hopefully this fellow knows his way around, and I'm sure he can direct you to people who can get you back home," Analytical I says.

"Maybe this guy is a serial killer, a real psycho. How do you know? He did hang up on you, didn't he?" Pessimistic I is trying to scare me again. "He lives out here in the woods like a hermit, and hey, what is this—the 1700s? No electricity, no phone. I think we're done for."

"That's a load of rubbish. He didn't have to call you in the first place, now did he? Sounds to me like he's going to help you get out of here and back to your life," says Optimistic I.

"Okay, guys. We're not going to argue out here on the porch. I'm tired from that long journey and just want to rest. Let's be positive."

"You've never been positive a day in your life!" Wise Guy I blurts out. I continue to listen to the I's until the exhaustion from the day's journey overtakes me and I fall into a deep sleep.

CHAPTER 23

I wake up with wet slobber all over my face. There are three dogs on the porch licking me and wagging their tails. They are obviously glad to see me. "Hey, hey, give me a break," I say. I wipe the slobber from my face and reach down to pet them. There is a springer spaniel, dark brown in color, a light rusty-colored Brittany spaniel with freckles all over his nose, and what looks to be a coonhound with big, floppy ears. I can't tell who is happier to see whom. They seem to be having a great time jumping all around me and running frantically across the porch. I too am glad to see them.

I look up the trail. From a little light cast from a dancing lantern, I can see the figure of a man casually walking toward me. I stand up out of the rocking chair, and as he gets closer, I can see that he is a large man; I guesstimate around six feet tall. He has an old brown fedora on his head and long black hair hanging down all around. He wears a dark brown hunting coat, the kind that has a pouch in the back for game and big bellowed pockets on both sides to store shotgun rounds. He's wearing blue jeans and black boots laced up over his ankles. He cradles a double-barrel shotgun in his left forearm. "Hello," he calls out to me down the path. "I see that you made it all right."

PART II

CHAPTER 24

I kind of freeze for a moment. This must be the guy. He sure has some great dogs. I'm excited and frightened at the same time. As he draws closer, I can see that he is powerfully built. The skin on his face is weathered. When he gets twenty yards from the porch, I lift my hand and wave.

He's now standing in front of me, and I can see that he has deep green eyes. Four eagle feathers hang down from inside his hat, which seems to be tied into his hair. His eyes are alive and warm, and this quickly puts me at ease. "I see that you met my friends," he says, motioning toward the dogs that are now sitting obediently in a line.

"Yeah, I must have fallen asleep. The dogs woke me up."

He looks up at me and says, "I guess so. They like you. They don't like everybody ..."

"Well, they seem awfully friendly to me, like they know me ..."

"Maybe they do," he replies with a slight chuckle.

I don't know what else to say. There's a long silence. I have so many questions to ask this guy, but for some reason, in his presence, I can't open my mouth. He walks up to the porch and pulls three pheasants from the pouch in his coat. He places them on what looks like an old wine barrel and looks back at me. "Are you hungry then?"

"I'm starving," I reply. I *am* starving.

"Well, I'd be starving too if I had nothing but beans to eat for the last three days," he says. How does he know about the beans or that I've been in the woods for three days? He turns and opens the cabin door, looks down at the dogs, and says, "All right, inside." They jump on his command and run into the house. I'm still paralyzed with fear, my usual scared response. "Would you like to be my guest for dinner?" he offers.

"Yes, I'd love to."

"Well, it's only dinner out here in the cabin, you know, not Park Avenue." He starts laughing. I don't know what to make of it, so I laugh with him, nervously. I start for the door when he turns and says, "Hold on. Be a good man and go around the back of the house and bring some wood in for the fire."

I just look at him. He smiles and winks. I turn and step off the porch and walk around to the back of the house. All the while, I'm thinking, *I don't know this guy. I don't even know his name. I don't know anything about him. And here he's got me fetching firewood.* When I get around the back of the house, I see cords and cords of chopped wood piled neatly, one log on top of the other, lying under a big roof. I fill my arms with as much as I can carry and head inside.

I find him over by the kitchen. He has removed his coat, but he's left his hat on. He instructs me to stack the wood over by the fireplace. "Throw a couple in," he says. "Then bring me a couple smaller ones so I can get the stove going."

I throw a couple of bigger logs into the fireplace and walk across the room with the smaller ones. He opens the trapdoor of the oven and tosses them in. Reaching up on the shelf, he pulls a match out of a tin can, puts his finger in the middle of the match head, and lights it John Wayne style.

"Hey! I know how to light a match like John Wayne too," I exclaim.

"John Wayne?" He chuckles. "Who the hell is John Wayne?"

He turns around toward me and says, "It's time to feed the dogs. In this corner"—he points to the right corner of the building—"you'll find a bag full of dog food. You see the three bowls over there? Fill each up and set them down exactly where you found them."

"Okay." I pick up the bowls and walk over to the bag of dog food. I turn back and look at him.

"Scoop's in there," he says.

I find the scoop, fill up each bowl, and walk back over to set them down. Without turning around, he says, "Make sure you put them back exactly the way they were. Don't want to start any fights, you know."

Now, I've had dogs all my life, and I've been around hunting dogs too. When I've had multiple dogs in the house, I know that each has to have his own bowl. You have to feed them in the same spot so they don't have any problems determining whose food is whose. So I know where he's coming from. He wants to keep the peace. But now here's the thing: the bowls are all very similar, just different in color, and I forget the order. At this initial stage of my relationship with this stranger, I don't want him to think I'm an idiot. So, I don't really want to ask him which bowl goes where. But then again, provoking a fight between this man's dogs wouldn't exactly endear me to him either, now would it?

I look at the dogs as they all stand in line, wagging their tails. This must be where they always stand at dinnertime. Now which bowl was which? I stand there for what seems like a very long time, and without looking over his shoulder, my host calls out, "The red one goes in the middle, the blue one's on the left."

What is this guy, a mind reader or something? I'm not sure if that was me or Wise Guy I.

"Don't worry about it. You'll get used to it," says my host.

Get used to it? What does this guy mean by get used to it? I'm getting out of here the first chance I get. I put the bowls down, and the dogs each sit in their spots facing them. None of them move a muscle. After a short while, in unison, they all turn their heads toward my host. He is over at the sink pumping water. Without looking back, he says, "Okay," and with that, each dog dives into his bowl. I stand there for a while watching the dogs eat. I don't quite know what I'm supposed to do next. I notice that the fire in the stove is going now, and the burners look hot. He is opening cans as he turns slightly toward me and says, "Why don't you go sit down on the couch and relax a bit. This will only take a little while."

I walk over to the couch with the two Indian blankets on it and flop down. My mind races with so many questions, but it seems I can't formulate them in my mind. The fire in the fireplace is going pretty well by now, and I glance out the window at the darkness. The dogs have finished their meals and are all lying on the floor. At once, they all come over to me. I finally blurt out, "These are great dogs! They're beautiful!"

He turns around and walks over to the mantel above the fireplace. Producing a match from a tin can he finds there, he strikes the match and lights the old-fashioned oil lamp. He adjusts the wick and sets it in the middle of the table. "Thank you. They are good dogs," he says as he walks over toward me. "Well, all except for old Bert there," he adds, gesturing at the coonhound. For the first time, in the light of the oil lamp, I get a really good look at him. He has taken off his hunting coat and is wearing a blue shirt and black leather vest that looks like it has seen better days. He has a blue bandanna around his neck with a string of orange and white beads. His hair is long and jet-black, with the four eagle feathers fastened on the left side. The lamplight illuminates a bracelet made of beads. He is still wearing that old brown fedora.

As he walks through the room, he repeats himself, "Yeah, they are really good dogs. Let me formally introduce you to them. The springer spaniel is named Polly; she, if you haven't noticed, is female. The Brittany spaniel's name is BB, and that old boy over there, that coonhound, his name is Bert." They are all standing there in front of me wagging their tails as if to say hello.

"Very nice to meet all of you," I say. "My name is Rich. I turn to the right where my host was, but he's already back over the stove cooking whatever it is he's whipping up for dinner. I call over to him matter-of-factly, "I don't think we've been properly introduced. My name is Rich."

Without turning around, he says, "Well, that's good to know. You can call me Jay. Dinner is on." He walks over to the table with two plates.

I get up off the couch and sit down at the table. "Well, I'm really glad to meet you, Jay." He sits down across from me and hands me a plate. I reach out to grab the plate, and our eyes lock. They are dark green; the whites of his eyes are crystal clear. They hold me in their gaze. I get the strange feeling that I have looked into these eyes before. They are mesmerizing; only through sheer willpower am I able to break their spell. I get a good look at his face this time.

His features are sharp and familiar. I notice his skin is like leather, although he has no beard and there is no sign that he has ever had to shave.

I am rather captivated by the whole scene, and there's a long silence. Finally, I hear him say, "Well, are you going to take the plate or not?" I snap out of it and reach up, grab the plate, and quickly put it down in front of me, feeling a little foolish. I look down at my dinner.

Beans! No, no, I think. I was hoping for some of that pheasant he brought in. To be honest, I'd be happy with anything else. After eating beans for three straight days, a food that isn't my favorite anyway, I'm sick of them. Seeing my reaction, he breaks out into a hearty laugh. "I thought you were partial to beans. Haven't you enjoyed them the last three days?"

I stare at him incredulously, my mouth hanging open. Rather than say another word, he begins to shovel hearty forkfuls of beans into his mouth. I look back down at my plate and also find two ears of corn, a small salad, and a biscuit exactly like the ones I found in the backpack. Without skipping a beat with his fork, he says, "You know, beans are a magical fruit."

"After the last three days, and especially nights, you really don't have to tell me how magical of a fruit beans are," I mutter. He chuckles to himself. Across the room, the dogs are lying on the floor, being very well behaved while we eat. I have my head down, refusing to look across at Jay.

"Aren't you going to ask him any questions?" Analytical I wonders. "How are we going to find anything out?"

"And who is this guy, a wise guy?" Wise Guy I adds. "Imagine, feeding you beans."

"Okay, guys, calm down. I just met this guy. I don't want to scare him off."

"You don't know this guy. He could be a cold-blooded killer," Pessimistic I says. "Better stay on guard."

"That's ridiculous. I'll get to the questions. I'll ask him what's going on. I'm just trying to be cool."

"Cool ain't gonna get you home," says Wise Guy I.

I look at Jay. He's munching on an ear of corn. He looks up at me and rolls his eyes in embarrassment. "How rude of me! I never offered you something to drink!"

"That would be great. I am a little thirsty."

"We have water, apple cider, and I think there's a little milk. What would you like?"

"How about some cider."

He gets up and goes over to what looks like a small, old-fashioned icebox and takes out a pitcher of apple cider, pours it in a tin cup, and sets it in front of me. He sits back down. I take a sip from the cup. My mind is scrambling. I have to say something, but I don't know where to start. Looking across the table, he has his head down while he eats, and all I can see is the top of his hat. Finally, I muster up the courage. "Jay, where am I?" He just keeps on eating. I ask again, this time more authoritatively.

"Here," he says without looking up and with a mouthful of beans.

"I know, but where is *here*?"

"Right here, sitting in my front room, having dinner."

"I know that. But where is *here*?" I ask.

With that, he looks up from his food with a serious expression on his face. His eyes are steely. "You're here. Right here. Sitting with me in my front room, and that's all I know." He catches me with his gaze, and I am speechless. I thought this guy Jay would have all the answers or at least help me find my way back.

"So, let me get this straight: you don't know where you are?"

He begins to laugh and says, "I know where *I* am. It seems to me that you don't know where *you* are, now do you?"

"Yeah," I say. "That's kind of the major problem."

"Well you're right here now. You should get used to that."

"Get used to that?" I repeat. "How can I get used to it? I need some answers."

His eyes become friendly, and his face softens. He chuckles a bit. "Maybe," he begins, "just maybe, you have all the answers. He stands up and takes my plate and his. Walking over to the sink, I hear him muttering something about not liking dirty plates in front of him. He puts the plates down in the sink, returns to the table, and picks up the pipe that has been sitting in the ashtray. My eyes never leave him. He turns to me and says, "I cooked, so it's your turn to do the dishes. I'm going out on the porch to have a smoke. When you're done, come out and have a cigar, and we'll talk."

Do the dishes? Here I am, totally confused, all out of sorts, desperate for answers, and he's going out to the porch to have a smoke? And doling out chores? My head is spinning, and all the I's are going crazy. My legs are so weak and wobbly I can hardly stand up. I feel afraid. I think I have to get out of here. I'm actually afraid of Jay. I have no idea what this guy is all about. Is he deliberately doing this to me? Is this some kind of game to keep me here? Suddenly, Jay walks in the front door, goes over to where he left the shotgun leaning against the wall, and picks it up. My heart skips a beat … maybe two. He puts it in the gun case, locks it, and returns the key to his vest pocket. It's as though he read my mind. I was just thinking that I might have to shoot my way out of here.

As he makes his way toward the door, he says, "Maybe we can make some sense of everything out here on the porch. Dishes first." I struggle to get to my feet, and as I make my way to the sink, I feel the full fury of my fear. I take hold of the handle and start to pump up and down maniacally. Though I've never used a pump like this before, I have a feeling of déjà vu. After a couple of pumps, the water comes gushing out. I pick up the dishes and put them under the stream of water. The water doesn't last long. I turn around and yell out to Jay, "Got any soap?"

"Under the sink. Open the door to the right," he replies.

I reach down and open the door, and to my surprise, there is a plastic bottle with dishwashing liquid in it. It looks just like the kind you would buy in any supermarket in the twenty-first century. The plastic bottle looks so out of place. Or perhaps out of time? Just then, I realize how much this bag of dog food looks like the one I have at home.

"He doesn't have any idea where he is? That's bullshit!" Wise Guy I says.

"Listen to him; he's right. There has to be a store around here. And a modern store at that. Where else could he have found that dog food and detergent?" Analytical I says.

"Don't let this guy give you any crap. We can take him," Courageous I says.

"Quiet down," I say. "You guys be quiet. I don't want to spook this guy. I'll make him spill his guts when I get out there on the porch." I pour a little bit of dishwashing soap on each dish, take a rag that I find hanging over the pump, and wipe both plates clean. I place them on the dry sink, take a deep breath, and walk toward the door.

I step out on the porch not knowing what I'm going to say. Jay is sitting there in the dark on one of those rocking chairs smoking his pipe. Even in the near darkness, I can see the smoke lingering over the porch. The only light comes from the doorway, and it takes my eyes a little while to adjust. As they do, I can just make out Jay in his chair and the dogs lying around him on the porch. He must have realized that the darkness is making it impossible to see, since he gets up, goes over to the side of the porch, and pulls a kerosene lantern off a hook. He scrapes a match along the side of one of the posts and lights the lantern. Not satisfied, he adjusts the size of the flame before returning the lantern to the hook. The porch is now illuminated, and I can clearly see the two chairs and the dogs lying on the floor. Jay returns to his seat. He looks up at me and says, "Don't you have a cigar left in your bag?"

"Yeah, I do in fact." The cigar! I totally forgot about the backpack after my earlier nap, and it's still leaning up against the cabin behind Jay's chair. I go over to it and, rummaging around a little, find the cigar and bite off the end of it. He hands me a match, which I run along the side of the cabin. Then I light the cigar. Using only a nod, Jay motions me to the empty chair.

I move through the cloud of smoke and find my seat next to Jay. We sit side by side, rocking and smoking in prolonged silence. Really, I don't know what to say or how to start the conversation. All I know is that I have an underlying feeling of resentment. I'm pissed that I am stuck in this place, and I direct my anger at Jay. This makes it difficult for me to formulate any questions. Finally, after what feels like hours, Jay speaks. "You must be tired from that long trip down here. You're quite a ways out you know."

"No, Jay, I don't know that I'm quite a ways out. As a matter of fact, I don't know anything! You won't seem to tell me anything." He just sits there, puffing away on his pipe and sitting in a relaxed fashion, his legs crossed and his arms folded in his lap.

"Well, Rich, I'll tell you whatever I do know. The fact is you might know more than I do."

"How could that possibly be?" I ask indignantly. "You live here, don't you? Don't you know where you live?"

"Of course I do," he replies. "I live right here."

"And where, exactly, is here?"

"Boy, Rich," Jay goes on, "you have a hard time dealing with *here*, don't you? This is kind of a redundant conversation, isn't it? You're here, and I'm here, and that's all I know."

I've become very frustrated listening to Jay. I start to rock really fast in the chair. "Why don't you just give me the phone so I can make a call and find out how to get out of here?"

Jay finds this hilarious. "You know, we aren't in a rocking chair race here. You might want to slow down a bit before you push yourself off the edge of the porch."

"No, I really mean it. I'd like to use the phone."

"What?" Jay says. "I don't have a phone. Did you see a phone hanging around here on the wall?" As a matter of fact, I hadn't. Now I'm really getting pissed.

"You must have a cell phone then. You called me on it."

"No," he says calmly. "I don't have a cell phone. Total waste of time. I don't have a phone at all. Whoever called you, well, that wasn't me."

"If you didn't call me, how did I get here, and who did I talk to on the phone?"

He goes on, "Now that you mention it, I don't even know how *I* got here."

"You don't know how you got here?" I ask more for my benefit than his.

"No."

I can't believe any of this. How does he not know how he got here? Or, for that matter, where he lives? I look back at him through the dim light thrown by the kerosene lantern.

"In all honesty, you don't have any idea where we are and don't know how you got here?"

"That's right, Rich."

"And you do not have a cell phone. Yet this morning, a cell phone

I found in that backpack there rang and told me to come here. You're telling me that wasn't you?"

He blows a big cloud of smoke and turns toward me, looking me straight in the eye. "That's right. That's about the size of it."

"Okay then. Who was that guy on the phone?"

"I don't know. It's your phone, isn't it?"

"No, no, no. That's what I'm trying to tell you. It's not my phone. I just told you I found it in the backpack."

"So, now," he says, "you don't have a cell phone either. So, if that's the case, how did I call you this morning?" I can't tell if he's being serious or not. He continues to rock in his chair as if nothing is going on. I can hear all the I's bubbling up inside me. They are going crazy, and I think my head may explode at any second.

"Look," I shout, "answer me this Jay: what state are we in?"

Jay doesn't answer right away. He just continues to smoke his pipe. After a long pause, he says, "It seems to me like you are in a state of confusion." His face immediately lights up, his features soften, and he chuckles a bit. "Hey, I think you could use a drink."

"At this point, a drink sounds pretty good."

"What will you have, tequila or whiskey? Take your pick."

"Whiskey, Jay. Make mine a double."

He gets up from his chair and goes into the house. I sit there in the chair shaking. The night air has gotten colder, but at this point, I can't tell if the shaking is caused by the temperature or the uneasiness in my mind.

"Boy, this guy's crazy!" says Wise Guy I.

"Hold on, try to get more information," suggests Analytical I.

"Keep an eye on him," Paranoid I recommends.

And not to be out done, Courageous I steps in with, "We're walking out of here tomorrow morning!"

"Can you guys just leave me alone?" I say. "I have to collect my thoughts."

The dogs were lying on the floor, but when Jay steps through the front door and back on the porch, they all jump up. He hands me a tall glass of whiskey and says, "This will straighten you out all right." I take the glass and see that his hands are empty.

"Nothing for you?"

"No," he replies, "never touch the stuff. Just keep it around for guests really."

"Guests? So, there are other people around?"

"Oh yeah, they come, and they go," he says matter-of-factly. He sits back down in his rocking chair and continues with his pipe. I take a big gulp of whiskey, and I must confess it's excellent. So, all I really know about Jay to this point is that he has great dogs and great whiskey. I take another drink. It's warm and soothing; I can feel it calming my nerves as it reaches my stomach. Jay glances over at me. "You feeling better now?"

"I do feel much better with the whiskey and all but not about my circumstances," I admit to Jay. "Please tell me what's going on here."

"Well, Rich," he says with a grin, "I can only tell you what I know to this point."

"Please enlighten me." I am starting to feel kind of tired, the kind of weariness brought on by whiskey, and as much as I want to learn as much as I can, my eyes are drooping, and I struggle to keep them open.

Jay begins, "I, like you, have no idea how I got here or where this place is for that matter. One day, I wound up on this front porch, just like that. There was a note on the door ..."

"What did it say?" I ask impatiently. Jay shoots me a stern look for interrupting, but I can't help it.

"It said 'Make yourself at home. I'll be back.' So I did just that. I went inside and made myself at home."

"How long ago was that?" I ask.

This time, there is no look from Jay. I think he may be giving up trying to scold me for all my questions. "I have no idea," he continues, "but it has been some time. I've been here waiting ever since. Of course, I've made some changes to the cabin over time. It was much smaller, and there was only half as much livestock. But I did find everything inside that I would need to survive. You see, Rich, I don't really know very much more than you do. One day I was where I was, and the next minute I was here."

"That's incredible!" I exclaim. "That's exactly what happened to me." I take another drink, draining the full glass of whiskey. "Except I didn't wind up at a cabin. I was out in the woods." At this point, I'm feeling pretty good. "Jay, who do you think wrote that note?"

"That is the question, isn't it?" he replies. "I don't know who, but I've been here waiting for someone. And I guess that someone is you." With that, he stands up and walks back into the house.

I wake up to a hand on my shoulder shaking me vigorously. I must have dozed off for a few minutes. Jay is standing over me, and in his hand is an old piece of paper. He hands it to me and says, "See, here's the note I found on the door." I look at it and try to focus my eyes. I must have only been out for a couple of minutes, and I'm still noticeably drunk. Jay reaches down, grabs the note out of my hands, and turns it right side up before handing it back. The faint light of the kerosene lantern conspires with the whiskey, but I am able to make out the words on the paper. They read exactly as he had said. I can also just make out the initials RLC in the right lower corner.

I almost jump out of my chair. Looking up at Jay, I exclaim, "You don't think these are my initials?" His face stretches into a large smile, and he asks me my full name. "Richard Lewis Corsetti," I tell him.

He takes the note out of my hand and looks down at me. In a calm voice, he says, "Welcome back."

"Welcome back? What are you talking about, Jay? You don't honestly think that I wrote that note?"

"We'll just have to see, won't we?"

"Why, that's impossible! Don't you think I would know if I wrote it?"

Just then, all the dogs stand up and start to bark. They take off running and disappear into the darkness. Jay walks to the end of the porch, yelling for them to come back. Still staring out into the darkness, he says, "Ah, they're out there chasing something, most likely a raccoon or a fox. They always come down here trying to get my chickens." It doesn't take much calling before all the dogs arrive back on the porch. Jay goes into the house and returns with another glass of whiskey. He suggests that I have another drink to ease my mind. I can't agree more.

CHAPTER 25

I come to in the big room, shaking my head, trying to get the cobwebs out. The fire in the fireplace is smoldering, and I'm covered with a blanket. My boots are off, and my head is killing me. What's worse: I'm alone. No dogs and no Jay. *Don't tell me I'm by myself again.* As soon as I sit up, the door comes flying open as though someone has kicked it in. All the dogs come running into the house followed by Jay. His left arm is filled with firewood, and he has a bucket in his right hand. "Oh, good morning," he says playfully.

I'm startled by the scene but manage to eke out a disingenuous "Good morning, yourself." I don't really see what's so good about it. I'm still here. He laughs as he walks across the big room and dumps the firewood next to the wooden stove. He opens the stove door, tosses a couple of logs in, and rests the bucket on the sink.

"How are you feeling?" he asks.

"Well, my head's about to explode, but other than that, I'm just fine," I say.

"You'll feel better after some breakfast." He takes a pitcher off the shelf and pours what looks to be milk out of the bucket and into the pitcher. The dogs have come over to say good morning as well, circling around and standing on their hind legs with their paws on top of my chest as I pet them. "Put your boots on," says Jay, "and get yourself together. We've got things to do."

I sit up on the couch and swing my legs over the side, leaving the blanket in my lap. The dogs are relentless in their affection and continue to lick my face as I explore the floor for my boots. "Okay, okay, all you doggies. Good morning," I say, pushing them out of my way and grabbing my boots. I get to my feet and find that I'm wobbling and my head is pounding. "How much whiskey did I drink last night?" I ask.

He smiles and says, "Enough, believe me. Enough. Shake it off. We have things to do."

"Things to do?" I echo indignantly.

A stern look comes over his face, and he turns and glares at me with those steely glass eyes. "There's plenty of work to do every day. We don't do that work, we don't survive. That blanket goes in the cupboard in the bedroom. I'm going out to feed the horses. Try to get that fire going in the oven."

"What time is it anyway?" I say as I watch him walk toward the door.

"Time." Jay considers the word for a moment. "What time is it?" he mimics before he starts laughing and disappears out the door.

I stagger over to the stove and open the trapdoor. The fire is going pretty strong, so I walk back over to the couch. I'm close to lying back down and closing my eyes, but I think the wiser of it and fold up the blanket and put it back in the cupboard as instructed. I walk over to the table and sit down. My knife and backpack are hanging on a peg on the coat rack next to the door. I sit there in a fog for some time, not trying to think because it's just too painful.

The door swings open, and Jay walks in followed by the dogs. He has his coat and hat on and looks a little chilly. He says, with a smile, "Oh, just sitting around, huh? I hope you don't feel as bad as you look. You'll feel better after a good breakfast."

"Jay, I can't eat anymore beans."

He seems to be much more cheerful than when he left. "Beans," he says. "I thought that was your favorite meal." His eyes are bright and playful. "We're not featuring beans this morning, although there will be some of my famous biscuits. We're going to have a proper breakfast."

Still not really knowing if I can trust him, I ask, "And what might that entail?"

"Well, what do you consider a proper breakfast?" A huge grin stretches his face.

"I always like eggs in the morning, maybe a little bacon and of course home-fried potatoes and a nice cup of tea."

"You're in luck. All of that happens to be on the menu."

"It is?" I say quizzically.

"Sure, we've got all the fixings." He motions toward the dogs, instructing them to lay down, and moves over to the sink, pulling a frying pan out from underneath. He takes some potatoes out of a bin and pulls a cutting board off the back of the sink. "Can I borrow that knife of yours so I can cut up the potatoes?" he asks. "I can't find mine." I retrieve the knife from the coat rack, pull it out of its case, and hand it to Jay handle first as he waits at the sink. When he takes the knife, he lets out a whoop and says, "Boy! This is some knife! I used to have one just like it, but I haven't been able to find mine for a few days."

"Well, technically, it's not mine," I say. "I found it in that backpack." Jay begins to laugh so hard I think he might fall over. I don't see what's so funny. But then again, my head is still cloudy from last night's boozing, and I might have missed something.

When he finally stops laughing, Jay says, "I'll take care of the potatoes and the bacon. I'll even whip up some biscuits. Your job is to go get the eggs."

"I thought you had all the fixings?" I protest.

"Well, Rich, there's chickens out there, and they aren't exactly going to deliver the eggs themselves. Go out to the coop and bring back some. Six should do nicely."

Chickens, I think. *I've never eaten fresh eggs directly from the chicken before, and I've certainly never gone into a chicken coop and collected them myself. I guess I'll have to take this as a learning experience.*

"Take that basket over there next to the fireplace and go around the side of the house. That's where the chicken coop is. Be careful. There's two roosters in there, and they can be pretty feisty." I stand up, and all the dogs stand up with me. "Don't take them with you. They like to chase the chickens around." The dogs must know that I am going outside; they all stand around by the door, wagging their tails.

"Uh, Jay, I don't think I can get out the door."

"Lie down," he says. "You guys aren't going anywhere." I watch the dogs reluctantly move back and lie under the table. Turning to me, Jay adds, "You had better put on your coat and hat. There's a bite in the air."

"What time of year is it?"

"What time of year do you think it is?"

"I don't know. Since I got here, I don't know anything. I originally thought it was summer, but now I wonder if it might be fall."

"Well, if you think its fall, then it must be fall," he says cryptically. "Things can change around here pretty quickly. The seasons are no exception."

I take the coat off the coat rack, grab my hat, and place it on my aching head. It's a gray, foggy day with an undeniable chill in the air. I start out through the door and make my way around to the side of the house. I can't believe what I see. While just yesterday all the leaves in the trees were green, they have magically changed color overnight. I'm surrounded by vivid reds, oranges, yellows, and purples. I walk back over to the front door and yell to Jay, "Hey, all the leaves changed overnight."

I hear a booming, hardy laugh that seems to shake the walls of the cabin. "You said it's fall, didn't you? That's what I heard." I could only shake my head. Things are awfully strange around here. I have no faith in anything anymore, including my own perception, and given the lingering hangover, I decide not to even bother. I find the chicken coop, which is surrounded by barbed wire. The coop has a series of small ramps rising into trapdoors that allow the chickens to enter and exit. I can't see any chickens outside and figure the cool morning air has forced them inside. I open the door. There are chickens in there all right, all said and done probably fifteen of them, thirteen hens and the two roosters. The whole place erupts as soon as I open the door.

Chickens fly every which way, though it seems they're mostly flying at me. It's unclear who is trying to defend themselves here, me or the chickens. I see eggs lying in various nests, but every time I approach, I'm scared off by an aggressive hen. And that's without even mentioning the roosters. I have all I can do to fight them off with my only weapon, the wicker basket, which I flail as wildly and unsuccessfully as Mrs. Hamshire back at the tennis club. I'm left with no choice but to retreat. As I turn to flee, I notice an unguarded egg in the nest closest to me. I reach down and pluck it up before running from the coop screaming. Feathers follow me out of the exit, and in my hasty flight, I trip, and the lone egg explodes on the wooden walk board.

"What's the matter? Chicken?" taunts Wise Guy.

"Are you kidding me? Those chickens are downright evil. They're trying to kill me!"

"Get your ass back in there and grab those eggs," says Courageous I.

"Not a chance. I'm not going back in there for nothing. I don't know how farmers do it."

I open the gate of the barbed wire fence and walk back to the house. Jay is standing on the porch wiping his hands with a towel and just looking at me. "What, no eggs?" he asks, laughing his ass off.

I stand there, spitting feathers from my mouth before calling out angrily, "I'm some source of entertainment, aren't I?"

"From where I'm standing, yes, yes you are."

"Oh yeah? Let me see you go get eggs from those psychotic chickens down there." He walks off the porch and comes over to me.

"Come on," he says, waving me on. "I'll show you how it's done."

We walk to the front door of the coop, and I adamantly profess that I am not going back in. He asks if I am afraid of chickens, and I tell him that I suppose I am, though I didn't realize it until a couple of minutes ago. He laughs again, so hard he actually falls to his knees, his hand over his stomach, which must be aching from all the morning's laugher. "The trick is you have to be nice to ladies." He opens the door slowly and walks in. I stay behind, peering anxiously into the coop. The chickens have calmed down and are now all sitting in their nests. Jay's reception can't be any more different from the bedlam I just encountered. In a soothing voice, Jay begins to speak. "Ladies, we need a few eggs this morning, but we won't take more than we need, and we thank you for the wonderful gift you give us." I watch as he reaches under several chickens and pulls out a total of six big brown eggs. He places them in the basket and, when he reaches the door, turns again to the chickens and says, "Thank you." They never moved an inch, nor did the rooster bodyguards. Closing the door, Jay turns and says, "These eggs are a gift, and we only take as much as we can use, and we thank the chickens for their gift." This seems ridiculous to me but, then again, I can't argue with results.

Back in the house, Jay goes straight to the stove. "Fried or scrambled?" he asks.

"Scrambled with just a little bit of milk, please. That's how I like them."

He breaks the eggs in an old bowl and adds a little buttermilk before scrambling them up and pouring them in a pan on the stove. "Like a cup of tea?"

"Sure," I say.

"Help yourself." On the table in front of me is a steaming pewter teapot. I take the cup from the place setting and pour myself some tea. Jay walks over with breakfast and hands me the plate, sitting down across from me. We eat in silence for a while. This is a real treat. As I've said, breakfast is my favorite meal of the day.

While we're eating, Jay breaks the silence, asking me if I'm feeling better. I tell him I am a little, though my head is still pounding. He gets up from the table and returns with some green, leafy herb in his hand. "Chew these leaves but don't swallow. They will take care of the headache." Almost instantaneously, my condition begins to improve, and I think this may be a good time for conversation.

"Jay," I begin, "what do you think is happening to us? I mean, what's going on here?"

He looks up, takes a sip of his tea, and answers, "I really don't know. What do you think is happening?"

"I don't know either. I haven't been able to figure it out. It's been four days now, and I know just as much as I did when I arrived here. All I know is one minute I'm at the club teaching a tennis lesson, letting my mind wander as it usually does, and the next thing I know, I'm in a clearing in the woods. Just like that."

All the dogs leap up and run to the door. Jay walks over and lets them out. Closing the door behind them, he informs me that they like to go out and have a run in the morning. He walks back over to the table, sits down, and continues to eat. I don't seem to be getting anywhere fast in the answer department. He's acting just as mysterious as he did last night. "Jay, tell me your story. How did you get here?" I ask. Perhaps questioning him will lead me to something.

He stares at me from across the table with a serious look and wipes his mouth with a napkin. "I guess if you're going to be stuck here with me, you have a right to know." I stop eating and look up, fully engrossed. He goes on, "Some time ago, being a full-blooded Mohawk Indian, I was sent out as a young man on a vision quest to find my true self and the meaning of life. As is our tradition, I was to spend three days alone in the woods, fasting, in the hopes that a vision would appear, and I would gain true knowledge of myself. My one true self, the whole of me, what I was to become. This would start me on a lesson path, and that would guide me to all the lessons life brings a warrior on his journey. The first day I left the village, I walked deep into the forest to a spot with a waterfall. It was a place of power that I had visited earlier as a child, and as soon as I arrived, I knew immediately that this was the place where I was to receive my vision. I sat on a rock beside the waterfall and immediately fell into a trance. I called the great spirit of the waterfall to show me the way. When I opened my eyes, I had been magically transported and was standing in front of this cabin. Like you, I had no idea what transpired. I felt trapped between two worlds: the world of reality and the world of imagination. That's when I noticed the note on the door telling me to come inside and make myself comfortable. Many days and many nights have passed since, more than I can count."

He continues, though the expression on his face becomes more solemn, "I, like you, tried to locate the way back over this time. I have walked many leagues in all directions, only to wind up back here at the cabin. Just as the clearing continuously pulled you back. And so I have been waiting here since for the one who left that note to return. He may have the answers." Jay takes a sip of his tea and leans back in his chair. "Well, there it is."

I'm dumbfounded. My mouth is gaping, and I imagine my eyes are pretty wide too. I finally stammer, "So you're an Indian?"

"Yes, Mohawk."

"I was wondering what those feathers in your hair were all about."

"Eagle feathers. I notice you have one in your hat as well," he says.

"Yes, yes, I do," I say.

"One day, you will have to tell me the story of how you acquired it. Let's get these dishes cleaned up. We have a lot to do today."

I'm feeling a little dizzy after the story he told me. It sounds so similar to what happened to me. "I need a drink of water, Jay," I say and make my way over to the sink. I start to pump.

"Don't drink the water from the pump!" Jay shouts.

"Okay," I say, pausing, "is there something wrong with this water?"

"I don't know. When I first arrived here, there was a note on the pump telling me never to drink the water." He gets up and walks over to a small cabinet under the gun case, reaches inside, and pulls out another note. He hands it to me, and I begin to unfold it, all the while looking at Jay. I open it, and sure enough, the note says, "Don't ever drink this water." I notice again that the initials RLC are inscribed in the upper right-hand corner. I look over at Jay.

"You don't still think these are my initials, do you? I'm telling you, Jay, I've never been here before. I have no idea, like you, what's happening or how I got here—and that's the truth."

He takes the note out of my hand, folds it up, and puts it back in the drawer where he got it from. He looks back at me with his eyes glaring and says, "We'll see, we'll see."

"See what?" I blurt out. "You've got to believe me."

At this, his face becomes friendly, and he says, "Trust is all that we should have between us, and in that trust, truth."

I sit there staring for a while. He puts on his coat and tells me that he's going out to feed the chickens and instructs me not to let the dogs back in the house because they'll be all muddy from their run. "Oh yeah," he adds, "one more thing. There's a jug of spring water on top of the windowsill there. Drink that." He goes over and grabs the jug off the windowsill and puts it on the table in front of me. "This jug is getting pretty light. We need to go fetch more. We will do that later." And with that, he's out the door.

I finish my drink of water, and my mind is still reeling. I can hear the I's in there talking, and they certainly don't believe Jay's story. But how can I not believe it? It's pretty much what happened to me. My head is still pounding a bit, and I take some of the herb that Jay left on the table for me and chew it. It has a funny taste to it, minty but sweet, so nice I almost swallow some, but I manage to spit it out at the last second.

Analytical I speaks up in a loud voice. "Go find Jay and find out more." Once in a while, he's right. I find Jay inside the chicken coop with a brown sack in his hand, tossing kernels on the ground. All the chickens are scrambling and pecking away, trying to get to each kernel first. I open the gate and walk inside, standing next to Jay. The chickens greet me as they did when I first walked into the coop, starting to go crazy, flapping, flying, and running toward me. I turn around and run back out of the gate. Jay looks at me, shaking his head.

"Come on back here and apologize to these chickens for trying to steal their eggs before." I look at Jay and can't tell if he's clowning or being serious.

"I'm not going to apologize to any chickens. After all, they started it this morning."

"I don't know, Rich," Jay says coyly. "It seems to me like you were trying to steal their eggs, and an apology is in order."

"Apologize to chickens! You've got to be kidding me."

"Well, if you want to have eggs for breakfast, you better get on their good side real fast. And I think for as long as you're here, your job in the morning will be to collect eggs." With this, he begins to laugh.

"Come on, Jay," I plead, trying to encourage him to have some sympathy for me.

"Do it," he says.

Trying my best not to roll my eyes, I concede. "Okay, I'll make a fool of myself in front of you and the chickens, but only for the sake of breakfast." I turn to the chickens. "I'm extremely sorry—"

Jay stops me right there. "Come inside the gate. Don't shout your apology from out there. It's not proper."

"Damn," I mutter as I open the gate and put my feet inside, still holding on to the gate in case another quick exit is warranted. "Chickens," I start, "can I have your attention please. It would seem that there was a misunderstanding this morning. I was not trying to steal your eggs, and for this I am very sorry. Please let us live together in peace." With that said, I step back out of the chicken area and close the gate.

Jay is roaring at my heartfelt apology. "Now, that is one of the best apologetic speeches I've ever heard. No doubt the chickens took it to heart. You can come back in here; I'm sure everything is fine now."

I open the gate slowly and put my feet back inside the pen. I look down at the chickens, but they don't seem to mind that I'm inside the fence. They continue with their breakfast. "You see," says Jay, "the chickens now trust you, and all you have to do is trust them in return." I stand there in the pen for a while next to Jay, watching him toss out the chicken feed.

Finally, I ask, "How long have you been here?"

He shrugs and replies, "I don't know. I have no idea."

"How old are you now?"

He turns and looks at me as if he has no idea what I just asked.

"What did you do when you first arrived here?"

"Like you, I spent all my time trying to find a way back, until one day I realized that it was futile. I just stopped looking altogether."

"Just like that, you gave up?"

"Oh, now, I never gave up."

"But you did just say you stopped looking for a way out of here."

"Yes. After many attempts and many failures and always winding back up here, I decided to wait," he says.

"Wait? Wait for what?"

Jay stops feeding the chickens, turns around, and faces me. I can feel the stare of his green eyes piercing right through me to my soul. "A warrior waits. He may not know what he is waiting for, but he knows when he has found it."

"But what could you be possibly waiting for?" I ask.

"The man that was here before me, he must know the way out, as he has not returned."

"Well, if he never returned, what makes you think he'll come back here ever again?"

With that same look in his eye, he responds, "The note said he would be back, so I wait for his return."

"How do you know who this guy is or that he wasn't lying when he said he would return? Or what if something happened to him?"

"I'll wait," he says very simply.

"Wait for whom?"

With a big smile on his face, he says, "For you."

I'm still standing in the chicken pen, and I'm dumbfounded. I think to myself that Jay is losing his mind. Or perhaps he lost it long ago. No doubt living out here alone for such a long time could do that to a man. How could he have possibly been waiting for me? I think all the time he has spent here has driven him insane. I hope this isn't what I have to look forward to. I start walking toward the porch. My conviction from the first night with Jay is becoming more and more affirmed. I have to get out of here.

The dogs return and, as Jay predicted, are covered in mud; they don't smell too great either. Jay is on the porch telling them how bad they have been. They are all hanging their heads as I hear Jay tell them none of them are allowed in the house until they clean themselves up. I walk out onto the porch, and all the dogs come running toward me, trying to escape the wrath of Jay. "Don't pet them," Jay says in a loud, commanding voice. "Don't even look at them. They're bad dogs, and besides, you won't be able to get that smell off you for a week."

I tell the dogs that I'm glad to see them but that they are a mess. Jay shouts at them to go lie down. They all find their spots and lie down just like they are told. I'm reminded of how well trained they are. They remind me of two dogs I once had, a Brittany and springer spaniel. I had them together years ago, so long ago that it seems like a past life. Never did own a coonhound though. A friend of mine, Bob, did and told me they were a handful.

Jay disappears into the house and comes back carrying a pail. He looks at me briefly, saying, "I'm going to water the horses. Why don't you go around back and chop some wood. Chop enough to fill the wood stand here on the porch. Oh yeah, don't forget to cut smaller pieces for the stove." And with that, Jay is on his way to the horse paddock. As I watch him walk away, in my peripheral vision, I can see three beautiful horses that appear to be Appaloosas. Two are mostly brown, and one is mostly white. They move through the paddock, looking at Jay as he moves toward them.

I walk to the edge of the porch, and from here I can see a small glimmering off the lake. Up in a sycamore tree, I spot my hawk. I'm glad to see him. With everything that has gone on since my arrival,

I've almost forgotten about him. I go around the back of the house and find an ax and two maul splitters next to an old stump. The stump provides a firm base to split the maul. I start breaking up a few logs when Wise Guy I comes to me. "Listen, we think this guy's lost his mind. He's sitting around waiting for—get this—*you*? Maybe we should get out of here."

"If we have to, we can take him. Besides, he can't hold us here against our will," Courageous I says.

"Well, if you look at it, he's not holding us against our will," Analytical I adds. "He's just going about his business. We're not prisoners."

"How can you be so sure about that? He just keeps talking about war," says Pessimistic I.

"No, no, no, he's talking about *warriors*," Analytical I clarifies.

"Well, warriors make war, don't they?"

I have to get in the middle of this. "I don't know about that."

"Besides all that," says Analytical I, "he says that he's tried every which way to get out of here, and we really don't know anything about that, now do we?"

"Okay, okay, that's enough, you guys," I say. "This is a lot better than being out in the woods, now isn't it? For once in my life, I need to trust someone else. Right now, I need to trust him. Conversation over."

"Okay," Wise Guy I says, "it's your neck."

I break up a lot of wood and bring most of it around to the front of the house, nearly filling up the wood stand, when I decide to sit down on the porch with the dogs and take a break. The Brittany spaniel, BB, and the springer spaniel, Molly, are both miraculously clean. Bert, the coonhound, is still a mess. BB comes over and sits in front of me. He puts his paw up on my knee, and as I reach out to pet him, I remember that my dog, Oliver, did the same thing when he was alive. I look down at him, and our eyes met. A feeling of déjà vu comes over me. I see myself sitting in Jay's chair, hat and coat on, petting BB. Or was it Oliver. I can't really tell which. I sit there, looking down into his eyes, and fall into a deep trance. Suddenly, I feel a hand on my shoulder shaking me, and I look up. It's as if I'm looking into a mirror. I see my own face staring down at me. As my eyes come into focus and my mind snaps out of my reverie, I see Jay's face staring back at me. He chuckles as he remarks, "No time for sleeping, Rich."

CHAPTER 26

"I-I wasn't sleeping," I stammer. "I was in some sort of a trance."

"This is a strange place," he says, "and you will find many strange things here." He laughs. "That's okay, though. The whole human race is asleep, and it's our job as men to wake up."

"Wake up? I'm awake. Just had some sort of déjà vu, that's all."

"Déjà vu," he says as he continues to laugh. "This place will give you plenty of that. We need to get some fresh water. I used up the last of it on the horses. Let's go. Get up. We'll take the horses from the barn. Get a couple of saddles and saddle two of the ponies up."

"I don't know how to saddle a horse. In fact, I don't even know how to ride one," I confess, rather sheepishly. "What's worse: every time I've ever been on a horse, I've fallen off. From what I can gather, it's not their fault."

Jay has a puzzled look on his face. He scratches his nonexistent beard. "We don't need any broken bones, that's for sure. But you will have to learn how to ride sooner or later. No time for that now. We'll take a canoe."

"Where do we have to go to get fresh water?"

"There's a spring on the other side of the lake near the waterfall. Go inside and get some water jugs and meet me down by the lake."

I go inside the house and manage to find three water jugs. The dogs follow me the whole way down. When we arrive at the lake, I see

Jay standing next to two canoes. He has two jugs in his hands, and there are two paddles in one of the canoes. This particular canoe is the largest I've ever seen. Perhaps more impressively, it looks as though it has been handmade out of tree bark.

"These are all the jugs I could find," I say.

"That's fine," he says. "We have enough. Load them into the canoe and then give me a hand. We need to push the canoe into the water a ways." After placing the jugs into the canoe, I grab hold of one of the gunnels on the side and start to push it slowly along the bank of the lake. It's heavy as hell, and I wonder how Jay has been able to do this on his own. When the front of the canoe hits the water, all three dogs jump in. "I guess they want to go for a ride," says Jay. Bert the coonhound is howling away; three dog tails wag excitedly in the morning light. Barking orders, Jay instructs me to get up front and grab a hold of a paddle. I get into the massive canoe and sit in the front seat, holding onto my paddle. Jay gives the canoe another push further into the water and leaps in.

As we glide out onto the lake, the sun has finally broken out, dissipating the morning fog. The lake is serene and flat; not one breath of air interrupts the placid water, and the glare from the sun skips across the surface. The water is so clear I can see the bottom. All the trees encircling the lake reflect the sunlight off their brilliant fall coats onto the water. I can see the waterfall off in the distance. Jay turns the canoe in that direction and instructs me to head for it. We paddle for a while in silence as Jay puffs on his pipe, producing plumes of smoke that must make us look like a steamer coming across the lake.

I don't want to break the mood, but I can no longer stay silent. "Any fish in this lake, Jay?"

"Oh yeah," he replies.

"What kind?" I ask as I paddle, trying not to turn around.

"Oh now, let's see. Three different types of trout: rainbows, browns and brookies, smallmouth bass and a few largemouth too, although not that many, Atlantic salmon, walleye, and I've even seen some very big pike."

"Really?" I say. "I'm a fisherman myself. I'd love to get a shot at this lake."

"I know you love to fish, Rich. You'll get your chance."

I turn to Jay solemnly. "I've got to get out of here, Jay. I need to get back to my life." I'm met with silence. He is still puffing away on his pipe, paying no attention to me as we paddle on.

"Did you hear me? I said I've got to get back to my life."

"What life?" he asks.

"My life back in New York, where I'm a tennis pro. People are going to be missing me. My students …" I break off, and a long silence ensues. Finally, I turn around again, angrily, almost throwing my paddle into the water. "Are you listening to me, Jay!"

"I'm listening," he says calmly. "Don't drop that paddle." He pauses briefly, as if he is searching for the right words. "Allow me to tell you something. With all that has transpired since you have been here, how do you know that the life you speak of is real? How can you be sure it exists at all?"

"Oh, it exists all right. I can remember it clear as day."

"Can you now?" he says.

"Can't you remember your life back before you went on your vision quest?"

"I'll ask this," he says. "What is memory? Is the memory that we have of the past accurate? How can we know that for sure? We only recall bits and pieces, and we try to assemble these pieces together in our minds, desperately trying to reconstruct what has occurred. I would say that if you ask two people to describe the same event, you would undoubtedly get two very different versions of what happened. If there are three people, you will get three different versions. And so on. As I said, we have only fragments, small pieces of what has passed. Those pieces don't always fit so nicely into the puzzle. So, what do we really know about the past? We know very little, if anything, for sure.

"I don't think about my vision quest as past," he goes on. "I think of it as present. I'm living my vision quest now. That's why I'm here in the now. I think that you will find that the past and future do not really exist and that all we have is now. This here"—he spreads his arms out—"this present moment." There is a liquidity to his voice, as if the words are flowing from deep inside him and he is merely the vessel for the knowledge that he is so desperately trying to impart to me. Nevertheless, I'm still not quite buying it.

"But, Jay, don't you believe that you were there then and now you're here?" I protest. I turn back around to look him.

"Face front and paddle," he snaps. After a short pause, he replies, "I don't know where I was or where I will be. I only know where I am, and I am here with you in this canoe at this very moment. That is all I have."

"That's all any of us have," I say, "but how can you live like this, knowing that something has occurred to bring you where you are? Something that took you away?"

The waterfall is getting closer, and I hear the rushing water. He speaks so loudly that I can hear him over the rumble. "I have to let that go. I can't carry the past around with me. Rich, you seem to be missing the point. Stay in the moment. Be there and be awake." He pauses. "Head for the right bank. See the break in the bulrushes? That's where we want to go."

I throw my paddle on the left side of the canoe and hold it up against the side, turning to face the break in the bulrushes that Jay pointed out. We both paddle hard, and I feel the canoe hit the shore. "Get out now!" shouts Jay. I jump out of the canoe and into a foot of water, pulling the canoe onto the shore. All the dogs jump out, and Jay stands up and walks forward in the canoe, holding both gunnels as he moves. When he is finally standing on the shore, he looks me straight in the eye and says, "A warrior makes the best of his circumstances." I look back into his eyes. They are fixed on mine. "These are the circumstances we find ourselves in, so make the best of it. Be a warrior."

He finally breaks his stare, bends down, and lifts the water jugs out of the canoe. His demeanor changes quickly. "Those circumstances right now involve us getting water. Pick up those jugs. Let's get up to the spring and do just that." With that, he starts up the gently sloping bank, a jug in each hand. I pick up the remaining water jugs and follow. The bank becomes steeper as we ascend, so steep in fact that we have to start walking diagonally. The waterfall is on our left-hand side, and it's so loud that it's nearly deafening. I have already lost sight of the dogs, who've scampered off into the forest, though I can still hear the howling of the coonhound, Bert, over the water's roar. We reach the face of the rock wall, and I follow Jay around to the right. There I see what looks like a large crack in the side wall of the rock face and water shooting out as if someone is spraying a hose from the other side.

"There it is," says Jay, "the best water you've ever tasted." He puts down the jugs and instructs me to do the same. He opens the top of one and begins to fill it with water. Turning to me, he says, "You see how this is done?"

"Yeah," I say, "very difficult." I roll my eyes.

"Well then fill up the jugs and take them down to the canoe. You'll have to carry them one by one. They can get pretty heavy."

With that, he takes off in the direction of the waterfall. I pick up one of the jugs, open its top, and hold it under the water. As I watch Jay walking away, I call out, "Hey, where are you going?" I don't think he hears me over the roar of the waterfall—or doesn't want to—and I watch until I lose sight of him. I fill up all five of the water jugs we brought and find out that he was right—they are extremely heavy. Taking his advice, I bring them down one at a time. I leave a couple of jugs just outside the canoe, wondering if it's strong enough to support their weight plus the dogs', Jay's, and my own. I wait there alone for a while. There's no sign of the dogs or Jay. Suddenly, I spot him at the top of the hill. He's waving for me to come up.

When I get there, Jay turns and starts to walk toward the waterfall, silently motioning for me to follow. We walk around a corner created by the rock wall, and I see a piece of flat ground between us and the waterfall. Rising from the ground is a wooden totem pole adorned with feathers, beads, and other various knickknacks. I notice a necklace of bear claws and what appears to be dried snakeskins dangling from it. Jay approaches the totem pole and sits down on the ground with his legs crossed. Without a word, he calls me over by extending his arm to the left and patting the ground next to him with his palm. I hesitate for a minute before joining him. We are both facing the totem pole as water crashes down the side of the rock wall some twenty feet away.

Jay sits motionless with both arms extended, his palms turned upward toward the sun. His eyes are closed, and through the deafening, crashing water, I can barely hear that he is chanting something. We remain in that spot for some time; Jay chants away, and I observe him. In a surprisingly quick move, he stands up and uses an arm to indicate that I should rise as well. Reaching into his vest pocket, he produces what looks like tobacco leaves and places them in a cup in front of the totem pole. He then turns around and faces the lake with both hands held up over his head. After I hear him chant something, he taps me on the shoulder twice and motions for me to walk in the direction of the canoe. We both walk down the hill in silence.

I don't know what just took place up on the hill, but it seemed to be some sort of ceremony. I have a lot of questions for Jay, but I know better than to speak. I'm not sure how long one must wait after a ceremony like that before breaking the silence. Jay picks up the remaining water jugs and puts them in the canoe. He then turns toward the forest and whistles loudly twice. "Where did those dogs get to?" he mutters to himself. He whistles again, twice, louder than before.

"Jay," I say, "what was that place with the totem pole?"

He glances at me slightly and places a finger over his lips, instructing me to be quiet. He pushes the canoe slightly back into the water and motions for me to get in. I jump in and move to the front of the canoe while he moves into his spot in the back. Jay begins to paddle backward, and I help. In no time at all, we are out of the bulrushes and into the lake. We both turn the canoe in the direction of the cabin and start paddling.

When we are halfway across the lake, I can't take it anymore and break the silence. "What about the dogs?" I ask. "Are we just going to leave them on the other side of the lake?"

"They'll find their way back," Jay says while lighting his pipe. "I didn't want to put them in the canoe with this much weight anyway. Besides, they'll probably be all muddy again." I figure it's okay to talk now, so I ask Jay about the totem pole again. "It's a place of power," he says, "our place of power. I was just introducing you to the spirits of the waterfall. They are very powerful spirits. They remember you."

I can't help but chuckle at this. "That's nice of them to remember me," I say, chalking this all up to some Indian mumbo-jumbo.

Behind me, his voice becomes stern. "Yes, it is very nice that they remember you. Because if they didn't, you wouldn't have found the cabin and be here with me." I'm too afraid to turn around.

"What … what do you mean I wouldn't have found the cabin?" I stutter. "What did the water sprits have to do with it?"

"I'll tell you if you are able to listen with an open mind. Are you capable of doing that?"

"I'd like to think I am."

"Don't think!" he shouts. "Know!"

"Okay, okay, I have an open mind. Please tell me about the water spirits."

"On the third day, your third day in the clearing, I went to that place of power at the waterfall to talk to the water spirits. I brought them tobacco in offering and sat quietly for some time. I received a vision. I saw you in the clearing. The water sprits recognized you. They showed you to me, and I spoke to you through them with what you perceived to be a cell phone." I open my mouth to speak, but he cuts me off quickly. "Do you want to hear this or not?"

I nod.

"I spoke to you without words. The water spirits told you the way. They also told me that it was good for you and me to meet in this struggle we call life and that this meeting would have powerful implications. At this time, you are searching. Searching for your true self, the real I, the whole of yourself. You have come on this vision quest to find this true self, and I am to show you the way. I talked to you that morning through the device you know as a cell phone. It was powered by the water spirits alone. So, it is through their providence that you have come to be with me today."

I was sitting in the canoe turned sideways, listening to Jay intently and watching him out of the corner of my eye. "Let me get this straight, Jay. The water spirits recognized me and told you where I was and that I should come here to you so you can show me the real me?"

Jay stops paddling and reaches into his pocket to get a match to light his pipe. I turn around to look at him, and with a glint in his eye, he says, "That's right. That's how it happened." I've never heard anything like this before, so I don't quite know what to make of it. Jay starts paddling again.

"Jay, what is this? Are we in some sort of dream?" He doesn't answer, just continues to paddle. I speak up louder. "Jay, is this all a dream? You have to tell me. I'm more than a little confused. I've been confused since I wound up in this place. Did the water spirits tell you what's happening to us?"

We are now near the shore, and he instructs me to paddle quickly. I feel the canoe drag on the lake bottom near the shore where we started out earlier today. I jump out and pull the canoe to shore. Jay gets out and, without saying a word, starts to remove the water jugs.

"Give me the paddles and carry those jugs up to the cabin," he commands. I do as I'm told. Before heading up to the cabin, I look back at Jay. He is looking at the other side of the lake.

"Where did those dogs get to?" he says.

Thoughts are racing through my mind. "Jay, did you hear me back in the canoe?"

"I heard you all right," he says and starts walking toward the cabin with both paddles in one hand and a jug of water in the other. I scramble to catch up to him, but with the weight of the water in the two jugs I'm carrying, I just can't seem to reach him. Jay goes around to the back of the cabin and tells me to bring the water jugs inside. When I come back outside, I find him standing on the porch, again looking out across the lake. I suspect he's trying to locate the dogs. When he sees me coming across the porch, he orders me to get the rest of the water jugs from the canoe. He then walks off toward the barn. I lug the two remaining water jugs up the hill and back into the house. When I get them all in, I head out to the porch and have a seat in one of the rockers. There's no sign of Jay.

"Do you honestly believe all that bullshit about water spirits?" Wise Guy I says. "I told you this guy is up to no good."

Pessimistic I says, "Water spirits. He's got to be out of his mind."

"How do we know he's even an Indian?" says Doubting I. "Just because he has some feathers in his hair? You have a feather in your hat. Does that make you an Indian?"

"We need to get to the bottom of this," Analytical I says. With that, all the I's begin to debate each other. Heatedly. I'm getting a headache.

Just then, I hear Bert howling, and, coming up the path, I catch a glimpse of all the dogs running toward the cabin. Before I know it, they arrive on the porch, muddy, wet, and glad to see me. I'm glad to see them too. After a few pets hello, I tell them to lie down, and they all stretch out on the porch. I'm rocking fiercely in the rocker, extremely stressed. I begin to contemplate what Jay meant when he said "true self." I am myself. Who else could I be? I'm not searching for anything like that. What I am searching for are answers so I can get the hell out of here and get home. What was it he said on our way across the lake? How do I even know that my life before exists? Of course it does. This is all too confusing. I sit there pondering my fate for some time, and after a while, Jay walks back from the barn.

When he reaches the porch, he looks at the dogs and says, "I told you they'd be muddy again. Don't let them in the cabin." He disappears inside the house as I rock myself into a stupor. After a short while, Jay returns with three bowls full of water and sets them down in front of the dogs.

"Jay, you never answered my question about the water spirits."

"All in good time," he says. His mood has obviously lightened. He even flashes a smile.

The light is getting low, and the sun is setting. I'm starting to feel a little hungry, and I tell Jay. I ask him what time it is.

"Twilight," he responds.

"I can see that, but what time is it actually?"

Jay walks over to me and sits in the vacant chair. His pipe is still going. Without looking at me, he says, "What is this fixation with time?"

"What fixation? I'd just like to know what time it is."

"There is no time," he says. "Time is an illusion created by man. The only useful thing about time is that it allows you to show up at a particular moment in a particular place for some particular event."

"What event are you talking about?"

"I'm talking about any event in which men compel you to do something or be somewhere, often to suit their own purposes. That's all time is good for." After a pause, he continues, "Truthfully, there is only light and darkness. The earth rotates, and as it does so, we receive either light from the sun or we do not. In this view, there is no time as you understand it. There is only light and dark. Furthermore, the earth not only rotates, it also revolves. The sun gives us more light or less light because of this. There are no days, no months. There are only seasons. With no months, there are no years, and with no years, no age. Nature is nothing more than a cycle of light and dark, birth and death. It recycles itself eternally. So, Rich, in light of all that, how the hell would I know what time it is?"

I think about this for a minute before saying, "How would I know what time to get up, and how would I know what time to eat? How would I know what day it is or how to keep my appointments?"

"Appointments are manmade. That is my point. You get up when you wake up, you eat when you are hungry, you wear more clothing when you are cold and less when you are hot. And that's it. Right now, the sun is going down, and it is becoming twilight, and you are hungry, so I guess it's time to eat." I scratch my head a little bit. In a funny way, it all kind of makes sense. "You are too used to the routines of the mechanical man who needs a time clock to function properly. Everything in your life is routine and designed around a clock. So, you see, the human race is really mechanical. We do everything based on time, and we do it by rote, everything over and over again in the same way. You see, you are mechanical. I am not. I have freed myself from those binds."

I start to speak, but he clasps his hand over my mouth to shush me. "You see, man is a machine. He is lost without his routine. He moves through his life in a mechanical fashion, repeating the same task in the same way over and over again. So what he calls a day is very similar to the last day and also the next. He eats and sleeps, walks and talks and acts like a machine in the routines of life. To become a real man, a warrior, one needs to break from his mechanized routine. First, in order to do that, he needs to observe this tendency in himself. Nothing can be changed without awareness."

Jay stands up and takes a pouch from his pocket. He fills his pipe with tobacco and strikes a match on a post. He lights the pipe and puffs it a few times, casting the dead match into the yard. He then walks into the house. I can hear him rummaging around inside. "Bring in some of that firewood you cut this morning so we can get the fire and the stove going. And don't let those dirty dogs in this place," he yells. I get up from my chair and go over to the wood box. I pick up logs of varying sizes and bring them inside, tossing the larger logs in the fireplace and heaving the smaller ones through the trapdoor of the stove. Jay lights a match and tosses it inside.

Just then, I hear the dogs barking, and they run off the porch in the direction of the chicken coop. They're making quite a racket. Jay is slicing up some potatoes when he turns to me and says, "Go see what all that fuss is about." I walk out the door and head across the porch toward the chicken coop. It is dusk now, the sky a backlight mauve. I can barely make out what is going on in whatever faint light is still lingering from the day. The dogs are howling, barking, and running all around. As I get closer, I hear a loud growling noise from the roof of the chicken coop. The dogs are pacing in circles, barking. Looking up, I see the large, shadowy figure of an animal atop the coop. Stepping a little closer, I recognize the outline of a mountain lion. The dogs have him treed. I take a step backward and freeze. The cougar's attention was on the dogs, but it quickly turns to me. Just then, Jay calls from the porch, "BB, Molly, come here now." The dogs hesitate before turning and running toward the porch, leaving me alone to face the cougar.

CHAPTER 27

I feel the fear. In fact, I can almost smell it on the crisp breeze that leaks out of the forest. No doubt the mountain lion can smell it too. I can't speak, and I'm hoping Jay will come down with his rifle. Instead, I hear a clamoring behind me, and to my surprise, Jay is walking toward the mountain lion and me, banging a wooden spoon against a metal pan. The cougar, obviously frightened by this commotion, leaps off the coop and runs toward the lake. I am still frozen in my spot when I see Jay standing next to me. He stops banging and says, "You going to stand out here all night?" He turns and starts to walk back toward the house. Without saying a word, I exhale all the air that I've trapped in my lungs and shuffle quickly to the porch and inside the house. Jay lets all the dogs back in and tells them to lie down as I collapse in a chair at the table. Jay resumes cutting potatoes as if nothing happened.

"Was that a mountain lion out there?" I ask, my voice shaky. "I could have been killed!"

Jay starts to laugh. "Oh, I don't know. I think he would have much preferred chicken to your bony ass. He comes down here now and then and tries to snatch a hen or two. He hasn't had much luck." He winks and pats BB on the head.

"Jay, why the hell didn't you grab your rifle and shoot him?"

"What!" he responds. "And kill a beautiful animal like that? A warrior would do nothing of the sort."

"But he could've jumped on me. He could have, you know, killed me." I must confess, I'm a little irritated.

"No, not him, he's afraid of a wooden spoon and pan. I think he knows by now that he'll never catch any of those chickens. Tonight I think he came down here for another reason: to have a look at you."

"Me?"

"You know, Indians believe that when an animal crosses your path, it is a powerful sign. Much more powerful than seeing another human. Animals bring you wisdom."

"Oh really?" I say incredulously. "What wisdom did that mountain lion bring me tonight?"

"Let's see," he says. "What would be the biggest characteristic of the mountain lion?"

"I don't know. I've never seen one before."

"Well, I think it's courage. Tonight, the mountain lion came to bestow courage on you. This is a wonderful gift."

"But, Jay," I argue, "I didn't have any courage. I couldn't even move."

"Yes, I know, but when you looked into each other's eyes, he gave you courage, courage that you will need to become a warrior. Use it wisely."

He then says that the dogs look hungry and suggests that I feed them. He reminds me to remember whose bowl is whose. I get up and fill each bowl and return it to the proper spot. "You're learning," Jay says. "Dinner is ready." He puts a plate down in front of me, and I look down.

Beans.

I look across the table at Jay. He has a devilish look on his face. "Jay," I say, "is that all we have around here? What happened to those pheasants you brought in yesterday?"

"Oh, the pheasants," he says as if he forgot about them. He chuckles a bit. "I cleaned them and hung them. They have to bleed out for a few days, or else they taste horrible. Besides," he continues, grinning, "we're having your favorite meal."

"I know I shouldn't complain, but ..." I start.

"Then don't!" he snaps.

"Well at least the biscuits are good," I say, trying to alleviate the tension and convince myself that I'm making the best of this situation.

We eat for a while in silence. I find it hard to formulate any thoughts with my mind contorted by Jay's earlier sermon. He seems to be enjoying his beans immensely. I, on the other hand, am barely choking them down. Finally, Jay looks up and asks if I would like some tea. He speaks so abruptly that it shakes me from my stupor.

"Fine, I'd like a cup," I say.

Jay gets up and pours some of the water we fetched earlier into a brass teapot and sets it on the stove to boil. He then returns to his chair. He sits silently, looking at me for a while before remarking, "You're awfully quiet tonight, aren't you?"

I take this as my cue to start a conversation, though I have no idea where this conversation will go. One thing I have learned about Jay is that no matter what I say or ask, he guides all of our discussion to what he feels we must talk about. And oftentimes he does so by responding to my questions with questions of his own. "Jay," I begin, "so you're an Indian?"

"What do you think?"

"Well you do have feathers in your hair," I say.

"Feather's don't make you an Indian. You have feathers in your hat, and you aren't exactly an Indian, are you?" It was the same logic Doubting I had used.

I think for a minute, trying to figure out how best to answer him without offending him. "Well, Jay doesn't seem like an Indian name to me. Is it short for Blue Jay?"

At this, he roars with laughter, and I can't help but laugh a little myself. "No, it's not Blue Jay, just plain Jay," he replies.

"What kind of Indian are you? I mean, what tribe are you from?"

"I told you that before. I'm Mohawk."

"You mean like the Mohawk Indians that lived in New York State?"

"I don't mean *like* them; I mean *them*." He goes on, "Jay is my name in the world of man, the world that you know. My name in the world of spirits, the world of the Indian, is Eagle Feather." With this, he removes his hat, sits straight up in his chair, and shakes his head a bit to show the eagle feathers that drape down from his hair.

"Are you a chief?" I ask, looking at him in amazement. "Or a medicine man?"

"No," he says. "I'm a warrior."

"Does that mean you've been in many battles?"

"Battles ..." He pauses and looks up toward the ceiling as if he's trying to clarify his thoughts. "I have not been in many battles."

"Well then, how are you a warrior?"

His face floods with a look of indignation. "Battles do not make you a warrior. Being a warrior is a way of life, a state of mind. Warriors accept their circumstances and make the best of them."

"What do you mean?" I ask.

"In the state of mind of the warrior, all is possible. He accepts only the present moment, whatever it may be. He is indifferent to all his surroundings, and because of this indifference, he is one with them."

"One with whom?"

"He is one with all of it. He accepts the world for what it is and is part of it all. He accepts the universe for what it is, as he is part of that also. Because he knows he is in the universe, he comes to realize that the whole of the universe is within him. Modern man has forgotten this and thinks that he is a separate entity. He thinks that he acts outside of the world, outside of the universe. This is why he has become so disconnected from himself. He acts as an independent, as if there is a disconnection between him and the universe. But a warrior comes to know that he is an intricate part of it all. Where man feels a disconnection, the warrior feels connected. He realizes he is connected to everything. And he acts accordingly. He moves through the world knowing that it is a mysterious place that he can never fully unravel. Yet still he walks through it in harmony."

"Are all the people in your tribe warriors then?" I ask.

"No, they are not all warriors."

I'm starting to become equally intrigued and confused by everything he is telling me. "How did you know that you should become a warrior?"

"When I was born, an eagle flying above dropped a feather to the ground near me, and my benefactor saw this. He was a man of great power, and he took this as a sign that he was to show me the warrior's path when I came of age."

"That's incredible. Jay, an eagle dropped this feather to me the other day." I gesture to the feather that I stuck under the band of my hat.

"I guess we shall have to take that as a sign," he says.

"A sign? What do you mean?"

"All through our lives, the spirits leave us signs that show us how to proceed, how to choose a path. We just need to be awake enough to recognize these signs and be ever vigilant because they can present themselves in many different manners."

"So the eagle dropping the feather for you wasn't the same as it was for me?"

"It was a sign, a sign of power. What it means is for you to decide."

"But, Jay, I'm no warrior," I say sheepishly.

"How do you know that?" he asks.

"I'm a tennis pro. I play tennis."

After this, there is a long pause. Jay gets up from his chair with the two dirty plates in his hands and suggests we clean up. I pop up from my chair like I've been sitting on a spring, take the plates from his hands, and wash them both quickly. I'm hoping we can continue this conversation after everything is clean. As soon as I'm done, I turn around to find Jay. He is on his way out the door and whistles for the dogs to follow. Without turning around, he invites me to have a smoke. Jay strikes a match, lighting a lantern, and I follow the light outside.

CHAPTER 28

When I get out on the porch, Jay sits in his rocking chair and lights his pipe with what's left of the match he used on the lantern. "I don't have a cigar to smoke," I say.

"Would you care for one?" he asks, puffing away on his pipe. I tell him I would love one. He gets up and goes inside the house. After he is gone awhile, I begin to wonder what he's doing in there and peek through the open door. Jay is seated at the table with his back to me. I walk inside and notice that he has tobacco leaves arranged in a pile on the table, and to my astonishment, he is rolling a cigar. He works efficiently, and in no time at all, he has one rolled up for me.

"That's incredible," I say. "Where did you learn how to do that?"

Without speaking, he takes out a small pocketknife and cuts off both ends of the cigar before handing it to me. He looks at me with a knowing, perhaps even sarcastic, smile and informs me that a warrior learns to do everything. Then he shoos me out to the porch, instructing me not to light it until I am outside.

I step onto the porch, and as I am lighting the cigar, Jay returns, sits down, and starts to rock away. All the dogs are around him, and he pets them softly. The night air has become cold, though not too cold for the crickets, who warble out the early favorites of fall. Jay tells me to sit down and relax, and I am happy to oblige, thanking him as I find my seat. As soon as I am seated, the dogs flock to me, competing for my attention. I am happy to pet them. I am struck by how friendly and well behaved they are.

I'm hoping Jay will engage me in more conversation about the way of the warrior, but he isn't saying much, so I let it be for a while. For the first time since my arrival a few days ago, I'm not so preoccupied with trying to get home; rather, I fix my thoughts on everything that Jay has told me about being a warrior. After roughly half my cigar has vanished, Jay begins to speak.

"You know, playing tennis in a tournament is very much like being a warrior." This gets my attention. I look at him and ask him how so. He goes on, "Well, you have to play under the conditions that exist, and you must continuously make adjustments to whatever is occurring. You have to clear your mind and focus your attention on the task at hand. Each point is a task in itself, and each shot is merely a task within that task. As a player, you need to stay in the moment. If you cannot, you lose the match. The parallels to the warrior's state of mind are obvious."

I am amazed at Jay's understanding of the mind-set one needs to play tennis. "Jay, that's astonishing. That is exactly where my head's at during a match, at least I hope it is, and it's exactly what I try to teach my students. Have you ever played before?"

He begins to laugh heartily, the same physical laugh that dropped him to his knees when he heard I was afraid of chickens. This easily goes on for five minutes. "I don't need to have ever played tennis before," he says through his chortling. "Every game that you could possibly play mirrors life. Every sport teaches you how your mind should operate as you proceed through life. It is unfortunate that this is only one of the few times when men act as warriors."

"I suppose you're right," I say. "We're, like you said, in the moment."

"It is more than just staying in the moment, Rich, though that is vital. The warrior's mind becomes quiet; he looks for signs and accepts the situation. He does this not only during competition but in all areas of life. Whoever can do this will be on the path to becoming a warrior. A warrior is always impeccable in this way."

"What do you mean by *impeccable*, Jay?"

"A warrior has full convictions and total attention devoted to the moment at hand. This is what I mean by impeccable. So, you see, Rich, you have acted as a warrior before. But you have only used that power in a small capacity, to play a game. Within this game, this play, is a lesson on how you should live your life. You, like many, have not seen this as a lesson; you have seen it only as a game."

I'm beginning to think Jay is amazing, brilliant even. How does he know all this stuff? It kind of makes sense. It's more or less what I was thinking back in the clearing before I got that strange phone call and found my way here.

"How about a drink?" he says and walks back into the house. Before I can even answer, as if he already knows that I will say yes, he yells, "Whiskey or tequila?"

"Whiskey," I answer. He tells me that I am predictable and that my mechanicalness is showing. He instantaneously appears back on the porch with a glass of whiskey. I think he had it poured before I answered.

"Why?" I ask. "Should I have tequila tonight or something?"

"No. We will not speak of mechanicalness tonight," he says.

"Jay, or should I say Eagle Feather—"

"No!" He stops me there abruptly. "You call me Jay!" he says in a stern voice.

I am kind of taken aback by his sudden change in tone. "Let's say I become a warrior. Then can I call you Eagle Feather?"

"In that unlikely situation," he says a little coyly, "yes. But that is a long way off."

"Tell me, Jay, how would I become a warrior?"

"Oh, do you think I can just tell you? Telling you would do no good. It would just be lip service, and you would be under the impression that you were a warrior without first walking the path. That's not why you are here."

I take another sip of whiskey and look back at Jay, who has now fallen silent and is sitting in his chair smoking his pipe. "So, Jay, why am I here? Do you know why? Do you actually *know* why I'm here?"

"Did you not hear what the water spirit told you?" he answers quickly and angrily.

I look at him quizzically. "No, I didn't hear anything. I didn't hear anything when we were at the waterfall, and I didn't see anything either. Just the totem pole."

"You're asleep," he snaps.

"That's kind of what I thought. I'm dreaming this whole thing."

"A dream. Yes and no. But that is not the kind of sleep I'm talking about. I'm talking about the sleep of the human race. Man comes into this world awake and then falls asleep. We are programmed, or perhaps we program each other, to fall asleep."

"So, let me see if I got this straight: I didn't hear anything from the water spirit because I'm asleep?"

"No, I did not say you couldn't hear the water spirit because you are asleep. You could not hear him because you are not a warrior. But, yes, you and the rest of the human race are asleep."

"Jay," I say, "I'm a little confused. You're telling me that everyone is sleeping, that I'm asleep right now."

"Yes," he says, "that is exactly what I'm telling you. The whole human race is asleep."

"So this is all a dream?"

Jay doesn't answer me for a while, instead staring straight ahead as if deep in thought. I'm thinking that maybe he doesn't have an answer. Finally, he turns his head toward me and says, "We're all in this dream that we call life. The sleep that I am talking about comes from life. Life keeps us asleep. When we are born, we are born of true essence. We come into the world as our true selves, but we do not remain this way for long. From the first time we begin to understand the world, the world plunges us into the deep sleep we consider to be life."

The profundity with which he uttered this last part intrigues me. I want to find out more about this metaphoric sleep he is talking about and how it relates to my situation. "So what exactly do you mean by *sleep*?" I ask.

"Life is an energy unto itself." His voice seems to perk up a bit, I figure because he sees that I am now engaging him. "Life's plan is to put you to sleep so that you serve life and not yourself, so that you become part of the mechanical circle of humanity."

I stop him right there. "This is why you told me that I was a machine and that I do things the same over and over again?"

"Yes," he says, "you are a prisoner of the mechanical circle of humanity."

"Are you a machine?" I ask.

He looks at me with a long, stern look and says, "I was once just as you are now."

"Well, if you're not a mechanical man, what are you?"

"I'm a spirit living in the conscious circle of the universe," he says matter-of-factly. After a short pause, he continues, "You see, the conscious circle of universe is composed of those spirits who have become conscious of their life while living. They have fought long and hard to break the bonds of sleep. They are truly warriors."

"So, all warriors are awake?"

"If they are warriors, yes, they would have to be awake," he says, starting to laugh. "You can't be a warrior and be asleep. To sum up what the water spirit told you today, this is your opportunity to wake up, to become a warrior and free yourself from the prison of life. This is your opportunity to gain this consciousness. Even though it is life that imprisons you, it is only through life that you can learn. Life is not only a great adversary, it can also be a great teacher and a great friend."

"Well, Jay, I don't know about this sleep you're talking about. I'm wide awake now and have been wide awake all my life."

With this, he takes a long pull from his pipe and blows a large cloud of smoke that engulfs me. "You cannot see anything through sleep, just as you cannot see outside this cloud of smoke. You are lost in the smoke, just as you are lost in life. You have been sent here to wake up, as the whole human race must. But the trouble lies in the fact that people do not realize they are asleep; you, for example, are only starting to realize that you have been asleep." Jay gets up from his chair, takes the empty glass from my hand, and disappears into the house. He emerges minutes later with a full glass of whiskey and hands it to me. He sits back down in his chair and asks if I am enjoying my cigar. I'm confused, and I stammer as I try to talk. I tell him that the cigar is great and that I'd like to learn how to roll them sometime. It is the only response I can muster while most of my mind is preoccupied with everything he just told me. I sit there for a while thinking about all of it; it's a great deal for me to process. I also think it's a bit crazy, that he's a bit crazy, crazy that he describes the whole of humanity as asleep.

I press him for more details. "I guess I'm just not understanding exactly what you mean when you say *sleep*."

"Well," he says, "sit back and enjoy your whiskey. I'll relate it to you just as it was related to me when I was trying to become a warrior myself. From the time that you are young and able to understand, you are affected—or perhaps I should say infected—by the world: your parents, society, essentially *other* people. You lost yourself. Because the people affecting you were asleep themselves, you too fell asleep. By listening to them, imitating or rejecting them, you became hypnotized. This problem perpetuates itself because it disguises itself. No one seems to know that they are asleep. You exist on one level of consciousness, and you think this level is the only one that exists. In fact, it is one of the lowest levels. Your mind is not working properly; it is not functioning at its full capacity. Something has gone awry. The present moment takes a back seat to thoughts dominated by the past and the future. In fact, only a very small portion of the mind focuses on the present moment. All these thoughts run into and out of your mind: thoughts of the past and thoughts of the future. You are so egotistical that you think that all these thoughts are important. As I've told you before, only the present moment exists. We spend so much of our mental capacity thinking about all that *has been* and all that *will be* that we miss what *is*. So, this is why I like to call it sleep; our minds are not where our bodies are. How can we say that we are awake when we are not even present in the moment that we are living? Is this not the definition of sleep? As a result, we become mechanical. We do everything the same way all the time and repeat the same thoughts and the same processes day after day. We don't have the attention it takes to break free from these cycles. You see, Rich, everyone you know and nearly everyone you meet in your life has been lost in this slumber."

Jay sits back in his chair, crosses his legs, and begins to rock slowly. I, on the other hand, am dumbfounded. "Jay, I'm having a hard time believing this. You're telling me that everyone in my life has been sleepwalking. And on top of that, I'm having trouble with the notion that—even though this place seems so real—I'm actually in a dream."

Jay chuckles. "Maybe you are, and maybe you aren't. But I assure you, Rich, everyone who isn't a warrior is sleeping. And I leave you this last thought: if everyone were conscious, there would be no war, no famine, no killing, and no problems with the atmosphere or with Mother Earth; life would be completely different."

Hearing this, I drop the cigar from my mouth and take one last sip of whiskey. The whiskey is starting to go to my head again. It's starting to spin … my head, not the whiskey. Jay gets up from his chair, walks to the door, opens it, and signals for the dogs to go inside. He turns back to me and says, "Rich, finish your drink. I'm tired. Let's get some rest." He starts to laugh and says, "I think it's a good idea that we go inside while you can still walk and I don't have to carry your ass in here again like I did last night." I get up and try to walk without staggering too obviously through the door. Jay points to the ladder and says to me, with a wisecracking tone, "If you climb that ladder, you'll find your bed up there." With that, he walks into his bedroom and closes the door. Then, through the wall of his room, he says, "Good luck and sweet dreams, Rich. Now get some *sleep*." He's laughing.

I somehow manage to make it to the ladder and climb it one rung at a time, holding on for dear life like I did when I climbed that ash back by the clearing. You know how I feel about heights. Even the whiskey did nothing to quell this fear. When I get to the top, I notice a fairly spacious area that runs the entire length of the house. There is a mattress on the floor with a blanket neatly tucked in and two pillows. I stagger over and flop down on the mattress, falling asleep instantly.

CHAPTER 29

A shiver runs down my spine as I am abruptly awakened by the sound of Jay banging a tin cup against the ladder. I sit up from my alcohol-induced stupor and peer down through the hole in the floor. I can see the top of Jay's hat as he stands next to the ladder. He looks up through the hole and sees me sitting up in the bed. At this point, I avoid eye contact. He calls up to me in a gravelly voice. "Let's get moving. It's the light side of dark, and we have a lot of things to do today."

I look down at him and can see that he has moved away from the ladder and out of my field of view. Although I drank a fair amount of whiskey last night, I didn't drink nearly as much as I did the night before, and I don't have quite the hangover. That being said, I'm still not feeling all that chipper. I get up and find that I am still fully dressed from head to toe. I surmise that has everything to do with my nosedive into bed last night. I didn't take the time to remove my clothes or boots. This saves me some time getting ready. All I have to do now is get down the ladder without killing myself.

On my climb down, I hear the door open and the pitter-patter of the dogs' paws out on the porch. By the time I hit the floor, I see Jay walking back toward the oven. Without turning toward me, he says, "We'll need some firewood for the oven if you want breakfast."

"Yup," I reply, still half-asleep. I make my way to the porch to retrieve the wood. Once I make it out the door, the morning sunlight smacks me in the face like a left hook. Squinting, I manage to gather an armful of firewood from the stand on the porch. I come back inside, toss the logs into the stove, and sit down at the table. My mind is still full of plenty of cobwebs from both the whiskey and the conversation with Jay last night. Although I haven't had much sober time to think about it, it still weighs heavily on me.

Jay turns around from whatever he's doing over by the oven and says, "Would you like some eggs?"

"Yes, eggs would be good," I reply sheepishly.

He points toward the door, saying, "You know where they are. Go get us some."

This snaps me back to my senses. I look at him, but he turns away from me and back toward the oven. "Jay, you know the chickens and I, we, uh, aren't exactly on the best of terms."

"I guess you're not in the mood for eggs then," he says. "I told you that you're in charge of getting the eggs each morning."

I start to whine. "You know those chickens don't like me. They put up such a fuss yesterday that I only managed to get one egg, and on my way out the door, I dropped and broke it."

"You're being ridiculous," he says. "Imagine, a grown man afraid of chickens. Besides, you apologized. This conversation is over. Get going."

I drag myself up and out the door. In no time at all, I'm back, with no eggs and a real bad attitude. Chicken feathers join the eagle feather in my hat. Jay chuckles as he stirs the dough that will soon become biscuits. "Well? The eggs?" he asks, extending his hand and grinning.

"Eggs?" I shout. "Why don't you ask your chickens? As I came through the door, they jumped me again. It was an ambush. It was all I could do to get out of there without being pecked to death."

Jay begins to laugh hysterically and tells me to come over to the table and sit down. He says, "It looks like it's just biscuits this morning. You can top them off with an apple if you want." He reaches over to the bushel next to the fireplace, plucks an apple out, and tosses it to me. Next, he comes over with two plates, nothing on them but biscuits, and sets them down on the table. He places two cups down and pours tea for both of us. "There you go—biscuits. Save some for tonight."

I look at him with disbelief. "You're not going to go out and get the eggs?"

Jay sits, munching on a biscuit. He takes a sip of tea and says, "Now, if I keep going out there to get the eggs, you're going to learn nothing. Getting the eggs is your job, and we do our jobs around here."

I'm in no mood for this. I'm angry, tired, and hungry. But without complaining, I finish a biscuit and start on the apple. Jay finishes his breakfast and heads out the door, calling back to me, "I'll be back. Chop some more wood and fill up that wood box." I'm infuriated and frustrated. I can't believe this shit. Here I am getting bossed around by this guy. At least when I was out in the woods by myself, I was the boss.

"Who does this guy think he is?" asks Wise Guy I. "He can't order us around like this."

"We'll find him and kick his ass," Courageous I says.

"Yeah, I'm with you guys," I say.

"Take it easy, everybody," says Analytical I. "This guy is all we have right now."

"I don't care. He can't talk to us like that!" Ego I snaps back.

I walk out onto the porch and throw the apple core angrily into the horse paddock. I storm back around the back of the house and start to chop wood as I listen to the I's conspiring how to escape Jay. It takes a good forty-five minutes of furious chopping before I calm down and return to my senses. I also notice that some of the I's have disappeared in the process. I've split so much wood that I have much more than I need to fill up the wood box on the porch. I find myself thinking about all that warrior stuff Jay was going on about last night. And about how the whole human race is sleeping and how I'm asleep. I decide that Jay is crazy; I'm awake and I always have been. At least as awake as he is. I go inside to have a drink. As I'm pouring water into a cup, the door swings open, and Jay appears with a bucket in one hand and mop in the other. He hands me the bucket and mop and says, "It's time to mop the floor. Do the entire floor, including the bedroom and the porch." He turns around and walks back outside, slamming the door.

CHAPTER 30

"I'd like to mop the floor with him," I mutter. I go over to the sink and begin pumping water into the bucket. After a short search, I find some sort of cleaning powder on one of the shelves, sprinkle it into the bucket, and start to mop. I'm having a really hard time dealing with this. Here I am doing his chores, mopping the floor like I'm in the military or, worse, like I'm a hired hand. He doesn't know who he's dealing with. I finish the whole inside floor and open the door to start on the porch. Just as I do so, the dogs fly into the cabin, tracking mud everywhere I just mopped. "Oh no," I yell, "not on my clean floor!" I sound just like my mother when I was a kid. "Out!" I yell as I chase BB, Molly, and Bert through the open door with the mop, just as my mother chased my brother and me when we were young and muddied up her clean floor. The dogs don't take much coaxing. In fact, they are much better behaved than my brother and me, who used to laugh hysterically and run just out of our mother's reach. After all the dogs are safely outside, Jay pops his head through the door.

"Nope," he says, "you have to do it over." He's gone in a flash. I find myself cursing under my breath. Just like my mother.

I'm out on the porch mopping. And I am not pleased. Jay walks up out of nowhere, picks up the bucket, and dumps the water all over the porch. "You're outside now. You don't have to be that particular about it." He walks off the porch toward the chicken coop. I can't help but think he is doing all this to get me mad. He's succeeding. When I finish the porch, I lean the mop up against the side of the cabin and walk off to figure out what I'm supposed to do next. I find Jay inside the chicken coop, feeding the chickens. I have managed to calm down a bit. "I see you're feeding those monsters you got there." Jay chuckles a bit and invites me inside. "No thanks," I reply.

"Have a seat on the rock over there and take a rest," Jay says, and I do just that. I start to notice that it's a beautiful day. The air is crisp, and a slight breeze whispers through the mottled, multicolored foliage. "Did you hear all those I's in your head calm down yet?" I can only stare at him. He goes on. "Boy, if it was up to them, I'd be hanging from a tree by now."

I'm taken aback. Is he reading my mind? I remember getting that impression the first night I met him. "I don't know what you're talking about," I say defensively.

"Oh, sure you do," he says. "You think you're the only one with all those I's running around in his mind? All those I's that take control of you and act in your name?" I'm astonished. That is exactly how they work. But how can he possibly know about them?

"What, so now you're a mind reader?" I ask, somewhat suspiciously.

He tosses the rest of the corn out to the chickens and comes over to the fence, leaning on it and facing me. "Are you so egotistical that you think you are the only one living with this problem? Man is a multitude of I's, each one vying for control over you."

I never thought about it this way before. Those I's are mine, and I just assumed I'm the only one who has them. I look up at him, catching a glimpse of his eyes, and ask, "Why, Jay, do you have these I's inside you that just keep talking and won't shut the fuck up?"

He snickers a little bit. "We all have those I's. We make them up as we go through life. We have hundreds of them, and they are all ready to take control over those minds and bodies of ours. They all want to be the one we listen to. So you sit there thinking that you are only one person. In fact, you are really a multitude of persons, and 99.9 percent of them are false, made up by you to react to your environment."

"Are you suggesting that I made all those I's up?"

"I'm not suggesting it. I'm telling you," he says.

"Why would I do something like that?"

"Because you are a victim of life, and you use all of these false personalities to be whoever you need to be in a particular instance. The I's are part of the sleep that we spoke of last night."

"So, now, not only am I asleep, but I have hundreds of personalities inside me? That's what you're telling me?" I pause for a minute. "I find this very hard to believe. You know what, Jay? I don't believe it."

He leaves the pen and begins to walk toward the porch. I follow. He stops suddenly in the middle of his stroll and turns to me. "Tell me this: do you not believe that you are all those I's? And are they not constantly battling in your head and stirring up trouble? Do they make it impossible for you to act decisively? Think about this."

We walk on in silence until we reach the porch. Jay walks into the house, while I sit down in one of the chairs. I'm in a state of confusion. I don't want to believe Jay, although I know he's right. I do obviously have those I's—more of them than I'd like to admit—and they do seem to take over.

When Jay comes back to the porch, I sit up straight. I've been waiting for him. "If this is true, what am I supposed to do about it?" I blurt out. "Is there any hope for me?"

He sits down and lights his pipe. "The first thing you need to do is observe these I's. Self-observation without judgment. Without observation, nothing can be changed."

"What do you mean? I should watch myself?"

"Yes," he answers, "this is exactly what I mean. Observe the I's in all situations. But do not judge them. Do not try to change them. Just observe. You see, once you pay attention to them, you give them power, and it is with this power that they control your actions."

"They take control over me?"

"Yes," he answers sharply. "You know this for a fact. You have been struggling with these I's for as long as you can remember."

"That's right," I say.

He continues, "You will need to consolidate all these I's into one I, the one true I or one true self. Then you will be whole."

"Will I be awake then?" I ask.

"Let's just say you will be well on your way."

"So how do I proceed with this observation?" I ask.

"First," Jay says, "it's necessary to split yourself in two: the observer and the observed. It is as if you are in a play. You must at once be the actor on stage and a member of the audience. Once you've accomplished this, you can start to pick and choose which I you would choose to give power to. You can eliminate all the I's that are of no benefit to you as you become your true self."

"So, what you're telling me is that I'm not only full of bad I's, but there are good I's too?"

"Yes," he says, "there are a number of good I's."

"Well how can I tell the difference between the bad guys and the good I's?"

"Oh," he says, "asking questions, now are we? Good. There are plenty of good I's, but for the moment, let's focus on the bad I's."

"What sort of bad ones?"

"Let's see," he says. "I'll give you a few examples. How about Jealous I or Proud I. Pride and vanity walk alone together. And here's one that you jump to consistently, Angry I. Or how about this one that you hear too often, Wise Guy I. There are so many that afflict the human race."

"Yes," I say, "I hear Wise Guy I all the time. He gets me in a lot of trouble."

"As do so many of these little I's, these personalities that you've made up for yourself. How about Pessimistic I? That's a big one in your repertoire. And I know you know this one pretty well too: Vengeful I."

I can't believe this. It's as if Jay is looking into my mind. "Stop! Stop, Jay. Enough already."

"Oh, I've got one more for you, one more out of the multitude that keeps popping up lately. Ungrateful I." I drop my head and feel the sting of Jay's remark. I know he is right. I have been ungrateful toward him and his hospitality. I've had moments in my life when I was unsure of myself, but this is different. I really feel guilty about my recent behavior and my constant griping. And now, to top it off, I'm starting to feel as though I don't exist, at least not as an I, more like an I by committee. It's as if I'm not in control of something that I thought I always had control over. And I tell Jay this.

"No, you don't have control right now. But control is merely an illusion. We really don't have much control over anything. This is something a warrior knows."

"Jay, does a warrior have all these I's inside him?"

He doesn't answer me for a while as he contemplates his response. Finally, he says, "When you truly take up the task of becoming a warrior, you must consolidate these I's into one, to become whole, to be the same one true person in all circumstance of life."

"On your way to becoming a warrior, did you complete this task?"

He takes a couple of puffs from his pipe and lets out a blast of smoke. He turns toward me and answers, "This task is never complete. This is a battle even a warrior must fight his entire life. We need to succeed in becoming one whole instead of several parts. You must stay vigilant and direct your power toward the one I and away from the legion."

I sit there in a daze, his words ringing in my ears. Jay stands up and tells me he is going to check on the horses. He invites me to have another apple if I am hungry, and he walks off the porch toward the horse paddock.

I sit alone for a while contemplating everything he just told me. I am overtaken by an incredible feeling of nothingness. It is as though I am no longer a man after what Jay just told me. At least certainly not a man in control of himself. Deep down inside, I know that he is right. I have been controlled by my I's all my life. I've made up I's so that my family and friends would like me or so that I would gain some advantage in a particular situation. I now realize that without all these personalities, I would be a completely different person, and perhaps that's Jay's point.

Just as I'm wondering how I could have allowed this to happen, I hear Wise Guy I. "You're not going to believe this guy, are you? Who would you rather believe: some strange Indian or us? You've known us your whole life."

CHAPTER 31

My stomach begins to hurt, and my head throbs. Just hearing that voice reminds me of all the others buried in there. And I now have the added torment of knowing that I have no control over them. Jay is right. He looked inside my mind and told me something that I've always known but couldn't face. Something I've never had the courage to face. In the next moments that pass, I hear many voices, and they all tell me that Jay is wrong. All of them tell me to ignore his nonsense, and each insists I should listen to him because he is the one true I. At this point, I fully expect to lose my mind because I no longer know who I am.

As I sit there in a stupor, I finally come to when I hear the whinnying of a horse. I blink and rub my eyes and look in the direction of the sound. Jay is mounted on a beautiful tan and white horse. In his hands are the reins of another horse, a striking chestnut brown that's fully saddled. "You seem to be lost somewhere in thought," he says in a playful voice. "The horses need some work. Mind getting up here? Let's take them out for a ride."

I stand up and look at the majestic, chestnut-colored mare, scared for my life. "I told you, I can't ride."

"Well," he says, "today is the day you learn, whether you fall off or not. Get on up. Sweetheart here's a lovely and gentle soul. She'll take good care of you."

I'm suddenly reminded of why I'm so against horseback riding. I had a beautiful blonde girlfriend back in high school who I was trying to impress. She asked me to take her riding one day, and I found a stable that rented horses, even though I had no clue what I was doing. I picked her up one day after school and took her out to the stable, never letting on that I had no idea how to ride a horse. On the drive, I learned that she had ridden horses dozens of times before and was pretty experienced. Things didn't look good for me. But I kept my mouth shut.

When we arrived, there was a man at the stable dressed like a cowboy, and he had two horses ready and saddled for us. He told us that there were a bunch of trails we could follow. It wasn't until the horses came close to me that I realized how massive they were and how afraid of them I was. From far away, they didn't look too big. But that all changed as they got closer.

Beth got on her horse like she was born to. The cowboy handed me the reins of my horse, and I put my leg in the stirrup and danced around for fifteen minutes trying to get my other leg over the horse. This provided great amusement to both Beth and the cowboy. They laughed through the whole ordeal, and it embarrassed the hell out of me. I finally managed to get on the horse, and off we went. To make a long story short, I fell off the horse three times, narrowly escaping injury each time. After all three times, it took me another fifteen minutes to get back on. So much for impressing Beth. Even though this was a girl I had lusted over for the longest time, my embarrassment prevented me from seeing her anymore. In fact, after that day, I hid from her at school.

So, now here I am, with Jay, facing the same situation. Of course, Jay already knows that I can't ride a horse. I told him so, and even if I hadn't, he probably would have just read my mind and found out anyway. Though Sweetheart looks very nice, when we are side by side, she is huge, and I feel the same fear I felt with Beth. Jay is snickering. He keeps trying to hand me the reins, and I keep refusing to take them.

Finally, he says, "It is always better to face our fears. Overcoming them with confirmed resolve is essential. It is okay to be afraid, but one must learn to overcome fear if one is going to succeed at the task at hand. It is mind over matter." I hear what Jay is saying, but given my last attempt at riding with Beth, my confidence level is very low. At that moment, I realize Jay is here to help. He knows I cannot ride a horse and is here to teach me a lesson, a lesson about fear and about controlling myself. I take the reins from his hand.

"Come on this side and put your left foot in the stirrup. Hop a couple of times while holding the saddle horn and throw your right leg over the horse's back."

I follow his instructions. The next thing I know, I'm on top of Sweetheart. "There you go," Jay says. He turns his horse and starts down the trail toward the lake at a slow walk. Without my having to do anything, Sweetheart turns and follows Jay. I'm bouncing all around, tense, and holding onto the saddle horn for dear life. Jay obviously senses this and turns around saying, "Relax with it. Rock your hips back and forth and become one with the animal." Become one with the horse? This is a strange concept. But I do as I'm told. I'm obviously very out of sync with the horse because Jay turns around and stares, roaring with laughter.

"Slow down," he says. "You have no rhythm. When the horse moves, you move. The trick is to start slowly."

I realize this is going to take a little concentration, so I slow myself down and try to feel when the horse takes a step and move forward and backward accordingly. I must be putting on a good show because Jay nods approvingly. Don't get me wrong though. I'm still terrified. The trail bends to the left, and fortunately, Sweetheart continues to follow. Knowing full well that I can't maneuver the horse, I call out to Jay, "How do I steer this thing?"

Jay kicks his horse and starts to move out faster. He yanks the reins, pulling them to the left-hand side, and the horse slows downs and turns so he's facing me, coming back with a trot. "It's not brain surgery," Jay says. "It's like driving a car. If you want to go left, pull her head to the left with the reins. If you want to go right, pull her to the right with the reigns. If you want to stop, pull back on the reins. And if you really want to go, let the tension off the reins and kick a little … just an easy kick."

"That's it?" I ask.

"Yup, that's all there is to it." He turns his horse and starts back down the trail. I decide to try this out. I pull the reins a little to the left, and Sweetheart goes to the left. I pull to the right, and she goes to the right. I pull back on the reins, and she stops. My mood lightens, and I actually start to feel some control over this beast. Jay has been watching all this out of the corner of his eye, and he kicks his horse and takes off down the trail. And it's at this point that my illusion of control disappears. Sweetheart, of her own volition, takes off after Jay and his horse, and it's all I can do to hold on by the seat of my pants. After fifty yards or so, Jay stops his horse abruptly. Sweetheart follows suit. Unfortunately, I do not. I wind up flying off the front of Sweetheart and landing on my back right in the center of the trail. Jay is laughing, and the horses start to whinny. Great. Beth and the cowboy all over again.

I get up, and Jay, through a smirk, asks if I'm okay. I tell him I'm fine as I brush all the dirt and trail dust off. I walk back past Jay and Sweetheart toward the cabin, muttering, "I told you I didn't want to ride a damn horse." Physically, I'm fine. It's my pride that hurts most.

I hear Jay shout out to me, "Giving up, huh? Looks like Ego I has taken control of you. I warned you about that one; he's a giant."

I stop in my tracks. I did hear Ego I in my head. I realize that Ego I is getting in the way of my learning how to ride a horse, just like he ruined any chance I had of a romantic relationship with Beth. I'm afraid now, as I was then, of humiliation, and humiliation is nothing more than the result of pride and fear mixing. I turn and look back toward Jay. I can feel his steely gaze looking right through me. "You have been controlled by fear and by pride already today. Ask yourself one thing: did you decide this? Did you make this conscious decision to surrender your will to theirs? Or did they wrest this control from you?"

I take off my hat and straighten the eagle feather, still brimming with pride and fear.

"If you want to keep that eagle feather, you had better get a hold of yourself. Otherwise you don't deserve it. It would not surprise me one bit if the eagle that so graciously gave you that gift returns and snatches it right off your head!"

I put my hat back on and walk toward Jay. Taking the reins from his hand, I put my foot in the stirrup, hop a couple of times, and get back on Sweetheart. I pull the reins so she turns completely around, and we start heading down the trail toward the lake. Jay finally catches up to me, and we ride in silence, side by side, for some time.

I fall off Sweetheart three times when all is said and done. Suppose that is my lucky number when it comes to falling off horses. Every time I fall, I feel fear and pride reemerging. Nevertheless, each time, I get back on, and by the end of the ride, I feel confident that I can ride a horse. At least a little bit. I have also learned something about myself, and I know that this is much more important.

CHAPTER 32

Beans again! I am sitting at the table when Jay plops down another plate full of beans and biscuits. What is it about beans? Are they the sacred fodder of the warrior? The dogs all lie around the table as usual.

"Beans again. Jay, don't we have anything else?" Jay is eating. If this beans-everyday-thing is a joke, it's gotten pretty old by now. "Is there anything else around here for dinner?"

"Stop complaining," he says. "You should be grateful that we have anything to eat at all! Complaining is a sickness, and you've been ill for quite a while." I don't have an answer to that. I'm reminded of when Jay described the I's to me and singled out Ungrateful I. A feeling of guilt shoots through me. We eat in silence, and I, in fact, am so hungry that I inhale the beans. Jay obviously notices this and remarks, "For someone who hates beans so much and points it out so often, you certainly seem to be cleaning up that plate awfully quickly. Take care of the dogs." And with that, he grabs both empty plates and goes over to the sink to wash them. I get up and feed the dogs, following the procedure Jay set forth.

I'm having mixed emotions. On one hand, I don't trust Jay. I have this idea in the back of my mind that he is keeping me here for some reason. But on the other hand, I'm becoming fascinated by his theories on life, and I have lots of questions. I want to learn more about the water spirits, the warriors, and all the little personalities battling it out in my brain. But the thing I most want to learn is how the hell I can get home.

"Go out to the barn, get a bale of hay down from the loft, and spread it out for the horses to eat," he says, refusing to turn away from the sink and face me.

I head out the door toward the barn. The light outside is fading fast, but I manage to glimpse my hawk as he flies above me and perches on the roof of the barn. I haven't seen him in a while, and it's nice that I'm back in the company of my only trustworthy friend. "Hello! Where have you been? Haven't seen you in a while," I say as if I almost expect an answer. But then again, I suppose stranger things have happened, especially around here. The hawk merely stares back at me.

As I walk toward the barn, I hear the unmistakable screeching of the crows. They are back and must have followed the hawk. The dive-bombing commences again, just as it did back at the clearing. The hawk stands by with his usual devil-may-care indifference. As I'm watching all this, Jay comes out on the porch.

"What's all that racket out here?"

I walk back toward the porch and point up at the crows. I begin to plead with Jay to intervene on the hawk's behalf. "These crows just don't seem to want to leave him alone," I say. "Maybe you could fire a shot in the air or something, anything to get them to disperse."

Jay motions toward the hawk with his chin, and I understand he wants me to look up at him. "Fix your gaze on the hawk," he commands.

It is a completely unnecessary thing to say. I haven't looked away from the hawk and blitzkrieging crows at all. "I know, Jay. I've seen them do this before. They're relentless."

"Look up at those crows but keep your eyes on the hawk. All the crows up there making all that fuss are like the I's in your mind. They make quite a racket trying to bait the hawk to attack or retreat. But the hawk knows that if he is to turn and fight or pay attention to the crows in any way, they will gang up and kill him. So, you see how he ignores them? He acts as if nothing is happening. He does not give power to the crows. He is not tricked into doing something stupid. That hawk up there is a wise old bird. A younger bird may turn and try to fight them and then find himself killed by the ensuing onslaught. Your hawk has learned that if he pays no attention to them, he will gain power over them, rather than the other way around, and the crows will ultimately lose interest and leave. You should take a tip from the hawk. When you find that your I's are bombarding you, try to ignore them, and in doing so, you will gain power over them, and they will go away." Sure enough, after a short while, the crows start to disappear.

I turn around to Jay and see that he has a big smile. "You should thank your hawk. He has come here tonight to teach you how to handle your I's," he says.

I walk to the barn and undo the big latch, pulling the barn doors back. It's dark inside. The only light I have to see with is the little bit that shines through the open doorway. I pause briefly, allowing my eyes time to adjust. I go over to the ladder and climb up into the loft where Jay stores the hay. As I begin my ascent up the ladder, I spot something in the right-hand corner of the barn that takes me by surprise. It's a truck, an old Chevy, that appears to be a faded red, though I can't tell for sure because it's covered in dust. It looks out of place. Or out of time. This truck looks to be from the 1950s. But then again, I remember seeing some modern things that first night I arrived at the cabin, the modern-looking bag of dog food being one, and so I guess I really have no idea exactly where and when I am.

The truck has a big flatbed on it with a tailgate that can be held together with chain loops. The body sits relatively high off the wheels, and I recognize that it must be four-wheel drive. I walk around to the driver's side and open the door. There is a full bench seat with no seat belts. I look down at the wheel hubs in the front of the truck and notice it has those locking hubs that old trucks have. They require the driver to manually turn them to engage the front wheels of the car for four-wheel drive. There is a stick shift and another smaller lever that puts the truck in four-wheel drive. I scan the interior, hoping to find some clue as to who the truck's owner might be. The dashboard looks wooden. I pop open the glove compartment and find a pair of work gloves, as well as four rounds of number eight shotgun shells and an old piece of paper. I grab the piece of paper and get out of the truck. Though I unfold it and try to hold it up to the light, it's so dark in the barn that

I can't read anything. I dash outside, hoping to find more light, but unfortunately the sun has dropped below the trees, and the fact that the paper is yellowed from age makes it even more difficult to read.

I return to my task at hand, throwing a bale of hay from the loft down on the floor of the barn, and I scamper down the ladder. I pick up the hay, rush over to the horse paddock, and cut the bale open, spreading it out for the horses to eat. Suddenly, I'm startled by a nudge in the back, and I turn to find Sweetheart standing behind me. I pet her between the eyes before making my way back to the cabin. This whole time, I'm thinking about the mysterious truck and becoming even more suspicious about Jay. He's keeping something from me. I'm sure of it. My mistrust of him continues to snowball until I finally reach the cabin. I'm not sure whether I should confront Jay about what I found or not. I decide I should at least try to read the paper before I say a word.

I see Jay sitting on the porch with the dogs lying around him. He's smoking his pipe and rocking back and forth. The kerosene lantern is lit. "Did you take care of the horses?" he asks.

I nod and walk right past him without saying a word. I close the door behind me, climb up the ladder, and sit on the bed. As I remove the paper from my pocket, my hands shake with anticipation. I'm hoping that it's going to tell me something important, something about how to get home. There's no light in the loft itself, but the light coming through the doorway in the ceiling is good enough, and I move closer to it. Written on the dirty, old paper are the words "Remember where you put the key." I read it over and over to myself. "Remember where you put the key." Who writes a note like this? Why not write down the location of the key itself rather than tell someone to remember where it was put? After some deliberation, I decide to go back downstairs and confront Jay. I fold up the paper and stuff it back in my pocket.

I find Jay on the porch and sit down in the empty chair next to him. The dogs jump up and come over to greet me, and I pet each one, returning the affection. I'm not sure how to begin this conversation with Jay. I'm equal parts upset, angry, and confused. I feel betrayed that he's holding back information from me. There's a long, uncomfortable silence, and I sense that Jay feels it too. Finally, he says, "I rolled up a cigar for you, Rich. It is on the bench over there if you want it."

"No, that's okay," I snap, which leads to yet another period of awkward silence. Finally, I can't take it anymore. I stand up and face him. "Jay, time for some answers here! You need to be truthful with me and tell me all you know about what's going on here. You're always going on about the impeccability of a warrior. Is truth not one of these virtues? What are you not telling me?"

He sits straight up in his chair and stops rocking. In a stern voice, he says, "Are you questioning my impeccability as a warrior? How would you know anything about impeccability or about truth for that matter? You are not, as of yet, even a whole person."

This makes me extremely nervous. Jay is already an imposing figure. The fact that he is staring me directly in the eyes makes him appear infinitely large. "I need to know what we're doing here," I say, my voice uneasy. "I need to know why I'm here."

Jay relaxes back in his chair a little. In a milder tone, he tells me to sit down and that he'll answer any questions I have to the best of his ability. I slump down into the chair and try to formulate questions that will lead to the answers I'm looking for. In my mind, I also prepare some questions that I think will trip him up. Hopefully, I can put some holes in his story. I hear Wise Guy I's voice: "Give 'im hell."

Analytical I speaks up. "There's no data to suggest that he's menacing in any way. I know you can be civil."

"Jay," I begin, "did you know that there's a truck in the barn?"

He chuckles a bit. "I've been in the barn many, many times. Of course I've noticed there's a truck in there."

"Yes, but whose truck is it? Is it your truck?"

"No, that truck has been here since I arrived."

"Well then, whose is it?"

"It belongs to whoever was here before me."

"Who was here before you?

"I have told you before, the man that wrote those notes. The one that said he would return and told me not to drink the water in the kitchen."

"Well," I say, "while I was in the barn, I took a look in the glove compartment and found this note." I take the note out of my pocket and hand it to Jay.

He sits up in his chair and unfolds the paper, holding it in the light of the lantern so he can read it. He reads aloud, "Remember where you put the key."

"What do you think it means?"

Jay smiles. "I don't know. But I think you might ..."

"And how would I know?" I ask angrily. Jay brushes off some dirt from the right corner of the paper and reveals the initials RLC. I look up at him. Suddenly I feel dizzy, as if all the blood has drained from my head; I feel faint. Jay looks at me with a funny expression and asks if I would like a whiskey. "I don't know," I reply. He disappears into the cabin and emerges with a full glass anyway, placing it on the bench next to my cigar. In a shaky voice, I repeat the initials to myself, "RLC."

There is a long, dead silence. I can hear all the I's scrambling inside my brain, trying to make some sense of this. None of them are able to come up with any explanation. I sit there unable to speak and watch Jay as he bangs his pipe on the side of the porch, dislodging the spent tobacco. He takes a pouch from his vest pocket, refills the pipe, and lights it by striking a match on the side of the house. The fire in his pipe reflects in his eyes, which are now gleaming, and he has a funny grin that I can't decipher. Finally, I formulate something to say. "Jay, I can't—and you can't—believe that I left this message in the truck as well as the other two messages you showed me. Just because someone signed them with my same initials? It has to be some sort of coincidence."

"A coincidence," he repeats quietly. "A coincidence is a convenient way out for men that do not understand how the universe works. There are no such things as coincidences. Everything happens for a reason. The trick is to decipher the reasons for these 'coincidences' and become a seer."

"Don't think for a minute you can tell me what I believe and what I don't believe. Jay, I'm telling you, I've never been to this place before, and coincidences happen all the time."

"Let me tell you what I think, or should I say *believe*," Jay begins. "People are so wrapped up in life that they seek to explain everything logically. In fact, there are no logical explanations for existence. Logic is a creation of humanity, a tool the blind use to trick themselves into believing they can see. There are many forces at work in what we call the world. You have the choice to tune into those forces and allow them to speak to you or to ignore them. Messages come to you in little riddles, rhymes, and signs as well as these things you call coincidences. This is all to show you your path—to show you how you should proceed in this life, how to choose the right road when you have proceeded so differently in past lives."

I interrupt him. "But, Jay, I thought I'm supposed to focus on the present moment? Why then am I supposed to learn from my past lives?" Admittedly, I'm being a little obnoxious.

This appears to frustrate him. "You still do not understand, and this is why I have resisted telling you what I am about to tell you. They are not past lives. I merely use those words to help you understand. Think of all those lives as happening simultaneously. When the forces of the universe speak to you and attempt to guide you, they are not coming from the past. They are coming into the present moment from another present. So, the coincidences that you are speaking of are merely the narrow vision of men that know nothing else of the world. Life has lulled them to sleep, just as I have told you." He hands me the whiskey.

"But, Jay …" I protest. He holds up his hand to stop me from speaking. I think he already knows what I'm about to ask.

In a joking voice, he says, "If you were not already sitting down, I would tell you to sit down now because what I'm about to tell you will require much whiskey. Your life is a recurrence, though not in the sense that it happens over and over again through time. As I've just tried to explain, your many lives are simultaneously recurring. Through this simultaneous recurrence, you reach different levels. This is achieved by elevating your conscious level. It is a process of learning, one of evolution. It is a cycle, and we human beings are responsible for the evolution of the universe, the evolution of our consciousness. So think of this, my friend: it is quite possible, perhaps even probable, that you have been here before; those notes are clues to that end." I take a long sip of whiskey.

My gulp is so big that I come up choking. Jay begins to laugh hysterically. He studies me with a comical look on his face and asks me if he should continue. With the whiskey burning down my throat, all I can do is nod. "So, would you like me to tell you the story of your recurrences? It's quite entertaining."

Choking back the whiskey, I grunt, "Yes." He continues to laugh and tells me he doesn't know if I've had enough whiskey yet for the story but that he'll tell me anyway. He clears his throat and begins.

CHAPTER 33

"The first time you arrived in the clearing, you were dressed in tennis clothes, whatever you had on, and you had nothing with you. After a few days of running around like a maniac, you died from starvation."

"What do you mean I died?" I ask.

"No questions now. Hear me out until the end of the story, or I will go inside and get some rest." I apologize immediately and tell him I will refrain from questioning until the end. He starts again, "The next time, you filled up the pack, and you were in the clothes you are wearing now. But you did not know which way to go. You tried to walk out of the clearing, and after several days and nights wandering in the woods, you once again died of starvation. The next time, you arrived with your pack and all the supplies, but after some excursions in the woods, you ran out of water. You drank from the stream without first boiling it. Several days later, you died from the parasites you contracted from the water.

"In the next recurrence, you came with your pack and your supplies. This time you had a cell phone, but it was not charged. And there would have been no one to call anyway. In trying to find a way out, you came upon the cave. You encountered the bear, and you became so frozen with fear that the bear—well, let's just say he did what bears do, and you died.

"After this, you arrived again with all your provisions and the cell phone with no charge. That is when I sent the hawk to you. You managed to make it for several days. You even managed to unstick yourself from that spot in the cave and escape the bear. At this point, I realized that there might be hope for you yet. So I contacted the water spirits and sought their help. Unfortunately, you did not face the bear down in the clearing. Instead, you ran up a tree. This made the bear angry, and he walked away vengefully. So on your way here, when you came across him again, he came out of the cave, smelled you hiding in the field, came down the hill, and stalked you for miles until he overtook you."

Jay stops his tale abruptly and blows smoke rings. I'm on the edge of my seat. I want to start asking questions, but I think better of it and sit in silence, anxiously waiting for him to start back up again. He begins again.

"Now, this next trip of yours is quite interesting. You arrived in the clearing and actually made it to the cabin, and I was not here. You found your way inside, and, thirsty, you drank water from the pump and contracted the same disease caused by parasites.

"Now let's see. I'm kind of losing track ... oh yeah. The next time, you did everything right, but you were killed by the mountain lion the night he was on top of the chicken coop. Even the dogs could not save you. And finally, everything occurred the way it had in the past few attempts, but like today, I sent you into the barn, and you found the truck there. Because you lacked patience and trust in me, you drove the truck out of here, trying to find your way back home. You drove for miles and miles until the truck ran out of gas. Trying to find your way back here to the cabin, you became lost and wandered in the woods for days until you finally died of starvation and exposure."

My mouth is gaping wide, and my eyes are as big as the moon. This is all incomprehensible. And I also realize I have finished my whiskey. Without another word, Jay gets up and takes my glass, goes back inside, and returns with another full one. "Jay, this is a ridiculous story. I'm not dead. I'm right here."

He pokes my stomach with his finger, as if to see if I am a ghost or not, and then laughs. He tells me we've had this conversation before. "Oh yeah, by the way, you wrote that note and put it on the pump so you'd know not to drink it. Which brings us to the note on the door. You wrote that one as well. And you *are* back, *aren't you*?"

I'm extremely dizzy at this point. I start to get tunnel vision, and my palms sweat along with the rest of my body. I'm either going to faint, or explode, or both. I have never heard anything like this before in my life. I just can't comprehend it. I look at Jay. He is sitting on the edge of his seat studying my face before he speaks. "And then, after a few more failed attempts, there is this recurrence. You may now ask questions."

The time has finally arrived, and I have so much to ask him. But the funny thing is I can't remember any of the questions I was formulating during the story. I can't even speak. I take another big gulp of whiskey, as if it's going to help. Finally, the power of speech returns all at once. "Jay, did I ever get past this point in any recurrence?" I ask in a voice that I don't recognize as my own.

He starts to smile. "That's all I can tell you. I can never go past the point of recurrence that you are in. This is because it is you who must do the work. It is you who must learn the lessons. But I will say this: every time you have returned, you've come back a little bit more conscious and a little bit better prepared to take the next step. So, in that regard, I have to say that you are *evolving*."

"Jay," I plead, "tell me what happens next. From what you've told me, my life literally depends on it."

He clears his throat again, as if he is going to say something profound. "It doesn't work that way. I just told you that you have to go on and see for yourself."

"Do I ever get back to my life?" I ask.

In a stern, cold voice, he says, "I will tell you this right now. You cannot leave this place without working on yourself. You are here to wake up from the sleep that life has put you in. You are on a vision quest, as I was, and the purpose of this quest is to wake up. This quest is the quest to become one, the one true I that you are. This can only be accomplished by following the path of the warrior. I'm here to show you that path, and you can either accept it or reject it. Rejecting it, for example, is trying to drive the truck out of here, and I've already told you how that ends up. You must put your trust in me."

CHAPTER 34

The next thing I know, I'm opening my eyes on the big couch in the big room. I figure Jay had to carry me here again, as he did the first night. In my grogginess, I can remember dreaming, or at least I think I was dreaming, that I continually mess up and awaken over and over again in the clearing. I sit up. My head is pounding. No one appears to be in the cabin except for me. Despite an underlying feeling of anxiety, my most immediate concern is the hangover. It's a killer. I try to get up, but I lose my balance and fall back over. I summon all my strength and stagger over to the door. I open it, and a cold breeze punishes my nose and cheeks. When I look outside, I see no one on the porch; there's no sign of Jay or the dogs. I see that all three horses are in the paddock, and the hawk is perched on the barn. I stand there for a while, letting the cold air revive me before shutting the door and making my way over to the sink. I am so thirsty. I grab a glass from the cupboard and start pumping. I fill the glass and lift it to my lips. Suddenly, I hear the door fly open. I turn abruptly and see Jay.

"Drop the cup! Drop the cup!" he yells. The sudden outburst returns me to my senses, and I drop the cup in the sink. I turn and look at Jay with a fearful expression as he stomps into the cabin in my direction. "What is the matter with you!" he exclaims. "Are you in such a big hurry to start your next adventure that you'd drink that water?" I just look at him as my body continues to shake. I grab a chair at the table and sit down. "You almost did it again! I can't let you out of my sight." I pick my head up and look at him. I open my mouth, but the words aren't there. He goes on. "Did you hear anything I said last night? Maybe it hasn't sunk in. Maybe you don't believe that it's got to be up to you. Like I said, I've been sent here to show you the way, so you better wake up quickly, or we'll be going through this over and over and over again. Lord knows how many times we've already done this."

In my present state, I really don't want to talk. I have a bunch of questions, but they will have to wait for later. I can't assemble the words well enough in my mind to pose any of them. Jay begins to chop potatoes. He turns to me and says, "You'll feel a lot better after you eat something."

"Jay, I don't know. My stomach isn't doing too well. Maybe just a drink of water will do."

He chuckles a little bit and says, "Drink the correct water this time." He pours me a glass from the jugs we retrieved from the spring and hands it to me. "Maybe if you move around a little bit, you'll start to feel better. I'm hungry, so I'm having breakfast. Get up there, go on out, and grab some eggs."

"No, Jay," I whine. "Not the chickens, not today."

"You're the official egg getter. It's your job to go out and get those eggs."

"But I told you I don't want any eggs. Do I still have to go out there and face those chickens?"

I am expecting him to be upset at this, but in a soothing voice, he says, "Go on out there and be thankful to those chickens for their eggs. Show them the respect that you have for them and your appreciation for their eggs. Go on. Off you go."

I get up slowly and make my way toward the door. "The next time I pack a bag, I need to put aspirin in it," I mutter loud enough for Jay to hear.

I walk out onto the porch and shut the door. From inside, I hear Jay call out, "And don't just *tell* them you respect them, *mean* it!"

The whole walk down to the chicken coop, I wonder how I am going to feel this respect for the chickens. What difference does it make anyway? I stop at the door of the chicken coop. There aren't any chickens outside in the yard, so I know they're all inside waiting for me. I compose myself and try to muster up any feelings of respect for poultry that I might be harboring. I tell myself that the eggs are provided by these chickens for Jay and me to sustain our life and that I should be grateful for that. When I feel as composed as I can be, I open the door and say in a very soft, almost seductive, voice, "Good morning, ladies."

To my surprise, the hens all remain in their nests. I take a quick look around and can't find the roosters. They're the ones I really need to keep an eye on. The roosters, I reason, couldn't care less if I respect them or not. I'm sure of that. In a respectful yet resolute manner, I walk around, reaching under several of the chickens and pulling out six beautiful brown eggs without so much as a squawk. I thank them kindly, turn around, and close the door behind me. With a sigh of relief, I walk back in triumphant glory to show Jay that he isn't the only one capable of bringing back the eggs.

Jay is standing on the porch. He looks in the basket and sees the eggs. Looking at me proudly, he says, "Genuine feelings are projected with your intent, and animals, as well as people, can pick up on these feelings. But it is only genuine feelings that will get you the eggs in life."

We both eat breakfast in silence. I'm still a little groggy from the whiskey, and I think about the conversation that took place last night. Although I have a lot of questions to ask Jay, I don't feel much like talking. When we finish eating and clean up, Jay goes into his bedroom and produces another hunting coat. He throws it to me and suggests I put it on, as it's getting pretty chilly outside. I like the coat very much. It is a tannish brown, and on the inside, it has what looks like a felt Indian blanket for a lining. It has two big, bellowed pockets on each side, with shell loops in them for shotgun shells. There's a big game pouch on the backside where you can put whatever you shoot during the trip. I have a similar coat that I use for hunting back in my other life.

I slip the coat on, and it fits perfectly. I thank Jay for it and tell him it fits great. "What a coincidence," he says before bursting into laughter. "No wonder it fits so well. It's yours." This makes me smile a bit. The fogginess in my mind begins to dissipate, and I'm beginning to think clearly again. Everything Jay told me last night floods my mind in detail.

We walk out onto the porch. Jay doesn't seem like he wants to talk, but I have a hundred questions to ask him. I think I can coax him into answering a few. "I saw the dogs earlier this morning," Jay says, "but when I let them out, they took off. Must be hunting up there in the woods. They'll be back." Now that I have him talking, I seize the opportunity to interrogate him.

"So back to what you were talking about last night, you know, with all my—what did you call them—recurrences?" He just looks at me sideways. I continue, "This morning, when I filled up the glass of water from the pump, was there a recurrence where I drank it and died … or did you come in and stop me?"

"What do you think?" he asks coyly.

"I don't know. That's why I'm asking."

"Well let's just say that you have made it to this moment, and that's that."

"I can't just leave it at that. I want to know about these recurrences, what they mean and what they are."

He takes the tobacco pouch out of his vest pocket and, holding the pipe in his right hand, fills the bowl. He strikes a match on the side of the house, lighting the pipe. "You know, we have a lot to do today, and I don't think we should just be standing around here playing twenty questions."

"Well," I say, "you might as well because I'm not letting you out of my sight. The way things are going, you're my only hope. I don't want to end up back in the clearing and have to start all this from scratch again."

"Okay, let's go back and chop some wood. Maybe we can make some sense of this."

CHAPTER 35

I break up wood for quite some time as Jay sits on an old stump smoking his pipe. After hours pass, he finally speaks. "Man is a funny animal. He learns through repetition. For instance, when you practice your tennis to become proficient in hitting a forehand, would you say that you have to hit the forehand over and over again thousands of times before you can repeat it effectively? Or let's say in school, when you need to learn a particular lesson, you have to read the lesson over and over again to fully understand it. Only by reading and rereading will you fully grasp the concept. This is, unfortunately, how we learn. So even though this is kind of a basic explanation, consider this: how could you learn life and all the mysteries of the universe if you only pass through here once? Would you not have to learn the lessons of life by experiencing them over and over again, as you have with all your other endeavors? You have to live the same life over and over again until you've got it, until you've found who you truly are. Then, and only then, can you move on to the next life. Failure is the best teacher."

With that, Jay gets up and walks around the front of the house. I immediately drop the ax and follow right on his tail. He glances back over his shoulder and says, "You aren't finished with the wood yet."

"I'm as finished as I'm going to be. I told you I'm not letting you out of my sight. If this recurrence thing is as real as you say it is, you're the only one who can save me from whatever is going to happen next."

Jay starts laughing hysterically. "I told you, I'm not here to save your ass. And what makes you think I even know what's going to happen next?"

"Well, you did burst in and stop me from drinking the water." It is amazing how Jay, in my eyes, has been elevated from slave driver and captor to my guardian.

"Yeah, I did," he says. "Maybe that was just a coincidence."

"Wait, you told me that there aren't any coincidences. You made it clear that things don't just happen."

Jay smiles. "Yes, that's right. You've learned something. You're actually listening." He goes on. "Let me tell you something. Don't be following me around here all day expecting me to save your life. Save yourself … that's up to you. But I will tell you this. All the times that you have been here and failed, you failed because you chose not to follow the path of the warrior. In other words, you didn't care to listen to anything I had to say."

Jay takes a bucket off the porch and heads to the corral. I follow right behind him, almost walking in his exact footsteps. I can feel the anxiety creeping up my back. When we reach the corral, Jay goes inside and takes a stool off of one of the fence posts. He goes over to one of the cows, puts the stool down, and begins to milk the cow. I'm standing right over his shoulder, watching his every move. "Fine. If you insist on following me around like a little puppy, you might as well make yourself useful. Do you know how to milk a cow?" he asks.

"No," I say, "and if I have to take care of the chickens, I think you have to take care of the cows."

"Well, that sounds fair," he says to my surprise. I stand there for a while before he speaks again, introducing me to the cows. "This is Maggie, and her sister over there is Bonnie."

I don't answer; I just stand there like a jerk. "Jay, do you think that if I live the warrior's life, I may have a chance to get out of here and get back to my life?" He doesn't answer; he just keeps on milking Maggie. I continue, "I mean, if I listen to you and learn the ways of the warrior, do I have a shot?"

He stops milking and turns around on the stool, locking those

RLC

steely eyes on me with a fixed gaze. "It is the only shot you have," he says coldly.

"Don't you want to get out of here?" I ask. "Don't you want to get back to your life or tribe or whatever?"

He continues to glare at me. "That is all a matter of perception. See, you think of yourself as stuck here. I, on the other hand, know that I'm here to perform a task. For that reason, I am not looking for a way out."

"How can you say that? Aren't you lonely here all by yourself … I mean, when I'm not here?"

"Oh," he says, matter of factly, "there are some visitors from time to time."

This excites me. It's been days since I've interacted with anyone except Jay. "Visitors? What visitors? You mean there are actually people around here."

"There are, and there aren't," he answers vaguely. "Besides, I'm here to perform a task, and a warrior does not question his task. He just performs it the best he can, and then he lets the spirits take over."

"What's this task?"

"As I told you, I'm here to teach you how to be a warrior, and you are here in search of your real, true self. Together, if you make the commitment, we can go in search of it. Perhaps we may just find a way out of here, and you may then return to your life."

"So, you mean it really is a way out of here?"

"That's up to you," Jay says.

"How could that be up to me? If that's the case, I would have been out of here already."

"If you don't watch your step, you will be out of here very quickly again," he says, laughing.

"I don't know why you think this is so goddamn funny," I say.

Jay finishes milking and puts the stool back on the fence. He heads toward the house with me right behind, trying as hard as I can to keep up with him. He puts the pail inside the house, then walks across the porch toward the chicken coop. I am still right on his heels. Chuckling to himself, he hands me a sack that I guess is full of grain and tells me it's time to feed the chickens. When we arrive at the open gate, I walk inside the fence. All the chickens are milling around outside. He tells me to toss the grain all around and that the chickens will find it. He then sits on a rock.

"Okay, Jay, I've thought about it. I'm willing to become a warrior," I tell him. "Tell me what I have to do."

Jay crosses his legs and lights his pipe again. "I don't know if you're sincere or not," he says in a stern voice.

I'm not sure what to say back to him. I think I sounded sincere enough. "What makes you think that?" I ask.

"We've had this conversation before," he answers.

This makes me wonder. Have I gotten to this same point before, feeding the chickens and pledging my allegiance to Jay's teachings before I'm derailed again and find myself back at the clearing? My mind is having a hard time wrapping itself around this notion of recurrence. "What I have to do is show you that I'm ready," I proclaim.

"You can only show me that through your actions."

"And what actions are those?"

There is a long pause before Jay answers. "The actions of a warrior. I have already talked to you about those actions, and since you are not yet a warrior, your first lesson is to act as if you are a one."

"How can I act like a warrior if I don't know how a warrior acts?"

Immediately, as if he anticipated my question, he goes on, "The first task as a warrior is stalking."

"And what would I be stalking?"

"You'll be stalking yourself. And since you're not an Indian, I will try to be more specific. I'll spell it out in terms you understand. As I told you before, you must observe yourself; you must split yourself into observer and observed. This means that you will need to watch your actions, thoughts, and feelings and resist the urge to judge them. You need only observe them."

"What will I be looking for? I mean, what will this show me?"

"This," Jay continues, "will show you what we spoke of before, that you are a multitude of I's. That you are not one person but many, made up of all those voices in your head. The voices that take charge of you in different situations. The artificial ones that are not your true self. Your job as a warrior is to observe these I's and see how they manipulate you and change you. All of these personalities are false, as we've discussed. You've created them over your life to deal with the many circumstances you have found yourself in. And now you are stuck with them."

I remember the earlier conversation Jay and I had when he surprised me with his knowledge of the I's. He goes on, "Those voices are a multitude. When you are ready, you must ultimately condense them into one voice. Into your one true self." Jay stands up and tells me to stop feeding the chickens. I have been so mindlessly throwing out grain while I'm listening to him that he warns me they will become fat. "Let's go," he says as he turns and walks toward the house. On the way, he says, "You see how this works? You feed the chickens, and the chickens, in turn, feed us."

Back on the porch, BB and Molly are standing around wagging their tails. Bert is nowhere to be found. I ask Jay where he thinks he might have wandered off to. "I don't know," he answers. "I hope he's not on the trail of that mountain lion. He'll come back around." Jay instructs me to put the sack of grain in the house, and when I come out of the door, I see him heading toward the horse paddock. I go running after him, still uneasy about being left alone. He begins to laugh when he spies me jogging across the grass in his direction. "Do you think that you can go over to the barn and bring a bale of hay over here without being so goddamn scared that you shit your pants?" he asks. I don't want to leave his side, but the barn is within his view from the paddock, and he nudges me, telling me, "Go on."

When I return to the paddock, Jay is inside brushing the horses. He tells me to cut the twine and spread the hay around. I'm about to ask him a question, but he abruptly cuts me off, telling me that warriors don't talk the entire day, they focus on the task at hand, and that it is difficult for me to pay attention when I'm constantly flapping my gums. I think he might be testing me to see if I am, indeed, really willing to become a warrior, so I keep my mouth shut. This, of course, doesn't keep the I's silent. Wise Guy I says, "This guy is up to something. I still think he's no good."

Ego I chimes in, "How can he boss you around like this? Doesn't he know who you are?"

Instead of letting them take charge of my mood—and it would be Angry I speaking if I surrender to any of my I's now—I find myself mentally backing off and watching. I watch the ways they try to sway me to act or feel certain ways. I do this for a few minutes and try to do as Jay has told me, to just observe. I spread out the hay for the horses in silence, but finally Ego I gets the best of me, and Angry I follows. I give in and become angry. "How do you expect me to learn to be a warrior if I can't ask questions?" I snap at Jay.

Jay turns around and looks to be a bit annoyed. "You're so in tune to those voices in your head that you can't keep your mouth shut for five minutes!" he says. "Do you not see how you are a slave to all of those false personalities that are going on in your mind?

I don't know what to do. He is right, of course. I decide to apologize. "I'm sorry, Jay."

"Sorry?" he says. "Sorry for what? It means nothing to me that your true self has been abducted by these I's, tied up and locked in the closet of your mind. You let these impostors take charge." With that, he turns and walks out of the paddock. I quickly finish spreading the hay around and run after him. He turns around and barks, "That's enough for today. Stop following me around." He walks into the house and shuts the door behind him, leaving me outside with the dogs.

Jay doesn't reemerge from the house for quite a while. I sit out on the porch petting the dogs, afraid to move. Thoughts of anxiety flash through my mind. I fear that at any minute I will be dead again and whisked back to the clearing, having to start all over again. I refuse to get out the chair, and I'm glad that I at least have the dogs there to keep me company. I'm a little worried about Bert. He still hasn't returned. I've had hunting dogs all my life, and as a general rule, I never let them out of my sight. That being said, Jay didn't seem to worry about Bert when he first disappeared, and I suspect he's done this before and, as Jay said, will be back later, safe and sound.

CHAPTER 36

As I sit there, I begin to think about what Jay said, about all the little personalities—these I's—that I have roaming around in my head. It occurs to me how different I could be when with different friends of mine. I would take on a whole new persona, oftentimes designed to make that person like me. As I sit there, reflecting on how I have conducted myself throughout the life I am trying to return to, I being to think how ridiculous it is that I should have to keep changing myself at the drop of a hat to please the person I'm with. And it doesn't even have to be in the presence of others. Even in different situations when I'm alone, this same phenomenon occurs. Up until this point, I never thought about changing this. But that is exactly what Jay is telling me, that there is one true I, a whole, and that's what I must find. But how can I arrive at this whole, this real me, when I've become so accustomed to living with the I's for so long?

While I'm trying to hash this out in my mind, I can hear all the I's trying desperately to be heard. They all seem to, in their own way, try to convince me that Jay doesn't know what he's talking about and that they are the one true I. This is going to be difficult. But if I ever want to make it home, Jay says this is the only way. I resign myself to put all my trust in him.

As if on cue, the door opens, and Jay steps out onto the porch with a shotgun slung across his arm. Both BB and Molly become energetic. They know we are about to go hunting. I look up at Jay and ask if that's the case. "I'm going to take the dogs, make a swing around, and see if we can locate Bert." I jump up out of my chair and volunteer to help. "Now you just sit back down there. It's not your time yet. Bring some wood up on the porch. It is going to get cold tonight."

As much as I don't want to stay here alone without Jay to keep an eye on me, I begin to think that something must have happened in another recurrence when I went searching for Bert. I yell out to Jay, asking if this is the case, but he just puts up his right arm to wave. I go around to the back of the house and grab some wood. As I carry an armful back to the porch, I start to wonder what would happen if I left with Jay to find that dog. Of course, this could all be in my head. I rationalize that he just wants some time away from me. He's probably getting tired of my following him around like I'm his little brother. I sit back down in the chair on the porch.

I must have fallen asleep. When I wake up, it is beginning to get dark. Jay is standing on the porch with BB and Molly. There is no sign of Bert. "I have no idea where he got off to this time. Not even the dogs could find him," he says before walking into the house and putting his shotgun back on the rack. I follow him in.

"Has he ever done this before?" I ask.

"Oh yeah," Jay says, "he's been out for days before. I just hope he's not tangling with that mountain lion. That's one tough cat, and Bert's just stubborn enough to make a stand." Jay begins to hurriedly make dinner and tells me to throw a ton of wood on the fire and get it going good. "It's going to be cold tonight," he reminds me.

I decide it's best to keep quiet. I can tell that Jay is concerned about Bert, and I really don't want to bother him with any of my questions. We sit down for another scrumptious meal of—you guessed it—beans.

"Jay, should we go back out in the morning and have a look for Bert?" I say.

"He'll be back," Jay says confidently. "He'll be back." We finish eating and clean up. Jay walks over to the couch in front of the roaring fire and stuffs his pipe full of tobacco. He asks if I would like a cigar, and I tell him I would. He returns to the table and rolls me a beauty in short order. We sit side by side on the couch, smoking away.

After a long silence, Jay says, "Only smoke in the house when the fire is going real good. It pulls the smoke up through the chimney." There is another uncomfortable pause as Jay continues to stare at me. It's as if he knows that I have about fifty questions for him that I've been bottling up. Finally, he says, "Okay. Fire away."

"What?"

"Ask away."

I'm a little surprised. I've been trying my best this whole time to act casually. But I see the opening and I take advantage. "Why did you not want me to go today? Did something happen in my last recurrence here?"

He looks at me, and I can tell that he's annoyed. "You can't keep asking me about everything that happens. That is for you to find out. Also, stop following me around like a little kid. Just go about your business."

"What business is that?"

"The business of becoming a warrior," he answers quickly and in a sharp tone.

"Oh, yeah, well I've been thinking about that ..."

"And what conclusions have you come to?"

"I've come to the conclusion that I'm going to put my trust in you and take your advice. I need to become a warrior. As a matter of fact, I've been trying to pay attention to all the voices that have been going on in my head, and I've noticed quite a lot of them. So, I've been stalking. What do I do about it?"

Jay blows a few smoke rings that float toward the fireplace. "The only way to free yourself from the overpowering suggestions of the I's is not to give them any force. You can only give them force by paying attention to them. If you do not go with them, they will become less and less significant; ultimately, they will surrender."

"What happens when they give up?"

"When this happens, you have cleared the path for the emergence of the one true I to take over. The real you. Then you will become a warrior, and you will be in command of yourself."

I'm quiet for a moment while I think about this. "This is not going to be an easy task," I say. "I've been listening to them my whole life. But I'll try to do what you're saying."

He chuckles a little bit. "Sounds like real resolve," he says sarcastically.

"How long is this going to take?"

"Don't be disheartened by this truth," Jay says, "but this is a process that will go on for the rest of your life. You always have to be on guard and aware. These I's can reemerge at any time in life. Thus, a warrior is always aware. A warrior is always stalking himself."

"How will I know the voice of the one true I?" I ask. It seems like a great question.

"You'll know by the quietness of your mind, and you will recognize the one resounding voice. It's a voice that you have heard before. That voice will become the prominent one, and it will not change in pitch or timbre, no matter what people you find yourself around and what situation you find yourself in."

I'm hanging on his every word. Somehow, I know that the warrior's path is the way out of here. And I realize that this one true voice has spoken to me before. "Jay, I think I've heard this voice before."

"Yes," he says as he stands up and tosses another log on the fire. He sits back down and stretches himself out. Turning to me, he says, "Tell me what happened when you were in the cave with the bear."

"How do you know about that?" I ask suspiciously.

"That is not your concern. Just tell me what happened in the cave when you were confronted by the bear."

I start to think back. It's a little blurry, but I definitely remember being stuck to the ground when I heard a voice from within myself. It was a familiar voice, though one I couldn't place. "When I saw the bear come around the corner in the cave, I became frozen with fear to the spot I was standing in. I heard a voice come from deep down inside, and it told me to run. Everything became crystal clear at that point, and, let me tell you something, I ran out of there like hell."

Jay starts to smile and says, "I guess you have heard that voice before, haven't you. This is good. If you hadn't, you wouldn't be sitting here today. You would never have come this far. You see, a warrior's voice has been inside you! You have already encountered the one true I!"

"If that's the case, how come I don't hear this voice all the time? If that's the one true voice, how come I don't live by it?"

There is a long pause again, as if he is calculating his words. After having spent some time with him, I realize that this is a strategic rhetorical move on his part to make me pay extra-special attention to the next thing he says.

Finally, he says, "You can't hear that I because your head is full of shit. The shit in there is all those false I's that you made up when you created the imposter that you are now! You're nothing but a con artist and a liar. You will never become a warrior, and we are stuck here, doomed for eternity!"

This pisses me off, to be completely honest. I hear Wise Guy I say, "What's this impostor business? Where is he getting this from? The only shit around here is the shit he's full of." I am about to speak when I realize that I'm listening to Wise Guy I again, and this is exactly what I'm not supposed to do. I almost fell into Jay's trap. I sit back on the couch and smoke my cigar for a bit, waiting for my anger to dissipate before speaking again.

Jay watches me like a hawk. His attention never leaves me the entire time. It's as if he's observing my aggravation melt away. I'm refusing to give in to Wise Guy no matter what, and if I can hold him and Angry I off, I know I'll pass Jay's little test. I smile, and Jay, seeing this, falls into hilarious laughter. I wait for him to calm down before I speak. "I heard those voices again, Jay, and I swear you almost had me. I must say my entire mood changed, and I was very angry about what you said, calling me an impostor and all. But I didn't go with the I's. I just sat back and refused to give them any force. I didn't feed them, as you suggested. I let it go. Sure, it did take a little bit of effort and a little time, but I did let it go."

He slaps me on the knee and says, "That's the first time I've seen you act like a warrior." He bangs his pipe on the side of the fireplace and walks toward the bedroom. Just before he disappears through the doorway, he adds, "I like it! There is hope for you yet! Good night."

CHAPTER 37

The morning is bright, and still a slight chill hangs in the air as I walk down to the chicken coop. Getting eggs is as easy as it was yesterday, and I'm starting to think the old girls in there like me after all. I get back to the cabin and start to fix breakfast. I haven't seen Jay yet, and the dogs are also noticeably absent. As if on cue, the door swings open, and both Molly and BB run in, just in front of Jay, who is yelling at them to go back outside. They are all muddy again.

"Good morning," I say, and Jay nods, placing his shotgun back on the rack. "Breakfast is ready." He takes off his hat and coat, sits down, and thanks me for making breakfast.

"Still no sign of Bert," he says a little glumly, "but he'll be back. I'm telling you." We sit down and eat in silence. If Jay is any more concerned about his missing dog, he is not letting on.

When we have finished eating and are all cleaned up, I tell Jay that I spent most of the night practicing my self-observation—stalking, as he calls it—and that every time I found myself listening to one of the I's, I would ignore it. I can tell that he's listening to me, though he isn't really responding. He puts his coat on and brushes his hair back, pushing the eagle feathers back to one side before he puts on his hat. He tells me that we have a lot of chores to do today. He reminds me, though, that my main chore is to work on my stalking. "Seeing as how you're working on being a warrior, this will be your main job," he says. He tells me to follow him and to grab my hat. As we are going out the door, he asks me to tell him the story of how I came into possession of my eagle feather.

I relay the story about how I reached the cave where I confronted the bear and how before I went into the cave, a bald eagle landed on the rocks. The eagle took off flying in circles over me, and at one point, the feather fell to the ground. I picked it up and put it in my hat for luck. On our way to the barn, he stops and asks, "What did you make of the fact that the eagle was there at that particular moment and that it dropped the feather to you?"

"I haven't really thought about it until now."

"Have you ever seen an eagle feather just lying on the ground before?"

"No, as I matter of fact."

He continues to walk toward the barn, and I follow closely. He suddenly stops again. "An eagle holds great power. The eagle that you saw that day was your higher self, and he was there because you were about to face your greatest fear, the bear. By dropping the feather, the eagle gave you power. I dare say that in no other recurrence have you arrived here with an eagle feather."

I stand there for a minute, looking into his eyes, which have taken on a shiny gleam. I don't know what to make of his statement, so I ask, "What was the power that the eagle gave me?"

"He gave you personal power."

"What sort of personal power?"

"Personal power," he goes on, "is not what most people think it is. It has nothing to do with physical attributes. Personal power is understanding."

"Understanding of what?"

He stops just in front of the barn, and again there is a pause. "Personal power is a warrior's understanding of the universe and of this world, his perception of it. The world is a mysterious place, and the perception of humankind is often false. A warrior understands that he or she has to look beneath the surface of all to understand. And, most importantly, a warrior grasps how this understanding fits into this perception."

"What do you mean 'perception of the world'?"

"The world is not what it seems to be. It cannot be grasped by the senses alone. Understanding means an acceptance, particularly the acceptance that there is no explanation, but rather everything is made up only of our own perception. A warrior discovers this on his path, and in knowing this, he realizes his place in the world and in the universe."

I stand there looking at him and waiting for more. He is straining, carefully searching for the right words. "A warrior knows he doesn't know. He acts in the moment. He is always present in the moment, and he acts with impeccability and indifference, and in this way, he receives understanding or personal power." Without saying any more on the subject, he opens the door to the barn and says, "Let's get that hay down for the horses. Get up there and throw a bale down to me."

As I'm spreading the hay across the paddock, Jay asks if I received any personal power from the eagle because, after all, I did have the feather. He asks me if I stopped to think why I received a feather in the first place and if I learned the lesson that the feather represented. Because if I haven't, he tells me, I am no better off with it than without it. As I spread the rest of the hay out, I try to think. But ultimately, I know I will have to ask Jay. Finally, I blurt out, "What was the lesson?"

"Do I have to figure everything out for you?" he says in a sharp tone. He stops brushing the horses and goes on, "You need to take the initiative." He walks out of the paddock, telling me to finish feeding the horses, and heads straight toward the cabin.

I think about all the events that happened on the day the eagle came to me, and although they are clear in my mind, nothing really jumps out as far as a life lesson goes. When I finish and get back to the house, Jay is nowhere in sight. I decide to go around the back and chop some wood for the fire. All the while, I go over the events that took place in the cave and try to figure out the lesson that I supposedly received. I guess along the way, I think I am trying to acquire some personal power. I finish with the wood and put it on the porch. With nothing else on my mind that needs to be accomplished, I resign myself to sit in the chair on the porch and wait for Jay.

After a short while, Jay comes around the corner and yells over to me, "The lesson was to run!" He looks at me a little sideways and says, "Well, that's a little piece of it anyway."

"Jay, please help me out here. God knows I need some personal power. If I don't acquire any, I'm never going to get out of here. I need all the power I can get."

He starts to chuckle and sits down to begin his explanation. "On the day in question, you were looking for your way out of this predicament, and you found yourself not knowing that there was much more to it than just walking out of the woods. Remember now that you reached the cave, and without hearing the voice of your one true I, the bear would have killed you in the cave and sent you back to the clearing to start over again. This time, the level of your consciousness was high, and the eagle came to you. You received a feather, and now you are supposed to reflect on the lesson that you are to learn."

"But I can't think of anything."

He puts his hand up to stop me from saying anything further. "When you went into the cave, despite your fear, and found the bear, you heard the voice of what we determined was your true self. It told you to run, and this time you listened. For a fleeting moment, you were one rather than a multitude of I's. The duress of the situation showed you that it is possible for you to find your one true self. So the lesson you should have learned is that it is possible, and that this should be your goal. Now you are working in that direction on your way to being a warrior. You received your first eagle feather to remind you to stalk yourself continually and find the one true I."

Jay goes into the cabin and comes back outside with a big towel and throws it to me. "Do you know what that is for?"

I think for a moment before answering, "You want me to use it as a blindfold so I can eliminate my sense of sight and perceive the world in a different way, thus gaining some personal power?"

"No. Go down to the lake and wash up. You've acquired quite a smell over the last few days."

I haven't noticed any foul odor coming off me. But then again, I haven't bathed since I left the clearing. I look back at him, lift my arm, and take a whiff. He's right. I start to make my way toward the lake when I hear him say, "Make sure you use this." I turn just in time to catch the bar of soap he tosses in my direction. "You stink." I'm well on my way to the lake when I hear him call after me, "Keep an eye out for snakes." He laughs loudly.

CHAPTER 38

The thought of snakes sticks in my mind the entire walk down to the lake. The I's have me possessed. They conjure up all kinds of images: snakes slithering across the grass and swimming in the water. I think this might be a new kind of I altogether, one that uses imagery instead of words to control me. All I can do is keep my eye on this particular I and all his treachery, as Jay has instructed me.

I come out of the woods to the lake where we used the canoes to cross the water. I scan the ground for any signs of snakes and, after a thorough investigation, conclude that the coast is clear. I take my clothes off and walk over the rocky shoal before wading into the water. The thought of snakes hasn't completely left me, and I keep looking through the crystal-clear water. It's a little cold—I rationalize too cold for snakes. Just in case, I decide to make this a short bath and lather up frantically.

My fear has all but subsided when I look back toward the bank and think I see something moving. I become very still and fix my gaze. I see even more movement. I take a step toward the shore, stop, and look again. The whole rocky shoreline around my clothes seems to have come alive. I gasp and look around me in the water where I spy a snake swimming about fifteen yards out in front of me. When I look back toward the shoreline, I realize it's crawling with snakes.

I enter full-blown panic mode. These are not tiny baby snakes, mind you, but monsters. Most look to be between five and six feet long.

All the I's in my mind begin to scream frantically, as if they all want out of there. I remember what Jay said and try not to listen to them. I quickly move back to the bank and onto the rocky beach. I'm now about twenty yards from my clothes, and I decide to retaliate. I grab a few small rocks and toss them toward my clothes, hoping to scare the snakes off and clear a path. This tactic backfires; in fact, it seems to agitate the snakes, and they begin to move faster. I look on the ground, find a long stick, and, brandishing it as a club, make my way along the dirt toward the rocky beach and my clothing. The stick is roughly seven feet long, and I use it to push the snakes away. This doesn't seem to work well; every time I push one away, two more get closer.

I'm considering giving up and running back to the cabin naked, but I don't want to face Jay like this. I know that seeing me in such a state will crack him up and lead him to say something like, "A warrior would never abandon his clothing." He'd be right of course. To make matters worse, my knowledge of snakes is somewhat limited, and I have no idea if these are poisonous or not. I guess that doesn't matter; I'm petrified of snakes regardless. When I reach my clothes, the snakes have them surrounded. I decide my best course of action is to try to pick up my clothes with the stick. This method works well. I manage to retrieve my shirt, sweater, pants, and even my socks, though I'm struggling to get my boots. After some time, I am able to loop the stick through the top of one of the boots, pick it up in the air, and fling it back behind me. As I try for the second boot, however, a large snake heads straight for me. I back up quickly, and it's then that I see the hawk—who I haven't seen through this whole ordeal—swoop out of the sky, snatch the snake off the ground, and fly off over the lake, dropping it somewhere in the middle.

I'm a bit stunned by this, and apparently the snakes are too. They begin to scramble in every direction, and I take advantage of the opportunity to grab my other boot. I dress faster than I ever have before, and once I have both boots on—I don't bother to tie them—I take off toward the cabin. The whole time I'm running, I'm half-scared and half-furious. I'm not sure why I'm so angry. Could it be that Jay sent me down to the lake knowing full well it would be teeming with snakes? It's kind of funny. I hadn't even thought of snakes until Jay put the notion in my head. When I'm two-thirds of the way back, I start to observe that I'm giving in to Angry I. I'm letting him take charge again. I stop abruptly and turn my attention to this. I realize that the I's are not just voices; they can be images and even emotions. I start to walk calmly toward the cabin and reflect on what I have learned by the whole ordeal.

When I get back, I am stunned to find a beautiful woman sitting on a white horse. Jay is on his horse next to her. The look of astonishment on my face is enough to drive Jay and the woman into fits of laughter. When they both calm down, Jay says, "Introductions are in order. This is Emma, and this, young lady, as you know, is Rich."

"How are you, Rich?" she says.

"I'm okay, I suppose," I say, "as okay as can be for somebody that was just chased off the lake by more snakes than I've ever seen in my life." They both begin to laugh again. I'm feeling a little embarrassed as well as ridiculous. I'm not sure what to say, so I default to, "It's nice to meet you, Emma. How are you doing?"

"Fine," she says, "but then again, I haven't had any run-ins with snakes today." This brings on another round of laughter.

When they both settle down, I ask Emma, "Are you from around here?"

"Well, you could say that," she replies and looks at Jay. "He doesn't remember?"

"No, we haven't gotten that far yet. He is still working on trying to stay in the moment."

"But he has a feather." I notice that Emma has an accent.

"I can see that," Jay acknowledges, "but he doesn't seem to know what it means. Why don't you stay here and get acquainted? Maybe he'll remember something. It is not unheard of, though it is unlikely. Plus, he doesn't seem that bright." Jay and his horse turn to me, and he says, "Listen to Emma. She has a lot to tell you. I'm going to ride around a little bit and see if I can pick up any signs of Bert." With that, Jay rides off, leaving the two of us at the house.

Emma gets down off her horse and ties the reins to one of the poles on the porch. As she gets closer, I get a good look at her. She has long, black, curly hair and beautiful deep-set eyes. She walks straight up with her shoulders held back, exuding confidence. Her lips are red and full, and her body moves athletically. If I had to guess, I'd say she looks to be around thirty years old, but sometimes with women, it can be hard to tell. She's quite striking. And I have to say she looks familiar to me, although I'm sure I've never seen her before. There's something about her and Jay; I feel as though I know both of them, although I know that I do not.

A strange thing happens. I have dated lots of women in my time and think of myself as quite charming. I hear the voice of Ego I telling me that I certainly could charm this woman. I then hear Romantic I telling me how beautiful this woman is and how wonderful it would be to know her. I stand there for a moment looking into her eyes. They are the kind of eyes that you could get lost in and not want to find your way back from. I watch myself become another person, different from who I have been since I found myself in this place. "Can I get you something to drink?"

"No, thank you," she says.

"Would you like to sit down?"

She says she would and walks along the porch, sitting down in the rocking chair usually reserved for Jay. I find my seat, and Charming I slips into action. I ask her if she would like to stay for dinner and tell her how nice she looks. She chuckles a bit and thanks me for the invitation and the compliment. "Are you from around here?" I ask.

"You asked me that already," she says and laughs softly. "I guess you could say I am and I am not."

"I noticed your accent is all," I say. "I can't quite place where it's from."

"Why? Don't you like my accent?"

"Yes, I do. It's actually very sexy."

"I knew that you would like this accent. Isn't it one of your favorites?"

I begin to think and decide that, yes, I would have to submit this to the list of my favorite accents. I love women with accents in general. This one almost sounds Russian. I ask her what she means by "one of my favorites," but she laughs and refuses to answer. There is a long pause in which she looks me straight in the eye. Finally, she asks, "Don't you remember me?"

"No," I say. I wish I did.

"Maybe that's why Eagle Feather asked me to stop by today, to see if you would remember."

"Who?"

"Eagle Feather," she repeats and then realizing, starts to chuckle. "You know, Jay."

"Oh yeah, Eagle Feather—Jay's Indian name. Is that what you call him?"

"Yes," she says in a serious tone. "What do you call him?"

"Jay."

There is another moment of silence, and she says simply, "I guess you haven't gotten to the point where he allows you to call him Eagle Feather."

"And he allows you?"

"Yes," she says a little sarcastically, "obviously."

With all this going on, I realize I have not been paying attention to Charming I at all. The topics are getting a little too close to home, and I need to find out what she knows about this place. Then she begins to speak again. "You and I have sat here before and had this same conversation, you know. Even though you don't remember it."

I begin to think. She must be talking about another recurrence, if indeed there are such things. "Is that why you asked Jay if I remembered?" I wonder.

"Exactly," she says, "and Jay also said you are slow-witted." And she starts to laugh again.

"So, you're saying that I have met you before, and we've sat on this porch and had this same conversation?"

"Yes, not word for word, of course, but basically the same thing."

"What are you doing here? How come you are in this place, and do you have any idea why I'm here? And what is it that Jay said you had to tell me?"

Her mood changes from light and pleasant to gravely serious. "We're both here to become warriors, as Eagle Feather has been telling you."

"Yeah," I say, "that's all he's been telling me since I got here. As a matter of fact, I think I've heard way too much about warriors. Are you a warrior?"

"Yes," she says.

"I didn't know that women could be warriors. I thought it was only men."

"Oh no. Women have been warriors since the dawn of time. They, like men, are on the path to find themselves. To find the true self, the one true I."

She is beginning to sound like Jay. "How long have you been here?" I ask her.

"Long enough to call Jay Eagle Feather," she says, and with that, her mood lightens, and she begins to laugh again.

I can feel myself start to become angry. She doesn't seem to be too forthcoming with any information. But at least she's much easier on the eyes than Jay. As if she senses how I'm feeling, she looks me in the eye and asks why I'm getting angry. I tell her I don't really like to be laughed at and that's all that she and Jay seem to be doing. Her facial expression changes, becoming stern. "There really isn't any reason to be angry. You take everything much too seriously," she says. "Jay and I can't understand why you can't enjoy this experience."

"Quite frankly, this experience is driving me crazy."

"Maybe you're viewing this the wrong way," she says sharply.

"Well, Emma, how are you viewing this?"

"I'm viewing this as a vision quest," she says, "as my opportunity to wake up. All my life, I've always thought there was something missing. I never really had control over my mind or my emotions, and I had sought an opportunity to wake up and to put the sleep of life behind me, to become more conscious and aware of myself in the search for the real reality that we live in. I wanted to break free from the perceptions I had been taught by everyone my whole life. It turns out that the way we are taught to view the world is a total fallacy. There's so much more to the world and to life. The world is a mysterious place, but through the perceptions that we have been taught, we lose the mystery. We take everything at face value when in fact nothing is what it seems."

"So, Emma, what you're telling me is that my perception of the world is incorrect and that it's been taught to me all my life since my birth."

There is a profound silence for a while before Emma starts back in. "That's right. You see, this is your opportunity to change that perception. You have arrived in this place to do just that. Eagle Feather is here to help you, to show you the way. The first step in this new perception is to find out who you really are. This is why Eagle Feather has you working on observing yourself, or stalking yourself as the Indians call it. Only through this stalking can you see yourself as you really are today and then make the adjustments you need to make to become the person that you can be, the person you must be. This change can only happen through observation. You must see how you act and why you act the way you do in certain situations."

"Have you been involved in this stalking yourself … um … yourself?" I ask.

"Yes," Emma replies, "very much so, and I found out a tremendous amount. When I arrived here, I was quite different. But through this practice, I've learned how to drop away the false personalities that are not me. Most of the useless parts have melted away, leaving me much closer to becoming a whole person. Eagle Feather told you that I had something to tell you, so if you can hold on to your questions until I finish and pay attention, you'll see that this is your next step."

She is so convincing and so confident that she has me hanging on her every word. I tell her that I've been observing myself for the past few days and have begun to notice a number of things about myself that I never knew before. I urge her to explain the next step to me. After a silence that feels like an eternity, she begins, "Your next task as a warrior is to remember yourself." I start to ask her what she means, but her stern look reminds me that this is not the time for questions. She goes on, "Remembering yourself means putting yourself in the moment. Remembering that you're there. So often, we forget ourselves, and we view the events that are taking place around us as if we are watching a movie or watching a play. All the action is taking place externally with all the players involved in the scene, and we don't feel that we are involved in any of the action. We are reduced to members of the audience. By remembering yourself, you put yourself in the scene; you become one of the players in the production. You remind yourself that you are there as well. You become part of the moment, and the moment is the only thing we have that is real. As far as the future goes, we have yet to arrive, and thinking of it takes us away from the present moment. The future will ultimately be transformed into the present moment, and we need not speculate on it. So, remembering yourself brings you heightened awareness. Your conscious level soars."

"This is kind of difficult, Emma. I'm having a hard time understanding what you mean."

"I know this is difficult to perceive, but if you ponder this scenario, you will find by observing yourself that you view the world as if you are a movie camera, only capturing pictures of all that is occurring and never really putting yourself in the scene. This is very important for you. If you can master the art of remembering yourself, you may start to remember what happened in your last recurrence. A warrior remembers himself and acts accordingly, and because he takes remembering very seriously, he catches glimpses of his past recurrences, and in so doing, he can change the outcome of events. So, remembering what happens in other recurrences is the way back to your so-called life. This is what I've been sent here by Eagle Feather to tell you. I think he sent for me to try to jog your memory. You and I spent a lot of time together, and we spoke many times and know each other very well."

"Emma, have you told me this before in another recurrence? I mean, have we had this conversation before?"

"Yes, I have told you this many times. I cannot remember how many." The look in her blue eyes is genuine, and in that moment, I believe her, though, I confess, I have been taking this business about recurrence a little bit halfheartedly. Besides, I like the idea that we know each other very well, and I wonder what that exactly means. I am hoping there is far more to our relationship, but then again, that could be Ego I talking.

She starts to laugh, as if she knows what I'm thinking, and I laugh a little myself. "So, what is this all about our relationship?" I ask.

"If you really want to know, I suggest you start remembering yourself, and maybe all that occurred between us will come back to you." She gets up.

"Don't go," I plead with her, but it's no use. Before I know it, she's back on her white horse. "I thought you were going to stay for dinner?"

She smiles. "I've had my share of beans. I'm not particularly fond of them."

"Well perhaps another time," I say.

"Perhaps."

And with that, she turns her horse and heads down the trail in the direction of the lake. I hear another horse coming from the direction of the barn and glance back to see Jay riding in. When I look back toward the trail, Emma is gone. As I pan my vision around the area, looking for her, I see the white horse back in the paddock. It's as if she disappeared. I look back to Jay and notice he has something draped over the back of the horse. It looks like Bert!

I yell over to Jay, "You found him!" He has Bert draped sideways over his saddle in the front. Bert has his head up, so I know he's still alive, but as they get closer, I can see that he doesn't appear to be in great shape.

"Help me get him down," Jay shouts as he throws his leg over and steps on the ground. I run over and hold Bert's head as Jay slides him off the horse and into my arms. "Take him in the house and put him on the couch."

I move as fast as I can, kicking the door open and placing Bert on the sofa gingerly. He's a little scraped up. One of his big, long ears is bleeding. I go grab some water and a towel. Jay comes into the room and walks over to the couch, sitting down and beginning to pet Bert. I come back with the water and towel and try to clean up his ear. "He'll be all right. He's really not that bad, just exhausted. Let him rest for a while, and then we'll give him some food," Jay says.

Bert looks up at me. "He was out there for a long time," I say. "Where did you find him, Jay?"

"He was down in one of the creek gullies, just lying there. I didn't see him at first. The horse almost stepped on him."

"What do you think happened to him?" I ask.

"I don't have to *think*. I know what he's been up to. He's been out there chasing that cougar all over the place. Looks to me like he had a little tussle with him too. Now he's all tuckered out. Let him rest a little bit and put some water in his bowl in case he wants a drink. He'll be okay."

I'm happy to see him. I've never had a dog go missing for days like that, and I've been pretty worried. As I pet Bert, he just looks up at me with large, melancholy eyes. "You're home now, boy," I say. "You're going to be okay." Just then, the other two dogs, BB and

Molly come running through the door. They are obviously happy to see Bert and start jumping all over. He is too weak to jump up but manages a couple faint wags of his tail. Jay stands up and tells me to leave Bert alone and let him get some rest. He ushers the other dogs out the front door, and I follow him out onto the porch.

"You sure he'll be all right?" I ask.

"He'll be fine. He just chased that lion so much all day and night that he ran out of energy and became exhausted. Just thank god that cougar didn't get a hold of him. This is nothing new; it's been going on for a while now."

"Maybe we should go out there and kill that mountain lion before he kills Bert first," I say.

Jay steps back and looks at me through his piercing eyes. He's obviously a little taken aback and annoyed by my suggestion. I can't pull my eyes away from his gaze. "Why would we kill such a beautiful animal?" he says.

"He's going to kill Bert eventually."

"The only things that are going to kill Bert are his own choices," he says gruffly. "He has a choice to chase after that lion or leave him be. That's purely up to him."

"Isn't he a coonhound? Isn't that what coonhounds do? Chase wild animals?" Our eyes are still locked.

Jay finally breaks his stare. "Only if they want to get killed."

I look at him quizzically. "What are we going to do about this?"

Jay sits down in his chair, and I grab a seat on the porch with my back against the wall. I watch as he shoves tobacco in his pipe and lights it.

"The cougar is like life. It's out there moving as nature intends. And ol' Bert here, his job is to chase life down. Or, if possible, to get that cougar up a tree so we can come along and kill him. If he accomplishes this, Bert feels as though he has succeeded, that he has accomplished what he's supposed to accomplish and bested nature in the process. And I'm here to tell you that none of us—not Bert, you, or me—can beat nature. Life is merely a game that we play. In the end, there are no winners. No matter how much wealth you may acquire, how successful you may be, how much love you may have for your fellow man, or how much love your fellow man may have for you, life always wins."

"So what good is life?"

"Well," Jay continues, "if we keep chasing after life like Bert and the cougar, not much good will come, and sooner or later, the cougar will win. But we can use life as a teacher. If we are able to see in every event the lessons that we have to learn, life becomes the teacher. Like Bert, we have a choice. We can go out and chase life. We can try to dominate it, to control it. Or we can let life come to us. We, as warriors, can observe the messages she sends and act appropriately. But that being said, it is important to note that life is not pedagogical: she never forces.

"So don't ask me to go out there and kill such a magnificent specimen. He serves a wonderful purpose. I'd suggest the time would be better spent convincing Bert not to chase him, but Bert is stubborn. He is not unlike you."

I sit with my back against the wall, digesting what Jay just said. It's obvious that his analysis of Bert's struggle is meant for me to apply to myself. He looks at me and says, "Life is merely a game. There are no winners; no one gets out of here alive."

I sit for a minute in silence, pondering Jay's dissertation on life. "Life's all a game?"

"Yes, the greatest game there is. And the only way to play the game is to learn—learn so next time around there are no mistakes."

We sit there in silence, and after a long pause, I speak up. "Jay, I'm a little befuddled. About Emma ..."

"Oh?"

"Where exactly did she come from? And where the hell did she go? She just disappeared."

Jay doesn't answer right away. He searches for the right words and then replies, "To tell you the truth, she just kind of pops in and out."

"What do you mean?"

"Let me see if I can make some sense of this for you. It might open your eyes so you can see." He sits back in his chair, puffing away at his pipe. "She's like the snakes you saw down by the lake."

My eyes widen as I try to process how, exactly, the lovely Emma could be compared to the horrifying snakes that accosted me at the lake. "When you were on your way down there," Jay goes on, "I'll wager that your mind was only focused on the task at hand:

bathing. So when I gave you a suggestion, the suggestion of snakes, this planted the seed, as it were, in your mind, and it rattled around a bit. When you arrived at the lake, you looked around thoroughly for snakes, and, not seeing any, you took off your clothes and got into the water. But your fear of snakes and the fact that you were out of your element and in the water made you leery. So when you turned around and looked back at the shore, you saw nothing but snakes. And then you saw snakes in the water, which, if I'm not mistaken, is your biggest fear when you're out in the water fishing."

I'm not sure how he keeps doing this. I'm deathly afraid of snakes, particularly snakes in the water, and when I'm out fly-fishing, I'm always vigilant. One time, I was fishing at one of my favorite spots, a spot where I always pull in a bunch of big trout. As I walked down the embankment, I was looking left and right for snakes. It was a warm day in May, and I knew that the water temperature had risen considerably, and this would increase my chances of encountering a snake. When I got to the water's edge, I looked down and took a few steps into the water. As I lifted my leg to take a final step, there, under my boot, I spotted a snake swimming along. I jumped back and turned to my left, only to spot another snake, this one swimming right at me. Looking upstream, I saw yet another and decided that three's a crowd, particularly when it comes to snakes (although truthfully, one was enough). I hightailed it out of there, not even bothering to remove my waders. As bountiful as the trout were at that spot and as close as it was to my house, I refused to go back until the following season. Jay seemed to know this story. How else would he have known to mention snakes?

As I emerge from my thoughts, I see Jay looking at me, grinning ear to ear. He has a twinkle in his eye and continues, "Now *you* tell *me*. Where do you think those snakes came from? Five minutes before you got in the water, everything was fine. Then suddenly they appeared." A ridiculous, incredulous look must have come over my face. I have no idea how the snakes got there. "Perhaps they were the world's fastest snakes, smelling your fear with their sensitive tongues?" He proposes this mockingly and busts out in a fit of laughter. I ask him where *he* thinks they came from. "They came from the same place Emma did," he answers. He gets up and goes inside the cabin, chuckling. He says he's going to check on Bert, but really I know he is leaving me alone so I can think about what he's said. I do just that: sit there and try to make heads or tails of all this.

Jay is inside for quite a while. When he steps back out onto the porch, I blurt out my answer. "My mind," I say. "The snakes came from my mind."

Jay freezes in his tracks and looks over at me. He says, in what I take to be a slightly condescending tone, "Learned something today, did we?"

"Well, it's the only logical answer I can come up with."

"That's some pretty good detective work," he says.

"Those snakes seemed awful real to me," I say.

"Yeah, and I suppose the bear seemed awful real to you too? And Emma?"

How could everything in my mind be manifesting itself? It's exactly what happens in a dream. Jay sits back down in his chair and starts rocking away. "Ninety percent of what happens to us happens in our minds, and only 10 percent happens outside of ourselves, in reality. A warrior knows this, and he knows how to use it to his benefit." I ask him how a warrior could use this knowledge to benefit himself—or herself, I add, given my conversation with Emma. "Well, here's the point," he says, "and what's really going to bake your noodle: if I hadn't put the thought of snakes in your head, they wouldn't have been there at all."

"I don't know about that," I say. "How can we possibly know that for sure?"

"Well," Jay says, "we can never know for sure. But I'll tell you one thing: a warrior would not allow himself to think negatively in any given situation. Don't you see how much you are a victim of your own mind? Don't you see that by not having control over yourself and your thoughts, you put yourself in great danger?"

"So how must I think, Jay?"

"A warrior thinks positively and acts decisively because a warrior is always in the moment. He doesn't allow his mind to be dominated by what-ifs."

"What-ifs?"

He makes a funny face and looks at me as if I have two heads. In a loud voice, as if to emphasize what he means, he clarifies, "In this case, *what if* there are snakes at the lake?"

"Oh," I say, still mired in minor confusion, "but you were the one who told me about the snakes in the first place."

"Yes, I showed you your fear. All I had to do is make the suggestion in your mind, and all the what-ifs started to roll in and compound like a snowball rolling down a hill, getting bigger and bigger as it goes. And what's worse is how given you are to such suggestibility. I bet if someone vomited next to you, you would vomit. Act like a warrior if indeed you really want to become one. This is the only thing that will save your ass in this place. And it will save your ass in your own life as well. Slam the door on the what-ifs. Slam that door before they start to snowball."

He gets up from his chair and tells me to bring in some firewood so he can make dinner. I get up and go around the back of the cabin, ruminating on our conversation. I grab a bunch of wood and try to slam the door on a particular what-if that just came over my mind: *what if Jay is making beans again?*

CHAPTER 39

I come back inside the cabin to find Jay at the stove cooking. He instructs me to throw some lighter pieces of wood on the fire and to set the rest down in the wood box. After arranging four or five nice-sized logs in the fireplace, I find a seat on the couch next to Bert. I'm relieved to see that food and rest have breathed some life back into him; he wags his tail more vigorously, and his head is upright, revealing his shining eyes. The other dogs sit on the floor under the table, where they spend most of the time while we eat. "He looks a lot better, doesn't he?" I say to Jay.

"Yeah," he answers. "Why don't you go over to the cupboard and get some biscuits. See if he'll eat some."

I do as Jay says, returning to the couch with two good-sized biscuits. I break one in half and offer it to Bert. He's a little hesitant at first, so I pet him gently to put him at ease, telling him that everything is going to be all right, that he is a good boy and that he should try to eat something. After a few minutes of coaxing, he finally takes the biscuit from my hand and gobbles it up without much chewing. He nudges me with his nose, indicating that he would like another. In short order, both full biscuits are gone.

I tell Jay that Bert's eaten both biscuits, and he says that this is a good sign, as he'll need nourishment to get his full strength back. I get up and fetch his bowl, put some dog food in it, and sit down on the couch next to him, placing the bowl just under his mouth so he can eat from it without having to get up. He doesn't eat at first but finally digs in and, slowly but surely, finishes all that I've given him. I replace the food bowl with his water bowl and watch him take a long drink. He then collapses, full and exhausted. I feel much better now.

"Let him get some rest," Jay says, "and give him some air."

I get up, find my place at the table, and sit down. Though I pet Molly and BB under the table, I never take my eyes off Bert, who is now snoozing on the couch. After a while, he begins to snore. Jay comes over to the table and plops down a plate of beans flanked by a biscuit and ear of corn. I look up at him and see that he is smiling that same devious smile. As tactful as possible and trying not to sound like I'm complaining—because I'm sure that a warrior never complains—I amiably mutter, "Not much of a varied diet around here, is there?"

Jay snorts a bit and, without looking up from his plate, says, "If you don't like the menu, why don't you do something about it? I'm not in the business of making sure you get fed. Any time you want something else, provide it."

This statement takes me by surprise. It hasn't occurred to me that I can literally bring home the bacon. I've taken for granted that we eat whatever Jay supplies. I mention that we ought to slaughter one of the chickens and roast it. This seems to annoy Jay a great deal. He looks up to at me. His lips press together, and his teeth clench in anger. "We don't kill chickens around here. They provide us with eggs. If I start to kill chickens every time I want something other than beans, there will be no chickens left and no eggs."

He goes back to eating, and I go back to thinking. "How about those pheasants you shot the other day?"

"They're not ready yet. They'll be tough as nails."

I have to say tough-as-nails pheasant sounds more appetizing than this limited menu of biscuits and beans. There's a long pause in the conversation, interrupted only by Bert's snoring. Jay finishes his meal and says, "You'd be in some fix if you had to live off the land." I tell him that I've never had to do that before; where I'm from, there are supermarkets and restaurants and delicatessens, and all you have to do is make up your mind about what you want to eat, and there it is. It's as simple as that.

"Out here, nothing is simple. Still, I can't believe that you can't find anything for us to eat in this lovely world. These supermarkets and such ... what kind of food do you get at these places?" Jay says.

"All sorts of things."

"Why don't you name a few?" he says with a grin. "Maybe it'll make the beans taste better."

"Oh, I don't know ... pizza, hamburgers, maybe some chicken, pasta, seafood."

"Seafood?"

"Like fish. I love fish."

His eyes get wide. "What kind of fish?"

"Salmon, trout, flounder, striped bass, cod, all sorts really."

He looks at me with a twinkle in his eye, and that familiar smirk drifts across his face. "What's your favorite fish?" he asks, almost jokingly.

"Salmon," I reply. I don't quite know where he's going with this, and it certainly isn't making the beans taste any better thinking about all those tasty dishes. He looks at me as if he's waiting for me to say something else. There is a long silence. I continue to look at him and then back down at the mound of beans.

Finally, he breaks the silence. "You're a poor excuse for a warrior!"

I look up at him. Obviously, I'm disappointing him in some way. "Why?" I ask.

"Because you've been complaining about the food that I've been preparing for you. When I ask you to do something about it, you tell me your favorite dish is salmon. Look out the window!" He throws back the shutter and points. "There's a beautiful lake chock-full of salmon, trout, and all other kinds of fish. A warrior would not need to be told this. He'd have figured it out for himself! He'd have scouted out the best places to fish. Instead of relying on my good graces to provide you with dinner, *you* should be providing both of us with a wonderful meal."

I sit back in my chair. Naturally, he's right again. I am a fisherman, and I've certainly caught loads of salmon and trout before. And the lake *is* right there. It could definitely put an end to the cavalcade beans. Maybe it's one of nature's signs. I jump out on the defensive, stating that I don't have any fishing equipment and that it would be impossible for me to catch trout or salmon without it.

"A good warrior would improvise," he says, effectively turning my excuse back on me. Nevertheless, I don't know how I can go about catching fish without a rod and reel. Before I can finish my thought, Jay instructs me to go into his bedroom and look behind the door. I get up and cross the room, waking up Bert and the other dogs in the process, who now watch me disappear around the corner. Once in the room, I check behind the door and find a rack with three fly rods, three fly reels and a number of boxes full of hand-tied flies, much like the flies I hand-tie for myself back home. This is wonderful. If only I had a pair of waders. Jay, reading my mind as he does, calls out to look in the closet on the opposite side of the room. I go to the door, open it, and find, hanging on a hook, a pair of waders.

"Try them on," Jay yells. "I'll bet they're just your size."

I sit down on the bed, take off my boots, and slide the waders on. The boot size is perfect. All the while, I'm still a bit miffed by his ability to read my mind and the uncanny fit of the waders. I can hear him chuckling in the other room. He yells out to me, "I guess that solves the fishing equipment problem."

"Yeah, I guess it does," I answer. I take the waders off and put them back in the closet. As I come out into the front room, all eyes are on me again as I cross over and sit back down. Jay has stopped laughing by now. "Can you believe you have such nice fly-fishing equipment? And those waders, they're the perfect size."

He gets up and takes the dishes off the table, walking over to the sink. "Do you really think it's so amazing that there's fly-fishing equipment here? Are you not a fly fisherman? Why is it so outrageous that those boots are your size?"

I scratch my head. I don't know what I think or understand anymore. Without turning to look at me, he says, "Weren't you just talking about fishing equipment?"

"Yes, I was."

"So why would you be so surprised to find fishing equipment? Have you learned nothing yet?"

"I don't know," I say. "You tell me. I actually don't know anything lately."

"Sometimes, the best lessons are taught by yourself. If I tell you everything, as it is occurring, these lessons will not have the same impact. Remember that."

"Come on, Jay," I plead. "I've been so confused since I found myself in this place. I need a little help."

He takes off his hat and sits down on the couch next to Bert. It is then that I really notice the four eagle feathers braided into his hair. You just don't seem to get the same effect when he has his hat on. "Let's see if I can explain a little to you, without actually explaining, of course. It seems to me that you want everything handed to you. But I'm not the kind that hands anything over easily. I'll show you the way. But you have to do the work, the work of becoming a warrior. This is kind of like the snakes that we talked about earlier."

I look at him with what must be a puzzled look on my face because he begins to laugh hysterically. This makes me a little angry. "What do snakes have to do with fishing equipment?" I demand.

"Come on," he says, "think a little bit. When you were walking down the trail to the lake, what happened?"

"You told me to watch out for snakes," I say angrily.

"And then a short while ago, in our conversation about eating something other than beans, you told me that your favorite meal is salmon. I told you that there is a whole lake full of salmon. But you told me that it is impossible to catch them without proper equipment. Tell me what happened next, in your mind?"

"I pictured all my fly-fishing equipment back home."

"And what did you find?"

"Fly-fishing equipment, complete with waders, just like mine."

"So, what's that tell you?"

I look at him for a minute, drawing a blank until I finally exclaim, "Are you telling me that whatever I'm thinking about just appears?"

His eyes become bright, and he sits up straight on the couch and looks me square in the eye. "Yes, that's more or less what I'm telling you."

"But how can that be? That doesn't happen in real life."

"Are you sure about that?" he snaps back sharply. He doesn't speak for a while, allowing me the chance to think. Then he says, "Think about it. You might find out that many things that have occurred here, as well as in your own life, have happened because of a thought. That, my friend, is how powerful your mind can be." With that, Jay gets up and strokes Bert's side a couple of times before going over and grabbing his pipe and tobacco pouch. He walks out onto the porch and closes the door. Jay certainly has a way of making these dramatic, silent exits.

I sit there for a while going over what we just talked about. I'm having a hard time accepting the notion that my thoughts create my reality. I never thought about this before, but it certainly explains the importance of getting my mind under control. After quite some time has passed, Jay comes back in and asks if I want a cigar. I tell him that would be great, and he goes over to the bowl where he keeps his tobacco and in no time at all produces yet another beautiful cigar. "If you want to smoke that cigar, you need to go out on the porch. It is not that cold out tonight."

We both move out onto the porch and sit down in our chairs. We sit in silence for a while; I smoke my cigar, and Jay smokes his pipe. I have a lot to work out in my mind between what Emma told me and my conversation with Jay at dinner. I don't know which way to turn. Jay sits there, causally smoking away and rocking back and forth. Finally, I speak up. "Do you think Bert's going to be okay?" I ask.

"He'll be just fine," Jay says confidently. "He's been through this before. He just needs a good night's sleep and a couple more meals, and he'll be right as rain." This is followed by another long silence before Jay asks, "What did Emma have to say to you?"

I'm becoming used to the manner in which he directs conversations. Though I anticipated this question, I think for a moment before replying, "She told me lots of things, most of which I didn't understand. But I have a question for you now that you bring up the subject."

"Okay, now is a suitable time for questions. Fire away."

"First, and most pressing, where did she go? I mean she was here one second and gone the next. Does she live around here?"

"Well, you could say that," he says as he bangs his pipe on the side of the chair, dislodging the used tobacco.

"Well then, can we go visit her?"

Jay chuckles a bit, as he seems to do every time I ask a question. I don't know why he seems to find everything so funny. Not everything, of course, only me. "No," he replies, "we cannot go visit her. I would not know how to find her. Besides, Emma, as I told you, is like the snakes, the bear, and pretty much everything else around here."

I look at him and say, "I know what you're going to tell me. You're going to tell me that she's in my mind." He reaches toward me with his fist closed and in one motion of his hand gives me a thumbs-up before sitting back and blowing smoke rings from his pipe. I'm trying to compute what he's telling me, though I find it unfathomable that this woman—who stood right in front of me in flesh and blood—is merely a product of my mind.

"Think about that," he says, though I get the impression that he already knows I'm doing just that. "Next question."

"Are we going to get to see her again?"

"Well, of course, that's up to you."

"You know, she reminds me of someone. I can't put my finger on it. She's beautiful: just the right size, the right eyes, pretty much the right just-about-everything."

"Why do you think that is?" Jay asks.

"I don't have a clue."

"It's because you created your perfect woman. You've taken everything about women you love and then turned that into Emma; you made her."

I stand up. "Jay, this is freaking me out."

"I warned you when you first arrived here that you would see a lot of things that are freaky," he says.

I sit back down and start to reflect on all that he has said. Jay doesn't seem to be doing any reflecting at all. He seems to know everything anyhow, so I guess there's no need for him to reflect. He resumes the conversation: "You still haven't told me what Emma had to tell you today."

"She told me a lot of things," I answer quickly. I'm starting to get a little annoyed with Jay. I can see that he's just fishing around for more things to laugh at me about. "How come she gets to call you Eagle Feather?"

"Because she's earned it," he snaps back. "Emma is a warrior. When warriors speak to you, there is power in their words. and you should remember that, and you should remember what they say to you because power is a gift; it is a gift that is not easily given. When you have the opportunity to hear those words, power needs to grab a hold of you. But instead, you were so busy looking at her—her eyes, her body, her physical form—that the power she was trying to convey to you was lost. She told you the most important thing you need to escape this situation." Here his voice crescendos into nearly a shout. "Don't you remember?"

Remember. That's what Emma was talking about. "She told me I have to remember myself."

"Congratulations!" he says.

"For what?"

"You actually remembered this important piece of the conversation."

"But that's it, Jay. I don't know what she means. Can you shed a little bit of light on this? What's this remembering all about?"

There is another long silence, the kind of silence that Jay likes to prefix his significant points or lessons with. He begins. "What Emma was talking about is that you need to remember yourself. This means that you need to put yourself where you are in any given moments so that you are awake and remember that you are on the warrior's path. By remembering yourself, you tune yourself into the one true I. It gives you a brief moment of recognition that the other I's are false."

"Well," I say, "I've been working on those I's."

"Have you now?"

"Yes. I'm not going with them as much as I used to. I'm trying to think for myself."

He looks at me, and a cold stare comes over his face. "Sooner or later, those I's are going to rebel and try to take back control, and the only thing that can stop it is for you to remember yourself."

Now I start to laugh. He waves his hand to stop me and continues: "As sure as I'm sitting here, there's going to be a rebellion. Those I's are more powerful than you think. If you can win that battle and take control, you can assert the one I that is truly you. Only through remembering yourself can you vanquish the false I's."

"But Jay, she said if I remember myself, I can remember what happened in other recurrences, and that will help me find my way out of here."

"That is true," he says, "but the practice has to start now, and you need to remember yourself at every given moment. Actually be there. This means that your mind, for the first time in your entire life, is to be in the exact moment and place in which your body is. In that moment of self-remembrance, the sun will pierce the clouds of your mind. Your internal dialogue pauses for a short moment, and in this brief pause, all the pathways of your body and mind become clear. Once you have experienced this pause, you can work on expanding it. Now practice with that," he says as he gets up and goes back into the cabin.

"Can I call you Eagle Feather now?" I blurt out.

"No," he calls out. "You need to earn more feathers."

I'm trying to figure out just how to remember myself because, in my way of thinking, this is the key to getting me out of this situation and back to my former life. But I also feel that it is necessary to keep me alive. I don't want to be killed, having come this far, only to find myself back at the clearing. I don't want to be a prisoner here forever. I have managed, to this point, to keep all the I's at bay. They're still there. But I've been managing to subjugate them by not paying them any attention and thus not giving them the force they need to overtake me and, as Jay would say, make me act like a stupid ass.

The thought of the I's attempted revolution is starting to worry me. But I have to admit, if I'm successful, this will lead me to become the one true I that I must. The more I think about this, the more I come to the conclusion that being a multitude of personalities is messing me up. I have to stave off any coup d'état that they are planning. But on the bright side, I get to go fishing tomorrow. It's something that always excites me. I want to show Jay that I can pull my weight around here and hopefully provide us with a wonderful salmon meal.

CHAPTER 40

I'm up early the next morning, and I find that even though I haven't been able to get a ton of sleep with all these thoughts running around in my head, I have a tremendous amount of energy. It's pretty clear to me that the prospect of my fishing trip has me running on pure adrenaline. When I spring down out of the loft, Jay is nowhere to be found, and I'm out the back door and back from the chicken coop with eggs in a flash. I get the fire going in the oven and scramble up the eggs. Then I take a few of Jay's famous biscuits and toast them up. I also fill the pot of water and brew some tea. I'm just putting the food on the table when Jay comes through the door with the dogs. It makes me feel good to see that Bert is now running around with the others as if nothing happened.

"Oh," Jay says, obviously surprised, "you're up early."

"Yeah," I say. "I'm thinking about trying my luck down at the lake. I'd like to catch us some salmon or at least a few trout for dinner."

Jay sits down at his place and starts to eat. "That sounds like a plan to me," he says.

"It looks like Bert is feeling much better."

"Oh, he's fine now. I told you a good night's sleep and some food, and he'd be his old self again."

"Would you like to come down to the lake and fish with me? You can borrow one of the rods, reels, and flies that I dreamed up." I add that last part for good measure.

"Another time," Jay answers, smiling. "But since you're going to go down and fish, I'll take care of everything around here."

At first, I think he's somehow agitated that I'm off to fish, leaving him here alone to take care of the chores, but he pulls his face into a smile that looks to be more of a smirk. I take this as a positive sign. "How big are the salmon in the lake?" I ask. He tells me the biggest one he ever caught was upward of fifteen pounds. "That's a nice fish," I remark.

"Let's see," he says. "There's also browns and rainbows and a few brookies. I think the browns top out around twelve pounds, the rainbows eight, and I've caught brookies over three pounds before."

With all this talk about the larger-sized fish down at the lake, I am wolfing down my food. Jay is watching me gobble everything up and says, "Slow down. The slow and steady always win." When I finish eating, Jay tells me not to worry about the plates and instructs me to pick out a good rod and reel. As I walk across the room, I ask Jay what line size he generally uses.

"There's a five weight, a six, and a seven," Jay calls from the sink. "If you're going after salmon, I recommend the seven weight and the eight-and-a-half-foot rod. That'll give you enough backbone to land a big salmon. There's a green bag in there with a shoulder strap. Take all the boxes of streamer flies and put them in that bag. Everything else you might need is already in there: clippers, scissors, and tippet material."

When I get in the room, I take all the fly boxes that he has stacked up on the table and stuff them into the bag. Then I head over to the closet and grab the waders and put on the boots. They are the same kind I have at home. These stocking-foot waders and hiking boots are the most comfortable you can have. I take the eight-and-a-half-foot rod with the seven-weight line and come out into the big room.

Now, the line size determines the thickness and thus the strength of the line. They start at six pounds and go up to fourteen. Fourteen is the thickest line; with that, you are able to throw very big flies and catch larger fish, like tarpon and sailfish. The seven weight, as Jay suggested, should be ideal to throw the proper size streamer flies and land me a nice, big salmon.

As I head out, Jay turns from the sink and wishes me luck. I thank him and hurry out the door, which closes behind me. I don't want to linger around long enough to hear anything derogatory, like a reminder about snakes. Besides, the weather is nice: a little overcast with a slight chill in the air. It's too cold for snakes, and I have a lot of confidence that I won't be running into any of them. I walk a half mile from the cabin to the lake and come out along the path at the spot where Jay keeps the canoes. But today, there's no need for canoes; I'll be fishing from the shoreline. I look around for a good place to start. The lake has the waterfall at the extreme end and a small stream in the left corner where it empties out and becomes the same stream I followed from the clearing. I think Jay calls it the River of Souls. I decide this will be a good place to start fishing, where the stream departs the lake. I've been a fisherman for many years, and I know that the pull of water out of the lake will attract the salmon, who will be holed up there searching for baitfish.

I make my way over to the stream. It's easy going. Most of the brush starts way back from the shore, so it's just like walking down the beach. When I reach the spot where the lake becomes the stream again, I open the bag and take out one of the boxes housing the flies. It is full of midsize streamers. The streamers are made out of feathers and tinsel, much like the tinsel that you would put on your Christmas tree. It mimics the action of small baitfish that salmon feed on. I think to myself that these flies look very nice, and I must say that Jay is a very good fly-tier. I flatter myself that I am as well. I spent eight years tying flies in a shop, and those flies were sold all over the world. So essentially, I'm a pro when it comes to tying flies, and Jay, I reckon, isn't too far behind.

Now a streamer fly is not an exact replica of those baitfish that salmon or trout feed on. It's merely a good suggestion to the fish that it's food. And it's this idea of suggestion you have to keep in mind when you're tying them. It is merely suggestibility that causes these fish to strike. Since it's an overcast day and not particularly bright, I pick a dull, olive-green color and a white fly with just a little sparkle provided by the tinsel. I'm trusting the tried and true adage of dark day, dark fly, bright day, bright fly.

I scan the water to make sure there are no snakes swimming around and to see how deep it is. I wade out about ten feet from the shore and start casting into the lake, maneuvering the fly toward the mouth of the stream. It feels great to be fishing. It is one time in this whole ridiculous situation that I find myself possessed with a deep calm. I am relaxed and enjoying myself. I guess you could even say I feel at home. Well, almost. I fish that spot for an hour or so, changing flies a few times and the way I fish each fly. But it's all to no avail. I get neither bite nor bump. The I's, on the other hand, are biting.

Wise Guy I suggests there are no fish in this lake. Analytical I suggests a strategic change of spots. Ego I reassures me that I am a great fisherman and my failure on the lake is due to Jay's lying and, as Wise Guy I has said, there are no fish in this lake. At that point, it strikes me that I haven't heard any of these voices recently; they seem to be absent when I'm with Jay. I get the impression that they're somehow intimidated by him and will not speak up in his presence. I decide not to give them any attention, as is my practice now. Nevertheless, I can't help but think that Analytical I is probably right and, before giving up completely, a change of scenery is in order.

I back out of the lake and reel in the fly, placing it on the hook keeper on the side of my rod. I decide to walk back in the direction of the canoes. When I come around the bend, I see the canoes sitting on the shore about a hundred yards away and someone standing next to them. As I walk closer, I see that it's Emma. It's hard to tell from a distance, but she seems to be wearing a baseball cap. She comes toward me, frantically waving her arms for me to come quickly.

CHAPTER
41

I stop in my tracks, startled by the sight of her. But as I stop, she begins to wave me over in a much more urgent fashion. I break into a trot toward her. She's holding two paddles and tosses one of them into the canoes. In a very authoritative voice, she says, "Get into the canoe! Quickly!"

We push the canoe into the water, and she jumps in and sits in the front seat. Picking up one of the paddles, she yells at me to hurry up and get in the canoe. I push the canoe into the water a little more, wading in a few feet and then throwing one leg over the side of the canoe. I hear a terrible screech behind me as a mountain lion bursts out of the underbrush, running at me. I look back quickly, turn, and jump into the canoe. Emma is already feverishly paddling. I reach forward and grab my paddle, flailing wildly away at the water. I turn around just in time to see the lion stop at the water's edge. Emma says, "He won't come in the water—I don't think. Just paddle hard to make sure." The cougar paces back and forth on the shoreline but never makes any attempt to swim after us. I am never so glad to know that cats hate water, and even mountain lions might avoid it. When we are about forty yards from the shoreline, we simultaneously stop paddling, without saying a word. The cougar disappears back into the underbrush.

"Don't mind telling you, but that scared the hell out of me," I say in a shaky voice. She looks back at me, smiling, and says we will go to the other side of the lake by the waterfall. We paddle for a while in silence. Finally, I say, "It's a good thing you came along when you did, or I would have been that cougar's lunch." She doesn't say a word, just continues to paddle. The thought occurs to me about two-thirds of the way across the lake that that could have been another demise for me; I could have had to start fresh, back at the clearing. I start to question Emma. "Was I killed by the cougar in the past?" She doesn't respond, and it's kind of upsetting. I ask again, "In one of my recurrences, did that cougar kill me here at the lake?" Emma turns around and looks at me with a solemn look. She turns away and continues paddling. "Come on, Emma," I insist. "There must be a reason why you came out here today." She turns around and says something that is inaudible due to the approaching, crashing waterfall. I yell back at her that I can't understand, and she motions for us to beach the canoe at the same spot where Jay and I landed when we came for fresh water.

We head for the opening in the bulrushes, as Jay and I did the last time. As soon as the canoe hits the ground, she jumps out and pulls it up onto the shore with me still inside. Though I didn't realize this before, she is not only very athletic but also very strong. I get out of the canoe and walk over to her. "Don't you think that cougar will come around the lake after us?" I ask.

"No, not at all. You got past your bout with the cougar today," she says.

"How do you know this stuff?"

"Let's just say that I've been around here a long time, and you and I have been together throughout."

I ask her again if that cougar killed me in a previous recurrence. She tells me that she can't divulge that information, adding, "I'm not supposed to interfere, you know. But I'm glad you asked." She says that she was worried that I was not remembering myself and thus not practicing the procedure that Jay told me about: trying to put myself in the moment and remember myself. She was worried that I wouldn't remember that while I was out fishing by the canoes, the cougar attacked, and I was forced back to the clearing to start all over. She explains that she went back to the cabin, and Jay sent her down to me to help me remember myself, and from here on out, it's my job to do that, so I can prevent further debacles.

"So, we're safe on this side of the lake?" I ask.

"I told you, I'm not supposed to interfere," she says. "I'm only here to show you the way, like Jay, but you have to walk the walk yourself." With that, she begins to walk toward the water spirit totem pole.

I follow, continuing to badger her. "So, we're safe now, right?"

When we finally reach the totem pole, she turns around and nods. Her nod relaxes my entire body, which, I didn't realize, was tense until this point. "You know, I haven't caught one fish all day. I'd really like to bring back some dinner for Jay—and for you, of course, if you'd like to stay."

"You can do some fishing after we visit the water spirits," she says. She sits down in front of the totem pole and crosses her legs, patting the ground on her right side and urging me to sit down next to her. After sitting, I try to cross my legs as she is doing, but I realize that I still have the waders on, and this is no easy task. She tells me to be quiet, as she is going to call the water spirits so we can hear what they have to tell us today. I sit there for a while in silence with Emma. I continually look over at her and see that she is sitting with her eyes closed in some sort of trance. After twenty minutes or so, she opens her eyes and stands up. She reaches down with her hands to help me up. She looks at me with piercing blue eyes. "Did you hear anything?" she asks.

"All I heard was the waterfall," I answer.

"It's not something you hear from the outside. Rather, it's a voice you hear from within."

"Emma, I have so many voices on the inside that I don't think there's any room for one more."

She giggles at this. "Your problem is that you're so crammed up in there." She points to my head as she says this, lightly poking my right temple.

"Well, did you hear anything?" I ask.

"Actually, I did. The message was for you."

"Tell me what the message was all about," I demand.

"You have to go under the waterfall, and there you will find a message."

"Under the waterfall? You mean I have to dive down into the water?"

"No," she says, "the water comes over the ledge. It's like the crest of a wave. You can walk underneath it and emerge on the other side."

I look up and notice that the water seems to hurl itself off the ledge, and there is, indeed, an opening, just like there is beneath the curl of a wave. She motions for me to go up there and have a look. I, being my usual self, am hesitant and afraid.

But like Jay, she seems able to read my mind. "There's nothing to be afraid of, you idiot. It's only water, and you're barely going to get wet. There's plenty of room underneath there."

"Have you been in there yourself?"

"Oh sure. Lots of times."

"Really? When?"

"When I was in your position and going through my own vision quest. There was a message under there for me then, just as there is a message under there for you now."

Slowly, I walk toward the waterfall, trying to summon all the courage I have. When I enter the tunnel created by the cascading water, I see how much it resembles a cave and reflect on my experience with the bear. There doesn't seem to be anything menacing about the waterfall at all now, and I feel a little foolish that I've ever had any fear of it. Perhaps I'm starting to buy into this mysticism. I now feel brave and walk in about halfway. Immediately, I notice an arrow carved into the side of the rocks. It points to the other side of the lake. Walking a little farther through, I see another carving. As far as I can guess, the carving depicts trees forming a circle with an open space in the middle. I continue to walk until I reach the other side of the tunnel. It isn't that far, perhaps forty yards at best. There I spot, sitting in a tree just in front of me, a bald eagle. Now I can't tell you for sure, but it looks likes the same eagle that I saw just before entering the bear's cave, the one that dropped me the feather. The eagle looks down at me, and I look up at him. After a long pause, he takes flight and, once again, drops a feather. Knowing this gift is for me and feeling elated, I run over and grab the feather. Looking up, I notice that the eagle has vanished.

I turn around and run back to the other side of the waterfall. When I emerge on the other side, Emma is standing there looking at me. I smile and hold up my prize, exclaiming, "Look! Another feather!"

"Yes, that's very powerful," she says, gesturing toward the feather in my hand. Her eyes become big, and she walks toward me.

"I know that," I say, "but what does it mean?"

"Haven't you noticed that Jay has four feathers in his hair?"

"Of course," I say. "I've been admiring them."

"Jay is a warrior, and a warrior is only a warrior when he has enough personal power. This personal power is signified by eagle feathers, four in particular."

I look down at the feather and look back at her. "Well, now I'm halfway there."

Pulling the feather out of my hand and the other from my hat, she tells me I did fine.

"How so?" I wonder aloud.

"Well, you earned that first one when you escaped the bear and faced him in the clearing, didn't you?"

"Yeah, I suppose I did. But what did I do today? Is it because I managed to escape the cougar?"

"You didn't escape the cougar all by yourself, did you?" she says with a sly smile. "I would say this feather has something to do with your working on consolidating your I's into one, accepting the path of the warrior." She takes both feathers and, producing a piece of red twine from her pocket as if she anticipated this, ties the shafts of each together. Now, I have been out in the wild a little while now, and my hair has grown to the point where it's becoming unmanageable. I'm actually thinking about cutting it or even putting it in a ponytail. Emma pulls off my hat and, using the same twine she used to tie the feathers, weaves them into my hair. Then she playfully shoves the hat back on my head.

"Hey, I'm beginning to look like Jay," I joke.

"I suppose you are ... but you have a ways to go yet."

I stand there and continue to look at her. Man, she's beautiful. The sun, now falling over the opposite side of the lake, bleaches her near-black hair and reflects off her face. She has a chiseled nose and large eyes that, in the reflecting light, are enough to make me melt. I stand there silently in awe for a second before she reaches over and pushes me by the shoulders, almost knocking me over and snapping me out of the trance.

"Aren't you going to fish?" she asks.

"Sure, sure I'm going to," I answer, remembering my plans for the day.

We walk underneath the waterfall together and down to the edge of the water. Looking out over the lake, I see a salmon trying to jump up. Then another and another. "Did you see that?" I say to Emma. "The salmon are trying to jump the waterfall and swim upriver." I look up and see she is giggling. This must be the spot I'm looking for. I run to the canoe and retrieve the rod and fly boxes, and I'm back in a flash. I wade out in the water a bit and make a few casts, letting my fly drift in the current created by the crashing water. While I stand there, I notice that a number of salmon are trying to make this leap. I've seen this before, and I know that it may take them many tries before they successfully make it. If they make it at all. I turn to Emma and say, "They don't seem to want to bite."

"Try a different fly," she suggests. She's right. The sun has come out now, and it's time for a brighter fly. I dig back into the bag and pull out a different box. When I open the box, I see a folded-up piece of paper. I take it out and open it. "Use the orange fly," it urges, and there, in the bottom right-hand corner, are the now-familiar initials, RLC.

I call for Emma to come over and have a look at the paper. She quickly points out the initials, and I say, "Yeah, I know." I'm starting to believe everything that Emma and Jay have told me about recurrence. Maybe I have been here before and left clues for myself, clues to get me home. "Well, what do you think?" I ask.

"I think you should use the orange fly," Emma says. She goes on to say that if it's me writing these notes and I'm the fisherman I think I am, I should certainly follow those instructions. I can't argue with that. I am the fisherman I think I am, as least as far as I can hear Ego I telling me. And, hey, maybe I did write this note. So off I go with the orange fly. I grab one of three apparently identical orange-colored flies and tie it onto the leader. I wade out into the water and cast. On the second swing, a tremendous hit! The drag in my reel begins to sing as the line flies off the spool. The fish is heading directly across the lake. All the fly line is off my reel in an instant, and I'm into my backing. This means the fish has traveled fifty yards in a matter of seconds. I'm holding the rod high in my right hand and keeping the left hand away from the spinning spool so my knuckles don't get busted up by the spool's frantic action. The fish feels the pull and takes off again, probably running another fifty yards off my reel before slowing down. I pump the rod again several times in order to gain back a lot of the line. This battle goes on for a good several minutes, which is quite a long time to fight a fish.

Finally, the fish comes near the shore and is obviously tired; he is lying on his side as I pull him toward the beach. It's a big one—probably in the neighborhood of fifteen or twenty pounds. A beautiful fish. Emma is cheering as I reach down and pull him up onto the beach by his tail. This is really the only way you can handle a salmon without the use of a net or a gaff. I'm feeling proud of myself and remark to Emma that it's one big salmon, possibly the biggest I've ever caught. Emma agrees, saying, "I think it's one of the biggest I've ever seen come out of this lake. We should thank the water spirits for giving us such a good fish and apologize to the salmon for taking him as food. Like the salmon, we too will one day die, and our remains will help nourish the earth." I look at her to see if she is truly being this morbidly frank. She has a deadpan, serious look on her face. "Go ahead," she urges. Following her advice, I thank the water spirits and apologize to the fish. Strange as it sounds, what else am I supposed to do?

"Maybe we should get another one," I say.

"No, that's a big fish, and you'll be eating off it for a while. Only take what you can use, and if you need to come back another day, perhaps you will have the same luck." I don't agree with her. I'm a catch-and-release fisherman and only plan on catching a few more for fun. But I imagine in Emma's thinking this would be cruel and torturous—catching fish for pure sport.

"Let's go," I say. "It's getting dark, and I want to be able to clean the fish and prepare it for you and Jay. That is, if you'll stay for dinner."

We walk down to the water, and I put the fish in the canoe. I push the canoe into the water and jump in as Emma follows. With a couple of strokes, we are off.

"What did you see under the waterfall?" Emma asks.

I describe the arrow and the circle of trees with the opening in the middle. "What do you think it means?" I ask.

"Those signs were meant for you and you alone. Only you can decipher them. But you can try to ask Jay when we get back to the cabin. He's very good at seeing the meaning in these things."

I decide to change the subject. "What do you think about that note?"

"I guess you have to believe that all these notes were written by you in another recurrence. And if I were you, I'd pay attention to them. I mean, the fly did work, didn't it?"

"That's true," I say and look down at the proof, in the person of the salmon, lying on the floor of the canoe.

We make it to the other side of the lake, and the canoe hits the beach. I look around for that cougar, but looking back at Emma, I can see that she doesn't seem to be the least bit concerned, and I take it as a sign that the danger has passed. We pull the canoe up on land and take the salmon out of the canoe, then walk the half mile back to the cabin. I keep my eyes on Emma the whole time, hoping she isn't going to pull another disappearing act.

When we get back, Jay is standing on the porch with the dogs. He walks over to greet us. I hold the salmon up in the air triumphantly and make a sort of Indian whooping noise that has never come out of me before. I'm so excited that I don't even consider it.

"The fishing was good!" Jay says with a smile.

"Yeah. Look at the size of the salmon I got. I think it's the biggest one I ever caught. And boy, let me tell you, he put up a good fight; he got into my backing and everything."

"Well, you did a good job," Jay says with a smile. "Now you have another job to do."

I look at him quizzically. "What's that?"

"Clean the fish."

"Jay, I'll do you one better. I'm not only going to clean him, I'm going to cook him for you and ... oh, by the way, I invited Emma for dinner."

Jay looks at Emma with a smile and makes some sarcastic remark about "Sunday best." Jay and Emma start to laugh. I take the fish into the cabin and quickly gut him, making several good-sized filets. I go out on the porch and grab some firewood for the stove while Jay and Emma sit in the porch chairs talking and laughing.

"Jay, what else do we have to go with this fish?" I call out from kitchen.

"We have some corn and potatoes. We can have some biscuits also."

"I can do the corn and potatoes, but, Jay, as far as the biscuits are concerned, you're the master."

"Relax," Emma says, getting up and laying a hand on Jay's shoulder. "I'll take care of the biscuits."

"That'll be fine. You do make a mean biscuit. Just don't burn any," he says to Emma.

"You should have a little faith in me," she replies. "After all, you're the one who taught me. It's really on you."

With this, they both laugh, and Emma comes into the kitchen where I'm cooking. She goes right to work and in no time whips up a batch of biscuits.

"The dinner is excellent, if I do say so myself. After all those days of beans, this salmon is the best I've ever had," I comment. "In fact, this might be the best *meal* I've ever had."

Jay and Emma start to laugh, and Jay says, "What happened? I thought your favorite meal was beans." This cracks them up again. I'm starting to get accustomed to their derision. I just wish I was laughing along with them. But I'll be laughing when I'm back home. The idea of getting back has never left my mind.

Jay rises to clean up, and I tell him I will handle it. I want him to relax. It's time for me to take care of everything. While I'm cleaning up, Emma feeds the dogs. I watch her out of the corner of my eye. She knows right where each bowl is to be placed. It's as if she has done it a hundred times before. When we both finish, we go out on the porch and find Jay. He seems to be in a good mood, smoking his pipe and rocking in his chair. He asks me if I want a cigar. Reluctant to smoke in front of Emma, I decline. Then to my surprise, he asks Emma if she would like one. Emma just laughs, and so do I.

"It's a good thing you caught that salmon because we're running out of beans, and worse, we're running low on tobacco. We certainly can't have that, now can we?" Jay says. Emma says we should have plenty of salmon to last for a little while. Then she says something that shocks me.

Turning to Jay, Emma says, "I guess we have to go into town for supplies."

CHAPTER

42

"Town? Do you mean to tell me there's a town around here? You never mentioned this to me, Jay?"

"Well, like just about everything else around here, there is and there isn't," Jay says.

"What the hell is that supposed to mean?" I ask. I'm trying to keep it together because Emma's around. Otherwise, I'd be shouting at Jay at the top of my lungs. These riddles have to stop.

"It's going to show up any day now, and when it does, I'll certainly let you know," Emma says. "Eagle Feather, will we be taking Rich with us to town?"

He doesn't respond immediately; he just continues to smoke his pipe. It's as if he's weighing the option. So I jump right in. "If there's a town here, you can be damn well sure I'm going. So what's this business about there being a town and not being a town? It *appears*?"

Jay looks at Emma as if to say, "Do you want to explain this or do I?"

"By all means, go ahead," Emma says. "He doesn't seem to remember anything."

"It's like this," Jay begins. "Every so often, a town appears, and that's where we go and get supplies. We get in there and get out of there before it disappears. That's really all I know about it."

"What's that supposed to mean?" I demand.

"I don't know exactly," Jay says.

"Eagle Feather, haven't you told him that he has to suspend his disbelief while he's in this life? Doesn't he know that anything is possible?" Emma asks.

"Yes, I covered that," Jay says. "He doesn't seem to be comprehending it though."

My blood is boiling. Jay and Emma are treating me like a child. "And another thing: I have two feathers now, if you haven't noticed. Can I call you Eagle Feather *now*?"

"I have noticed that," Jay says, "and it's quite an accomplishment to have two feathers. But that merely means you are on the path to become a warrior. Two feathers does not a warrior make." Then he adds, slyly, "Three feathers, though ... I suppose that will do." Both he and Emma start to laugh hysterically.

"Well, she doesn't have any feathers," I say, pointing to Emma, "and she calls you Eagle Feather."

"Emma has fulfilled her vision quest. She's left this place and has returned only to help you. Don't you forget that and be grateful," Jay says calmly.

This stops me in my tracks. I decide to try to find out more about this mysterious, disappearing town. "Tell me more about the town."

"Well, it's like this," Jay says. "The town appears at a certain spot from time to time, and that's where we get many of the supplies we need to survive. Take the dog food, for instance, or those lovely beans, or the tobacco. We also get shotgun shells and a few other items. But then, just as mysteriously as it appears, the town disappears."

"Are there people there?" I ask.

"Oh, there's people there all right. That's what worries me."

"Why does that worry you?" I prod him.

"Because, first off, you can't remember anything. Secondly, you're not whole yet. You still have all those I's dancing around in your head, and that certainly wouldn't be a good thing in town. But, then again, it hasn't appeared yet, so we'll worry about that when the time comes."

"How does it happen? How does a town just appear and then vanish like that?"

"Not sure," Jay says, chuckling a little bit. "I don't pretend to know how everything happens around here."

Changing the subject, Emma says, "Why don't you tell Eagle Feather about the signs you saw under the waterfall?"

"That's a good idea," I say. But before I can start, Jay stops me with a lift of his palm and asks first if I heard anything from the water spirit. "No," I say. "Unfortunately, all I could hear was the roar of the waterfall."

"So how did you know to go under the waterfall?" Jay asks.

"Emma. Emma heard the water spirit and told me to go underneath there."

Jay looks at Emma sternly. "Emma seems to have taken a liking to you again. She seems to be interfering a bit." Emma just smiles.

"Don't give her any grief," I say. "She saved my life."

"She's not supposed to do that. And she should know better. But I'll let it go this time. Now, tell me what you saw under the waterfall."

"I saw an arrow carved on a rock wall, pointing to the other side of the lake. When I walked farther in, I saw trees carved in a circle with an opening in the middle. What do you think it all means?"

Jay sits back, takes a long pull from his pipe, and says, "What do *you* think it means?"

"I'm not sure. The arrow looked to be pointing to the other side of the lake. But then again, it could have been pointing to that next picture of trees."

"Well, I guess you'll just have to think about this for a while," he says. "When you come up with an answer, tell me. Is there anything else?"

I tell him about the note I found, and Emma takes the note out of her pocket, unfolds it, and hands it to Jay. He points to the initials in the corner. "I know," I say. "You keep telling me that those initials are mine."

"I think at this point you should try to accept the fact that these notes have all been written by you in your past recurrences in this world. Then, if you can remember yourself by practicing, you may be able to find the answers that these clues are trying to help you find and thus find your way back to your former life," Emma says.

"We all should see clues from our past, signs. They come to us in all sorts. We see an ad fly by on the side of a bus and don't realize that it contains a message for us. We see an image of a place in our mind, and we don't know why, but we know we would like to visit there, and when the image persists, we take a trip there. When we arrive, we find a sign of some sort or a lesson that we must learn. But so often, these signs go missed, the lessons obscured, because we are asleep in life. A warrior, because of his practice of being awake in the moment at all times, sees these signs, learns these lessons, and acts accordingly. And this helps him to change his life, change it to the life he wants, change it to the life he deserves.

"You, on the other hand, Rich, are a very strange warrior, or a very clever one. I can't decide which. You refuse to leave it to chance that you will see these signs for yourself and insist on leaving little notes for yourself that help you on your way through this recurrence. You have been able to keep them from me since last time you were here. You may have thought that I would consider this interfering, as I consider what Emma did today, saving you from the cougar, interfering."

He pauses for a moment, and I can see the wheels in his head turning, as if he's mulling this over. He continues, "I have decided that because this is you writing to yourself, these notes cannot be considered interfering. So, we will let that be. If only you could remember yourself by practicing you would be able to find the answers to all this and much more."

I complain that I *have* been trying to remember myself, but as far as remembering what there is to come, well, I'm not psychic.

Emma says, "Being psychic is a very funny thing. Maybe you should understand it in this way: psychic people are people who remember their past recurrences, and in doing so, they see what is about to happen in their lives as well as the lives of anyone that comes to them."

"How can they know what will happen in other people's lives?" I wonder aloud.

"Because," Emma replies, "they have encountered these people in other recurrences, and through these encounters, they see what is happening and what will happen. In the same sense, if you remember yourself, you will continually see yourself where you are. The world will open up to you, and you will be able to change the future. And in changing the future, you will change the past. This, of course, can only happen while you live completely in the present."

I have to think about all this for a while. I'm confused and definitely in need of some whiskey. I get up and go inside the house, inviting Emma in for a drink. She declines, and when I come back outside with a full glass of whiskey, she's gone. "Where did she go?" I ask Jay.

"It was time for her to go."

"Go where?"

"Into the ether."

I just look at him. We sit in silence for a while as I try to make sense out of all this. Jay speaks up suddenly, obviously startled. "Go inside, to my room, and have a look at those two feathers in the mirror."

I get up and walk into the bedroom. On the far side, I spot a small mirror, roughly the size of an eight-by-ten picture, hanging on the wall. I haven't seen myself in days, and I'm curious to see how long my hair has grown; it has never been this long in my entire life. As I stare into the mirror, I see that the hair on my head has grown quite long, but I do not have any facial hair. I stand in front of the mirror and take a good, hard look at myself. As my eyes come into focus in the dim light, I'm shocked to see not my face but Jay's staring back at me through the mirror. I back away, close my eyes, and shake my head a bit. I take another look, and my first glance is confirmed. Then, quickly, all of Jay's features change, and I see myself. I run out of the room and onto the porch. Jay is nowhere to be found.

When I come back inside, I find him sitting on the couch. "How did you do that?" I yell.

"Do what?"

"Put your reflection in the mirror when I was looking in."

"Why? What did you see?"

"I saw you!"

He is smiling from ear to ear and chuckling. "Are you sure?"

"Yes, goddamn it, sure as I'm standing here now." *What kind of Indian sorcery is Jay up to?*

"Are you even sure that you're standing there now?"

I have to think about this. "No, I suppose I'm not."

"That's right," he says. "In life, you can't really be sure of anything."

"But that doesn't change what I saw."

"That's quite a sign. I think it's supposed to show you something. Maybe you should think about that."

"Sure. Why not. I have so much to think about it will take a lifetime just to digest it all."

He doesn't seem willing to talk about the subject any further. He tells me that he has given me a lot to think about and that I should go to bed.

"Is that what you're going to do?" I grumble. I look around for the dogs and see that they are down for the night. So, mumbling to myself, I climb the ladder to the loft. When my head hits the pillow, I'm out like a light.

CHAPTER 43

I have the most vivid dream—unlike any other dream I've ever had in my entire life. I guess you could call it a vision. In the dream, I find myself peering out of what appears to be a window. Ominous shadows approach me. They are faceless and formless; they are ghosts. Somehow, though, I know exactly what they are and that they are coming for me. They are my I's.

I find a rifle slung over my shoulder and take aim at the closest figure. I fire, and the shadow disintegrates into smoke-like dark matter that lingers in the air. I do this to all the I's, and the same thing happens to each. After I shoot the last of the apparitions, all the black smoke combines into a large, swirling cloud. It floats toward me.

Suddenly, a figure emerges from the cloud, and I can see that it is Jay. He has a calm look on his face as he approaches me. All the fear I have trapped inside dissolves. When he's standing right in front of me, Jay grabs both of my wrists. In that moment, I see everything that he has experienced on his own vision quest. I see how important it is to turn off my internal dialogue and clean out all the unimportant thoughts in my head. I see how to wake up. I also feel what Jay feels; I feel the daunting task of remembering myself at every point of my life. I understand, as Jay must, the ways in which the universe opens up to us with signs that urge us in the correct direction. I feel a sharp pain in my temple and reach up. I find four feathers tied into my hair. Jay is gone. But, without having to look in a mirror, I can tell what has happened.

The next thing I know, I'm back at the cabin and am myself again. I look off the porch and see Jay coming toward me. Then, where the forest opens up, I see my I's, again in shadow form, materializing from the darkness. They too are coming toward me.

CHAPTER 44

I wake up in a completely different frame of mind. I sit up on the bed. What I must do is abundantly clear. I must become a warrior if I am ever going to find my way back. I have to find Jay and tell him that I'm fully committed, either in this life or my other, to becoming awake. I scramble down the ladder only to find that Jay and the dogs are gone. I'm surprised to see that he has already gathered eggs, and I decide to make breakfast.

In the middle of cooking, Jay and the dogs burst through the door. The dogs immediately run toward me, and I pet them all good morning. Jay's expression is foreign. It's as if he knows all about my dream. He has a seat at the table, and without wasting any time, I begin to tell him all about it.

Jay listens attentively. When I finish telling him all that I saw and felt, he tells me that the dream was indeed a vision. "What kind of vision?" I ask.

"It is the kind of vision that some Indians spend eternity in search of. You have been shown how to conduct your life. If you are to succeed, you must practice everything that I have been teaching you about the warrior's path."

"I'm ready, Jay," I say confidently. I tell him that I accept him fully as my teacher now and that I will do whatever he asks of me.

He looks me straight in the eye and studies my face for a while.

He must be trying to judge if I'm truly sincere this time. Finally, he says, "I accept you as my student. From now on, you will call me Eagle Feather. Your training begins this very moment. I will teach you the ways of the warrior, just as they were taught to me when I was a young man."

"What would you have me do first?" I ask.

Jay seems a bit taken aback by my eagerness. I'm not fooling around anymore. I realize that I am a mess, both here and in my former life. I am a multitude rather than an individual. I am determined to change all this. He looks me up and down again and says, "Okay, first thing's first. Let's clean up the breakfast mess, and after that, I want you out there chopping wood."

I pop up and grab our dirty plates. I have to confess that I didn't think his teaching would involve chopping wood, but I am dedicated now, and I know I must do whatever he tells me. When I finish the breakfast dishes, I go around back and start in on the fire wood. After a while, Jay comes around and sits down on one of the stumps. He sits quietly, watching me chopping away. Finally, in a booming voice, he says, "Who are you?"

He's caught me off guard, and I don't answer right away. My reply is tentative at best. "Rich L. Corsetti?"

"Where are you?" he continues.

"I ... uh ... don't know."

"What do you mean you don't know?" he asks indignantly. "Where are you at this moment and what is your task?"

"Chopping wood," I answer.

"Okay. Let me be a little clearer: what is your task in life?"

"To wake up. To become one. To become a warrior."

"Good," he says. "This is called remembering yourself. You are aware of your physical place at this moment. You are aware of who you are and what you are doing while still keeping in mind your ultimate task. Whenever I ask you to remember, you should easily be able to answer these questions. Keep yourself focused on these points so that your mind will fly to them when prompted." He gets up and walks away in the direction of the barn.

I stop chopping wood for a few minutes to take a break and think about everything that Jay has just said. Over and over again, I repeat that I must remember the moment I'm in, who I am, what I am doing, and what my task in life is, hoping I can learn it by rote. I easily chop a cord of wood while my mind cycles through this mantra for a couple of hours.

Jay comes around to the back of the cabin and makes a funny gesture, as if he is taken by surprise at my productivity. "Is that enough, Jay?" I ask, gesturing toward the wood.

He chuckles a little and says, "That will do for now. As I told you, I'm no longer Jay. From here on out, you are to refer to me by my proper Indian name, Eagle Feather." This is followed by one of his theatrical pauses, the ones he orchestrates before he is about to make a point. He looks me straight in the eye and says, "Remember yourself."

In my mind, I start to go over, point by point, all the things that he wants me to *remember*. He looks at me and, in a loud voice, tells me to say what I am supposed to remember out loud. I begin, "I'm standing here behind the cabin, holding onto the ax, and looking at you. I remember who I am: Rich Corsetti, and my task in life is to wake up."

"Now in addition to saying all this, I want you to visualize yourself as you look now, standing where you are. Look at all the surroundings as well; I want you to have a mental picture of where you are."

"So, while I'm saying this, you want me to also think of myself."

"More than that," Eagle Feather says. "Visualize. Take a snapshot photograph of yourself in this instance. See yourself standing where you are; see your surroundings and picture yourself. This picture must be a picture of you now; it cannot be a picture of you from ten years ago or what you think you might look like in another ten years. The picture has to be crystal clear. It must be a picture of you and your actions in this moment. Your task has to be remembered fully so that you can complete it."

I struggle for a moment, trying to get a mental picture of how I look at this moment, and without too much effort, I am able to see myself and my surroundings in the moment. I am standing there looking at Eagle Feather. I remember that my task is to wake up from the sleep of life.

"How's it going?" Eagle Feather asks.

"Not too bad," I say. "I had a little trouble trying to envision myself at first, but now it's not hard at all." I ask him what the purpose of this exercise is.

Eagle Feather sits down on the stump and tells me to pay attention because he doesn't want to have to repeat this to me a hundred times. He begins, "Your mind, like everyone else's, is a time traveler. It wanders around in the past and flies into the future. It rarely ever exists where your body is. With this exercise, we are trying to put your mind, spirit, and body all together in a particular place and moment. This is what I mean by making you whole. It is the only way a warrior can live. He must constantly be on guard so he can make sure his mind, body, and sprit are all together in the present moment at all times. This is the remembering yourself exercise; the Indians call it stalking yourself, as I have already mentioned."

He pops up off the stump and tells me to follow him around the house. We head into the barn, take a bale of hay out, and begin to feed the horses. I know this routine well by now, and as I am spreading the hay out on the floor, Jay asks me to remember myself and to do it out loud. Immediately, I visualize myself spreading out the hay. I see the surroundings, and I see myself there at that moment. "Now out loud," he commands, and I do as he says.

The rest of the day is spent doing chores in every conceivable place, and at least once during each chore, Jay has me remember myself. He never lets up. Later that evening, while I am cooking dinner, he asks me four times. He has me remember myself three times while we eat and once while we are out on the porch smoking the little tobacco he has left. Finally, when the day has ended and it's time for sleep, Eagle Feather tells me that this is the first day in my life in which I have been present in all that I have done. I tell him that I have never been so aware of myself and my actions. He tells me that this exercise has to be lived and that I can't just turn it into lip service. No matter how long it takes, I must commit this into my being. I must follow the procedure because if I forget myself at any time, I will be falling back asleep.

"This is really difficult," I complain lightly. "Tell me it gets easier."

"Life is difficult, and anything worth doing is difficult," he explains. "Being awake is worth the effort."

With that, we both go to bed.

CHAPTER 45

Over the next few days, Eagle Feather concocts all sorts of different chores for me to do. The whole time, he is right on top of me, prompting me to remember myself. These times, however, he tells me not to verbalize them. He tells me it is more important to internalize and ruminate than to just talk. One particular time, I am brushing the horses, and Eagle Feather, sitting on a small bench in the paddock, asks me to remember myself after each stroke. I become a little overwhelmed and tell him that he's going too fast. He laughs with a hardy laugh from deep down in his belly. "I have to move faster and faster so that you will become accustomed to remembering yourself at every given moment. In this way, all these tiny snapshots will turn into a moving picture. It will be like a movie, a movie in which you will now be the director and the audience, as well as the star." He smiles at the suitability of his simile. He then tells me to think about this.

Emma doesn't appear at all during this time, and I am kind of missing her. I hope that she will materialize like she always has before. I figure that Eagle Feather has cautioned her from coming by at this stage; he wants me to concentrate on remembering myself and knows Emma will only serve as a distraction. To my surprise, she does turn up after three days, and Eagle Feather suggests that she and I go for a ride so I can practice my riding.

I am delighted by this, and Eagle Feather tells me that Emma is a very accomplished rider and that she could certainly teach me a few things. "I'm sure she could teach me a whole lot," I say excitedly. They both laugh at my unintended innuendo, and even I have to crack a smile. I'm excited about the ride. I want to spend time with Emma, and this is a great opportunity to escape Eagle Feather and his constant insistence that I remember myself.

But if it's a break from Eagle Feather's austere teaching that I'm seeking, no such luck. Emma continues Eagle Feather's drilling every chance she gets. In fact, she might be tougher than Eagle Feather. Nevertheless, it's so good to be with her, and we have such a good time that I don't mind her nagging as much. And to top it off, the process is becoming easier. Every time she asks me to remember, my mind flies in accordance. She is obviously impressed and tells me that Jay's allowing me to call him Eagle Feather is a huge step in the student-teacher relationship. She tells me that in Indian liturgy, referring to a warrior with his warrior name means that he has accepted you as an apprentice and a warrior in training. I feel very proud about this, and I tell her that I have made a commitment to do whatever it takes to become a warrior. On my way back to the cabin, she asks if I have remembered anything from the last recurrences I have spent here.

"Just a little," I say.

"The more you remember yourself in the moment, the better chance you have at remembering your recurrences. At some point, this will happen."

We ride back the rest of the way, and she continues to prod me to remember myself. In between those times, I wonder when and how my memory of past recurrences will happen. When we arrive back at the cabin, I ask her how I will remember the past. I'm surprised by what she tells me. "Don't try to figure it all out. And it is not the past that you are trying to remember. The universe is a mysterious place, and everything cannot be known to us. These things just happen."

CHAPTER 46

I sit on the porch with Eagle Feather and Emma; both of them are in the rocking chairs, while I'm on the floor with my back up against the wall. Eagle Feather has his pipe going with what little tobacco we have left. Suddenly, Eagle Feather speaks. "I want you to understand the true meaning of being one, of being in the moment, of remembering yourself." I look at him in the golden light of the lantern that dangles from the ceiling. He looks shiny and luminous, even ethereal. "A warrior," he continues, "lives in the sun. That is the light of the sun. Not like the ordinary human being who lives like the bugs under a rock. When you pick up the rock and the sun hits the ground, all the little vermin scurry off into the darkness. Man lives in the darkness of his mind. He is never where his body is. By practicing remembering yourself, you are putting your mind and your body in the same place, and you are awake in life and living in the sun. These last few days, you have been more aware and more alive, much more present than you have ever been."

I know this to be true. In the few days that I have practiced self-remembering, I have become more aware of every movement I have made in every task I perform. I feel like I never felt before. Eagle Feather continues, "A warrior is always on guard; he is always stalking himself and does not slip back into the sleep of life. And when a warrior is in the state of remembering himself, only then does he have true power."

"What kind of power are you talking about?" I ask.

"The power over life. You are no longer a victim of happenstance, and you are on your path of destiny. In so being, you have control because you can remember your recurrences and can change the outcome of the past by changing the future."

I ask him what he means by "happenstance."

He explains, "In life, all that happens does so in the only way that it can. Those who are not warriors become passive victims of life. Warriors, on the other hand, are active because a warrior has intent; he is there in the moment and knows that he has been there before, and he catches glimpses of what is to come. In this way, he is able to affect the outcome of any event."

I have to sit back and think about this. I am beginning to see that if I practice remembering myself, at some point I will remember my last recurrence. I think to myself that if I can just do that, I will remember what will happen next. And I think that sounds funny, *remember what will happen next*, but the way that Jay and Emma have explained it to me, it makes sense. I ask Eagle Feather if this is the case.

"Exactly," he says. "That's exactly what I'm saying. Only through practice is this possible." I ask him how long this will take. "It will take as long as it takes," he answers cryptically. I shake my head in disbelief. Eagle Feather and Emma look at one another in that golden-lantern light and start an unusually loud and unexpected laugh. "Shaking your head, huh? In disbelief, are you? I hope that one didn't shake you up," says Eagle Feather.

All I can do is nod my head yes. He leans forward in his rocking chair as eddying smoke from his pipe billows up to the ceiling, forming a great cloud in the lantern's light. I just look at him. In a loud voice, he says, "Practice the willing suspension of disbelief."

"I'm not too clear on that statement," I say.

"Let me clear things up for you. You need to willingly suspend your disbelief in anything that we have told you here. When you can do that, you will definitely be on your way."

In a half-joking voice, Emma says, "Try it. You have nothing to lose and everything to gain."

I don't know how to respond to that. She is, of course, correct on both accounts. I don't have anything to lose, and if I can possibly suspend my disbelief of everything that's occurring, I might gain the necessary insight to become a warrior.

As if she's reading my mind, she goes on, "This is very difficult because we have been taught our whole life to believe that life is what society, our parents, and history have told us it is. In fact, it's all a bunch of crap, and human beings are capable of much higher levels of that consciousness that makes infinity possible. It is a warrior's job to seek higher and higher levels of consciousness." When she has finished speaking, she gets up, walks off the porch, and vanishes into the darkness.

Jay sits there looking at me and chuckling. I guess I have an astonished look on my face. I get up and tell him that I'm tired and am going to bed. I'm going to need some time to think all this over. He tells me to ponder it. I have to look at it from all angles. He, as Emma did on our ride, warns me against trying to figure it out. He tells me that the universe is a mysterious place and that it is beyond our comprehension to figure these things out; acceptance is the key. He tells me to remember to accept everything that happens, even if it seems impossible.

"Okay," I say, "I'll practice the willing suspension of disbelief." I climb the ladder to the loft, yelling back, "Acceptance is key."

CHAPTER 47

The next few days go on as the last few. Eagle Feather continues my training in self-remembering as I do all the chores around the place. I have to admit that he's quite a drill sergeant and could have easily been a marine. He never lets up on me and asks me to remember myself at every possible moment and in every possible way. I must say, with all this constant repetition, I find myself quite competent with the procedure, so much so that I find myself remembering myself at moments even when Eagle Feather is not prompting me.

One morning, I wake up with a strange feeling of anxiety. I have had anxiety before, of course, but this is different; it hangs over me like a fog. As I descend the ladder from the loft into the big room, I feel as if there's some impending doom hanging over my head. Eagle Feather starts right in on me while he makes breakfast. He announces that today will be different. Once we leave the cabin, he will no longer ask me to remember myself; it's up to me do so on my own now.

All through the day, while I complete all the necessary chores, I have to remember myself at every moment.

That evening, after supper, Eagle Feather remarks that our provisions are getting dangerously low. I offer to go fishing again so that we don't have to eat what little beans we have left. Eagle Feather announces that he is taking the dogs out hunting, and they will try to rustle up some grouse for tomorrow's supper. I become excited at the thought of hunting and ask if I can go with him. A strange and concerned look comes over his face, and he tells me point-blank that no, I am to stay in the cabin with Bert. He hastily puts on his coat and hat and pulls his shotgun from the case. He calls for BB and Molly, and the two bird dogs meet him at the door. I notice a strained look on his face, almost a look of concern. He looks me straight in the eye and tells me to take care of everything and that he will be back shortly. He turns and opens the door, and the dogs run out in front him. Before closing the door, he takes one last look at me, as if to say, "Good luck."

This is strange behavior, and it heightens my anxiety. What does he know that he's not telling me?

I sit in front of the fire with Bert, waiting for Eagle Feather to return. I glance out the window and notice it's getting dark. I think to myself that this is a curious time to go grouse hunting. This time in the evening, they usually go to roost up in pine trees. You don't have much of a shot at them then, and the dogs will be useless. But then again, I wonder if Eagle Feather knows where the birds go to roost and is trying to cut them off before they make it to the trees.

Just then, in the middle of my thoughts, Bert stands up alertly and goes to the door. He begins to whine and paces back and forth. My first thought is that he has to go outside to use the potty, and I get up and make my way over to let him out. As I do this, I have a vision; it is almost like a movie playing in my mind. I see myself opening the door and letting Bert out, but instead of relieving himself, he runs directly toward the chicken coop, howling. I see myself out on the porch, trying to see what all the fuss is about. It's not until I make it to the edge of the porch that I hear the mountain lion's snarl.

I start down the edge of the porch after Bert and see that the mountain lion is already on top of the coop. I run, horrified, toward Bert as the mountain lion leaps off the roof of the chicken coop and on top of Bert. The dog and the mountain lion begin to struggle, and by the time I reach them, Bert is a goner. The mountain lion now devotes his attention toward me, leaping right on top of my chest. I see myself fighting: throwing punches, kicking, and screaming in pain. My mind goes black.

I snap out of the vision and realize I am still standing near the door. For some unexplained reason and despite my vision, I open the door anyway. Just as I saw, Bert runs toward the chicken coop. I hear the scream of the mountain lion, and I run the length of the porch, on my way grabbing the broom that is leaning up against the side of the building. When I get to the edge of the porch, I see the mountain lion preparing to leap on top of Bert, and I leap over the railing, landing just outside the chicken coop. In a quick motion, I push the broom into the side of the mountain lion while he's in midair. I push with all my might, and the mountain lion falls to the ground, rolling over twice. I grab Bert's collar, trying to pull him out of harm's way. The mountain lion regains his balance just as I lose my grip on Bert. Bert lunges at the big cat. The mountain lion stands on his hind legs, roaring and swiping at Bert with his front paws. I pick up a rock from the ground and heave it, hitting the mountain lion on his side. The great cat once again topples to the ground.

With reckless abandon, I run forward and grab Bert again by the collar. I get ahold of him and pull him back. The mountain lion now jumps the fence and into the chicken coop. I tug Bert's collar, fighting him all the way back onto the porch and finally managing to get him inside the house. I close the door behind me. Outside, I hear the chickens making quite a racket. I have to do something to protect our eggs. I run for the gun case and grab a twelve-gauge shotgun from the rack. I pull open the drawer and grab a handful of shells. I make my way toward the chicken coop. Hearing the pellets rattle inside, I know that all I have is birdshot. I know it might not be powerful enough to kill the animal, but I hope it's enough to put a hurting on him and force him to retreat. As I get to the end of the porch, I load each barrel and hurry down the path to the chicken coop. Inside the fence, I can see the mountain lion raising hell; feathers are flying everywhere. When I get to the coop, I see the mountain lion has one of the chickens in his mouth. He turns in one quick motion and glares at me. I make a whooping sound, a sound like an Indian war whoop. The bloodcurdling cry seems to shock the big cat, and he drops the chicken without taking his eyes off me. He turns and once again jumps on the roof of the coop.

I now have a clear shot at him. I was hesitant to shoot with the fence between us for fear that it would disperse the birdshot and render it ineffective at hurting or at least discouraging the cougar.

He stares down at me with cold, doll-like eyes and gives me the impression that he's making a stand and will, at any minute, leap down on top of me. I raise the shotgun and aim it right for the middle of his chest.

Just as I'm about to pull the trigger, I hear a voice inside me. It's not one of the usual voices, the nagging I's that I have been trying to suppress. I recognize it immediately as the voice that told me to run from the bear when I was inside the cave. "The mountain lion is a beautiful creature, and it represents life. You cannot defeat life." I remember immediately what Eagle Feather said about Bert and his decision to stop trying to beat life; it's Bert's decision alone to stop chasing the mountain lion. Just then, the mountain lion moves to the edge of the roof, and I recognize immediately that he's positioning himself to leap toward me. I raise the shotgun above his head and fire one round. Obviously startled by the noise, the mountain lion turns, and with a single, long bound, he lands on the other side of the chicken coop and disappears into the woods. I watch his silhouette vanish into the darkness.

It is now that I feel the fear in my body. Up until this point, I haven't felt anything; I've been acting on autopilot, not even concerned for my own safety. Trembling, I sling the shotgun onto my back and make my way to cabin, feeling confident in the fact that I still have another round left in the gun.

When I get back inside the cabin, I find Emma there with Bert. Both come rushing toward me. Emma gives me a big hug and a kiss I will never forget. I look her in her eyes and see that they are teary. We kiss again. The door swings open, and Eagle Feather steps into the room. I look up at him and see that he has a sort of reserved smile on his face. "You made it," he says.

I manage to muster a simple, "Yeah."

"I heard the shot," Eagle Feather says. "Did you kill him?"

"No, I shot over his head. He's too beautiful an animal to kill." I have the feeling that in my last recurrence, it is the mountain lion that does the killing. Emma and Eagle Feather both look happy to see me and Bert standing there in one piece. I don't think either of us made it the last time. "It didn't go so well the last time, did it?" I ask, looking directly into Eagle Feather's eyes.

"No," he says. "But you made it this time. Sit down here on the couch and tell me about it." Emma follows me over to the couch and sits down next to me. I point to the table where I realize I threw the dead chicken. "I'm sure he put up a hell of a fight, but he wasn't as lucky as you and Bert," Eagle Feather says.

I go on to tell him about my vision, the one that saved me and Bert. How just seconds before the event occurred, I was offered a glimpse into what I can only imagine was my last recurrence and how this time I was better prepared for what was about to transpire. Eagle Feather is ecstatic. He tells me that my remembering practice has been successful. Emma explains that she and Eagle Feather knew, as warriors, that this was going to happen and confessed that both had their doubts as to whether I'd succeed. I tell her that I'm kind of happy about it myself, downplaying the whole situation, and joke that Bert is probably pretty happy about it too.

Emma gets up and goes over to the desk, opening one of the drawers. When she comes back over, she has an eagle feather in her hand, and she promptly ties it in my hair with the others. "Now you look more like a warrior," says Eagle Feather. "One more ought to do it." At this point, I feel that my nerves need calming, and I'm ready for some whisky. We spend the rest of the night talking about what happened. The whisky never tasted so good, and I, for the first time, feel like a peer to Emma and Eagle Feather. Almost.

CHAPTER

48

In the days that follow, I find myself becoming more and more like a warrior. Eagle Feather has dropped his drill sergeant routine, relying on me to remember myself at all times. Emma and I are becoming very close. We spend most of our time riding, and she teaches me all that she knows. I'm becoming increasingly proficient at remembering myself; just as Eagle Feather and Emma told me, the snapshots I'm taking of myself are slowly coming together and turning into a motion picture. I'm no longer remembering myself from moment to moment. It now feels like the process is flowing throughout the whole day. It's an unbelievable feeling to be awake and alive.

On the negative side, however, our food and tobacco situation is becoming grave. I go fishing a few more times, but the fishing isn't great, and ultimately we find ourselves down to our last can of beans. There isn't much tobacco left for Eagle Feather's pipe, let alone enough to roll a cigar. One evening, I'm sitting on the porch with Eagle Feather when I have another vision. I see myself sitting in the front seat of the truck I found in the barn. I look pretty much the same as I do now, but I only have two feathers in my hair. I watch myself take out a piece of paper and write the words "Remember where you put the key" and then my initials, RLC, in the right-hand corner. I then pull the key out the ignition and jump out of the truck, making my way across to the cabin. Once inside, I take a plate and place it on the table. I grab a can of flour off the shelf and place the key in the middle of the plate. I then dump the flour onto the plate, key and all, and pour it back into the flour can, replacing it on the shelf as if nothing happened.

At the conclusion of this vision, I run back into the cabin and grab the can of flour, dumping it on the table. Sifting through the flour, I find the key and go back out to the porch to show Jay what I discovered. "Look," I say. "Look what I found in the flour."

He takes the key from my hand. He looks back up at me and, recognizing what the key is for, asks me where I found it. I relay the vision I just had to him. He reminds me that the visions are all a product of my ability to remember myself. He goes on to say that I put the key in the flour so I would not make the mistake of trying to drive the truck in search of civilization, a move that he has already told me resulted in my running out of gas and becoming lost in the woods before dying of starvation. He goes on, "But you have found the key at a very opportune time because you now know that you can't drive out of here and make the same mistake that you made in the past."

"What good is the key then?" I ask.

He smirks and simply replies, "You never know when that key might come in handy. Put it some place where you can find it again, and that way, it will be there if you ever need it." He hands the key back to me, and I take it inside and bury it under the couch cushions. It seems as good a hiding place as any.

CHAPTER 49

The next day after dinner, Emma appears again. I'm happy to see her and think we might go riding again. I'm beginning to enjoy riding; finally I'm actually able to stay on the horse. She seems extra excited today and quickly reveals why: the town is about to appear. She doesn't know exactly when, but she went to the water spirit this morning, and he told her to keep a watchful eye. Upon hearing this news, Eagle Feather leaps from his seat at the table, puts on his coat and hat, and starts out the door. Still sitting at the table, I call out to him, "Where are you going?"

"Sit tight with Emma," he says. "I'm going to get the horses and take a look."

"A look? A look for what?" I ask.

"For the town, dummy. What else would I be looking for?"

Out the door he goes. Emma sits down on the couch and begins to pet the dogs. They are always happy to see her, but no one is ever happier to see her than I am. I ask her to explain what she was told about the town. She explains that she went to the water spirit in the morning and sat in meditation. During her mediation, she saw the town appear, and she took this to mean that it would not be long before it would once again manifest itself. I ask her if she knows when this will happen, and she tells me that she has no idea, but it should be soon, and it will be our opportunity to go and stock up on supplies. We continue to sit there chatting for a while. She is fun and interesting to talk to, kind of like a female version of Eagle Feather. She tells me many interesting aspects of the warrior's life. As we sit there chatting, I continue to move closer and closer to her, until our shoulders are nearly touching. I think this is a good opportunity to kiss her again. She turns toward me, and our eyes lock. I lean forward—you know, that lean forward so your lips are close and you're hinting at a kiss. She looks deep into my eyes, and I look back into her big blue eyes. She leans forward, and I feel the warmth of her lips on mine. At just that inopportune moment, the door bursts open, and we both jump off the couch like embarrassed teenagers whose parents just got home.

It's Eagle Feather, of course, and he's laughing. "Not the best time to come home?" he says.

"No," I say, "not at all." Then, changing the subject, I say, "What about the town? Is it there?"

"No, I didn't see it anywhere."

"Well, where does it usually appear?" I ask.

"It doesn't appear in the same place every time," Emma answers.

"That's right. We have to go out and find it. It can be quite a chore sometimes, and it may take days," Eagle Feather says.

"What should we do?" I ask.

"You and Emma clean up, and I'll scout around a bit more. Hopefully we'll locate it in short order because, god knows, I need the tobacco"—he looks at me and smiles—"and I know you're dying for more beans." He takes off on his horse again.

I turn to Emma and say, "Maybe we can pick up where we left off?" She just laughs. I grab her and kiss her passionately. I must say there is no hesitation on her part. But after a short period of kissing, she pushes me away and tells me that will do for now.

"Let's get the horses out and have a look around for ourselves," she suggests.

We saddle up the horses. It's getting dark, and I mention this to Emma. She tells me that this is the only reason the town will be visible. This seems counterintuitive, and I ask her why. She explains that, for some reason, the sunlight makes the town and people disappear, so it only appears in the darkness of night. "How are we supposed to see the buildings from a distance if it's dark out?" I wonder aloud.

She looks at me as if I'm truly pathetic. "We're going to look for the lights, you dummy."

We start out by making a big sweep of the area, circling around for a bit. She tells me that the last time the town appeared, it was close to the cabin—so close, in fact, that they could see the lights from the porch. The last time, they had been out searching for three days only to see it when they returned to the cabin. "Remember, though," she says, "the town doesn't always appear in the same place. Just because it will be appearing soon does not necessarily mean we will find it tonight or even tomorrow. It might take weeks." We continue to circle around like two great birds in search of prey; the radius of our search gets larger and larger.

Emma keeps insisting that I look for the lights, but I don't see any. After about three hours of riding—very slowly, might I add, so we don't run into any trees or topple over any cliffs in the heavy darkness—we come to the top of a hill. At this point, it begins to rain, lightly at first and then heavier and heavier. From our vantage point high atop the hill, we can see the vast forest in every direction. The rain continues to beat down on us, and I'm becoming soaking wet and discouraged. I want to joke that the rain must be the water spirits telling us to turn around, but I know that to Emma and Eagle Feather they are no laughing matter. "Maybe we should head back. I'm drenched. Maybe Eagle Feather had better luck."

Just then, looking down in a valley between two hills, I see a glimmer of light. "Look! Look!" I exclaim, pointing toward the image of the lake. "There's a light!"

"Where?" Emma says, leaning forward in her saddle.

"Look down in the valley. You can just make it out through the rain. Small glimmers of light."

I begin to think this is the first light in the woods that I have seen since I found myself here. Emma, scanning the periphery of the forest with her eyes, finally sees what I'm talking about. "That's it!" she exclaims. "That's the town. It looks to me to be about eight to ten miles away, but it's hard to judge in the dark, especially with the heavy rain." She tells me to mark the spot—look at our surroundings and note in which direction I'm looking. On the ground, I see an outcropping of rocks and a fallen tree that looks as though it has been struck by lightning. She tells me to use these as landmarks so that we can find our way back tomorrow.

"It's only one light though. How do we know it's a whole town?" I ask.

She says that the other lights from the buildings are probably blocked by trees and land formations. I ask her what the town looks like. "I don't know," she replies. "Every time it appears, it's different."

"Different?"

"Yeah. One time, it looked like a small New York City. Another time, I remember it looking like a small strip mall. It's also looked like a suburban town. We don't really know what we're going to get. That's up to you."

I shake my head in disbelief. "It's up to me?"

Without answering my question, she turns her horse around. "Let's get out of this rain. We're getting soaked," she says and takes off.

When we get back to the cabin, we find Eagle Feather sitting by the fire with his rain slicker still on. "Did you have any luck?" Emma asks.

He turns and looks at both of us standing soaking wet in the doorway and laughs. "No, not at all. I didn't spot a thing."

I'm unable to contain my excitement. "We saw it! We saw the lights! We found the town!"

"You saw it?"

"Yeah. We were up on a hill north of here, and we saw the lights through the rain!" I say.

"Well, we actually saw only one light, but I'm pretty sure the town is there," Emma clarifies.

"How far off?" asks Eagle Feather.

"I don't know," I pipe up. "Emma estimated the distance to be eight to ten miles, but it's tough to tell at night and in the rain."

Eagle Feather stands up. "Did you mark the direction?"

"Yes, we can go to the hill tomorrow. There's a downed tree that looks like it was struck by lightning and a small but characteristic rock formation. We noted the direction where we saw the town and got ourselves back here and out of the rain." I nod, corroborating everything she just said.

Eagle Feather sits back down and pulls off his rain slicker. Emma moves over to the couch and has a seat next to him.

"What are we waiting for?" I shout. "We can see the lights! Let's get going!"

My enthusiasm is met with silence. Finally, Eagle Feather turns toward me. "First of all, we don't know if we can make it before the sun comes up. Secondly, there is a bit of necessary preparation before we go. We will spend tomorrow morning making these preparations, and by the afternoon, we will make our way to the hill, find your mark, and move in the direction of the light."

"Tomorrow afternoon?" I protest. "I thought the town is only visible at night."

He looks at me sternly. "This is true: the town is invisible in daylight. But if we must travel eight to ten miles before we reach it, darkness will fall during our journey, and we will know precisely where we have to go. If we start at night, it is possible that we will not arrive until sunrise, and the town will disappear."

This makes sense to me. I start to think about these preparations, and curiosity is getting the better of me. "What do we have to do tomorrow morning to get ready?" I ask. "Can't we just ride down there, pick up our supplies, and head back?"

Eagle Feather looks at Emma and then looks back at me. "If only it were that easy," he says. "You don't quite seem to understand what this town is all about."

"No, I guess I don't," I say. "Isn't this town just a town?"

Emma and Eagle Feather exchange glances and then laugh that laugh that I recognize follows something I say that they think is ridiculous or foolish. Emma says, "Well, as I told you before, we don't quite know what the town is going to be like … or should I say *look* like. Every time it appears, it's different. Like I told you before, sometimes it's a big city, sometimes it's a little town, and sometimes there's only one or two buildings; we rarely know what we are going to get. It all depends on your imagination."

I scratch my head and must have an incredulous look on my face. "My imagination?"

Eagle Feather shakes his head. "You still don't seem to understand that this is all imaginary. Most importantly, it's all *your* imagination.

So tomorrow, whatever you're thinking about or whatever you imagine the town to be, it certainly will be."

I look at him and Emma. They are both smiling cynical smiles. We are all quiet for the longest time. I am thinking about what they said about my imagination. Finally, I say, "So, you two are telling me that whatever I imagine this town to be, it will be?"

They look at each other. Eagle Feather says to Emma, "My god, I think he's getting it."

"Yes," Emma says to me, "whatever you imagine is what we are going to get."

"So, if I imagine my hometown, that's what will appear?"

"More or less," she says.

"Yes," Eagle Feather goes on, "but it really comes down to what's in your subconscious."

"What do you mean?"

"Just what I said: whatever is in your subconscious mind will be manifested tomorrow in the form of that town," Eagle Feather says.

"Why my subconscious mind? What's wrong with my conscious mind?"

"You see," Eagle Feather begins, sitting back to make himself more comfortable, "the conscious mind is too busy with all the details of day-to-day life. It isn't the creator of things; rather, it serves as the caretaker. By this, I mean it takes care of the moment. Whatever is happening in that moment, your conscious mind is dealing with it; it helps you get through it, enjoy it, hate it, whatever the case may be. But now your subconscious mind is, in fact, the creator of all things. It serves as the artist, the inventor; this is the power that you have to manifest events, relationships, material things, and so on. Through your subconscious mind, you have the power to create anything that you would like to have happen in your life. The problem is that we don't all know how to tap into the subconscious mind. Those who learn this trick are able to create any event, situation, or thing that they would like to see in their lives. Now here's the caveat: this can only be done for the greater good of all concerned."

I am listening attentively. "So, Eagle Feather, how do you tap into the subconscious mind if we all possess this ability? And how is it so powerful that it's able to do all that you say?"

"Those are interesting questions," Eagle Feather says, "and they deserve interesting answers. The subconscious mind is a part of the conscious circle of humanity. This conscious circle of humanity is all-encompassing. It is the power that holds the universe and all that there is in it. The subconscious mind is both a part of this whole and a smaller version of this whole in itself. So, you see, in every one of us, there is this power over the whole, the whole universe, but unfortunately, only a few have found the secret to tapping its power."

"How can I tap into this power?" I ask.

"That's what this is all about," Eagle Feather says. "This journey that you have been on, a journey that includes your time here and indeed your entire life, is a journey toward this knowledge. We've been focusing on this work here, the work of getting your mind under control."

"How so?"

"Well, staying in the moment is part of the equation, clearing the noise out of your mind and becoming one I instead of several. Remembering yourself is a huge part. When you combine these parts of the process, your mind will be clear, and only then are you able to hold a concise thought of what you wish to manifest in your mind until it comes to fruition. Without this discipline, your mind is out of control; whatever you are trying to accomplish becomes muddled up in your mind. Only by being as clear and present as possible are you able to tap into the subconscious and use it and all its power to create what you would like."

"Well," I say, "I've tried to make things happen before, like winning the lottery. I keep that in mind, but it never seems to happen. Explain that to me."

Eagle Feather squints his eyes. "I'll explain it to you this way: the reason that you never seem to win the lottery is because you are trying to make it happen rather than asking for what you would like and then allowing your conscious mind to get out of the way of your subconscious. Once you've cleared your mind and gotten yourself out of the way, you are in the right position. Ask and you shall receive."

"You mean to tell me that I'm supposed to ask for something and then not try to make it happen?"

"Well, yes and no," he says. "You have to ask and hold that

thought in your mind and then be conscious enough to look and see the signs that will tell you what you need to do. Then you must follow these signs without trying to make anything happen yourself. Just follow these signs and observe the process for as long as it takes, and what you have asked for will come to fruition."

At this point, Emma gets up and walks toward the door. "I believe tomorrow's going to a big day," she says, "and I need to get some rest." With that, she is out the door again and gone. Eagle Feather gets up and walks toward his room.

"Where are you going?" I demand. "We haven't finished this discussion."

"Oh, yes we have," Eagle Feather says. "I told you what you need to know; now you think about it and go up into the loft. I'm going to bed. Emma is the only one with any sense around here. She's right. Tomorrow is going to be a big day, and we need all the rest we can get. Good night."

He disappears through the open door, just as Emma did. It's enough to make me wonder. Emma seems to disappear completely, so when Eagle Feather goes through that door into his room, is he even still there? I'm about to get up and have a look, but I look down at the dogs, see that they're fast asleep, and realize I'm tired myself. I decide to save the mystery for another day. Besides, I have so much to think about after our discussion. I climb up into the loft, strip off my wet clothes, lie in bed, and fall fast asleep.

CHAPTER 50

I toss and turn all night, waking up on several occasions. My imagination is running wild with all sorts of visions of places I have been throughout my life. This town is whatever I imagine it, and I wonder what I'm going to make it. I imagine towns, villages, and cities. Anywhere and everywhere I have ever been. From homes to family vacations.

I'm also excited at the prospect of meeting other people. I am conscious of the fact that I haven't met anyone other than Emma and Eagle Feather since I found myself at the clearing. I am both excited and anxious at the prospect of returning to some semblance of civilization. And maybe, just maybe, someone in that town can help me make some sense of my situation, even help me find a way out and back to the life that I once knew.

I am awakened by sounds from the kitchen. I can hear the clanging of pots and pans as Eagle Feather is preparing breakfast. I sit up groggily and unsettled, with a little bit of anxiety about what the day's adventure will usher in. As I get dressed, I hear Emma's unmistakable voice down in the kitchen. Emma and Eagle Feather are engaged in a conversation, though I can't make out a word of it from where I'm sitting. I creep closer to the ladder and perk up my ears.

"I hope he doesn't make the same mistake he made last time," I hear Emma say. "It seems like he's made such progress this time."

Eagle Feather laughs, saying, "Well, we've taken him as far as we can to this point. It's all up to him now."

I sneak onto the top rung of the ladder, but the wood groans under my weight, and the conversation below me goes silent. This only adds to my anxiety. I make my way down the rest of the ladder and notice that sunlight is just barely creeping though the window in the front of the house. The light catches my eye as I look out the window. It's a gray day. Without looking up from the stove, where he's scrambling eggs, Eagle Feather says, "Well, good morning. It's about time you got yourself out of bed."

I look out the window again, then back at Eagle Feather before muttering a sarcastic, "Good morning. It looks like the sun is just coming up."

"That's right," he says. "Nobody can pull the wool down over your eyes." Emma and Eagle Feather both laugh.

"Good morning, Emma," I say.

"Good morning, Rich," she answers.

"So, what's all this business about making a mistake?"

Emma and Eagle Feather exchange glances. They then look at me, clearly surprised that I heard any of their conversation. "Oh, nothing really. We were just chatting," Eagle Feather says a little sheepishly.

I look over at Emma, and she has a funny look on her face. "Didn't just sound like chatting to me," I mumble as I make my way over to the table. "I have enough anxiety without having to worry that something is going to happen today. Don't tell me this is one of the days when I get killed again."

"Oh, Rich, don't be so dramatic," Emma says, already seated at the table.

I sit down, and Eagle Feather hands us each a breakfast plate. As he bends down to hand me my plate, he looks me straight in the eye and says, "You'll find out soon enough."

I return his glance and reply, "That's what I'm worried about. So, tell me, what's going to happen today?"

"Never mind about that. You know things don't work that way.

We certainly can't tell you anything. You have to figure this out on your own." He sits down, and we eat in silence.

When breakfast is finished, Emma gets up and begins to clear the table. The anxiety in me was building throughout breakfast, and the silence only makes it worse. I can't stand it any longer, finally blurting out, "Why can't you just tell me? Why does everything have to be such a big secret? Why does it all rely on me when you both clearly have all the answers? Just tell me already!"

Eagle Feather remains calm in the face of my outburst, merely replying, "Now that would take all the fun out of it, wouldn't it?"

"Well, I don't know about either of you, but I'm not having any fun, and I don't find this funny either."

"I think it's hilarious," Eagle Feather replies.

I am now furious. I start to stammer, but in my frustration and agitation, I can't even utter a coherent sentence. Eagle Feather looks at me with those stern eyes of his. "Don't even begin to complain. It will do you no good. Whatever the day brings, whatever scenario you face, you must endeavor to be impeccable, an impeccable warrior. And you will do whatever is necessary. Now I won't hear any more of it."

I don't know what to make of this. Eagle Feather goes on, "We have a lot of preparation, and we don't have time for whining. Let's get things together so we can get moving at the appropriate time." He throws his coat over his shoulder and puts his hat on his head. In no time at all, he is out the open door. I turn and look at Emma. She is looking at the door, watching Eagle Feather make his way out.

"Are you really going to let me go into this blindly?" I ask her. "You're really not going to give me any useful advice?"

She turns toward me with the same fixed expression and stern eyes that Eagle Feather just showed me. "We have both given you all the advice you need, so you're not going in blindly. All you have to do is remember all the techniques that Eagle Feather and I have been teaching you. Remember yourself and find the signs that you must find, and you will come through."

"Okay, okay," I say. "Just answer one question: the last time we got to this point, in my last life here, did I make it through?"

"You're not going to get anything out of me," she says with a stone-cold expression. She stands up and looks at me, continuing,

"Maybe if you quiet your mind and your mouth and remember yourself, you will do a lot better." She leaves the room, and I find myself alone with the dogs.

I look at each of them and consider asking them what's going to happen to me today. But they're Eagle Feather's dogs; they probably won't tell me anything anyway. They know I'm paying attention to them, and they all come over to where I'm sitting. I go to pet them, but they pass me by, congregating by the door. I get up and open it for them, and they all rush out.

I look out the door toward the barn and horse paddock. Eagle Feather is not in sight. The day is gray and chilly, and a light mist is falling. I close the door slowly. I'm still in kind of a daze. I have no idea what's about to occur. I look down and see, to the right of the door, the backpack that I had with me at the clearing. All those provisions are still in there, and I think how easy it would be to pick it up and head back out into the forest, escaping whatever danger awaits me in this town. But, no, I decide this isn't a wise idea at all; I would just be wandering blindly through the woods and probably find myself back at square one, the clearing.

I head back over to the table and sit down, burying my head in my hands. My mind continues to scramble, and all the I's, the personalities that I've managed to suppress with Eagle Feather's teaching, come racing back. Optimistic I is telling me that this is my opportunity to find out where I am and what has happened and that the people in this town may be able to answer these questions. Wise Guy I, on the other hand, is telling me that because I have been ignoring him and all the other I's and only listening to Eagle Feather, I am about to get what I deserve. A fight ensues between Optimistic I and Wise Guy I, and I jump in. "Quiet down. What do you mean I'm going to get what I deserve?"

"Oh, you'll see," is all Wise Guy I answers before I hear the door swing open and see Eagle Feather walk into the room carrying three saddlebags. He flings them on the table next to me, and I look up at him startled. All the I's become silent again.

"We'll put these on the horses so we can carry back all the supplies we need," he says.

I look up at him and then back down at the table where the

saddlebags are lying." Are we going to be able to put all the supplies in those three bags?" I ask.

"They'll do," is all he answers.

"What's with all this preparation? Aren't we just going to ride down there, fill up these bags, and come back?"

Eagle Feather walks over to the table and sits down across from me. "That's about the size of it. But that's only the physical preparation."

"What other preparation is there?"

He looks at me with those steely eyes again, a look I have gotten to know well. "There's also psychological preparation," he says. "I guess this is as good a time as any to get into that."

"What do you mean?"

"Well, stop talking and listen to what I have to say." I just sit there waiting for him to speak. The expression on his face suggests he's contemplating his words and searching for the right way to proceed. After a long pause, he begins, "This is a critical juncture in your stay here. We are about to go to town, and everything we encounter, from the town itself to its inhabitants, will be of your own making."

I'm not sure where he's going with this. "What are you trying to tell me?" I ask.

"I have to be careful here," he goes on. "It's of paramount importance that you understand my words." He pauses briefly, then says, "Every event that occurs in one's life, every scenario that plays out, is put there by that individual. In this case, that individual is, of course, you. So, my friend, everything that you see and everything that happens in that town depends on you."

I'm not sure how to react to this. I stare into his eyes, searching for something, as if the answer or some clarification lies somewhere in that steely gaze. I see nothing that seems helpful. "I know that you have tried to tell me all this before," I say, "but it's such a jump from what I've been led to believe about how the world works that it's unbelievable for me."

He starts to chuckle and says, "Hold on to your hat. You're about to get a real big taste."

"So this town lies in my imagination and everyone there is imaginary?"

"That's about the size of it. And not just that, your whole life is made up by you. Well, not *you*, per se, your subconscious."

"Well," I respond after a period of standing there, staring at him with my mouth gaping, "what would you have me do?"

"I'd have you do nothing at all," he says. "All you can do at this point is get on with it."

"Do you have any advice?" I ask.

"Yes," he answers, "and pay strict attention to this: keep your mouth shut. I know this is particularly difficult for you, but try not to say too much while we are there."

"But I have so many questions that I'd like to ask the people in that town about this place."

He gets up and hunches over the table, bringing his face very close to mine. "No one, and I mean no one, in that town can give you answers—and I mean that." He pulls himself away and stands up. "You seem not to realize that the only one with any answers is *you*." He picks up the saddlebags and begins walking to the door. "I'm going to bring these bags down to the paddock and give them to Emma so she can put them on the horses. While I'm gone, go down into the root cellar and get the last bit of tobacco; I'd like to smoke my pipe on the ride."

"Root cellar?" I had no idea we have a root cellar.

When he reaches the door, Eagle Feather turns back and says, "Walk around behind the ladder that leads up to the loft. In the floor, you'll find a trapdoor. Pull the ring, and the door will open. You'll find a ladder leading down. You should find the last bit of tobacco hanging from the ceiling. Now get going. I'll be back in a bit."

CHAPTER 51

I get up and make my way over to the ladder, the whole time trying to process the idea that my entire life and all that is and was, everyone and everywhere, is just a creation of my mind. I look down on the floor and find the ring. When I pull it up, the floor opens. I look down. The hole is about four feet wide, and there is a ladder that runs down, disappearing into the darkness. I go back over to the fireplace, take an oil light off the mantel, and find some matches in a cabinet. After igniting the lamp, I slowly climb down the ladder into the root cellar.

The oil from the lamp gives me just enough light to see my way down into the room. It is about eight feet by eight feet and ten feet deep. The walls consist of earth that has been shaved down flat, and there really isn't much down here except for a few barrels of unknown contents. I look up at the floorboards of the room above and see one tobacco leaf hanging from a nail that has been banged into a two-by-four. I walk across the earthen floor to the other side and see a small window that is also carved out of earth, though it does have a piece of glass that I guess serves to keep the varmints out.

I grab the one tobacco leaf off the nail and head back over to the ladder. When I get there, I notice, pinned to the wall, a piece of paper. Holding the lantern up to the paper, I see that something is written on it: "Don't forget to bring a strong rope. You'll find one in the barn." At the bottom, as I expect, are the initials RLC. And If I have learned anything in my time here, I should do as these notes says. When I get to the top of the ladder, I find Eagle Feather back in the room. I grab a hold of the ring and drop the trapdoor back into the floor.

"Did you find the tobacco?" he asks.

I'm starting to think that he had an ulterior motive in sending me down there. "I did. Here you go," I say, handing him the tobacco.

He takes it from my hand and puts it up to his nose. "Smells like a good one. I saved the best for last," he comments. My eyes follow him over to the drawer where he grabs his pipe. Breaking up a piece of tobacco from the leaf, he uses his thumb to stuff it into the bowl of the pipe. Then, producing a matchstick from his pocket, he lights it John Wayne style. He looks back at me, and I look at him. He stands there in his hunting coat and fedora, the smoke from his pipe curling up into the air. We stand like this for a while.

I can't help but think that if it wasn't for this man, I wouldn't be here right now. I'd be dead. I have tremendous respect for him. He has all the answers, and yet he prefers that I discover them for myself. Isn't this the mark of any good teacher? I don't know how long we stand there eyeballing each other. I can't help but wonder what he's thinking but whatever it is, he seems to be taking a great deal of pleasure in it—and in smoking that pipe mixture.

The door opens, and Emma walks in. "Why are you all standing around?" she says. "Don't you think we should be on our way?"

"Just sizing up your man," Eagle Feather says with a big smile.

Emma laughs. "So now he's my man?"

"Well, he's certainly not mine," Eagle Feather says, laughing.

"Wait a minute," I chime in. "I'm nobody's man."

They continue laughing, and Eagle Feather jokes, "That's what we were hoping you'd say. We're hoping you have become your own man." Emma starts out the door, and Eagle Feather turns to me and says, "Let's go. It is time."

All three of us head out the door and onto the porch. Emma brought the horses around front and tied them neatly to one of the posts on the porch. Eagle Feather and Emma mount their horses, but I, remembering the note, take off in the direction of the barn.

"Hey, where are you going?" Emma shouts after me.

Without turning back around, I shout, "The note." I run across the grass, past the horse paddock, and into the barn. I open the big front door just wide enough for me to get in. I look around and find, next to the truck and hanging on one of the nails, two ropes. Both are curled in circles. Now to find the "sturdy" rope. I look at both, and the one on the bottom appears to be made of twine. The other one, the top rope, is blue and white and has a snap hook fastened to it. It's much larger than the rope on the bottom. It looks as though it would be used for mountain climbing. As I get closer to the post, I see another piece of paper tacked in between the coils of the top rope. I pull the paper down and read it. This note says, "This one, stupid." Again, I see my initials at the bottom.

I pull the rope down and throw it around my shoulders. Running out of the barn, I push the door closed. I make my way back over to Eagle Feather, Emma, and the horses and, once there, toss the rope over the saddle horn and mount my horse. Eagle Feather remarks that the rope "looks like a good one." He turns to Emma and says, "Which way?" Without a word, she starts off in the direction where we saw the light last night.

CHAPTER 52

We ride in silence for twenty minutes. We reach the bottom of the hill and start upward, winding our way back and forth steadily. When we reach the top of the hill, Emma rides over to the landmarks that we used to mark the direction. She stops in front of the downed tree and points in the proper direction. Eagle Feather and I are following her, and we both reach the top of the hill at the same time and look out in the direction she has indicated. Eagle Feather dismounts his horse and suggests that we get down and have a rest. He takes the canteen that he has strapped to his saddlebag and takes a long drink of water before offering the canteen to me. My mouth is so dry from nervousness and anticipation that I can barely drink. I take a quick pull and hand it to Emma.

"What do you think we're going to find down there?" I say.

Eagle Feather turns around and looks at me. "I don't know. You tell me. All I know is that we need to find this town."

We continue looking in the direction that Emma has indicated. Eagle Feather estimates the town to be about ten miles from where we stand. "We'll take our time and get ourselves safely down into the valley, and hopefully we will begin to see the lights just after dusk. That being said, we should arrive there just as it appears, and we'll have plenty of time to get our supplies and get the hell out of there."

I'm still kind of puzzled by this. Obviously, there's some kind of danger in this town. There's something they're not telling me. And it seems the longer we stay in the town, the better chance there is for something to go wrong. I doubt either of them will answer my question, but I ask it anyway: "What are you both so afraid of?"

"I already told you there are no answers down there. And the less you say, the better off you will be." After Eagle Feather says this, he mutters something about them not liking Indians. I think this last fact won't make any difference to me; I'm not an Indian. As though Eagle Feather has read my thoughts, he asks, "Have you looked at yourself in the mirror lately?" I shoot him a look. I actually haven't seen a mirror in quite some time, and the last time I did, I didn't believe what I saw. "Well, it's too late now," Eagle Feather says.

"For what?"

"To take those feathers out of your hair," he replies.

I reach up with both hands and feel the feathers that Emma tied into my hair. I got so used to them that I forgot they were there; they've become a part of me.

"You sure look like an Indian to me," Emma says, laughing.

"Oh god," I say. "Anybody got a knife? I need to cut these feathers out of my hair."

"We're not cutting any feathers out of anybody's hair today," Eagle Feather says in a booming voice. "You worked hard for them, and they were a gift. Wear them with pride." He shifts gears after a brief pause. "Okay, let's mount up and get down off this hill and into the valley. We need to be there at the right time, just as the town appears. No dillydallying."

I get back up on my horse, and I'm not feeling too good about this whole thing. I haven't really thought of myself as an Indian, Eagle Feather tells me they don't like Indians in this town, and with these feathers tied into my hair, I'm going to be hard-pressed to convince anyone that I'm not one. As we ride down the hill, Eagle Feather again reads my thoughts. "You're dressed for the part, so you might as well play it. Oh yeah, and by the way, this is the part that you picked; play the role with impeccability."

The face of the hill is quite steep. Eagle Feather rides on ahead, with Emma and me following closely behind. The hill is so steep, in fact, that we have to weave our way down between boulders and small shrubs. Small pebbles, rocks, and all sorts of bric-a-brac slide down under our horses' feet. The decline forces me to lean back while riding, a technique I learned from Emma, which is very uncomfortable for me as a novice rider. Riding up the hill, I had to do the opposite. But the ride down is far worse; I have the constant feeling that I'll fall head-over-heels forward, with the horse toppling over me. Also, Emma encouraged me to just allow the horse to find her way down, but I, ever the control freak, have the idea that I also have to steer. So, while trying to lean back as far as I can, I am also making efforts to move the reins left and right. It's very uncomfortable. Fortunately for me, Sweetheart knows where we need to go. Emma turns around and tells me to the give the horse her head. In horse lingo, this means that I'm to stop steering her and let her go where she wants to go.

"How the hell am I supposed to do that?" I yell.

"Stop pulling back on the reins. Just loosen up," she replies.

I do as I'm told. Sweetheart realizes that I'm not trying to fight her anymore, and we both make our way downhill without any problems. Once we reach the bottom, I turn around and look back up. I come to the realization that if I had to try and walk down the hill without the horse, it would have taken me a long time and would been awfully treacherous. I probably would have even needed that rope.

As I've mentioned, most of the horses I have been on in my lifetime—which is not that many, mind you—have done their best to get rid of me. They never seem too comfortable with the fact that I'm sitting on their back. Couple this with the fact that I'm a lousy rider, and I usually wind up on the ground.

As I'm reflecting on this, I have a memory of my father, my brother, and myself on horseback at a place that I loved to go as a child: Frontier Town. It was in Upstate New York and about an hour's trip from where we lived. It was set up as a town that you would find in the Wild West. A long dirt road ran straight through the town and was flanked by several buildings, the kind you would expect to see in the Wild West. There was a saloon, a blacksmith, a livery stable, a general store, a Wild Western inn, a telegraph office, and even a sheriff's building complete with a jail. There were several other buildings, and the road ended at a white church with a tall steeple. On both sides of the road, both up and down, horses were hitched to posts. A stagecoach made its way into and out of the town every half hour or so. The workers—probably out-of-work actors—were all dressed in the familiar cowboy garb. There was a sheriff, shopkeepers, blacksmiths, and the like. They would stage shootouts between the outlaws and the sheriff and his deputies. Every afternoon, the Indians would raid the town. All these little performances were put on to entertain the people that came out to Frontier Town for an afternoon, to make them feel as though they were actually living in the Wild West.

I was somewhere between the ages of eight and ten at the time, and my brother was younger than that. Every year, we would beg our parents to take us to Frontier Town, and when they would finally give in, we would insist that they buy us cowboy hats and six-shooters so we could participate in the action. After the Indian raid was put down, as it always invariably was, my father, my brother, and I would go down to the stable for horseback rides. My father always told us that he could ride a horse, and he did look pretty good up there. My brother was at that young age where he was fearless, and he too got along pretty well on horseback. But this wasn't the case with me; I was afraid of falling off the animal from the get-go. Nevertheless, I still always tried to ride them. You can't be John Wayne if you can't ride a horse.

But somewhere along the way, I would always fall off the horse. This would upset my mother, who would not ride and preferred to watch from a bench. She'd run over and pick me up off the ground while I cried my eyes out and my brother giggled from his saddle. My mother would tell everyone around that this was it for me as far as horseback riding went. My dad, on the other hand, was old-school, and he would get down off his horse, brush me off, and send my mother back over to her bench. He would spend five minutes trying to talk me back onto the horse. I remember complaining—in the midst of crying, of course—and the horse would keep walking along. I'd never really fall off in any dramatic fashion, and I was still at the age where I was accustomed to falling anyway. My father would offer encouragement like, "You can't learn to ride a horse if you're not on top," and the now clichéd "If you fall off, get back on." After a few minutes of fussing, crying, and pouting, I would get back on the horse, still whimpering, and finish the ride. After that, I would feel pretty good about myself, and it was time for ice cream and time to bid goodbye to Frontier Town for another year.

One of these times—I'll never forget it—was my father's turn to fall off his horse. I don't know exactly what happened, and it's a point of contention to this day. My father, who claimed to be an accomplished rider and was every bit the cowboy in his own right, suggested that a horsefly bite had caused his horse to buck wildly, and although he stuck on as long as any real-life bronco-buster, he ultimately found himself tossed off. At least this is his account. I don't remember it that way. My recollection is that the horse in question went left, and my father went right, and the result was him falling on top of his new cowboy hat.

My brother and I were hysterical, but it was nothing compared to my mother's reaction; I don't think she ever laughed so hard before or again. I jumped down off my horse and ran over to my father. I brushed him off, as he had done so many times for me, and with a twinkle in my eye, I said, "If you fall off, get back on." His reply was a simple "Shut up," and to his credit, he was back on the horse in no time. That, my friends, marked our last-ever trip to Frontier Town.

CHAPTER 53

The land now falls away into the valley in a much gentler fashion. The trees and brush open a bit, and the sparser vegetation, in addition to the more gradual decline, makes the riding much easier. We still move along slowly and ride single file for some time. Occasionally, Emma, riding directly in front of me, peeks behind to make sure I'm okay.

Although I appear calm and collected on the outside, I'm a mess on the inside. Eagle Feather's demeanor is not helping the situation any. Although I can only see the back of him, he keeps looking from side to side as if he's expecting an ambush any minute. And the fact that he hasn't spoken to me in a while is also unnerving. This is just the kind of situation I don't like to find myself in; I suspect it's the kind of situation that nobody likes to find themselves in. I have no idea where we're going and what we'll find when we get there. I've never really been a good traveler. This is basically torture.

After riding for some time, we come to a riverbank. The river doesn't appear very wide across, maybe fifty yards, and only seems to be—from where I'm standing anyway—to be no more than two or three feet deep. Eagle Feather walks his horse back and forth along the bank, looking out at the river as he does so. He goes downstream about twenty yards and then back past us and up another twenty. For the first time in a long time, he speaks. "This looks like a good place to cross. I think we can just go off here. It doesn't appear to be that deep. Then he looks at me, adding, "Besides, horses can swim."

I don't like the sound of that at all. "What do you mean they can swim?"

He starts to laugh as he makes his way out to the river. He calls out, "If it gets too deep, the horses will swim to the other side. Just hold on." I look at Emma, and she looks back at me and smiles. "Okay, let's go!" Eagle Feather yells.

"Hold on," I say. "Emma, I appreciate you taking all the time to teach me how to ride and all, but I just don't know if I'm up for this."

"Just hold on, silly," she replies, "and let the horse do the rest." With that, she's off.

I stay on the bank for a minute, watching them. It appears that the water isn't so deep. I grab a hold of the saddle horn and hold on tight. I give Sweetheart a little kick, and off we go. When we get about two-thirds of the way across, I look and see four heads protruding from the water. Two belong to the horses, while the other two belong to Emma and Eagle Feather. I don't know exactly what to do. If we stop in the middle of the river, I have no idea how to get out of there. To my amazement, the next thing I know, Sweetheart begins to swim. Even more amazing, I'm still on top of her. I hold on for dear life, and we continue to move forward without issue. It's actually quite nice, Sweetheart swimming along, both of us buoyed by the water. I look ahead and see Eagle Feather and Emma come out of the river, still on their horses. Before I know it, I feel Sweetheart's hooves touch solid ground, and we rise up out of the water and join Emma and Eagle Feather on the bank.

Emma and Eagle Feather are both looking at me. "That was great!" I exclaim. They both start to laugh. "I came across that river like John Wayne."

Eagle Feather pulls his pipe from his mouth and says, "The horse came across the river like John Wayne. You had very little to do with it."

"Hey," I say, "I didn't drown."

"No," he says, "you didn't, thanks to that horse." He moves up the bank and onto a flat plateau about ten or twelve feet above the river. Here he dismounts. "We'll have lunch here," he says, tying up his horse. Emma and I do the same.

Emma goes into her saddlebag and produces hard-boiled eggs and three cans of beans. "This looks very familiar to me," I say. "Who packed this lunch?"

"Why?" Emma responds. "I did."

"You have anything to do with packing my backpack? You know, the one I had when I first arrived in the clearing?" She just smiles.

Emma goes back into the saddlebag and takes a blanket out. She spreads out some of the loose dirt in the clearing and opens the blanket. We all sit in a circle to eat our meal. Eagle Feather still doesn't seem comfortable. He keeps looking around in all directions, and I find this behavior peculiar. I take one look at the beans and get up to gather some sticks to make a fire, since it appears that no one else is going to take the initiative. Eagle Feather watches as I move around the clearing, picking up small sticks. "Where should I make the fire?" I ask, apparently too loudly.

My question is met with a resounding "Shush!" from both of my companions. Eagle Feather goes on to say, "Keep your voice down! We're not making any fires."

"No fire? Those beans taste a lot better when they're warmed up—believe me," I say.

"No fire. Cold beans," Eagle Feather snaps back at me.

"Cold beans? But it'll only take me a few minutes to build a fire and warm them up. You guys know I have some experience with this. And another thing. Why are you looking around so much? Are you expecting company?"

"Stop talking so loudly!" he snaps again in a loud whisper. "I told you—no fires. Now open the beans. We eat them cold."

I throw the bundle of sticks I've been cradling to the ground. It makes quite a racket, and Eagle Feather glares at me.

"What?"

"Sit down!" he commands. "Stop making all that noise and moving all about."

I don't immediately sit and observe him as he continues to make roving eye movements and turn his head sharply at each crackling twig and whisper of breeze in the forest. Finally, I can't take it anymore. "What are you looking for? You know there's no one else here except for you, me, and Emma."

"Oh, is that what you think?" he says. "Sit down, and we'll have a talk … quietly."

I sit down and take my knife out to open a can of beans. "Will you please tell me what the hell this is all about?" I ask. "You're acting very strange. What exactly are you looking for? What do you expect to see out there?"

He turns toward me and says, "Indians."

My jaw drops. "Indians!"

"Be quiet," he says. "Can't you keep your mouth shut? If you feel you must talk, do so in a low voice."

I'm becoming a bit agitated, both from Eagle Feather's reprimanding me like a child and from this newfound knowledge that there are Indians lurking. "I thought there was no one else here except for you, me, Emma, and these townsfolk—that is, the night that the town shows up."

"I'm looking out for Indians," he says again.

"Indians. What sort of Indians?"

"Hostile Indians."

I look over at Emma, who has been silent during this entire exchange. "Are there are hostile Indians out here, or is he just pulling my leg?"

She looks up at me from her hard-boiled egg. "No, I'm afraid he's not pulling your leg. There are Indians out here all right."

I drop the can of beans I'm holding and look at her in amazement. "You mean to tell me that there have been Indians out here all along?"

"Oh no, not all along. Only here, around the village, and only around the time the village appears," she says.

"Really?" I look back at Eagle Feather. He is continuing to eat his cold beans and scanning the clearing from side to side. "Well, you're an Indian," I say to him. "What are you worried about?"

"They are not of my lineage or even my tribe," he answers. "They are different from me."

"What kind of Indians are they?" I ask. This subject has piqued my curiosity.

"They are Algonquin. My ancestors and their ancestors have been feuding with one another for generations."

"And you're Iroquois, right?" I ask.

"It doesn't matter what I am!" he snaps. "All you need to know is that we do not get along. And let me tell you something else: if they are not of my lineage, then they are not of your lineage either."

"What are you trying to say?" Is Eagle Feather insinuating that I am somehow related to him?

"Maybe it's time we get down to what is going on around here before you get yourself scalped. You and Emma are both of my lineage, whether you like it or not. You were once an Indian, and you are now an Indian again. Do you think it is all happenstance that you were born where you were born and live in the place you call home? The place you call Croton? You have existed there in spirit and have played out your life experiences at different times in the evolution of the world and the human race. You, like everyone else on this planet, have a spiritual home; it is a home in which you have lived many lifetimes. You see, you were once an Indian living in Croton and have spent many lifetimes there in various incarnations. You lived in that same Croton as a person in the 1700s, again in the 1800s, and now you are in this incarnation in the twentieth century. It is not happenstance that you keep recurring in the same location. It happens by infinite design.

"We see people travel great distances and then make a home in a place that seems to speak to them. They are traveling to find the geographical spot in which they are supposed to be. They come into this world through the only gateway they can find. If it is not the correct spot, they move. Once they find the particular area where they have spent their past lives—their spiritual home—they settle down. You see, you have been here throughout infinity and will continue to be here indefinitely."

"Hold on a minute," I say. "If that's true, why do we recur in the same place?"

"Because that is where all your lessons are and everything that you need to evolve as the human race evolves."

"So, why then have I, in my current incarnation, evolved to relive this Indian life?"

"That's a good question," he replies. "All of what you are and all of what you have been is still contained in your being. It's all still there. And, as your Einstein once said, all time happens at once. Your mind has chosen to show you this wonderful aspect of evolution, so you have jumped back in what you call time to find yourself here again, perhaps to remember who you are and where you came from."

"Oh no—my ancestors came from Italy. And I really don't think I was ever an Indian."

"Well, you certainly don't act like an Indian," Eagle Feather says and begins to laugh. His demeanor has shifted and become more playful. "As far as those people coming from Italy, it was their time to reincarnate, and the portal through which they did so was through Italy. Perhaps, for whatever reasons in the universe, Italy was the only portal open to them at the time. But as I said, as far as you are concerned, it is no coincidence that you have found your way back to Croton, back to your spiritual center."

"So, Eagle Feather, we have been together before?"

"Closer than you think," he says.

Just at this moment, we hear a twig snap somewhere way off in the brush. Eagle Feather quickly turns his head in the direction of the sound. He gets up slowly and turns toward us, saying slowly and quietly, "Get up off the ground, pick up the blanket, and pack what's left of the lunch in the saddlebags. We are walking out of here real … slowly."

Eagle Feather goes over to his horse, unties him, and starts walking off in the direction of where we all believe the town will be located. Emma and I follow suit. We walk for some time in an erratic fashion. We start out going several yards to our left and then turn and go several yards back to our right, always proceeding in the same general direction. Eagle Feather continues to look back over his shoulder and to his left and right. I catch up with Emma, who is just ahead of me, and ask her why we are walking in such a bizarre manner. "Don't talk so loudly," she says. "Eagle feather thinks the Indians are following us, and he's trying to make it difficult for them to stay on our trail."

Upon hearing this, I decide to go up and talk to Eagle Feather. I'm beginning to be generally concerned. And god knows I upset easily. I walk a bit faster to catch up with him and stop when we're walking side by side. "That twig that snapped came from the other side of the river. I think they've been trailing us since we left the cabin," he says. He takes off his coat and drapes it over the saddle of his horse.

He quickly turns back around and looks over his shoulder. I look at him and notice two Colt forty-five revolvers tucked at his sides in a sash that he wears like a belt. Stuck in another sash that hangs from his back, I spy a tomahawk. The sight of the Colts sends a chill down my spine.

"What's with all the hardware?" I ask him. He continues to walk without responding to my question. I have not known Eagle Feather to carry any sidearm, nor have I ever seen him with a tomahawk. The only firearm I've ever seen him with is the shotgun that he draped over his arm when he went hunting. I press him again. "What are you doing with those pistols and the tomahawk?"

"Will you be quiet?" he says angrily. "Shut your mouth. I don't have to explain myself to you or anyone."

We walk for a while in silence, still zigging and zagging through the brush. Finally, Eagle Feather turns toward me and stares at me with his piercing blue eyes. "If those Indians catch up to us, you will be awfully glad I have these pistols and tomahawk." He starts off walking again, and I stand dumbfounded. I didn't consider the fact that we might have to fight other Indians or anyone else for that matter. As my fear begins to mount, I hurry to catch up. I glance over my shoulder at Emma and observe her walking along calmly.

I clear my throat and say, in a very authoritative voice, "Don't you think I should be carrying a gun also?" Eagle Feather looks over at me and squints. He walks on. Again, I plead my case. "No, really, Eagle Feather. Where's my Colt?"

He chuckles at my request and says in a voice that is both low and emphatic, "No."

I begin to protest. "I'm handy with a gun, and I could be useful if we find ourselves in a fight."

This brings a big smile to his face. Without turning sideways to look at me, he says, "There's a big difference between knowing your way around a firearm when you're out in the woods shooting at pheasant and when you have people shooting at you." He takes a quick look at me and says, "Pheasant don't shoot back."

This all seems ridiculous to me. I try to defend my position. "I've fired forty-fives before."

"What, at paper targets?"

"Yeah, and I'm pretty good too from fifty yards out," I boast.

"Those paper targets hardly ever shoot back. You'd probably wind up shooting yourself in the foot—or, even worse, shooting me in the foot—if you actually had to return fire." Then, changing the subject, he says, "Okay, mount up." He slings his right leg up over his horse, and Emma and I do the same.

As we ride along, I think about all the new things that have been thrown into the mix. There's the conversation about being an Indian and all that stuff about a spiritual home and living in the same place where recurrences happen over and over again. And how people travel the world over to find this place. And now I've got hostile Indians.

As I ride along on Sweetheart, I try to sort everything out, as I have been doing since I first arrived in this strange place, and I feel as though I have found few or no answers. At this point, all the I's return. I thought I successfully got rid of them, but, like Eagle Feather said, they never disappear completely.

First, I hear Wise Guy I. "This guy is going to get you killed out here in the woods with all these Indians hot on your trail. Lose your scalp for sure."

Analytical I sounds a little befuddled. "What's with all this business about being an Indian in your past recurrences and always living in the same location?"

Ego I is offended by Eagle Feather's suggestion that I'd shoot myself in the foot and reassures me that I'm a good shot, even with weapons much larger than those forty-fives.

Then Paranoid I, the one I seem to listen to all the time, puts his two cents in. "You're out here in the woods with a bunch of crazy people and hostile Indians that are trying to kill you. You should just get the hell out of here. Just turn that horse in any direction and ride like hell. Get out of here as fast as you can."

I shake my head. "I don't have time for this, and I'm not listening to you guys anymore. Nope. Not listening. Leave me alone."

"Okay," Wise Guy I says. "Have it your way. You'll get your's soon enough."

I kick my horse so that she speeds up, and I move up alongside Emma. I'm hoping that if I engage her in conversation, it might quiet my mind and free me from the nonsense that I'm listening to. "Emma," I say, and she turns to me and suggests I speak in a low voice. "How do we know exactly where this town is? I mean, we could have passed it by now. You know, even though we saw the lights from the top of the hill, it's pretty hard to judge distances at night, especially when you've just got a few lights off in the distance to go on. For all we know, those lights could have been fifty miles away."

"Have a little faith in Eagle Feather," she says. "He's an accomplished tracker, and he knows what he's doing. He'll find that town; you can bet your life on it."

I look at her with concern. "That's what I'm afraid of."

She smiles and looks over at me. "How about a drink. Looks like you could use one." She reaches behind her and pulls the canteen off the saddlebag, unscrews the top, and hands it to me. I take a long, slow drink and feel the cool water refresh me; somehow, I manage to put the canteen down. I hand it back to Emma, and she screws the top back on and returns it to her saddlebag.

Just then, Eagle Feather kicks his horse into a trot, and Emma and I, seeing this, do the same. We are moving along at a pretty good clip; the land is quite open, as it is only dotted by some small brush and trees. I can see the river on my right-hand side. Eagle Feather, just in front of me, bobs up and down on his horse. We ride on like this for some time.

I realize that we have come a long way down into the valley. Eagle Feather rides into a clearing on the side of the incline, and we have a pretty good view of the rest of the valley as it stretches out before us. We can see the river running along on our side and widening as it makes its way into the middle of the valley. The spot that Eagle Feather has chosen to stop has two large trees with boulders between. All in all, there are four large boulders that appear to have rolled down the hillside; two of them sit so they block any view from the hill.

Eagle Feather dismounts and ties his horse to a smaller tree just to the left of the rock formations. He signals for us to do the same. He then makes his way into the space between the two boulders I just mentioned. I get off my horse along with Emma, and we follow Eagle Feather, finding him seated on a smaller rock. The boulders and trees in front of us and the two large boulders behind us form a clearing that is about forty square yards.

Eagle Feather speaks quietly. "This is a very good place for us to wait until dark. We're sheltered and protected from the front and back. Should anything happen, we can make a stand here. It will be getting dark soon, and from this vantage point, we should be able to spot the lights that you both saw last night."

"Are we close?" I ask.

"No way of really knowing," Eagle Feather answers. "We may just be right on top of it."

I notice that he has finally ceased his nervous head movements. He sits quietly with his back up against the rock and his pipe in his mouth. There is no smoke coming from the pipe. Emma sits across from him with her back up against one of the boulders that lies between the trees. I sit on Eagle Feather's left with my back up against the rock adjacent to them. It is late in the afternoon, and golden light from the sinking sun effuses through the trees leaves.

I may look a bit like Eagle Feather did on his journey; I keep looking back and forth between Eagle Feather and Emma, waiting for one of them to say something. We sit in our respective spots for some time in silence. Finally, in a low voice, Eagle Feather says, "Why don't we have a little something to eat. It's going to be a long night." He motions for Emma to go over to the horses and get what little food we have left. She makes her way over deliberately, returning with some food and a blanket. She spreads the blanket out and puts down a few hard-boiled eggs and some jerky. We all take a piece of jerky and an egg to have what appears to be our meager dinner. Again, we sit silently. The jerky is so salty that it forces me to go over to the horses and grab the canteen. Seeing me do this, Eagle Feather instructs me to walk slowly and keep my head down. I do as he says, return with the canteen, and take a sip. I pass it to Emma, who, in turn, passes it to Eagle Feather.

The light is fading fast, and Eagle Feather wipes his mouth after a long sip. "It's time we have a little chat," he says.

"Great," I say. "The silence is killing me."

"I think I misrepresented myself. We're not really going to chat. I'm going to talk, and you're going to listen. Now pay strict attention to what I have to say because, I kid you not, your life may depend on it." I can tell that he's talking exclusively to me, and the graveness of his words gets my attention. "Every event, every happening in this life we call reality comes from our minds. Look around," he says, making a sweeping gesture with his arms. "Everything you see here and everything you have seen in your life is born in thought. These trees, the boulders and rocks, and the birds flying in the sky, even Emma and I, are products of your thoughts. For example, the cabin was a thought you had before it appeared in reality. Do you understand?" I nod even though I'm still kind of confused. "About everything that's going to happen this evening is going to be a product of your thoughts."

I stop him right there. "Let me get this straight: you're telling me that I thought up both you and Emma."

"Yes," he says most emphatically, "that's correct, and what's more, this whole place, everything you see around you and everything that has happened here, every event that you have endured since you arrived here has been a product of your thoughts."

I lean over and pull Emma toward me. She giggles. "You seem pretty real to me," I say. "I thought this was all just a bad dream." Emma giggles again.

"It's no dream," Eagle Feather says. "It's as real as you sitting here right now. Your mind is the most powerful thing in the universe. Everything and everyone is connected, it is true, but you are the creator of your own reality. The Indians have known this since the beginning of time. Most men, though, have lost their way and try to rely on their senses to tell them what is real and what is not. Whatever you think and whatever emotions you feel couple together, and as this continues to happen over time, reality is formed. I'm telling you this now because everything that goes on in this town is going to be coming from you: your mind, your thoughts, and your emotions. I want you to be aware of this because this knowledge will be the most powerful weapon you have this evening, more powerful even than my revolvers or my tomahawk."

"Well, thanks, Eagle Feather. I need all the help I can get. Wait a minute, wait a minute. We've been through this before. Tell me right now. Have we been through this before?"

Eagle Feather leans over closer to me so that his nose is touching my head. "Many times have we been on this journey. And many times have you awakened in the clearing."

I pull back away from him, reeling from the profundity of

his words. "So if this has happened before, then tell me what the outcome is now." Eagle Feather does not speak. "He's not going to tell me anything. Please tell me," I beg Emma. She looks back at me, devoid of any expression. "If you don't tell me, I'm doomed. I'm going to repeat what has happened over and over again for eternity. Don't just sit there. Help me out."

Eagle Feather puts up his finger. "There is something you can do," he says. "You don't have to keep going around and around and over this ground over and over again. Every recurrence is another opportunity. It is another chance for a different outcome. But there is something that you need to do in order for a different outcome."

"And what is that?"

"In the moment in which all is occurring, remember yourself."

PART III

CHAPTER 54

The light is dissipating quickly. We sit in silence, waiting for darkness to descend upon us. Eagle Feather's words lead me to go through all the progressions of remembering myself. I mean, he said something about life or death, so I'm really concentrating. I remember my aim: to get to the town and procure supplies. I visualize where I am in the moment: sitting with my back up against the rock. I scan the area with my eyes and notice the trees, which are now merely shimmering branches etched into a bright, blue-gray sky, backlit by a sunken sun. I see Eagle Feather sitting on the rock. I see the slowly swaying heads of the horses. I see Emma. While I'm going over this all in my mind, I feel in the moment. Still, I'm not having any visions of what is about to occur.

Eagle Feather tells us that he is going out on foot to reconnoiter. I take this to mean that he is going to scout around. He says that he will be back shortly and tells us that we shouldn't move around much or make a lot of noise. I open my mouth to speak, but he quickly clasps his hand over it and chastises me with a stare. "Speak softly," he says.

"Where are you going?" I ask in a whisper that is hardly audible.

He looks at me as if I am being ridiculous. "To find the town," he whispers back.

"Isn't the town just going to light up? Why not just stay here and wait for the lights?" I'm half-arguing. I know he's going regardless of what I say. But I don't want him to leave. I know the Indians are still out there, and he's the one with the guns.

"The town could be hidden by trees or a small hill. There is no way of knowing. I'll make a sweep of the area and come right back. Is that all right with you?" he says.

In the waning light, I spot his eyes. I imagine the woodpecker, the one I heard when I first arrived here, has eyes just like that. "Don't worry," he says. "Emma will take care of you."

Eagle Feather starts to make his way out of the rock formation. He stops and turns to me. "At some point in this, you're going to have to be a warrior. Don't let it take too long. It could be your ass— or mine." I watch as dark forest swallows him whole.

My mind flashes back to when I was a kid. I remember watching the *Lone Ranger*. I move toward Emma and sit down next to her. "This reminds me of a show I used to watch on TV as a kid," I say.

"How so?"

"I used to watch this show called the *Lone Ranger*. The Lone Ranger was a law man who wore a mask to hide his identity and had an Indian sidekick named Tonto. They roamed around the West fighting injustice and a particular bad guy named Butch Cavendish. In these episodes, the Lone Ranger always sent Tonto into town to find information. Tonto would then get caught by the bad guys, and the Lone Ranger would have to come and rescue him."

"What are you trying to say?"

"I'm just saying it seems awful familiar to me: we sent Eagle Feather, an Indian, into town …"

"We didn't *send* him into town. He told us he was going. He's not your sidekick. And besides, he's a great warrior. He'll be fine."

"I suppose you're right. At least I hope so …"

"Don't talk so much. And for god's sake, don't worry so much."

Emma and I sit in the darkness in silence. It's amazing how quickly it becomes dark. And astonishing how quickly it becomes silent. I try again to engage her in conversation, but she just shushes me and tells me to keep my ears open. I remember the Indians that Eagle Feather said were on our trail since we left the cabin. I sit there for what seems like an eternity, straining to hear any minute sound that might signal their presence.

Just then, without making a sound, the shadow of a man slides through the opening of the rocks and stands in front of Emma and me. I gasp at the sight of him, but as I look up and my eyes adjust to the light, I see Eagle Feather standing there in front of us. He squats down and says, "I've located the town. It's about a mile and a half from here on the other side of the ridge that runs along our right. We can't see the lights from here, but it's there nonetheless."

I stand up, but Eagle Feather grabs my sleeve and yanks me back down to the ground. I'm surprised by how fast he executes this maneuver. "Let's get going," I say.

"Be patient," he says in such a low voice that I can hardly hear him. "We are going to move toward the town slowly and cautiously." I can't help but think he's being melodramatic about all this. But these thoughts are displaced by my realization that he knows more about this than I do and that, in fact, it is probably best to proceed cautiously.

From his crouched position, Eagle Feather moves back over and sits down on the same rock he was sitting on before he left. I find it odd that he did not stand up. "What did you see out there? What does this town look like?" He puts his finger up to his mouth, signaling for me to be quiet; I take this to mean that I'll find out soon enough. "Did you see anything else?" I ask.

"The Indians. There are about twelve of them, and they have moved out toward our left and are making their way toward the town. We'll give them a wide birth when we leave. Sit quiet for a while, and then we will make our move."

As I sit there, I am overcome by strange feelings of anxiety and apprehension. I lean over to Emma and whisper, "I'm having déjà vu."

"That's because we've all done this before," she whispers back.

"Well, if that's the case, how come I'm not seeing any visions like before?"

She tells me that I don't have enough personal power to summon up those visions at any given time and that they will come to me sooner or later. Despite her reassuring me, my mind is still not put at ease.

Suddenly, Eagle Feather stands up and quietly motions for us to do the same. "It's time. Let's get going." As we begin to untie the horses, he says, "We are going to walk with the horses single file. Stay behind me, and when I stop, you stop." He starts to move off in the town's direction.

The valley is steeped in darkness and silence. We walk so slowly that the usually heavy pitter-patter of the horses' hooves sounds like light raindrops. Eagle Feather, Emma, and I weave single file through shadows cast by the trees and brush. As we come around the ridge, I finally see the lights of the town casting a bright halo on the dark sky.

Eagle Feather stops abruptly and motions for us to come up beside him. "There it is," he says. "We are going to ride around the right side behind the buildings and stay just past the tree line in order to avoid those Indians on the left side." He pauses briefly, just long enough to take a deep breath. "Okay, let's go. Mount up now and stay behind me. Single file."

As I ride forward on top of Sweetheart, the lights from the buildings become increasingly bright. We ride deliberately, and when we make it to the back of a row of buildings, I can see that the street is illuminated with gas lanterns, the kind that someone would have to go around and light up from the outside. When we reach the last building, Eagle Feather hops off his horse and gestures for us to do the same. "Well, there it is," he says.

I poke my head around the building and look down the street. It all looks so familiar to me. Light from the gas lanterns illuminates the entire street. I can see a white church at the end of the town, followed by a blacksmith shop and, on the other side of the street, the general store, several other small shops, a saloon, and what looks like a jailhouse. Lining the street, in front of all the little shops, are hitching posts.

Suddenly, like a smack in the face, it comes to me. This is Frontier Town. I shake my head; I can't believe it. I close my eyes and open them again, almost expecting to see something else. But when I reopen them, just to confirm what I'm seeing, I notice a sign that reads, "Welcome to Frontier Town." I turn and look at Eagle Feather and Emma. Both are wearing ridiculous smiles. "It's Frontier Town!" I blurt out.

Eagle Feather's smile breaks into hardy, though quiet, laughter. "It appears that, for the first time since you've arrived here, you know where you are."

CHAPTER 55

I poke my head back around the building and look down the street. All the buildings are just as I remember them, hatched from the time capsule of my mind. All those fond childhood memories come flooding back. "This is that Old West town where I used to fall off the horse all the time."

Eagle Feather's eyes shine. "Yes, we know. You've told us that many times before."

I look back down the street, and the town seems to come to life. People dressed in cowboy outfits move up and down the street, going about their business just as they did during all my past visits. "See those people? The ones in cowboy clothes. They're all just actors," I explain.

"Yes, we're all actors, actors in this ridiculous play that you have cast us in," Eagle Feather says sardonically. He reaches down and pulls Emma and me back around behind the building. "Okay, get on your horses. We're going to go down to the other end of the street where the general store is and get our much-needed supplies. Then we're going to get the hell out of here."

"But, Eagle Feather," I protest, "maybe these people can tell us where we are. Maybe they can help us."

"What makes you think," Eagle Feather says forcefully, "that in this town—a town you thought up, mind you—that those people out there know anything you don't already know or can help you any more than you can help yourself. I told you on our way here that the best thing you can do is keep your mouth shut."

We ride out from behind the building and down the street very casually. The townspeople seem to pay no attention to us. We pass the jailhouse, the saloon, and other little shops until we reach the end of the road and the general store. We dismount and tie our horses to the hitching posts out in front of the shop. Glancing across the street, I recognize the bench in front of the stable where my mother used to sit during those childhood horseback rides with my father and brother.

"This is very strange," I say to Emma.

"If you think this is strange, just wait until later tonight," she replies.

All the shops have big wooden porches that run the entire length of each building. The general store has two gigantic windows on either side of the front door. Two cowboys sit on a bench on the porch just next to the door of the general store, one tall and one short. As we walk up onto the porch, Eagle Feather tips his hat to them, and both nod back in acknowledgment.

Inside the shop, the floorboards are made of big wooden planks that squeak and groan when we walk on them. The shop is very large and crammed with all sorts of paraphernalia, pretty much everything that you might need out on the frontier. Kerosene lanterns dangle from the ceiling and are flanked by wicker baskets and iron bear traps. The walls are lined with picks, shovels, and assorted canned goods. I spy a case full of Winchester rifles, shotguns, and Colt .45 revolvers. I notice the now infamous Boston baked beans that I have been surviving on since my arrival. In addition to all these typical Wild Western items, I notice a number of things that seem out of place: plastic bottles with dishwashing liquid, bags of dog food, flashlights, even batteries. Above the counter, hanging on the wall, is a stuffed bear head and several deer heads complete with antlers. There are also the toy six-shooters and the cowboy hats that my brother and I had to have during every visit to Frontier Town.

Eagle Feather turns to me. "Should I buy you a hat and six-shooter?" he asks before he and Emma break out into laughter.

I thank them for the offer and decline. Pointing to the stuffed bear head mounted on the wall, I say, "I thought you said there aren't any bears around here."

Before Eagle Feather can defend himself, the clerk turns quickly and says, "That's the last bear anyone's seen in these woods. Shot almost forty years ago."

"Oh yeah? I don't think that was the last bear."

"Oh, no," the shopkeeper says. "I can assure you it was."

I look at Eagle Feather and Emma. "Then what was that chasing me through the woods just a short while ago?" Eagle Feather laughs his face off while Emma struggles to hold the laughter back.

"Can I help you with anything?" asks the shopkeeper. He's wearing blue jeans and a blue shirt with a black bowtie. He has a visor on his head and garter belts holding up his sleeves. There is something familiar about him. "Can I help you with anything?" he repeats.

Eagle Feather produces a folded piece of paper. "I have some items here that I'd like to purchase," he says as he unfolds the paper.

"That'll be fine," says the shopkeeper, and Eagle Feather hands him the list. "Let's see now ... I think we have all of these items in stock. The shopkeeper then proceeds to ask Eagle Feather a tremendous amount of questions about every item on the list. "Shotguns shells ... Remington or would the dynamics do better? And what gauge, twelve or twenty? Because, you know, if you're using these for birds, then twenty ought to be plenty. But for anything else, you might want twelve. What type of beans would you care for? We have quite a selection. Now the original Boston baked variety happen to be a little bit more expensive but open easy and cook real fast. How are you cooking them, open fire or a hot stove? What type of dog food would you care for? We have several different brands ... all depends on the type of dogs you got."

Eagle Feather patiently addresses all of the shopkeeper's questions, though I'm confident he could have easily walked around the store and found everything he needs without the inquisition.

As the shopkeeper and Eagle Feather work their way through the list, a tremendous ruckus erupts outside: war whoops, people screaming, gunfire. The two cowboys that were sitting on the bench burst through the front door. "Indian raid!" they yell as they turn around and take position on either side of the doorway. They draw their six-shooters and begin to fire out of the open door, ducking inside for cover after a few shots. Instinctively, I drop down and crawl to the window with Emma following. The shop clerk yells for us to get down as he slumps behind the counter. Emma and I take cover behind a couple of wine barrels that are up against the window. I can hear the unmistakable sound of horses galloping up and down the street, and I muster up enough courage to poke my head up above the wine barrels and peer out the window.

Indians are firing bow and arrows from atop their horses, which move up and down the street at blazing speed. I see the townspeople scurrying to take cover and returning fire with their colt .45s and Winchesters. The shorter cowboy turns to me and tells me to keep my head down before it gets shot off. I take his advice and scan the shop trying to find Eagle Feather. To my astonishment, Eagle Feather is carrying about his business, browsing the store as if nothing out of the ordinary is occurring. He walks around picking items up off the shelves and examining them as if he is oblivious to the melee that is going on just outside the door. I yell at him to take cover, but he merely laughs and tells *me* to take cover before I get my ass shot off.

I can't resist the urge to take another look out into the street, and I put my head back up, albeit a bit more cautiously this time. The Indians are magnificently dressed in feathers and war paint. Their ponies are similarly adorned, and the Indians ride without saddles, displaying incredible technique and horsemanship. As I look out on the street, a thought occurs to me that this is much more intense than anything I ever saw as a child at Frontier Town.

I turn to Emma, who is sitting with her back to the barrels, and say, "This isn't like the Frontier Town I remember."

She laughs at me. "How do you mean?"

"I mean this looks pretty real to me."

"Do you *believe* it's real?" she asks.

"Yeah!" I say. "Look, there's a townsperson over there with an arrow stuck in his chest being carried across the street by several other townspeople."

Emma takes a quick look at me. "If you believe it's real, then it is real."

From where we sit, I can see the jailhouse down the street. The sheriff and his deputies flood out into the street and take up positions, firing at the Indians. All at once, the Indians turn and make their way up the street. I'm not sure exactly what they are after, but it appears that they have stolen a few horses from the corral. I watch the sheriff and deputies mount up and take off after the Indians, chasing them out of town. The two cowboys fire their final shots at the Indians as they ride by.

Smoke and the smell of burnt gunpowder hang in the air inside the shop. It is quiet once again. I watch the two cowboys reload their six-shooters as I make my way over to the door. The taller cowboy turns to me and says, "Don't you go out there. You don't know what might still be lurking. You might get yourself scalped."

"Why would anyone want to scalp *him*?" asks the shorter cowboy. "They'll just be stuck with that stupid-looking hat."

I peer out the door before declaring, "The Indians are gone."

"What, do you think we should invite them back for dinner?" says the shorter, sarcastic cowboy.

I take a good look at him. He's a tough-looking guy. He turns and spits tobacco out the door, wonders aloud what I'm looking at, and asks whether I want to make something of it. Just then, Eagle Feather, who has been selecting his tobacco, stands between the cowboy and me. "Now, gentlemen," he begins, "this is no time for any more ruckus. I'm sure my friend here was just upset by all the excitement. Let's let bygones be bygones." I can see Eagle Feather stare sternly into the shorter cowboy's eyes while he speaks.

Right then and there, the cowboy backs down and starts walking toward the door. "I'll let it go this time because I don't want that pretty little girlfriend of yours to see you get your ass kicked." With that, he disappears through the doorway.

The other cowboy turns to us and says, "This is a dangerous place. You really need to be careful or you could be killed." He follows the other cowboy out.

Eagle Feather looks at me and smiles.

"Man, those guys are just full of sunshine," I say. "What's the matter with them? It's like I did something wrong."

Eagle Feather chuckles and says, "Well, as far as they are concerned, maybe you have. Just ignore them."

I hear the thumping floorboards and the jingling of their spurs as they walk away down the porch. The shorter cowboy yells back, "You'll get yours."

CHAPTER 56

Eagle Feather has completed his business with the shopkeeper, and I watch him pay with several silver dollars. He tells Emma and me to take the supplies out and load up the saddlebags. After we have the horses loaded, I notice the town again seems very quiet. Eagle Feather comes out on the porch and announces that he has some business to attend to over at the livery stable. I tell him that I am going down to the saloon to grab a couple of bottles of whiskey, as we ran out at the cabin. I ask Emma to accompany me and see her look back over toward Eagle Feather with a strange look. Eagle Feather climbs onto his horse and turns around. "Okay," he says, "but be very careful." He then looks over at Emma with a grave look. He hands me five silver dollars and tells us to take the horses with us. We set out with the horses, walking down the street while Eagle Feather heads off toward the livery stable.

As we walk down the street toward the saloon, all the townspeople stare at us through the windows of the shops. All the shop walls seem to have arrows stuck in them, remnants of the Indian raid that just took place. Emma keeps telling me that it might not be such a good idea to go into the saloon. She insists that we should stick close to Eagle Feather. I am still hung up on the notion that we are in the Frontier Town of my childhood, and I am determined to finally make it to the saloon. Turning to Emma, I say, "Don't worry about it. We're just going in for a sec. I'll buy you a drink."

Emma stops walking and turns to me. "I don't drink."

"Really? How about some tea then?"

She doesn't answer but continues walking. "Emma, how did we wind up in Frontier Town?" I ask.

"Have you thought about this town recently?"

"Actually, yeah, on the ride here."

"There must be a reason," she explains. "Deep down in your subconscious, there must be something that you have to learn from this place."

"Have we been here before? In any of my past recurrences?"

"More times than I can remember," she answers. "Do you have any recollection of being here before?"

"Only when I was a child," I answer.

"Maybe you should be practicing your remembering techniques; maybe something will come to you."

We walk on in silence as I try to remember myself in the moment. I'm going over the technique that Eagle Feather taught me. When we arrive at the saloon, Emma asks if any visions of the last time we were here have come to me. "No," I say. "I'm not getting anything."

"Nothing at all? Well, keep your eyes open, and maybe we'll get a sign."

"What kind of sign?"

"The kind of sign that will tell us what to do."

Outside the saloon, like the general store, is a big wooden porch with benches. Big, wide floorboards make up the porch, extending right into the saloon itself. There are two big windows on either side of the door. Over the door is a big sign that reads "Full Moon Saloon." The doors are the batwing, swinging type that roughly run from my knees to my chest so that, even if you are standing on the porch, you can see into the main room. As we make our way up the squeaky steps, I confide in Emma that as kids we were never allowed into the saloon, and I always wanted to venture in. She chuckles a little bit, saying, "Well, you've been in here before."

The cowboys on the bench look at us with fascination. We pause before entering, and I peer over the top of the swinging doors and into the main room. There are a lot of people inside, and I can hear a piano. People are laughing and milling around. Off to the left, in a corner of the room, I see five men playing cards at a table. As we push our way through the swinging door, the floorboards wince a little under our weight.

The room is rather large. To our right, a bar stretches from the back of the building to the front. There is a staircase on the far wall that winds itself up to a second floor. A cowboy stands at the bar, talking to a dance hall girl. Behind the bar is a big mirror, and above that, a moose head is mounted on the wall. The bar is beautiful, wooden with a nickel-silver top and sandwiched by spittoons. As we walk across the room to the bar, the music stops, and all chatter ceases. I can feel the stares. As soon as we reach the bar, however, the music resumes, and everybody seems to dive back into their conversations.

While walking over to the bar, I have this cowboy thing going on. I put my foot up on the foot rail and spit toward one of the spittoons, missing badly. The bartender has his back to us at first, but I recognize something familiar about him when he turns around. He's a tall man with a handlebar mustache, white shirt, black vest, and an apron tied around his waist. "Hello," he greets us. "It's a beautiful night out there, now isn't it? The Indian raid's been put down, and to tell you the truth, I was never worried about them at all."

I turn to Emma. "Man, this guy's all sunshine and roses, now isn't he?" He's so overly jolly, in fact, that I wonder if he hasn't been sampling some of his wares.

Suddenly, the cowboy that has been standing to our right pushes his companion, the dance hall girl, out of his way and leans in toward me. "Those bloodthirsty Indians will be back. And we'll probably all lose our scalps."

"Don't listen to him," the bartender, whose smile has never faltered, advises. "Everything's always the end of the world with that fellow."

"Oh yeah," the cowboy says, "well, things don't always work out for the best, like you seem to think. Not in this town, anyway." I recognize him as the taller cowboy from the general store. Apparently, his outlook on the future hasn't changed a bit. I'm fortunate that he seems to have lost his wise guy friend.

"What'll it be?" asks the bartender.

"I'll have a whiskey for myself and a cup of tea for the lovely lady," I say. The bartender continues to stare. Without taking his eyes off me, he points to a sign on the wall above the corner of the bar: "There will be no sale of whiskey to Indians by order of the sheriff."

"Can't you read?" the bartender asks me.

"Yeah, I can read, but I'm no Indian."

"Well, from where I'm standing, you sure are," he says. With that, he reaches over the bar and pulls the hat off my head, exposing the three eagle feathers tied into my hair. "Sure you're no Indian?" he asks.

"At this point, I'm not sure about anything," I reply.

"Well, that's the law."

I look at Emma; she's giggling. He continues to stare, and I start to feel very uncomfortable. "What are you staring at?" I ask him loudly.

He shakes his head abruptly. "I have something for you," he says. He turns around and goes to a drawer behind the bar and produces an old, tattered envelope. "This must be for you," he says and hands it to me.

"Why would there be an envelope here for me?" I wonder aloud.

"A while back, I can't recollect how long ago exactly, a fellow came in here that looked a lot like you, and he gave me this envelope and told me that if anyone came in here looking exactly like him, I was to give him this envelope. You, my friend, are the spitting image of that fellow, so I suppose it's yours."

I take the envelope from his hand. It's old and dingy with smudge marks all over it. I turn toward Emma, holding the envelope up so she can see it. "What do you make of this?" I ask her.

She shrugs. "Go ahead and open it."

I pull the top part of the envelope off and turn completely around so I can read the note without letting the bartender see what is written on it. Emma leans toward me as I pull the letter out of the envelope. I unfold the note, which is just as dingy as the envelope it came in. I hold it up to the light thrown from the kerosene lantern. "If you don't want to be hanged, get out of the saloon. Fast." Glancing up at the right-hand corner of that note, I see the familiar initials, RLC. I look at Emma and see that's she's staring back at me.

"Emma, this is another note from me!" I exclaim.

"Yeah," she says. "Looks like we got the sign we were looking for. Let's get the hell out of here."

I grab her hand and take a step toward the door. Just at that moment, a vision flashes through my mind. I see that wise guy cowboy from the general store and the sheriff with all his deputies coming through the door. The wise guy points at me and says, "There he is, that's him. He's an Indian and a troublemaker, and he won't listen to any of us anymore." The sheriff and all his deputies wear silver stars on their chests. The sheriff's has something written on it that starts with a C, though I can't quite make it out.

"So that's the one we've been after?" the sheriff asks the wise guy.

"Yup, that's him."

The sheriff raises his right hand, points at me, and says, "All right, boys, get 'im." And with that, all the deputies jump on me. I put up a struggle, but then again, it's six on one here. I see them dragging me out of the saloon while onlookers gape. I hear the wise guy suggest that I hang tomorrow.

Just then, the vision ends, and I snap back into the present moment. Eagle Feather comes through the door and walks toward us with a stern look on his face.

"Eagle Feather—" I begin, but he interrupts me.

"I know. Let's get out of here. Fast."

I hear grumbling of boots on the wooden porch just outside the saloon. The door swings open, and in comes the sheriff, followed by his deputies, who spread out in front of the door and encircle us. The wise guy from the general store pushes his way through the deputies. "There he is!" he shouts, pointing at us. It looks as though my vision is coming true. "They're Indians, and he's the one causing all the problems." But unlike my vision, instead of pointing at me, he points at Eagle Feather instead. Come to think of it, I don't recall Eagle Feather being in my vision at all.

"This is the guy?" asks the sheriff.

"Yup. The tall one there. He's causing all the problems. He has the little guy there ignoring us."

"Okay," the sheriff says, "we'll take him in." He raises his arm and points at us before yelling, "Get 'im, boys."

The deputies swarm Eagle Feather, jumping on top of him, and though he puts up quite a fight, he is badly outnumbered and easily subdued. I grab a chair from one of the tables and fling it through the big picture window on the side of the door. Glass shatters and rains to the floor. I grab Emma's hand, and together we jump through the broken window and out onto the porch. This startles the cowboys that have been sitting on the porch, and they jump up. One of them runs toward us, but Emma is able to grab his arm and flip him over the hitching post where our horses are tied.

"Get the horses!" yells Emma, and we both jump off the porch and mount up. Emma grabs the reins of Eagle Feather's horse, and we take off down Frontier Town's main street at a swift gallop. Though I'm mostly trying to hold on for dear life, I manage to turn around and spot the mob dragging a handcuffed Eagle Feather across the street toward the jail.

Just before we get out of earshot, I hear the wise guy yell, "We got him now, boys. He'll hang tomorrow night." We ride down the street toward the forest and into the night. I'm doing my best to follow Emma, who is moving awfully fast considering she's not only riding her own horse but also has Eagle Feather's in tow. Once we reach the woods that skirt the town, we slow down. Visibility is now an afterthought in the pitch darkness, and we struggle to find the spot where the big boulders are, the spot where we waited earlier for night to fall.

I manage to catch up to Emma finally and pull up alongside her. "I don't remember where those big rocks are where we were hiding out before," she says. Suddenly, the spot flashes into my mind. I tell her to follow me, and we reach the boulders without much difficulty. We tie the horses to a tree and scamper back to the safety of the rocks.

CHAPTER 57

"What was that all about?" I exclaim.

"Stop talking so loudly," Emma says. "And sit down."

"Sit down? How can I sit down? They've got Eagle Feather, and tomorrow night he hangs." I can't relax, and I begin to pace back and forth frantically. I can't believe what I've just witnessed. "What is going on here?" I demand.

Emma tackles me to the ground and, while lying on top of me, says in an almost imperceptible tone, "Keep your voice down. They may still be looking for us." Even if I want to speak, I'm unable. The force of her landing on top of me has knocked all the wind out of my lungs. As I lie here, pinned to the ground and gasping for air, she says, "I'll let you up. But you have to promise not to speak." She climbs off, and we both scramble to the rocks in front of us and peer out into the black of night, straining our eyes and ears, trying to catch any faint notion of our pursuers.

"I don't see anything," I say in a whisper.

"Don't be so sure they're not out there."

"I can't see a thing. It's so dark."

"Use your ears."

We remain there for some time with our chests up against the rocks and our heads peering out into the woods, looking for any signs. The gray light of the early morning begins to make itself known. Emma relaxes, sitting down with her back up against the rocks. I, on the other hand, remain anxiously vigilant.

"Why don't you sit down and relax," she says.

"Relax? I can't relax right now."

"The sun is coming up. It's early morning now, and we don't have to worry about the sheriff and his deputies coming after us any longer. Remember, the town and all its inhabitants disappear in the daylight."

"So you're telling me that we're safe now?"

"Yes, we're safe from them now that the sun is up. They're all gone."

I slide down the rock and sit next to Emma. The forest grows brighter by the minute. "Now all we have to worry about is the Indians." The Indians. I forgot about them in all the excitement. "If we keep our heads down and don't talk too loudly, we'll be okay," she says.

We sit in silence for a long while. My mind is having a hard time comprehending the fact that the people—or whatever they are—have captured Eagle Feather. I wonder, if the town and all its inhabitants have disappeared with the rising sun, where Eagle Feather is right now. Emma gets up finally and makes her way over to the horses. She returns with a canteen, and we both take a long drink. "What are we going to do now?" I ask her.

"I don't really know," she replies.

"Come on, Emma. You told me that you've been through this more times than you care to remember. Why don't you just tell me what's going to happen so we can figure out how to proceed?"

"That would be useless."

"What do you mean? If I know what's going to happen, then we can concoct some kind of plan."

"That's just it," she says. "There are so many possibilities, so many futures, and our actions in the present moment determine what future will coalesce. So, you see, though we have been here many times before, our actions in the present moment will dictate what path the future will take. There is only one action that will lead us forward, that will lead us to an outcome that we haven't lived through before."

"So, you're trying to tell me that what we do now or at any one time can lead us forward to some new future?"

"That's exactly what I'm telling you. The only way to the break the recurrence is to find the path that has not been traveled before."

"And so, Emma darling, if we find this path, will it lead me out of this place and back to my other life?"

"Well, if you haven't traveled this path before, it would certainly not be part of the recurrence that you keep living over and over again here, now would it?" she replies.

"If that's true, then that would mean if different aspects of the recurrence are handled differently and events begin to change, then we would have changed the path of future events and even the recurrence itself."

"Yes," Emma says, looking me straight in the eye. "That would alter the outcome and change the path that we're on."

"And that path could lead me back to the life that I was living before?"

"Yes, the correct changes—or should I say correcting the faults and missteps of this recurrence—would lead you back there."

"Emma, how will we know if anything is different? How can we tell if anything has changed, or, for that matter, how can we change anything if we don't know what happened in the previous recurrences?"

"That's where all the work on remembering yourself comes in. Eagle Feather told you that if you practice remembering yourself, you will be able to catch glimpses of what has occurred in your past recurrences, and only then will you have the knowledge necessary to change those events. Think hard, Rich. Is anything different?"

"What do you mean? Oh … wait a minute. When we were back in the saloon, right after we read my note, I had a vision. I saw the sheriff and his men come into the saloon, and in the vision, the wise guy pointed at me, and I was captured. This time, the wise guy pointed out Eagle Feather, and I escaped. So we've already broken with the recurrence."

Emma looks at me with a strange expression. This is followed by a long and, if you ask me, very awkward pause. "Well it is, and it ain't," she says.

"What the hell is that supposed to mean?" I snap. "You sound like Eagle Feather. What do you mean *it is and it ain't*? Can't you and Eagle Feather ever give me a straight answer?"

"No," she says. "When it comes to your situation here, we really can't interfere."

"Well isn't that just lovely? Are you going to be any help or not? It's bad enough that those guys have Eagle Feather and they're going to stretch his neck tonight. And I'm thinking that I've made some progress in this recurrence, and you, Eagle Feather's apprentice and my close friend, can't offer any guidance." Emma just stands there looking at me. "I guess you really aren't going to help," I say glumly before going back over to the rocks and sitting back down. I have nothing else to say to her.

I sit with my back up against the rock and continue to stare over at Emma, who is now peering over the top of the big boulders. Looking for Indians, I guess. Every time she turns around and begins to open her mouth, I look away, disinterested. I have nothing to say to her. I need to gather my thoughts about this whole ridiculous conundrum we've found ourselves in. And she isn't offering any help anyway. So, I sit for quite some time trying to make sense out of this whole thing. The more I ponder it, the more I realize that there isn't any sense to be made of it. There are only a couple of things that I think I know: those people in the town have Eagle Feather, and something in this recurrence has changed from the last. Changed for the better or worse, I have no idea.

"Well, what are you thinking?" Emma asks without turning around to look at me.

"That this dream, or whatever it is, has turned into a nightmare."

Emma chuckles before finally turning around to look at me. "Good dream, bad dream, they're pretty much the same."

I look at her with bewilderment. "You've got to be kidding me."

She smiles and slides down the rock, landing in a seated position so she faces me. "You've been sitting here for so long. Have you come to any conclusions?"

I just glare at her. I'm pissed off that she's taking this so lightly. Finally, I say, "The only conclusion I know is that we have to somehow rescue Eagle Feather. And I'm sure if I knew what you know, that would be a much easier task. Oh, yeah, and another thing: who are those guys in the town?"

Emma looks at me, her face contorted into a wry smirk. "They're just a figment of your imagination," she says.

"How the hell would my imagination have concocted *this*?"

Emma walks over and sits so she's right in front of me. "Is it so unbelievable?" she says. "Your imagination just pulled this whole town out of your memory, didn't it?"

I think for a moment. "Yeah, I guess. But I don't remember meeting those characters from the town before."

"Oh really?" she says. "How can you be so sure? I'll tell you this: you've known them your whole life, and they know you."

"What do you mean by that?"

Emma, apparently done explaining for the time being, gets up and walks over to the horses.

"Where are you going?" I call out.

"I don't know about you, but I'm hungry," she answers. "And if I'm not mistaken, there's still some food left in the saddlebags." I watch her walk out of the circle of rocks.

Emma returns quickly with the whole saddlebag. She takes out the blanket and spreads it across the grass. She then pulls out hard-boiled eggs, the beef jerky that gives me gas, some biscuits, and a couple of apples. "Eat something," she says. She doesn't have to tell me twice; I'm starving. "We'll eat half of what we have now and save the rest for later." She then pauses before shouting, "So, what are you going to do?"

"I thought you said we had to talk in a whisper," I say.

"That's true, but I had to wake you up somehow."

"I don't really know. Give me a chance to think, will you please?"

Emma gets up and takes what is left of the food. She folds the blanket and puts it back in the saddlebag along with the rest of the food. She then stomps over to the horses with an air of indignation.

"Where are you going?" I ask.

"I'm going to take the horses down to the water," she says. "They could probably use a drink."

"Be careful," I say. "Remember, the Indians." With that, she rides off with the horses in tow toward the river, leaving me seated at the rock to ponder my circumstances. I think of the strangely familiar townsfolk, how to save Eagle Feather, and how I'm ever going to return home. The townsfolk, Emma said, are figments of my imagination, but they seem much more like hallucinations. I go over their faces, their words, and their actions in my mind. I also rack my mind for a way to get Eagle Feather out of jail before his impending execution. But most of my thoughts focus on the people in the town.

In all the excitement, I haven't realized how tired I am. I have, after all, been up all night, journeying into the town and ultimately being chased right back here. I pull the brim of my hat down, Indiana Jones style, close my eyes, and slump down on the rock. I am asleep within minutes.

CHAPTER 58

I am awoken suddenly by an extremely forceful tap on the shoulder. This startles the hell out of me, and I jump to my feet quickly to defend myself. I am standing face-to-face with Emma. "Having a little leisure time?" she asks sarcastically.

"Oh, no, just resting my eyes a bit," I say equally sarcastically.

"What do you think? We're on a picnic?"

"No, believe me, this is no picnic. Did you see anything?"

"Not until I got to the river. There were a bunch of horse tracks in the mud."

"Horse tracks?" I repeat.

"Yeah, easily fifteen or twenty sets of them."

"What do you make of that?"

"Well, the tracks were from un-shoed horses, so Indians would be my best guess. The only thing that's bothering me is that the tracks were coming out of the river on this side."

"Really?" I say.

"Yeah. So, let's just sit back down, try not to move around too much, and, for god's sake, be quiet." Emma inches her way over to the side of one of the rocks and lies down so she can look out from the clearing. She then turns to me and says, "So, what are you going to do?"

"What do you mean?" I know what she meant, but I need time to stall my answer.

"Well, obviously we seem to be in this predicament. What is your plan?"

"Plan?" I have no answer to her question. "Honestly, I spent most of the time you were gone thinking about those strange folks down in the town."

"Listen," she says gravely, "we have much bigger fish to fry. We need to rescue Eagle Feather before they kill him. What's the plan?"

"I really wish you'd stop asking me that," I say.

"You'd better come up with something—and soon. We're burning daylight here, and as soon as that sun goes down, we have to act."

I know Emma is right. I have to think of something if we're going to keep Eagle Feather's neck out of the hangman's noose. That being said, I'm coming up blank. The stress and the sleepless night have rendered my mind mashed potatoes.

"Well that's just peachy," Emma replies to my silence.

"What we need is constructive thoughts, not snide comments."

"Well, excuse me," she says. "A warrior would have a plan. A warrior would look at this whole situation from top to bottom and meticulously come up with a plan. And then, at the opportune time, he would throw his whole being into it." She slides down the rock on her back and continues to glare at me.

"I guess we need a warrior," I say glumly.

She stares back at me, and I can't help but notice the ultra-serious expression on her face. "Yes, we do need a warrior. It's your time."

I'm no warrior. I don't even feel close, despite all of her and Eagle Feather's teachings. I look back at her, dumbfounded.

She stands up and walks toward me, putting her face so close to mine that our noses almost touch. I can feel her breath. "It's time for you to become a warrior," she says again, staring into my eyes before repeating, "It's time." She slowly backs up to the rock and sits down again, never breaking eye contact with me.

I am taken aback by her comments and the forcefulness with which she proposed them. I stammer back, "But I'm no warrior."

She continues to stare back at me with the same steely eyes that I know from Eagle Feather. "It's your time."

"But—"

"You've come this far. You've learned your lessons well. You've earned those feathers. Now you must finally become the warrior you are to be and save Eagle Feather. That is why you have come to this point; that is why you have made it this far in this recurrence. So pull yourself together and formulate a plan."

My mind is rambling. I almost miss the unfriendly advice of the I's, who have been silent for so long. "But, Emma, I might have earned these three feathers here, but a warrior has four, like Eagle Feather."

There's a long pause. Emma looks at me, and I look back at her. Finally, she speaks. "Go over to the horses and bring back Eagle Feather's saddlebag." Without questioning her, I get up, move over to the horses, remove Eagle Feather's saddlebag, and return to the circle of rocks. I try to hand Emma the bag, but she won't take it. "Oh no," she says, "the saddlebag isn't for me. It's for you. Open it up and have a look."

I undo the leather strap and open it up. I reach inside and pull out a tomahawk. "Anything else in there?" Emma asks. I reach back in and pull out an eagle feather. My jaw falls open, and I look back at her.

"Are you sure Eagle Feather is ready for me to have this?"

"The question is, are you ready for it? And you are." Emma takes the feather from my hand and pulls out some red twine from her pocket. She quickly ties the fourth feather into my hair. "There it is: your fourth feather. I officially pronounce you a warrior."

"But, Emma, I'm none of those things that a warrior must be."

"Yes, you are those things. There's a warrior inside each and every one of us. All we have to do is get out of its way and let it out. All you must do to be a warrior is act like a warrior."

She then takes Eagle Feather's red sash, ties it around my waist, and puts both Colt .45 revolvers into the sash, just as Eagle Feather wore them. She takes Eagle Feather's tomahawk and places it in another sash wrapped around my back. Finally, she takes a couple of steps back, as if to admire me.

"How do I look?"

She goes into her saddlebag and pulls out a mirror. Handing the mirror to me, she says, "You sure look like a warrior. Have a look."

When I look in the mirror, I see a much different image of myself than I have ever known. I have to admit, with that fourth feather, tomahawk, and red gun belt, I do look like a pretty formidable warrior. I look confident. I look like Eagle Feather.

"Do you like what you see?" Emma asks.

"Actually, I do." I hand the mirror back to Emma. "So, what would a warrior do now?"

"Who am I to tell you what to do? You are a warrior now. All you have to do is believe that to be true."

My mind flies back to all the conversations I have had with Eagle Feather about the acts of a warrior. I remember him telling me that a warrior is always decisive and acts accordingly. "Emma, I have to save Eagle Feather, and to do that, I have to come up with something, and I have to execute that plan decisively."

I sit down with my back up against a rock and cross my legs as I saw Eagle Feather and Emma do when they called on the water spirit. I close my eyes and fall into a trance. In the ensuing vision, I am suddenly at the jailhouse, looking around my tiny, claustrophobic cell. Through the lone, barred window at the back of the cell, I see Eagle Feather riding up with my horse, Sweetheart, in tow. Suddenly, I hear a voice in my mind. "Reverse the roles," it says. It somehow sounds like both Eagle Feather's voice and my own. I recognize the voice. It's the one I heard when I encountered the bear in the cave and the one that told me to stand my ground in the clearing. I know immediately that this is my one true I. At this moment, I am suddenly outside the barred window. I look into the cell and see that it is now Eagle Feather, not me, behind bars. And I know exactly what I need to do.

Just as suddenly as I entered the trance, I emerge from it. When my eyes open, I see Emma sitting in the same position that I am, facing me. I swear I see her mouth say, "Reverse the roles." But when I ask her what she said, she merely replies, "Nothing."

After a long pause, Emma finally asks what I saw. "I know what I'm going to do," I say. "I know how to rescue Eagle Feather."

After another long pause, she answers, "You are a warrior, and it is now time for you to take charge." I relate the full vision to Emma and then uncross my legs and sit back against the rock. The power of the vision still clouds my mind as I struggle to regain full consciousness.

I sit there for some time, trying to clear my head. Not much seems to be happening; it feels a bit like a hangover in which my mind is somehow stuck between two (or perhaps more) recurrences. But by and by, I start to return.

"Emma, what should I make of the fact that it's initially me in the cell and then Eagle Feather? It's like they captured the wrong person this time."

"Don't think for a second that they captured the wrong person. I think you missed the entire point."

"Missed the point?" I say sarcastically.

"Yes," Emma says and climbs up a rock. "You need to widen your gaze. A warrior, as the expression goes, can both see the trees through the forest and the forest through the trees. You're only seeing a small part of everything. You need to widen your gaze." And as if to demonstrate her point, she turns her head from side to side, looking out into the woods.

I sit there muttering to myself, "Missed the point … widen my gaze … small part of everything."

"Grumbling will get you nowhere," she says, her head still turned away from me. "A warrior doesn't grumble."

"What exactly do you mean, Emma? Are you going to help me or just keep speaking in riddles?"

"Rich, you know I can't interfere. You need to figure this out on your own. It is, after all, your dream."

"Whoa, whoa, whoa. This is not my dream. In my dream, you and I are sitting in hammocks on the beach of some tropical island sipping piña coladas. And you're in a bikini."

As I look up at her, I see her side shake. She's giggling. Maybe this is my chance to turn on the charm and get her to give me a little more direction. "Please," I implore her, "come down off that rock and sit down." Once more, she slides down the rock and faces me. "You know," I say slyly, "there must be times when a warrior needs to seek counsel. Right now, I'm seeking the counsel of a very wise and beautiful warrior. Can you please help me hash this out?"

A smile overtakes her face, and her eyes ignite. I keep up with the flattery. I might be really laying it on, but with the daylight waning and night about to fall, I know I need to act soon. "All right," she says, "I grant your request for counsel." She half-giggles.

"So, in my vision in the saloon, I was the one captured, and that's why I'm arguing that they captured the wrong person. And you just told me that I should not believe that in capturing Eagle Feather and not me, the wrong person was captured. So, logically, I have to assume the person that is supposed to be captured is Eagle Feather."

"Hang on, hang on, not so fast," she says. "We need a proper counsel fire. Go out and round up some small sticks.

"What about the Indians?" I ask, considering that the smoke from a fire would potentially draw a band of murderous Indians to our campsite.

Emma just commands me to follow her instructions with a wave of her hand. "Do what I say. We do not have to worry about the Indians at this time."

I get up and walk out into the brush to collect sticks for the fire. As I'm coming back into the clearing, I pass Emma, who is on her way to the horses. "Put the sticks in the hole that I dug out," she says. In the middle of the rock circle, I see a small hole that has leaves and dried brush in it. Around the hole, Emma drew a circle. I deposit the sticks in the middle of the hole and look up. Emma is back, carrying the saddlebag from her horse. She reaches into the bag and pulls out a box of matches similar to the matches I had when I was out in the clearing. She strikes a match on the side of one of the rocks and lights a fire in the hole. She then produces a long, ornately carved, and feather-decorated pipe; it looks like a peace pipe that I would see Indians smoking in a Western. She breaks apart the last of the tobacco, putting some in the pipe and casting the rest into the fire. She takes a couple of puffs, and I watch the smoke spiral up, up, up above our heads. She then offers the pipe to the east and then to the west. She hands me the pipe and tells me to do the same. When I'm finished, I hand the pipe back to her, and she puts it down next to her.

"What's this all about?" I ask her.

"Be quiet! Don't interrupt. You asked for counsel, and we are having a proper counsel."

She begins to chant something in a language I don't understand. She closes her eyes, and when she reopens them, she appears to be in a trance. "Now you may ask me questions. I will try to direct your own thoughts to answer those questions. You must remember that the answers to all your questions are already inside of you, and this counsel will only illuminate those answers."

"Okay. Is there anything I should call you—you know, some kind of Indian name?"

"Rich, don't be overly dramatic. Just call me Emma."

"Emma, was Eagle Feather really the one they wanted to catch?"

"Yes."

"Why would it be Eagle Feather and not me as I saw in my visions?"

"I can only say this: save Eagle Feather, and you will save yourself."

"Save Eagle Feather and I will save myself," I repeat. After this, a long silence ensues. I decide to move on. "So, what did that voice mean exactly when it told me to reverse the roles?"

Emma takes a deep breath. "You are here with me. Eagle Feather is captured and sits in jail. You must take on the responsibility of a warrior and save him."

"Yes, that's what you told me earlier. But you also said that I'm missing the deeper meaning."

"Yes," Emma says, "it is true that you have missed the deeper meaning." Silence then ensues again.

"Well, what do you have to say?" I ask in a loud voice. Emma just sits there, motionless and silent. "You aren't being very helpful," I point out.

"Counsel does not exist to tell you what to do. That is up to the warrior. I am, however, indulging your questions sufficiently so that you yourself will be able to see their answers."

"Okay, okay, I get it. You're not allowed to interfere. Let's move on. What about those people in the town? They're so strange to me and yet so familiar. It's as if I've known them my whole life."

After this question, there is a long pause. It's the kind of pause I'm used to from Eagle Feather that almost always proceeds some huge point. Emma then speaks. "Every person in our lives has been brought there by us. We make them all up as we go along. They serve the purpose of showing us our faults. They also show us the positive aspects of our character. It is ridiculous for you to ask me who they are, as they have been created by you yourself."

"*I* created them?"

"Yes, as I've told you and Eagle Feather has told you, you have created everything that you see around us. This includes Eagle Feather. It also includes me."

Admittedly, this counsel is not going according to plan. I thought for sure that I could charm Emma into revealing some real answers. Instead, she has created more questions. "Enough of these questions. You yourself will have to answer them," Emma says. "The fire is going down. Fetch some more sticks and build it back up."

I leave the rock circle to find more wood. Emma sits still with her legs crossed. She is still in some sort of trance. I return moments later with a bit more wood. The fire, which was just smoking a bit, bursts back into flames when I toss the wood into the pit.

"It is time to concentrate on your plan," Emma says in a deep voice that seems to emanate not just from her mouth but from all around the rock circle. It forces me to look around and try to find the source of the voice.

"I'm going to have to go with what I saw in my vision."

"And what is that?"

I repeat to her what I saw. "There will be deputies inside the jailhouse at this time," Emma says.

"Yeah, that's right," I say. "I saw them all in there just before the Indians raided the town. I see what you're getting at. I'll have to get the deputies out of the jailhouse before I make my move. All I need is a diversion. Hmm ..."

"Rich, this isn't just any town. This is Frontier Town. This is your town."

"That's right. I made it all up."

"And what happens every day in Frontier Town?"

"Oh, there's a number of things: a gunfight at the okay corral, a stagecoach robbery, a—wait a second—I got it! There's an Indian raid, and this forces all the deputies and the sheriff out of the jailhouse to fight the Indians. Eagle Feather will be left unguarded!"

"There you go," Emma says. "And remember: trust in your vision."

After saying this, her head drops to her chest and hangs there for quite a while. When she finally lifts it up, I can see that her eyes have lost that shine, and she is out of the trance and back to her old self. She stands up quickly, instructs me to put out the fire, and reminds me to find a good stick to rake the pit and make the earth look just as it did before our counsel. I get up and head out of the circle of rocks. Emma follows close behind me and then heads back over to the horses. "Where are you going?" I ask her.

"Never mind that," she answers. "Just take care of the fire pit."

As I begin to cut some branches down to serve as a makeshift rake, I notice that dusk has already set in. The light is fading fast, and I know all too well what this means. The town will soon be appearing, and in a short while, I will have to spring into action if I am to save Eagle Feather. I'm still preoccupied with that profound thing Emma said. "Save Eagle Feather, and you save yourself." Perhaps saving Eagle Feather is the key to returning to my old life.

When I return to the circle of rocks, Emma tells me to extinguish what's left of the fire with water from the canteen and spread the dirt so it looks pretty much as though nothing occurred. Emma returns from the horses carrying a small cloth that appears to have something wrapped up in it. She unwraps the cloth, and I see two small clay rocks, one red and one white. She puts the two pieces of clay down on a flat rock and, taking the canteen, sprinkles a little water on each. As she does this, they turn into a kind of paste. She sticks two fingers into the red paste first and comes walking toward me. I continue to stare at her, trying to figure out what she's up to. When she reaches me, she raises her hands to my face. I catch her by the wrists before her hands can reach my face.

"What are you up to?"

"I'm going to turn you into a proper Indian, a proper warrior."

"What's that on your hands?"

"War paint." She shakes her wrists from my grasp and slaps two fingers across my right cheek. She dips her fingers in the red paste again and slashes two fingers across my left cheek. She repeats this whole process with the white paste, never breaking her gaze into my eyes. Her eyes are mesmerizing, and I can't look away. They seem to have so much power in them.

When our gaze finally breaks, I ask her why I need war paint. "The answer is twofold," she says. "First, you will blend in much better with the raiding Indians once you reach the town. Second, while it is true that those revolvers, that tomahawk, this war paint, and even those feathers in your hair are not what makes you a warrior, it is important for a warrior's physical appearance to match his spiritual appearance. In fact, the red sash you are wearing with the Colt .45s, the tomahawk, the feathers—all these things are yours, not Eagle Feather's. While they do not make you a warrior, they are the tools of the warrior." She pauses here before continuing.

"A human being is a vibration. He or she is nothing more than a vibration of energy that flickers like the flame on a candle or a tree branch in the breeze. Increase the level of vibration, and the human being's consciousness rises. When this consciousness reaches its pinnacle, all things are possible. Clarity of mind is obtained. Physical prowess increases infinitely. Agility and stamina are heightened. And most importantly, understanding of the universe becomes possible. This is the natural state of the warrior." Emma moves even closer so that our noses are barely touching. The tone of her rhythmic voice transfixes me. "At this moment, it is paramount that you increase your level of vibration to that of a warrior."

I am trying to speak; I am trying to ask her how this is possible. But no words form in my mouth. She sees that I am struggling to speak and puts her hand over my mouth to shush me. She continues: "If you place a boiling pot of water next to a pot filled with water that is not boiling, soon both pots of water will boil. The pot with high energy, the boiling pot, transfers its energy, its vibration, to the low-energy pot. Just as this is true with water, it is also true with the energy of human beings. Higher beings can increase the level of vibration in the lower and, in so doing, increase their consciousness.

"When two people melt physically together, their vibrations mingle. This is the magic of love. It is the magic spoken of through all the ages of human history. It is the single most powerful magic in the universe. A warrior knows this and is capable of using this magic to increase the level of vibration in every living being."

Emma leans forward and puts her arms around me in a loving fashion. She kisses me passionately. I am taken so completely by surprise that I don't even return the kiss. She presses her body firmly into mine and kisses me passionately again. I return her affection. I can feel the heat from her body radiating into mine. Each time she kisses me, she pulls me deeper and deeper inside her. My mind is reeling from the passionate embrace. But at the same time, everything becomes clear. I feel a tremendous surge of energy throughout my entire being as though until now I have been left completely outside of myself. I feel Emma moving deeper and deeper inside me.

Finally, she breaks her embrace, puts her lips to my ear, and whispers, "I love you." She takes a step back, her eyes now a fiery blue, and says, "You are now a warrior. This is your time and your place. You and I are now one." She pulls herself back into my body, holding me tightly and kissing me again. When I finally open my eyes, she is gone.

CHAPTER 59

I am alone again. Truly alone, like when I was in the clearing. Emma has pulled one of her disappearing acts. In the past, I would have been terrified. But it seems that Emma's kiss, as she predicted, turned my level of vibration up to warrior status. I feel at peace; I feel confident. I climb the rock that Emma was perched on. When I make it to the top, I crouch, peering into the forest, on the lookout for Indians. My mind is infinitely clear. It seems that I can answer any question I may pose.

If I'm responsible for everything in this world, the mystery of the townspeople finally clears. They are all me, made up from my own mind. They are my I's. The lesson that Emma said I came back to Frontier Town to learn becomes clear. I didn't realize it before—perhaps I was too young—but it was during my childhood in Frontier Town that these voices first started running around inside of me. These voices would soon take control, and I would come to refer to them as my I's.

And now, throughout this whole ordeal, journey, dream, or whatever this is, I have come back here to vanquish them—of course, with the help of Eagle Feather, who has taught me the meaning of the I's and the method to become one. He told me that at some point the I's would revolt and that I am not to dismiss them entirely. I didn't quite know what he meant at the time, but I see it all clearly now. To save themselves, they must defeat Eagle Feather. So then, it is no mistake that they captured him and not me. Because, as the big guy in town told the little guy, "He's not letting him pay no attention to us." And, as Eagle Feather has told me, the key to vanquishing my I's is ignoring them, refusing them power and paving the way for the voice of my one true I.

And now my mind flashes back to that voice, the one I heard in my vision, the one that said, "Reverse the roles." With Emma's help, the warrior's vibration that she passed on to me through her kiss, the roles have been reversed. I am now the warrior, and I must save Eagle Feather. I look up and see, in the fading light, the hawk circling high in the sky above me, what's left of the sun gleaming off his brilliant red tail feathers. I raise my arm to salute him, and I take his appearance to be a sign of power. No doubt his presence serves as a sign that I will win the day.

I slide down the rock and pull both revolvers from my sash. I open each one and spin the barrels to make sure they are fully loaded. When I am satisfied that they are, I return both to the sash. Night is coming on quickly; already the faint lights of the town are beginning to manifest. All the while, I go over the plan in my mind. I need to be in position across the street when the Indian raid commences, and my timing has to be perfect. While I'm going over the plan, I hear horses' hooves about one hundred yards to my left. The Indians are massing for their attack on the village. It is time. I have to move quickly.

I head out of the rock formation and take the reins of both Sweetheart and Eagle Feather's horse. I remember to grab the rope; I'll be needing that. I start to move into the woods along the ridge, towing the horses behind me. It is remarkable how stealthy and confident my movements are, and I chalk this up to my newly acquired warrior status. In no time at all, I reach the backs of the buildings that line the street. Here I become extremely cautious, carefully keeping an eye out so I can avoid being seen at all costs. I quickly reach the last building at the end of the street. I poke my head around the building, and I can see, across the street, the jailhouse where they are holding Eagle Feather. All the lights in the windows are lit up. There is a small porch in front of the building, like many of the other buildings in the town. Both front windows are barred, and a big sign that reads "Jail" sits centered over the front entrance.

I stand in place, not moving a muscle, when I hear the first war whoop from the other end of the street. As I turn my head and direct my attention toward the sound, I see the Indians come charging down the street, whooping and hollering with bloodcurdling sounds. At this point, all the townspeople run out of buildings and start firing at the passing Indians. Knowing from all my previous visits to Frontier Town that the deputies and sheriff will be on their way out of the building shortly, I mount Sweetheart and, still holding onto the reins of Eagle Feather's pony, wait for my opportunity.

Quite a spectacle develops: guns going off every which way and arrows flying high through the air. The Indians eventually reach my side of town, as they always do, and turn, charging back down the other direction. It is at this point that the sheriff and all his deputies come running out of the jailhouse with their guns blazing. As predicted, the Indians turn and head back through the town away from me. So much gun smoke hangs heavy in the air. This is my opportunity. As they go by me, I charge out onto the street like I'm one of them, and indeed, with my feathers and war paint, I must look the part. I quickly ride up behind the jail and to the barred window. Slipping the rope through bars, I tie it securely to Sweetheart's saddle horn, as I saw in my vision. I see a head pop up in the window, and though I can't make it out through the lingering gun smoke, I hear the familiar voice of Eagle Feather. "What took you so long?" I give Sweetheart a solid kick, see the rope become taut as she strains, and finally hear the clanging of the bars as they pop off the window.

Eagle Feather scampers out and stands in front of me. "Well, it's good to see you!" he exclaims.

"Didn't think I would come for you?" I ask with a smile.

"One never knows. Every other time, it was I who came for you. I can see that Emma has done her job." Eagle Feather quickly walks around to his pony and takes the reins from my hand. He goes to his saddlebag and produces two Colt .45 revolvers and a tomahawk, just like the ones I'm carrying. He places both revolvers in his red sash and the tomahawk in the sash around his back. He then pulls out two sticks of clay from his bag, one red and one white, wets them, and dabs his fingers into each, applying his own war paint. We now look more or less identical.

"Let's get out of here," I suggest.

But Eagle Feather has another idea. "Not so fast," he says. "Enjoy this moment. This is where the fun starts. He mounts his horse and motions for me to follow him. We slowly creep around the side of the building. We now have a view of the entire street. All is quiet: the Indian raid has been repelled by the deputies and the townspeople, though both are still lining the street. I look over at Eagle Feather and see that he has a funny look in his eyes.

"Let's just back out around the building, take to the woods, and get the hell out of here," I say quietly.

He sits up in his saddle and turns to me. "No, that won't do for two warriors such as ourselves. We need to make them remember who they're messing with." He motions for me to move up so that my horse is adjacent to his.

"What are we going to do?" I ask.

"We're going to put on a little show here in Frontier Town," he replies. "We're going to charge down the middle of the street and rough these boys up a little bit." Perhaps it is the warrior in me, or whatever Emma did to me, but my blood is up, and I am all for it. "Do as I do," Eagle Feather instructs. He takes the reins of his horse and puts them between his teeth. He pulls both Colt .45 revolvers out of his sash and holds them in each hand, pointing the barrels up to the sky. I mimic him. He looks right at me, and I look back at him. We both kick our horses at the same time and go charging headlong down the middle of the street.

I hear the familiar voice of the wise guy yell, "There they go! The prisoners are escaping!"

Prisoners? I wonder. It was only Eagle Feather that was locked up.

Guns go off simultaneously from both sides of the street. Eagle Feather, who is slightly ahead of me, fires both Colts. I begin to fire too as we fly down the street. I am riding faster than I ever have in my life, and yet somehow I am in complete control. The bullets fly all around us like angry bees who've had their nest knocked over by a bear. When we reach the other end of the street, I hear the sheriff yell, "Get to the horses, men! After them!"

We crash into the darkness at the edge of the town. As we do,

Eagle Feather lets out a chilling war whoop. And in response, I hear the same war whoop come from me. We make our way through the woods, bobbing and weaving our way around brush and trees. The only light we have to navigate by is cast by a crescent moon, which throws deep shadows everywhere. This makes the going all the more difficult. The horses break into a trot, and we continue for about another hundred yards before Eagle Feather whirls his horse and comes to a stop. I come up beside him, and just as I reach him, I hear the bell ringing in the church tower back in Frontier Town.

"What's that all about?" I ask Eagle Feather.

"The sheriff's rounding up a posse. In no time at all, we'll have all of Frontier Town out here looking for us."

Eagle Feather reaches into his saddlebag and produces a handful of .45-caliber bullets. He hands a bunch to me. "Reload," he says loudly. "There's going to be a hell of a fight tonight. It's either us or them." I do as he says, taking the bullets from his hands. I pull both Colts out of my sash, open their breaches, reload the chambers, and spin both revolvers shut. Eagle Feather does the same.

"What do you mean, hell of a fight? I got you out of jail. Let's just get the hell out of here."

Eagle Feather chuckles as he always seems to do. "Oh, make no mistake about it. This ain't over by a long shot. I told you there would be a revolt. And I also told you that those I's are not just going to give up and go away." As he speaks, I hear the thunder of horses' hooves coming our way. "What did I tell you?" Eagle Feather says. "Well, so what's your plan?"

"My plan?"

"Yes, your plan. You're a warrior now, and you've successfully executed the first part of your plan—rescuing me. So, what's next?"

"Well, to tell you the truth, I haven't thought this far ahead yet," I say sheepishly. "My plan kind of ended with breaking you out of jail."

"Not very thorough," he mutters under his breath.

The sound of the horses is drawing closer. "Let's get the hell out of here," I suggest.

"That sounds like a plan to me," Eagle Feather says. "Follow me. We need to get to the river."

I agree with him, from one warrior to another. We move out into a trot, ducking and swerving to avoid the low-hanging branches and brush on the forest floor. All the while, the sound of our pursuers' horses' hooves chase us as we thread our way through the darkness.

"Do you have any idea where the river is?" I ask Eagle Feather.

"No," he replies. "But you'll find it. It's your time now."

"What do you mean?"

He pulls the reins hard on his horse and stops. Seeing this, I also stop. In that faint crescent-moon light, I feel Eagle Feather's eyes lock onto mine. "You are the warrior. This is your war party. You lead, and I'll follow. It's up to you now." I open my mouth, take a deep breath, and begin to speak, but before I can get a complaint out, Eagle Feather growls back at me. "What do you think we've been doing this whole time? And don't think for one minute that Emma wasted all that energy on you back there. You are the author of all this. Now take your rightful place as a warrior and lead us out of here."

Even in the faint light, I can see the seriousness in his eyes. My resolve stiffens. I kick Sweetheart and say, "Follow me." As far as I can gather from my sense of direction, the town we left behind is on our left. That's also where the sound of the horses is coming from. And if I'm correct, the circle of rocks where we set up camp is just about 150 yards ahead of us. I remember Emma took the horses to the river, and though I didn't watch when she took them, I'm convinced that the horses moved out of the circle toward the right. I turn Sweetheart that way, and we continue on through the dark night.

Now confident that we are going in the right direction, I turn back to Eagle Feather and yell, "What will we do when we get to the river?"

"I don't know," he answers, "but I'm sure you'll think of something." The voice in my vision told me to reverse the roles. I guess we have now come full circle—Eagle Feather playing my part and me playing his. In true Indian fashion, the student has become the teacher.

We crash through the brush and emerge on the riverbank. Not only have I found the river, but we came out of the woods in the same spot where we crossed the river the other night. I quickly ride up the side of the bluff above the river to get a view back toward the direction we came from. Eagle Feather rides up and stops beside me. As we gaze back in that direction, I see two lights moving through the woods toward us. They look like the headlights of a car, though they are spread too far apart. "Look," I say to Eagle Feather as I point at the lights coming toward us. "Those cowboys have flashlights."

"No, no. Kerosene lanterns," Eagle Feather says. "They're tracking us through the night, using lanterns to stay on our trail. And if I know the sheriff, he's enlisted some of those Indian braves to help him find our trail. Those Indians are the finest trackers around; they could track a duck through a marsh in a monsoon."

As we look down at the lights, they seem to be moving at quite a fast pace. They are right on our trail, moving almost exactly in our tracks. "If we don't do something quick, they'll be on us in no time," I say.

"Well, what's your plan?" Eagle Feather asks. It *is* a fair question.

"Plan? I don't have a plan. I'm making this stuff up as I go along."

"Well then make something up quickly," he says.

I pull the reins of Sweetheart and ride down the embankment. Kicking her gently, she wades out into the water. Eagle Feather and his horse follow close behind. "Stay in the water," I instruct Eagle Feather. "I'm going to ride upstream and find another place to cross. As long as we keep our horses in the water, we won't leave any tracks for them to follow. With any luck, they'll cross here, and when they don't find any tracks on the other side, they'll have to split up. This should confuse them and buy us some time. At the very least, we'll have a smaller group to fight."

Eagle Feather chuckles as we ride on. "I think you're getting the hang of this warrior thing," he says.

CHAPTER 60

Water splashes under the weight of the horses' hooves as we slog on up the river. We make our way rather slowly. I can still see the lights from the lanterns moving through the woods. I happen to catch a glimpse of Eagle Feather as he rides behind me. He seems to be riding in a casual fashion, even whistling a tune as if nothing much is happening. I find this odd.

I remember, as a boy, in my backyard back on Croton Street, playing cowboys and Indians. I was almost always a cowboy chasing after Indians. It now seems like the cowboys are chasing after us. Talk about reversing the roles. Believe me, the game was a lot more fun in my backyard.

After about a mile, the river widens. Here it is much shallower and easier to cross. I turn Sweetheart out into the river, and we make our way across. Eagle Feather follows along behind me, still whistling away. I can't for the life of me understand how he can be so calm with the sheriff and all of Frontier Town hot on our trail.

We come out of the river and move along the riverbank before riding up a high bluff that overlooks the entire river. We dismount and tie our horses, taking cover in a rock formation in the middle of some pine trees. From our vantage point high up on the bluff, we can see back downriver where we first entered the water, the last place we left tracks for the cowboys and their Indian trackers to follow.

The light thrown from the kerosene lanterns of our pursuers still bobs through the woods exactly along the trail that we left.

Eagle Feather comes up alongside me in a leisurely fashion and sits down on a rock next to me. He pulls out his pocketknife, opens it up, finds a stick on the ground, and starts to whittle. I turn and look at him in amazement. "What the hell are you so goddamn calm about? Don't you realize we're in mortal danger?" He just snickers. There is a period of silence that follows as he just sits there, whittling away.

Finally, he speaks. "I have total confidence in the fact that you will figure this all out."

His statement is so ridiculous that it causes my mouth to fall open. "Figure it out? You have total confidence in me figuring *this* out?"

"That's right," he says and continues to whittle away. "And when that posse arrives at the tracks we left at the river, we'll see if your plan to have them split up is a good one." He resumes his whittling. I have nothing to say. I just look out at the river, waiting for those dancing lights to emerge on the riverbank.

Finally, I break the silence. "What happened to Emma?"

"What do you mean?"

"She just disappeared. She was there one minute and gone the next."

"Oh. She returned to the source."

"Returned to the source?"

"That's right," Eagle Feather says, "back to the source of all that is."

"Well, I thought she was going to help me out—you know, lend me a hand in breaking you out."

"She did."

"How so?"

"She gave you strength. She turned you into a warrior—or, should I say, she brought the warrior out in you."

I look at him. His eyes are dancing as if he anticipated my question. "Really?" I say. "All she did was mumble a few things in some Indian language that I didn't understand, kiss me a few times, and then off she went.

Eagle Feather laughs uproariously. "You think that's all she was doing?"

"Well," I start, but he will not let me finish my thought.

"Were those kisses she gave you not the best and most impactful that you have ever received in your life?" I nod. "She was giving you her energy. She was melting with you and increasing your vibration to that of a warrior. And, I must say, seems like she did a pretty good job. So now she's returned to the source."

I shake my head. His eyes are still dancing. I can see that he is thoroughly enjoying this. "You knew that we kissed," I say, suddenly remembering Eagle Feather's omniscience. "How did you know? How do you know everything that happens in my head?"

He laughs again. A jolly laugh. "Never mind that now. We have a bloodthirsty posse on our hands. How can you be so engrossed in your silly questions?" He goes back to whittling.

Eagle Feather is acting mysteriously, if you ask me. It's almost like he doesn't care whether we're caught or killed, one way or another. I look back down at the river. The lights are getting closer to the bank. I look back at Eagle Feather and watch him whittle for a few minutes. "What happens if they catch us?" I wonder out loud.

"Catch us." He snickers. "They don't want to *catch* us."

"Then what are they doing out here chasing us?"

"They don't want to catch us because they are out here to kill us."

"Kill us? What would they want to kill us for? I mean, I thought those were all my I's down there. If I die, wouldn't they die with me?"

"Well, I suppose that is true, but just for a short while," Eagle Feather says.

"What do you mean?"

"Well, let's just see if you can't figure that out for yourself."

"This is no time for your games," I say gravely, staring him straight in the eye.

"Okay, what happens if you die?"

"Then I'm dead."

"No, what happens if you die—in this place?"

"Well, in this place, you told me that I go back to the clearing and start over again, start another recurrence."

"Ah ... yes, that is correct. And when you were back in that clearing, do you remember those I's having complete control over you? You did whatever they said and even tried to mediate between them when they argued about your next course of action. You were a slave to them. If they manage to kill you, they send you back to the clearing and regain their dominance over you. I believe that is their plan now, and ultimately, they would like to influence you so that you remain in the clearing, never reach me, and are slave to them for all of eternity. This has been their plan before."

"It has?"

"Yup. They've killed you many times before."

I gasp, and then all the air leaves my body. "And when does this happen?" I ask.

"Let's not focus on that. You have made it here in this recurrence. And we still have an opportunity for you to make it even further, and maybe, just maybe, you will succeed and return to your other life."

I look back down at the river. The lights still haven't reached the riverbank. Finally, another question comes to me. "Well, that does explain why they would want to kill *me*. But why would they want to kill *you*? Answer that one for me."

"It's like this," Eagle Feather begins. "I've been the one providing you with the power to resist them. If they can get me out of the way, they think they will regain control of you. It makes perfect sense. I'm the one you listen to now, and I've taught you how to pay no attention to them."

"Seems like we're in a lot of trouble," I say. "There just doesn't seem to be any way out."

Eagle Feather glances back down at the river and then looks back at me. "That's where you're wrong. There's something that they don't know."

"And what's that?" I ask.

"You are a warrior now, and you possess your own personal power. As far as I can recollect, they haven't had to deal with that yet."

CHAPTER 61

The lights burst out of the woods and onto the riverbank. As I look on, I see six Indian braves carrying lanterns and walking along the riverbank, the posse following right behind them. From our vantage point on the high bluff above the river, I count thirty men in addition to the sheriff and the braves. I see the braves discover our tracks leading into the river. The braves then mount their horses and cross with the posse in tow. As soon as they reach the other side, the braves dismount again and walk up and down the beach, using their lanterns to try to pick up our trail. I watch the sheriff ride up with the Indians. He has a brief conversation with them. The sheriff then rides back to the main body of the search party and, after wildly waving his arms, points both down and upriver. The posse splits into two with three braves and half the party heading downriver and the other half of the posse and three braves heading upriver toward us.

"Look," I say, "they're splitting up, just as I hoped."

"Yup," says Eagle Feather, calmly whittling away, "they took the bait. Now what's your plan?"

"My plan is like I just told you: we got them to split up, and we have the high ground. When they find our trail and follow it up to us, we'll be able to pick them off one by one. Although I hadn't really planned on there being so many of them …"

"I told you the sheriff would have the whole town after us. Remember, everybody has a stake in this."

I turn to Eagle Feather and ask him to go back to the horses and get the rest of the ammo we have with us. He chuckles a little bit and continues to whittle. "All the ammo we have is in the pistols we're carrying."

I didn't count on that either. "Well, I guess we'll just have to make every shot count."

"Ah, so you're a sharpshooter now," Eagle Feather says sarcastically.

"I don't think you're taking this very seriously."

"Oh, really?" He turns his head and looks back downriver. "In no time at all, those Indian braves will pick up our trail, and they'll all be on us. Then things will get a bit more serious."

I look back down the river at the posse moving in our direction. My eyes become fixated on the kerosene lanterns held by the braves out in front of the party, and I fall into another vision. I see the braves discover our trail and signal for the posse to move up. When they reach the trackers, a member of the posse, who I assume is the sheriff, raises his arm and fires a single shot in the air. Downriver, the lanterns turn about, and the second group starts moving quickly back toward us. The posse that was down below us stays on our tracks, moving upriver.

"Here they come," I say, still in the vision.

I see them close in quickly, firing, the first rounds ripping through the pine trees all around us. Eagle Feather and I return fire at the shadowy figures. I see some of the sheriff's men pull out there Winchester rifles and move to our flank, trying to establish position and keep us pinned down where we are. I am firing at anything that moves, but it does nothing to slow the overwhelming spray of bullets exploding all around us. In a matter of minutes, Eagle Feather and I are both out of ammo. I watch him pull the tomahawk out from behind his back and let out a war whoop. He dives head-on into the approaching posse, but the onslaught is too much. The second wave of pursuers has already reached the hill, and we are so outnumbered that Eagle Feather's last stand is futile. They shoot him down with several shots and scalp him. Seeing this, I jump to my feet and run for the horses, but before I can reach them, I too am shot down.

As soon as I collapse to the ground in my vision, my mind flashes back to the present moment. I hear the gunfire from the first party that discovered our tracks. I look at Eagle Feather, who spins the barrels of his Colt .45s, making sure they are loaded. I look at this, and he returns my glance with a funny look.

"Well," he says, "are you ready for the big fight? It's a good day to die." With that, he laughs maniacally.

"Bad idea, bad idea," I mutter to myself.

"What do you mean?" he asks.

"You know, that idea about splitting the parties up and picking them off one at a time."

"Yeah ..." he answers.

"Extremely bad idea," I add.

I look back down the hill. The posse is almost right on top of us. I look back at Eagle Feather. He is still sitting there in a casual fashion. "Well, what should we do now then?" he asks.

"First, we're going to get the hell out of here as quickly as possible. And then, if I don't get my ass shot off, I'll try to think up a new plan."

"I take it you didn't like what you saw," says Eagle Feather as we sprint for the horses.

"Absolutely not—no, not at all," I reply. "How did you know that I had a vision or that I saw anything at all?"

"Maybe I saw the same thing," he says, cracking a wry smile.

"This would be an opportune moment for another vision," I say.

Suddenly, a thought comes to me.

"We need to slow them down a bit," I say to Eagle Feather, "or else they'll be on top of us before we know it. Can you cover me a sec? I'm going to try to shoot out those lanterns."

"Sure, sounds like that ought to slow them down a bit," he says. "Ride to the edge of the hill, and when I start shooting, take your best shot."

We turn the horses and stop abruptly at the top of the hill. I pull out my Colt .45s and take aim at the lantern that is closest to us and moving quickly up the hill. I fire three times, and finally, with the third round, the lantern is snuffed out. I then take aim and fire down the hill at the second lantern. Incredibly, with the one shot, I manage to take it out.

"I told you you were a sharpshooter," Eagle Feather yells. We both turn quickly and kick our horses, making our way toward the woods. As I look back, I see the first batch of bullets pepper the pines where we just were. Being on horseback, we are able to get out of there fast enough to avoid being shot.

"That levels the playing field," I say to Eagle Feather. "They'll have a hell of a time following our tracks in the dark."

We ride on toward the valley in silence. All the while, I'm continuously spinning around to see if we are being followed. When we make it to the bottom of the hill and seem safe enough for the time being, we stop to take a breather. Eagle Feather suggests that we dismount and give the horses a break. He goes to his saddlebag and pulls out a canteen of water, and we both take a drink.

"You think they're still out there?" I ask. "Maybe they gave up and went back to Frontier Town. I'm sure those Indian braves are having a hell of a time tracking us in the dark."

Eagle Feather takes a seat on a rock and, to my astonishment, pulls his pipe out of his vest pocket. He stuffs some tobacco into the pipe and lights it. He then pulls out his stick and continues to whittle.

"I thought you ran out of tobacco," I say, "and with all the commotion and you being captured, when did you have time to take any supplies with you?"

He chuckles a little bit. "You know that business about a dying man's last wish?"

"Yeah."

"Well, I decided to ask for some tobacco." He pauses and takes a puff before continuing. "Oh, and by the way, they aren't just going to quit and head back to Frontier Town. That's not in the cards. Not tonight. So, take a rest my friend while we have the chance. We're really going to need it."

We sit there in the dark quietly. I keep peering out into the darkness, straining my eyes and ears for any sign of our pursuers. All is quiet except for the sound of Eagle Feather's whittling and the sizzling tobacco in his pipe; he nonchalantly blows rings of smoke as if we are on the front porch of the cabin.

Suddenly, Eagle Feather stands up as if he has had some sort of premonition. "Let's get moving," he says.

With that, we both walk over to the horses. I put my left foot in the stirrup to mount Sweetheart, but Eagle Feather says, "No, no, we're going to walk the horses up the hill. We'll give them a little bit longer break, and besides, it will be much quieter."

I walk around Sweetheart and grab the reins, and we start up the hill on foot. It is an arduous climb; I didn't realize how steep the hill really is. When we reach the top, we stop and stand by a tree that looks like it may have been hit by lightning. From our vantage point high up on the hill, we can see the whole valley. Off in the distance, the lights of Frontier Town only wink through the wind-swept branches.

"Look!" I exclaim. About a hundred yards out, down at the base of the hill, I see two lights lilting through the woods in our direction. "Look, Eagle Feather! There's those goddamn lights again."

The lights stare back at us through the darkness, moving along at a quick, determined pace. "They must have been able to repair those lanterns," I say to Eagle Feather.

"Is that what you think?" Eagle Feather says.

"Yeah. What other explanation is there?"

Eagle Feather doesn't answer right away, and there is another of his long pauses. "No, they brought extra lanterns with them. You know, you and I are not the only ones who have been through this recurrence before." After speaking, he glares at me.

His statement shocks me. I hadn't thought that those I's down there would have the wherewithal to remember all the situations of our last recurrence and then actually be able to capitalize on them. "You mean they know what's about to happen? Are they having visions just like I am?"

"Not in the full sense, no. Remember that they are a part of you, so they are only getting bits and pieces."

"Which bits and pieces?" I ask.

"How the hell am I supposed to know?" Eagle Feather says. "I guess they got that bit about the lanterns though." He laughs uproariously.

"Well, this is no good. I thought we had an edge over them."

"Edge? There's thirty of them out there looking for us, and you're talking about *us* having the edge. We'll just have to try to stay one jump ahead of them."

"That's just lovely," I say.

"Remember, you are able to see the entire vision while they can only see a small portion of the event," Eagle Feather says.

"We have to figure out a way to throw them off our trail," I say. "Or we have to outrun them."

Eagle Feather glances back down the hill at the lanterns, which have now advanced to only fifty yards away.

"Outrun them? Throw them off our trail?" he says in a surprised voice. "How do you run away from yourself? How do you throw yourself off of your own trail? No matter where you run, there you are. They could track us to the ends of the earth, and, believe me, they would find us."

I'm getting pretty antsy now. The posse is a little too close for my liking.

"Well," I say, "we'll just have to outrun them until daylight, and then they'll disappear." I like this response and am surprised I didn't think of it sooner.

Eagle Feather turns toward me with a stern look in his eye. Shaking his head, he says, "There is no daylight. There is no daylight coming at all."

"What are you talking about? What does that even mean?"

"I mean it ends tonight. Either they kill us and you start all over again, or you find your way out of here and return to your other life."

I turn and grab Sweetheart by the reins and mount her quickly. Eagle Feather follows suit. As he mounts his horse, Eagle Feather turns to me and says, "So, you see, we can't go on running forever. Sooner or later, they will catch up to us."

"What would you suggest?" I ask angrily.

"Eventually, we'll have to make a stand and let the chips fall where they may," he answers.

"Well, one thing I know from that last vision is that we're outmanned and outgunned. If we're going to make a stand, we're going to have to do it on our own terms. We pick the time, and we pick the place."

"So …"

"So, lead the way to the cabin. I thought there was a reason why you cut those gun turrets in the window shutters and the front door."

Eagle Feather grins and turns his pony in the direction of the cabin. "I can see, just like in your tennis matches, you like home court advantage."

"I like any advantage I can get," I say.

Just as we reach the bottom the hill, I hear rifle fire and feel the cool air around my head move as a bullet whizzes by. Too close for comfort. As if on cue, Eagle Feather and I both wheel our horses around and return fire, emptying our pistols into the dark night and praying we can keep the posse at bay long enough for us to get out of range.

We ride headlong into the cover of the night. As I look back, I see the lanterns at the top of the hill begin their descent. We move at a quick clip through the pitch black, barely able to see the noses in front of our faces and desperately trying to close the nearly two-mile gap between the bottom of the hill and the cabin before the posse overtakes us.

As my body is occupied trying to stay on Sweetheart and dodge the trees and low-lying branches, my mind keeps going over the two scenarios that Eagle Feather just laid out. The fact that there will be no daylight and one of those two scenarios will come to fruition has me a bit concerned. I have to choose one, and I am certainly not going to choose the scenario in which we are both killed and I have to start all over from the clearing. Naturally, I'd rather select the path that lands me back in my life. But how am I supposed to pull that off? Throughout my entire time in this strange place, there has been no solid indication of any way home. And now, in one night, however long that night may be, I have to find my way out. Because the alternative is unthinkable.

CHAPTER 62

I leap from my horse, unbuckle the saddle, and toss it onto the porch. Eagle Feather slaps his pony hard on the ass, and I do the same to Sweetheart and watch both horses disappear down the road toward the lake. Eagle Feather goes over to one of the windows and closes the shutters. Following his lead, I do the same to the window on the other side of the cabin. We burst through the door, and Eagle feather turns around and slams it shut as the first few rounds from the posse pepper the front of the building.

"Throw the bolts on the shutters and lock them," he calls over to me as he makes his way over to the fireplace. He returns with a heavy wooden beam that he lays across the door onto two L-shaped metal bars. He then goes over to the gun cabinet, reaches into his vest pocket, pulls out the key, and unlocks the case. He pulls out two Henry repeating rifles and throws one across the room to me. I catch it with my left hand and deftly open the lever with my right. It is empty.

I look at Eagle Feather. He opens the bottom of the gun case and pulls out a box teeming with ammunition. "Load up," he says, "and don't forget to load your pistols also."

Bullets crash against the outside of the cabin. As I load my rifle, I peer out of the slots in the shutters. I can see two lanterns glowing and the shadows of men behind them. Smoke fills the air.

"Loaded?" Eagle Feather yells, and I nod affirmatively. "Remember," he goes on, "squeeze the trigger—don't yank it back. And when you take aim, aim small, miss small."

I rack a round into my Henry rifle, slide the muzzle out of one of the turrets, and fire. And I continue to fire repeatedly. As does Eagle feather. But I realize I'm just shooting really; I can't see what I'm firing at. The return fire from the posse is unbearable. The lead slams the side of the cabin so repeatedly that the wood seems to cry out in pain.

As Eagle Feather reloads his rifle, he suggests we go for the lanterns again. "If we shoot the lanterns, we may be able to see the sheriff and his men a lot better in the moonlight. They've positioned the lanterns out in front, and we only seem to be shooting at shadows."

I aim for the lantern closest to me and fire a couple of times, successfully extinguishing it. Eagle Feather hits his lantern with one shot and lets me know about it with a wink and a smile. Now looking out of my gun port, I can clearly see the silhouettes of the sheriff's men. I begin firing at targets rather than indiscriminately discharging my weapon. I'm not sure what the results are, whether I'm hitting any of them or not, but it seems that Eagle Feather is having a ball. After every few shots, he lets out one of his war whoops and makes a notch in the wall with his knife.

"Just like at the shooting gallery!" he calls out.

Even though Eagle Feather claims to be hitting the men he's shooting at, it does little to quell the barrage of bullets; the firefight rages on for quite some time. And then, as quickly as it began, it is over.

Eagle Feather turns and sits with his back up against the wall next to the window. I do the same.

"Well," he says, chuckling, "looks like round one is over."

I exhale a deep breath, remove my hat, and use it to wipe my brow. I look around the cabin.

"Where are the dogs?" I ask Eagle Feather.

He shoots me a look of shock. "Those dogs are too smart to hang around here with all this ruckus going on."

"I can see that. But where did they go?"

"Oh, they're with Emma."

"What do you mean?"

"They went back to the source."

"The source?" I say, hoping against hope that he might finally elaborate.

Eagle Feather shoots me a disapproving look. "The source. You know, the source of all this," and he rotates his arms in a slow fashion. "The source of all there is." He then stretches his face into a big smile. He pulls his hat down over his eyes and says, "Get some rest before round two starts."

"Whoa, whoa, whoa. Hold on a sec here. Tell me about this source."

Without bothering to lift his hat over his eyes, he starts, "The source ... the source of everything you see and all events that take place. All comes from one source. In this life as in the other life, it is the source that thinks everything up, that creates and projects it all out into the space that we call reality. All the characters and all the events play out according to this source."

I just look at him. He looks ridiculous, pontificating from underneath his down-drawn hat. I bet he tells me to think about it next.

"Think about it," he says.

But before any actual thinking about it can occur, the silence is broken by a voice. "Hey, you in the cabin." Then again, "Hey, you in the cabin. We want to have a parlay with you."

CHAPTER 63

I turn back around and glance out of the turret. Out in front of the cabin, I see a tall man, a short man, and two Indian braves. The short man is standing there, waving a stick with a white handkerchief tied to it. Eagle Feather does not move, with the exception of pulling his hat back up off his eyes and grinning at me.

"Now what's this all about?" I ask him.

"Looks to me like the sheriff wants to come in and have a little talk with you. You know, a powwow."

"Well, what do you think?"

"That's up to you. You're running the show now."

"What the hell can they possibly want?"

"Go ahead. Invite them in and find out. I mean, they did go through all the trouble of tying a white bandana to a stick, didn't they? Hey, it can't hurt." He smiles.

"All right, let's see what this is all about."

"Good idea," says Eagle Feather, chuckling.

"Throw down your weapons and approach the door unarmed," I call out. I turn to Eagle Feather and add, "I don't trust these guys. Keep an eye on them."

Eagle Feather sits up and turns around, looking out his peephole. We watch as the taller man, who I presume is the sheriff, and the shorter man both drop their gun belts. Their Indian accomplices gingerly lay their bows and arrows on the ground.

"This ought to be entertaining," says Eagle Feather through a smirk. "Getting more entertaining as the night wears on."

"Entertaining my ass," I say. "What do you suppose is really going on here?"

"I'm guessing they want to come in for a look-see; they want to gauge what kind of guns we have, how much ammunition, our food situation—you know, try to see how long we can hold out. Oh, yeah, and this is the best part: they're going to try to talk you out of this whole thing."

"Talk me out of what? They're after *us*, remember?"

"You'll see. Let's not keep them waiting." He pushes his chin out to suggest I have another look out of the shutter.

"All right," I yell, "you, out there in the yard, start walking for the door real slow-like. Don't try any funny stuff, or I'll shoot ya down where you stand."

"I love it!" says Eagle Feather, who laughs until I think tears are going to roll down his face. "Just like John Wayne!"

When they reach the porch, I stick my Henry rifle out through the hole and insist that they keep their hands where I can see them. Eagle Feather gets up and goes over to the door. I stand a few paces back, with my rifle in my hands, while Eagle Feather removes the beam that secures the door. Two rather impressive Indian braves walk in first, feathers in their hair, war paint, and the like. They are followed closely by the sheriff and the runt that I recognize as the wise guy from Frontier Town.

"All right, stop right there. Keep your hands where I can see them. Now what's this parlay all about?"

Before the sheriff can answer, Eagle Feather begins speaking to the Indian braves in a language I have never heard before. This is followed by a lot of posturing and hand gestures. Eagle Feather points to me several times and also at the sheriff while talking to the Indians in what I can only assume is their native language. He pats himself on the chest with his right hand. He also makes motions with his left hand. The Indian braves do little speaking; they mostly listen … and look back and forth at me and the sheriff several times.

Eagle Feather goes over to his quiver of arrows. He pulls an arrow out and, walking back over to the braves, holds the arrow up with both hands over his head. He then breaks the arrow in half in front of the braves and hands one half to each of them. Each brave takes their half in their left hand and places their right hand on Eagle Feather's left shoulder. This must signal the end of their discussion; both braves turn and leave. I watch from my vantage point, looking through the open door as the two braves round up the rest of their Indian companions and ride off toward the lake.

"Okay, floor's all yours," Eagle Feather says to me.

"So, what's this all about?" I say. "You have come to have a parlay, so go ahead, parlay."

The wise guy is the first to speak up. "We don't want to talk in front of this Indian here. Tell him to go into the other room."

"First of all, don't come in here and dictate to me what to do," I say forcefully. "Secondly, I don't tell him what to do. He does what he damn well pleases."

"That's right, he does," replies the wise guy. "He's the cause of all this. He told you not to pay any attention to us—that we were no good and that we didn't have your best interests at heart. Well, that's a load of crap. We want things to go back to the way they were, the way they have always been."

"That's enough," says the sheriff to the wise guy. "Shut your mouth. I'll do the negotiating around here—and don't you forget that."

"Damn," mutters the wise guy.

"Well, what do you have to say? Make it quick," I say. "You're interrupting our dinner."

"There's no need for all this fighting. There's no need for anybody to be killed. We just want you to come back with us. We'll take you back to town and take good care of you. We'll simply forget this little misunderstanding we've had, and after a while, you'll forget about this fellow here," he says, gesturing toward Eagle Feather, "and all the foolish notions he's been filling your head with. And we'll go back to the way things were before. Back before you met this crazy man."

There is a short pause. The air is so heavy you could, as a fellow says, cut it with a Crocodile Dundee knife.

I look at the sheriff sternly. "Is that all you have to say?"

"No," he snaps. "I'll just say this. You have a choice to make tonight. You either come back with us and have things go back to normal or we're coming after you with everything we have."

"What does that mean?" I ask.

"That means either you join us, or you die."

"And your Indian friend," chimes in the wise guy.

"Well, what do you say?"

I can feel the sheriff, the wise guy, and Eagle Feather all glaring at me. In this moment, I realize that I have come a long way. I am much better off living the life of the warrior than being a slave to those I's. I have no intention of going back.

"Kill me? Kill Eagle Feather? I should shoot you two down right here and save us all the hassle. Only because you came under a white flag, under a sign of truce, am I allowing you to walk out of here alive. Turn around and get the hell out of here."

"You're making a big mistake," yells the wise guy as he walks out. "We're going to kill you both."

"I guess you'll just have to kill me then. Get the hell out of here."

When they have both left the cabin, Eagle Feather slams the heavy wooden door behind them and quickly replaces the beam that reinforces it. We ready ourselves for round two.

Through the hole in the shutter, I watch the backs of the two men as they disappear into the dark. I then turn back around and sit with my back up against the wall. Eagle Feather does the same. There is a long silence in which neither of us speaks.

CHAPTER 64

Finally, Eagle Feather turns toward me and says, "I guess you told those boys."

"I'm not going back to the way things were," I say. "I'm not going to be that person any longer, with all the confusion in my mind and all those voices talking to me. I don't want to be controlled by anybody. I want to become, as you said, whole. I want to become the one true I that I can be. If that means they have to kill me and I have to go through this all again, so be it. No matter how many times it takes, I am going to be whole."

Eagle Feather stretches his arm out in front of himself, makes a fist, and then pokes his thumb straight up in the air, giving me the sign of approval.

"Eagle Feather, when do you think I will become the one true I? I mean, where is he and when do you think I'll hear that voice?"

"Oh, he's been with you here all along," Eagle Feather says in a serious tone. "And you have heard his voice. It's obvious that you have; otherwise you would not have been able to keep all those I's at bay. Also, you would not have been able to hear and understand the teaching that you have undergone since you arrived here. He's here with you now, and if you stay true to your lessons, he will be here with you for the rest of your life … for however long that may be." With this, he begins to chuckle.

346

I look over at Eagle Feather, and he seems to glow with an incandescent light. "I know that you talked to me about the two scenarios, the two possibilities that could play out tonight. But as far as the second scenario goes, I have no clue whatsoever about how to get back to my other life." Eagle Feather remains silent. "Any thoughts on that?" I ask.

"If you stay true to your aim of becoming one, you'll be shown the way."

"I know, and next you're going to tell me to think about that." He lets out a laugh. "Oh yeah, and by the way, what did you say to those Indians? After you were finished, they just picked up and left."

Eagle Feather reaches into his vest pocket and produces his pipe. He strikes a match John Wayne style and uses it to the light the pipe. "Remember a while ago when I first talked to you about the I's and how negative they were and how destructive they were to you? You asked me if any of these I's were good—the kind of I's that would look out for you and help you on your journey to becoming the one true I. Well, those Indians out there are your good I's. They were merely duped, tricked by the townspeople. They were told that you were here to destroy them all. I just had to set them straight. I told them who you really are and why you are here, that you are on a vision quest to become one. Once they realized this, they could no longer help the townspeople, and they rode off."

Just as Eagle Feather finishes speaking, a barrage of bullets slams the shutters. Startled, we both jump up. I try to peer out of my gun turret to see what's happening, but the onslaught of bullets is too much. I can barely see out let alone get my rifle out to return fire.

"Looks like you really pissed them off!" Eagle Feather yells. "Here they come."

Though I can barely see out the peephole, I manage to catch a glimpse of four men rushing toward the cabin. Using a large wooden beam as a battering ram, they charge the front door over and over again. Each time they crash into the door, it trembles. The bullets insistently pound the sides of the window, making it impossible to shoot out. After several charges, the front door looks as though it won't be able to withstand another blow. If we don't do something soon, the whole posse will overtake the cabin, and we will be done for.

"Get the ten-gauge shotgun out of the gun case!" Eagle Feather yells, and I do as he says. "There's two rounds in the desk drawer. Load it!"

I pull open the drawer and put the two rounds through each barrel of the ten-gauge. "What do I have in here?" I call out to Eagle Feather.

"That there is double-0 buckshot. You can stop an elephant with that."

"Get to the door," I say, "and when you're ready, open it."

Meanwhile, the men outside the cabin have continued to slam away at the door. Now the hinges are shaking, and the large wooden bar is vibrating back and forth. I know it is not going to hold up much longer. Eagle Feather pulls the bar off in one quick motion and flings the door open. Immediately, all four men drop the beam and rush the door. I aim the shotgun out of the open doorway and pull the trigger, firing both barrels at once. The men outside crumble, reeling in pain before falling to the ground dead. Eagle Feather reaches over, slams the door shut, and replaces the beam. I drop the shotgun, run to the shutters, and look out. The hail of bullets has stopped, and the four men lie dead on the porch.

I look at Eagle Feather, and he looks back at me. I can feel my throat swelling as I hold back tears. "I have never killed anyone before," I say.

He looks at me with sympathetic eyes. "It couldn't be helped," he says. "They were going to kill you. Besides, have a look out there. Go ahead, cast your eyes back out there on that porch."

Again, I look through the peephole, expecting to see the horror of what I just did. I'm astonished to see the four men that had been lying dead just seconds before come back to life, jump up, and run back out into the darkness. I am taken aback and turn to look at Eagle Feather.

"Those are hard sons of bitches to kill," he says, his eyes dancing.

"But how can that be? You and I both watched them collapse in pain and die."

Eagle Feather lights his pipe, the smoke billowing up to the ceiling. "Those I's out there can't be killed. There's no way to vanquish them completely. You created them, and they've been with you for countless lifetimes. The only real weapon you have against them is your attention. Notice that it was when you felt guilt over their deaths that they were able to spring back to life and retreat. It's only when you are able to ignore them that their power is useless." He pauses for a second, probably to let this all sink in. "So, you see, my friend, this fight is not about life or death. It's about control. All those men out there, and all the people in the town, they seek control over you. If you deny them this control, you deny them their life. They have nothing. But they cannot be eradicated."

"If they can't be killed, then what's the sense of wasting all this ammo on them? And if that's the case, why don't they just storm the cabin and overtake us?"

"Well, that is a good question," he says. "Fortunately, they are like everybody else in that they do not know that there is no such thing as death. What you just witnessed was not a pleasant experience. For a brief while, they did die, and they did experience all the pain and agony that goes with death. And believe me, they don't like that. But then the life force returns, and they are back to where they were before. You, on the other hand, as the complete entity, are differently affected by death. You will return to the beginning, to the clearing, and have to start this whole journey over again." He chuckles. "Guess you've just seen your first glimpse of recurrence."

Eagle Feather sits back and smokes his pipe. All is quiet outside the cabin, and I sit for a while, thinking about what Eagle Feather just said. Finally, I turn and say, "It's awfully quiet out there. Maybe they've had enough and have gone back to town."

"You can bet your bottom dollar that they're still out there. They are desperate. They are ruthless in their desire for control, and they will stop at nothing to obtain it. In fact, I don't really like this prolonged silence. They're up to something all right. And I expect we'll find out what soon enough." He continues to smoke away.

"I thought you told me there's no smoking in the cabin?" I say.

"I reckon in a little while it won't matter much," he answers.

I lean back up against the wall of the cabin. Meanwhile, the eerie quiet outside persists. Eagle Feather suggests that we try to get a little rest while we still can.

"I think we have a kind of Mexican standoff," I say. "They're outside and can't get in. And we're in here and have no way out."

Eagle Feather pulls his hat down over his eyes and leans back. "Maybe so. We'll see how it goes. Now get some rest."

It's been an extremely long night. As a matter of fact, it has quite literally been the longest night I've ever been through. With this thought hanging in my mind, I pull my hat down over my eyes, lean back, and fall into a deep sleep.

CHAPTER 65

I awaken to a ruckus out in front of the cabin. I hear shouting and the sounds of something being thrown up against the cabin walls. The sounds are not gunfire but something else—soft, dull, and, I fear, something possibly more insidious. Though I'm still groggy, I turn around and peer out the peephole. I see men running toward the cabin, tossing bales of hay on the porch. Before I can see what they're up to, shots begin to hit the shutters. I duck just in time as one of the bullets whistles through the peephole and clangs against one of the hanging frying pans across the room.

"Here we go again!" yells Eagle Feather. "I think these boys have little patience for a Mexican standoff!"

He begins to fire out of his hole in the shutter. I poke my rifle out as well, but the barrage of bullets is too much. Eagle Feather continues to fire away in defiance; it is as if he is daring them to shoot him through that tiny gun turret. I manage to get another look out and see two men lying dead in front of the cabin. But what I see next is what really horrifies me: the men are running up to the cabin with flaming torches and heaving them onto the porch. I watch as Eagle Feather successfully shoots two more of them before they can reach the porch. But our defense is hopeless as several torches land on the porch and ignite the bales of hay. I watch the two dead men spring back to life and flee into the woods as flames shoot up the sides of the cabin.

The hay is a tremendous catalyst, and to make matters worse, the walls of the wooden cabin—ash, I think—are extremely combustible. Instinctively, I jump up and run for the water pump, grabbing a bucket from under the sink and frantically pumping water into it. Once the bucket is full, I toss it onto the smoldering walls. Eagle Feather is working his own bucket, but it is hopeless; the fire is outpacing our efforts. Now the entire front side of the cabin is engulfed in flames. Smoke, choking smoke, pours into the little room.

"Don't bother with that water anymore," Eagle Feather cries out. "It won't do much good. Goddamn bastards are going to smoke us out."

We are now kneeling in the middle of the room, coughing and gagging, our eyes burning from the relentless smoke. Eagle Feather looks at me, and our gazes meet. His eyes are glowing, though I can't tell if it's from the reflected flames or some other supernatural cause.

"You are a warrior now," he says. "Make no mistake about that. Get to the water spirit. There you will receive guidance. Keep steadfast in your mind the life you wish to return to. Don't entertain any negative thoughts and use all your intuition to guide you. Time for you to become whole, to become one. Heed that one single voice as it guides you toward your one true self. You and I have come as far as we can go."

The illumination in his eyes draws me in, and I am unable avert his glance. Or speak. Through the darkness and smoke of the burning cabin, Eagle Feather himself begins to glow. He reaches out his hand and puts it on my left shoulder while still looking intently into my eyes.

"I am about to give you the last bit of the puzzle, the last bit of power you will need. There is help along the way. And at the end of your journey, a friend will come to help you. Now it is time that I return to the source. Our time together in this life can go no further. I will always be with you, and you will always be with me. Now I return to the source of all that is."

With that, Eagle Feather vanishes. The flames have spread to the roof, and bits and pieces of flaming timber crash to the floor.

The smoke is so black that I can hardly see, let alone breathe. I throw myself to the floorboards and feel my way to the trapdoor of the root cellar. Struggling a bit, I manage to pull the door open and descend the ladder. When I reach the bottom, I again hear that same voice that I heard when I was in the cave with the bear. But the voice sounds different now. It sounds clearer and more a part of me. "Remember where you put the key," it says. "Use the key and take the truck to the lake."

Groping along the walls of the dark cellar, I manage to find the ladder as I hear large sections of the cabin's roof crashing down above me. Once I make it safely to the main floor, I crawl to the sofa, now ablaze, and feel around under the cushions until I locate the key. The smoke is too overwhelming, and I make my way back to the ladder and descend into the root cellar, closing the trapdoor. I hear several loud thuds, which can only be the rest of the roof caving in.

I collapse to the floor, gasping for what little oxygen is left in the pit. An overwhelming feeling possesses my entire mind and body. It is a feeling unlike any I've ever had. I get the feeling that I have died here before. Suddenly, I find my consciousness floating above my body. As I look down, I see my body lying there on the root cellar floor. Visions of the clearing on that first day I arrived return to my mind. I see myself there as I was that day: confused, alone, and with all the I's scrambling through my mind again. It is as if I am being pulled back to that place.

My resolve stiffens. I can't let this happen again. I summon all my willpower, all my emotions and my intellect, and I struggle hard to pull myself back into my body. It's as if I'm swimming upstream against a raging torrent. With all my being, I press hard. The struggle seems to last for an eternity.

Finally, I see nothing but darkness. I open my right eye and see my hand move in front of my face, and I know I am back in my body again. Coughing, gagging from the smoke and now unbearable heat of the floorboards of the cabin, I struggle to my feet. Through the murky darkness, I see a single small beam of light. The window!

CHAPTER 66

Struggling, I somehow make it to the source of the light. I reach behind my back and pull the tomahawk from my sash. With a few swings, I manage to clear all the glass from the tiny window and, gathering every last ounce of energy, I manage to pull myself up and squeeze through the tiny opening. Still choking with my smoke-filled lungs, I lie there on the ground.

My mind is in a fog from near asphyxiation. Even in my semi-coherent state, I know that I have to get out of sight. I spy the row of firewood piles that line the back of the cabin and crawl on my belly the thirty or so yards until I reach the closest pile. It seems a good enough spot to wait until I can get my wits about me.

I remain there for quite a while, and just as I'm starting to feel a bit better, I hear voices coming around toward the back of the cabin. As they come closer, I recognize one of the voices. It is the voice of the wise guy and one of the sheriff's deputies. They must have been sent out to patrol the back of the cabin and make sure that neither Eagle Feather nor I have escaped. I pull both my pistols and cock the action. In no time at all, I realize that the only thing separating us is the woodpile.

I have the tremendous urge to spring up from behind the woodpile and shoot both of them right there on the spot. After all, the wise guy was one of the major instigators here in this life. And come to think of it, he caused me no small amount of trouble in my other life. Without any doubt, he is one of those I's that has to go. But I decide not to go through with it. I realize that my Angry I is silent, and I take this as a sign that I have truly taken control of myself. I elect for the more pragmatic approach: hunkering down in hopes that they will pass right by. Firing on them would undoubtedly bring the rest of the posse down on me. And from what I've seen, there'd be no sense in shooting the wise guy, as he'd just come right back to life.

So there I lie, hoping not to be discovered. I hold my breath as they stand just a few yards from me. After a while, they continue to walk out around toward the other end of the cabin. I exhale as I hear them moving away and unlock the pistols, returning them to my sash.

My mind seems to be freshening, and I poke my head up and watch them get farther away around the still-burning cabin. As my mind clears, I remember the last things Eagle Feather told me: that I would receive help on my way back to my other life and that I should seek guidance from the water spirit. Looking around, I follow the woodpile as it stretches along the whole back of the cabin and wraps around the building's far side, which is just across from the barn.

The barn! I remember the voice that I heard in the root cellar telling me that I should retrieve the key to the truck and take it to down to the lake on my way to the water spirit. I reach down and pat my pocket and am glad that the key is still there despite all the excitement. Staggering to my feet, I realize that these woodpiles that Eagle Feather had me construct will provide enough cover for me to safely make it to the barn and the truck.

I begin to, ever so cautiously, leapfrog from one pile to the next. When I finally reach the last pile, I crouch down and see that only forty yards separate me from the barn. I look to my left in the direction of the front of the cabin. There the sheriff and his entire posse stand, cradling their rifles and admiring what is left of the blaze. This will afford me the opportunity to make it to the barn. But I know that as soon as the fire has dissipated, the sheriff will order his men to search for our bodies in the rubble. Of course, what they do not know is that there will be no bodies to find, and this will prompt the men to scour the entire area, searching for us.

I crouch down behind the woodpile, taking care to stay out

of sight, and look at the barn. I have to make my way across forty yards of wide-open ground with nothing to conceal me. While the dark night lingers on, the cabin flames throw enough light and shadows that I can easily be spotted. As I crouch there, I begin to think. *Where the hell is the help that Eagle Feather told me I would receive?* Nevertheless, deep down inside myself, I am comforted by the feeling that something will occur to help me on my way. At this point, I don't quite know what. But I just know.

I remember that Eagle Feather told me to keep the idea of returning to my former life in my mind at all times and that I am to banish any negative thoughts along the way. I begin to think back to the tennis club, the last place I was. And I even think how wonderful it would be if I were suddenly back there now, finishing up that lesson with fat, old Mrs. Hamshire. Suddenly and without warning, I hear a tremendous roar. Poking my head up and glancing to the left, I see all four walls of the cabin come crashing down on top of one another, sending smoke, ash, and glowing embers soaring toward the heavens. The men in the posse seem transfixed by the sight, and I hear them cheer. This is my opportunity.

I leap from behind the woodpile and sprint across the open ground, hoping the men's attention is dominated by the collapsing cabin. I reach the barn without incident and squeeze through a slightly ajar barn door. It is the same barn door that I fastened and locked on the day we left for Frontier Town. I find it a bit curious that it's open now, as it would have taken some time to unlock it and pull the large door open. But I'm certainly not one to look a gift horse in the mouth—not right now.

It's quite dark inside; the barn is lit only by the light of the surviving flames that are filtered through a few small windows. I quickly make my way to the truck, swing open the cab door, and hop into the driver's seat. I pull the key from my pocket and put it in the ignition.

"Use the four-wheel drive. Lock the front hubs," says the voice inside me.

I jump from the cab of the truck, move to the front, and lock both hubs. Now the truck will be in four-wheel drive, a necessity on the rocky and bumpy dirt road that runs from the cabin to the lake. Holding my breath, I turn the key and ... nothing.

CHAPTER 67

Nothing happens. Just a slight clicking noise. *Damn. I hope this thing starts.* I don't even know if there's any gas in the tank. And god knows the last time this truck has run. I depress the gas pedal a couple of times and push the clutch down before turning the key again. *Rorr rurrrr rurrr.* It sounds as if the engine is trying with all its might to turn over. "God damn it!" I yell as I slam my hands down on the dashboard. "Come on, you old piece of junk. Start for me." I pump the gas a couple more times, push the clutch down, and turn the key again.

"Rurr rurrr rurrr," answers the engine, obviously gasping for air and making those same tired, heartbreaking groans. I reach up and yank my hat down over my eyes in frustration. I can't believe that I was able to make it to the truck, and now the damn thing won't start. I think about getting out and opening the hood, but then again, I've never really had a mechanical I.

"Pull out the choke, pull out the choke," the inner voice urges.

I lift my hat back up over my eyes so I can see what the hell I'm doing. Looking down on the dashboard, I see a round knob just to the left of the steering wheel. And, fortunately for me, written plain as day across the knob is the word "choke." I reach down and pull the knob out as far as it is willing to go. I then turn the key and pump the gas pedal a couple more times. With a much more confident and tremendous roar, the engine ignites.

Looking out toward the front door, I see a head pop through the opening. I pull out the light switch on the dashboard, and as soon as the lights click on, I see the face of the wise guy. The lights startle him a little, and he starts to yell, "Here they are! Here they are in the barn!"

I let off the parking brake, push in the clutch, shift the truck into first, and hit the gas. This sends the truck through the barn doors, knocking them off their hinges. I make a right turn in the direction of the lake. Just then, I see the wise guy running alongside the truck and doing his best to avoid the debris kicked out by the falling barn doors. I pull a pistol from my sash and lean out the window. Knowing full well that I can't kill him, I shoot the little bastard in the ass. After a quick peek in the rearview mirror, I see the wise guy hit the ground hard. He struggles to his feet and starts to limp in my direction. I laugh—a laugh that sounds hauntingly like the ones I've heard so many times from Eagle Feather.

I'm now moving quickly toward cabin and the posse. The sheriff and his men jump out of my way at first but then quickly gain composure, and in no time, bullets are slapping against the side of the truck. I have to duck as a bullet flies through the cab and manages to take my hat off. I feel my long hair and four eagle feathers floating in the breeze as I shoot down the dirt road toward the lake.

"Get to the horses, men!" I hear the sheriff yell. "There he goes! After him!"

I hang on for dear life as the old truck lumbers down the bumpy dirt road. But I'm moving pretty good; I'm able to open quite a distance on the posse. Everything's going great until the truck starts to make several popping noises, sobbing as it seems to be running out of power. I look down at the gas gauge and see the needle languishing on E. Fortunately, I'm now just yards from the lake. I jump out of the truck as it comes to a rolling stop.

I run off toward the canoes, but once I reach them, I realize that they are far too large for one person to drag into the water. Instead, I pull the kayak off the blocks it's resting on and manage to easily thrust it into the lake. Grabbing a two-sided paddle, I hop into the seat and start paddling frantically out onto the lake toward the water spirit on the other side. Behind me, I can still hear the not-too-distant pitter-patter of horses' hooves as the posse comes closer and closer to the lake. As I intensify my paddling, water splashes up turbulently, yet I don't seem to be making any headway.

"Calm down. Calm down," I hear my inner voice say. "Paddle in rhythm."

"Thanks," I answer.

I must confess that I really am starting to enjoy having one voice speaking to me rather than the legion of I's. I shuffle myself around so that my back is firmly against the backrest of the seat and place both my feet on the supports at either side of the kayak. I start to paddle in rhythm, and the kayak begins to move along at a nice clip.

When I am about sixty yards out, I hear the report of several rifles, all firing at once. Bullets splash all around me in the water, and some fly just over my head. The posse has reached the beach and opened fire. I now know the true meaning of the expression *sitting duck*. I begin to zigzag the kayak, trying to make myself a much harder target to hit. Nevertheless, despite all the chaos, a calm comes over me once again, and I get the feeling that something will happen to help me on my way. Something will occur that will help me across the lake safely. I don't know exactly what; I just know.

I paddle first left, then to the right as shots land all around me. Just then, as if on cue, a heavy, dense fog descends on the lake. Snugly enveloped in the fog, the kayak and I disappear from the sight of the attackers. The shooting ceases.

Not that I'm not thankful for the fog—I am—but I still have to find that opening in the bulrushes on the other side of the lake. By keeping the sound of the waterfall on my left, I know I'm heading in the right direction. However, the bulrushes engulf the entire side of the lake, and this makes it paramount that I'm able to find that small canal so I can land the kayak on the shore. My plan is just to reach the bulrushes and paddle up and down them until I see the opening.

I happen to glance over my shoulder and see a light way back on the other shore that is starting to move in my direction. They must have commandeered one of the canoes. There's also another light moving around the outskirts of the lake on my right, probably a few of the men on horseback. Those damn lanterns again. How many of those things do they have? We shot them out on two different occasions, and yet here they are again, chasing me to the far side of the lake.

CHAPTER 68

When I reach the other side, I emerge from the fog precisely at the spot where the bulrushes open up. I take this as a stroke of luck, but then again, I've been told that there is no such thing. I paddle hard until I feel the kayak hit the ground, and I push it all the way up onto dry land. I quickly jump out of the kayak and drag it down the shore before shoving it into the bulrushes to conceal it. I don't want my pursuers to see where I have disembarked.

I run up the hill, in the direction of the water spirit totem pole, but I bypass it for the freshwater spring. I stand there washing my face and drinking until I choke. When I've had my fill, I run toward the totem pole, pausing briefly to look back out onto the lake. I can see the light from the canoe, which is now a third of the way across and moving in my direction. Looking to my left, I see that the portion of the posse on horseback has only reached the river of water that flows out from the lake. I know that it will take them a long time to reach me; those in the canoe will be here much sooner. I can only hope that they have trouble making their way through the bulrushes and landing on shore.

On my two previous trips to the water spirit, I heard nothing, and thankfully Eagle Feather and Emma were along to translate the messages I was meant to receive. I sit down and cross my legs as both my teachers instructed me to do on my previous trips. Yet

I hear … nothing. My mind is racing, jumbled from all the events of this night of living hell. I close my eyes and sit for what feels like quite some time, waiting for something to happen. I'm only able to think about the posse arriving on the shore, finding their way through the bulrushes and ultimately to me. Why is nothing happening? Surely by now I should have heard a voice or received some direction. I open my eyes on a couple of occasions, expecting to find myself back in my other life. But each time, I find myself in the same predicament, sitting at the base of the water spirit's totem, anxiously awaiting the posse to overtake me.

I stand up in a panic. Turning toward the lake, I see that the fog is dissipating and that the lanterns from the canoe are now halfway across the lake. And when I turn and look toward the shore, I see that the other part of the posse has crossed the river and is now on my side of the lake. A shiver runs through my entire body.

Now filled with anxiety, knowing that I am running out of time, I begin to pace back and forth in front of the totem pole. Where the hell is all the guidance that Eagle Feather promised me before he disappeared?

"Calm down, calm down," my one true I tells me. "Clear your mind."

I take a deep breath. I remember that I am now a warrior and that a warrior is capable of incredible things. And I remember both times I was here with Eagle Feather and Emma. On both occasions, they gave the water spirit an offering. I obviously forgot this, and given my current, exceptional circumstances, I don't feel like I should be to blame. The water spirit is all-knowing, right? Surely, he's understanding. I have nothing to give. But maybe that's why he's not listening now. Maybe he—or she, or it, or whatever the water spirit is—needs something from me. And obviously, right now I'm in no position to give.

"Are you that selfish?" I yell up to the heavens. "I have no offering." I'm angry at Eagle Feather. He should have known. He should have prepared me for this. How could he have taken me this far only to forsake me when I need him the most? I raise my fists above my shoulders and shake them in rage. It's death for me now. The posse will be on me in no time, and I'll be back in the clearing again. I stop shaking my fists and let them drop, pounding them hopelessly into my hips.

It's then that I feel something. I reach into the right pocket of my coat and pull out a wad of tobacco. Out of the left pocket, I produce a box of wooden matches. *Eagle Feather, you sly dog!* Sure, the jacket is one of his, one that he gave me, but I don't remember feeling either the matches or tobacco in the pockets before. He must have slipped them in at some point. I put the tobacco in the dish reserved for the water spirit's offerings and, for good measure, strike the match John Wayne style. I drop the lit match in the offering bowl, sit back down, and cross my legs. As the smoke billows, I close my eyes, relax, and try to clear my mind.

CHAPTER
69

"Listen to the water. Listen," instructs that voice from deep down within me, and I cast my full attention to the sound of the water as it cascades down into the lake. What I hear is hypnotic. In the speech of the waterfall, I hear the primal violence of the mountain lion that perched atop the chicken coop, the crackling brush of the bear that once chased me, and the derisiveness of my Wise Guy I. But I also hear the serenity of the silent clearing when I first arrived, the voice of Emma, and the impossible tranquility of my one true I. The best way I can describe the feeling is one of peaceful bliss, a blankness in which everything in my universe has found its counterpoint. I sit there for what feels like an eternity. I don't want to break the spell.

Suddenly, like a dying vagrant that has traveled through the desert, found an oasis, and drank until he got his fill, I stand up. When I open my eyes, I remember that Emma said that the water spirit does not speak with voices but with feelings. I recognize that I am not to be sent back to my life there and then. I remember Eagle Feather's insistence that I keep the goal of returning to my former life resolute in my mind and know from his teaching that I must allow the process to unfold. If I do this, the idea will begin to take shape and form and ultimately become reality. And I know that this process is unfolding through this long, dark night.

I now know how the water spirit will offer me the next piece of guidance. I am to walk into the tunnel created by the waterfall and look on its walls. While the images I saw there before were incomprehensible to me at the time, I now know that I am ready for the wisdom they will offer me.

Suddenly, I hear a thud and a series of voices, words that I cannot make out. I recognize it to be the sound of the posse's canoe hitting the shore and scraping the banks of the lake to a halt. From my position, I can see the lantern lights shining through the gap in the bulrushes. The posse has arrived, and I'm making out their disembodied, meaningless voices. It's only a matter of time before they discover my haphazardly hidden kayak.

"Spread out, men. See if you can pick up his trail," I hear the sheriff say. "I want him taken into custody—dead or alive."

I quickly run up to the mouth of the tunnel created by the waterfall. Looking inside, I can see that it is extremely dark. Stepping into the darkness, I trip over something that was leaning on the rock wall. I'm startled and, in the darkness, can't quite make out what I've fallen over. Bending over, I pick up what seems to be a stick, and groping it in the darkness, I feel a rag that has been tied to the top of it. Someone has left me a torch.

I quickly reach into my pocket and again pull out the matches, using them to light the torch. Now with aid of the torch, I am able to move through the tunnel. I soon come across the arrows that I saw the last time, pointing to the other side of the lake. As I walk deeper into the tunnel, the water rushing just over my head, I see the circular carving of trees. But I now notice something I didn't on my last trip: there is a carving of what appears to be a big rock off to the left side but still circumscribed by the trees. I swear that the last time I saw the carving, there was no such rock in the picture.

As I continue to ponder the carving and its new addition, my mind shifts back to my other life. And I'm now more confident than ever that I will return there. I now recognize that the strange images depict the clearing where I first arrived. I have no idea why, but I realize that I need to find my way back there before I can return home.

I look up and to my left and see another carving of an arrow pointing to the other side of the lake. I take this as a sign that my journey must continue in this direction, even though my original trek to the cabin came by way of the opposite side of the lake. As I move through the remainder of the tunnel, in the direction signified by the arrow, I reflect on the fact that it took me a full day to find my way from the clearing to the cabin, and with this unending darkness, it will undoubtedly take me much longer. I need only to make my way back to the river and follow it. But as simple as that sounds, the cavalry chasing me will soon pick up my trail and easily overtake me.

But then again, I get the feeling that something will occur. Don't ask me how. Perhaps it is the new warrior mentality I'm sporting, but I know something will happen. Something that will aid me on my quest.

I come out of the water tunnel on the other side of the lake. While it has aided me a great deal, I know the torch will ultimately give me up. I toss it down into the waterfall, allowing myself to hide in the darkness. I hurriedly move up the bank. When I finally reach the top of the hill where the bank levels off, I freeze in my tracks.

CHAPTER 70

Standing ten yards in front of me are twelve Indian braves mounted on horseback. Like me, they have eagle feathers woven into their hair and war paint splashed across their faces. By the dim light of the moon, I can see the vapor from the horses' breath billowing up in the cool night air. My initial thought is to retreat into the tunnel, but then I'll find myself trapped between these Indians and the posse on the other side. And not only that, I have had enough of being chased through this cold, dark night. My resolve stiffens. I reach into my sash, pull both Colt .45s, and cock the actions. If it must end here, I'm taking a few of them with me.

One of the braves kicks his pony and inches closer to me. I raise my pistols. He stretches out his arm in front of himself, and I can see that he is holding two pieces of a broken arrow. I recognize him as one of the Indians that Eagle Feather spoke too back at the cabin. While I didn't know it at the time, Eagle Feather's breaking the arrow was a sign of peace. I'm relieved to realize that there will be no fighting between us.

I drop my pistols, un-cock both actions, and return them to my sash. The brave motions for me to come closer. It is then that I notice the Indian directly behind him is holding the reins of an unmanned horse. Even through the darkness, I recognize the horse as my horse; it is Sweetheart! I move closer.

The Indian brave begins to speak to me. He speaks in the same language that I heard him speak to Eagle Feather back at the cabin. As he continues, I realize that I can't understand a word he's saying. Nevertheless, he repeats the same phrase over and over again. As I listen attentively, somehow, as if by magic, my mind becomes accustomed to the strange language. Suddenly, I begin to understand him.

"We've come to take you where you want to go," he says. "Wherever you need to go next to fulfill your quest, we are here to help you see it through."

I don't answer. I'm taken aback. Up until this point, I have been told to avoid the Indians. Eagle Feather himself admitted that they are hostile. I'm not quite sure what to make of this sudden turn of events. But then I am reminded of what Eagle Feather told me about these Indians. They are my good I's.

"No longer will we help the townspeople," the Indian with the broken arrow tells me. "They told us that you were sent here to destroy all of us. They told us that we needed to help them, or we too would be destroyed. Thus, we stopped making war on them and joined them to track you. When we met the great war chief Eagle Feather in the cabin, he told us that you are questing to become the one true I, to become that which you really are. He explained that we have nothing to fear from you because we too desire this for you. So, we've come here to take you wherever you need to go."

I begin to speak, but the words that come out of my mouth are inconceivable, even to me. I hear myself speaking in the Indian's native tongue. I tell him that what I truly desire is to return home, back to my other life. I tell him that he can take me there. A look of astonishment comes over his face.

"We have no such power."

I kind of laugh. I didn't think they did, but, hey, I thought I'd give it a shot anyhow. The Indian brave holding the reins of Sweetheart moves forward and hands her over to me. As he does so, he points behind me, in the direction of the water tunnel. As I turn around, I see the curl of water that creates the tunnel illuminated with light. I recognize this to be the posse's lantern. They came up the hill, passed the totem pole, and picked up my trail to the water tunnel.

They are now working their way through to the other side. I quickly mount Sweetheart.

"Where do you want to go?" the Indian with the broken arrow asks. He seems to be their leader.

"I need to go upriver, to a place where the river shrinks into a small stream that runs through a clearing. Do you know this place?"

"Yes," he says. "It is a holy place. It is in this place that we first found the great war chief Eagle Feather."

"Found Eagle Feather?" I say in a voice that must betray my surprise. "My Eagle Feather?"

"The very same."

He kicks his pony, and all the Indian braves follow, as do I. We ride along a flat piece of ground and then down a sharp embankment and into the woods alongside the river. As the darkness swallows us whole, I peer back as the first lantern emerges from the water tunnel. We ride into the dark night, trying to open a gap between us and those damn lanterns that are pursuing us, always keeping the river in sight. We move upstream in the direction of the clearing, the place I know I must reach. I'm not quite sure what I must find when I arrive there, but I'm confident that it holds some clue on how I am to get out of this place.

The Indian braves are excellent horsemen, and we move along the riverbank at a good pace. I'm praying that the posse will be confused when they see all the horse tracks; I wasn't mounted when they initially picked up my trail at the water spirit. I'm hoping against hope that this will be cause for them to pause and allow us to get well out in front of them. Occasionally, I turn back to pick up the flow of the lanterns as they bob up and down through the woods. We seem to be opening quite a margin on them. And the addition of the Indian escort makes me feel much safer than if I were traveling alone. When we appear to be a comfortable distance from the posse, I decide to address the Indian who appears to be their leader.

"How much farther is the clearing?"

"Twelve of your leagues, perhaps more."

"My name is Rich."

"I know."

"What is your name?"

"Running Bear."

So far, not much of a conversationalist, this Running Bear.

"I'm a little afraid of bears," I admit.

"I know," he says again. Then a smile creeps across his face, stretching the war paint on his cheeks. This whole time, he has been riding with only one eye open. "But you have nothing to fear from me. You have nothing to fear from any of these warriors."

"How is it that you know my name?"

"Your coming has been foretold for many moons by Eagle Feather."

"How so? And why do you call Eagle Feather a great war chief?"

"Your many questions have also been foretold for many moons by Eagle Feather."

Running Bear elects to not answer either of my questions, and we ride on for quite some time in silence. Finally, he speaks.

"I will tell you the tale of the great war chief Eagle Feather. Perhaps this will help you to understand. Many moons ago, we came upon Eagle Feather in the clearing, the very same clearing that we now journey to. He was here on his own quest. He told us that he had been sent ahead of a great warrior that was to come. He was merely here to pave the way. To pave the way so that this great warrior could become one. In order to do this, he told us, it was necessary for him to gain much knowledge, specifically the knowledge of how to wrestle control away from the townspeople. Many times, we followed Eagle Feather into battle against the townspeople. Many times, Eagle Feather fought bravely and was vanquished. But then, just as before, we would find him back in the clearing, and his quest would start all over again. Finally, after many attempts and many attacks and many deaths, he came to the realization that the struggle between positive and negative I's would not be won by the physical act of fighting. He came to the realization that the townspeople would have to be dealt with in a different manner. They could not be permanently vanquished. No matter how many times he would engage them in battle, no matter how many he managed to kill, they would always be there. So, you see, the battle did not lie in the physical realm. It was a battle in the mind of the warrior."

"Hold on, hold on, Running Bear. You're telling me that Eagle Feather faced the same problems that I do now. If I understand correctly, every time he was killed, he awoke in the clearing and had to start all over again."

"Yes, that is true," replies Running Bear without turning around. "The Indians have a saying."

"What might that be?"

"It is a very ancient saying," continues Running Bear. "It says 'the spirit comes before us.'"

With that, Running Bear stops talking and turns his horse around, coming to a stop. All the braves follow suit.

"We'll rest the horses and walk for a while," he says. His eye never opens.

With that, he turns and continues on foot, guiding his horse by its reins. I quickly move up alongside Running Bear. I am totally engrossed in his story and want to learn more.

"Tell me more about Eagle Feather."

We continue to walk for quite some time in silence, and finally Running Bear continues the story.

"After many attempts and many new starts, Eagle Feather eventually gained the knowledge that there is a choice to be made. The choice is a simple one in concept but much harder in practice. The only way the townspeople have any power is when a warrior pays attention to them. By giving the townspeople attention, they receive power, and this leads to the confusion of many tongues talking. Thus, it is by denying the townspeople attention that the mind becomes free. And only when the mind is free can the warrior hear the voice of the one true I. Eagle Feather then left us and no longer bothered with the townspeople. He built his cabin in the woods and became a recluse, waiting for the day when the great warrior would come."

Running Bear falls silent, and we walk on for a bit. Finally, I speak up.

"Running Bear, am I the great warrior that you and Eagle Feather speak of?"

Running Bear does not answer. Rather, he turns to the braves and instructs us all to mount up. We continue to ride in the direction of the clearing. As I look back, I see that the lights of our pursuers have picked up considerable ground on us. To make matter's worse,

I am confused and need to think about all the information Running Bear just imparted to me. I decide to press him further.

"If all this is true, I still don't understand why Eagle Feather told me to avoid contact with you. He said that you were not of our lineage and that there would be a fight if we ever came face-to-face."

"Eagle Feather believed that in this quest it is important to first gain control over the I's of confusion. After the mind is clear, it will become easier to recognize and pay attention to the positive I's. For this reason, he told you that we were hostile and that we would fight you to the death. This is far from the truth."

"But Running Bear, is it not true that tonight you both raided the townspeople and later helped them track Eagle Feather and me? I don't quite get it."

Running Bear sits up in his saddle.

"As I said before, we raided the townspeople, trying, as Eagle Feather had, to vanquish them. It is to no avail. You see, we had lost contact with our good friend Eagle Feather. After you arrived in town, the sheriff and the annoying short man came to us and told us that you were not the one that Eagle Feather spoke of. Rather, you were here to destroy us all. Although we knew it was their nature to lie, they deceived us, and so we decided to help them. That is why you saw us tracking you. But when we met Eagle Feather in the cabin, we learned the truth. At that time, we left and would not help them any longer."

We ride on in silence, working our way in the dark through heavy brush. At no time do I recognize any landmarks that I remember from my trip to the cabin. But then again, we are on the opposite side of the river this time. All the while, the lights continue to make up ground on us. Finally, we emerge from the thickets, and there, stretched out in front of us, is the swamp. It is that same swamp that I remember took me so much effort to cross. Running Bear looks back and decides that the only course of action we have is to continue through the swamp; with the lights approaching so quickly, we do not have the time to go around it.

Initially, I think the horses will make traversing the swamp that much easier. But to my surprise, they seem to be sinking in the mud. We move forward a little bit before the decision is made to dismount and make it easier for the horses. One of the braves comes up alongside me and advises me to keep an eye out for quicksand. We continue on like this, riding for a bit, then stopping and dismounting so the horses can free themselves from the mud. All the while this is going on, thoughts continue to run through my mind. While I am now starting to believe that these Indians are indeed my good I's, I have no idea what a good I actually is. Eagle Feather spent so much time discussing the negative I's and how to overcome them that he never delved into the intricacies of the good I's.

Finally, after a while of fighting through the muck, we reach the other side of the swamp, and the ground becomes firmer. We make our way up a small bank and onto a flat portion of land. We are not far from the clearing. A quick glance back shows me the woods illuminated just on the other side of the swamp. While the posse has continued to make up ground, I'm sure they'll have their fair share of difficulty making their way through the swamp.

Running Bear kicks his pony and rides off to find the clearing. The forest on this side of the swamp is sparse, and the riding is easy. Running Bear slows his horse, waiting for Sweetheart and me to come up alongside him. As if he knows what is in my mind, he begins to speak.

"Eagle Feather has done well with you."

"Yes," I say, "there is no more confusion in my mind. I don't hear all the I's speaking anymore."

"That is true," he says. "You have learned well. You have learned to control your mind. The many tongues have stopped."

"I still have one voice that speaks to me."

"This is the voice of the one true I," he begins. "This voice has been with you all along, all through your life. However, you could not hear it well until Eagle Feather taught you to control your attention. Now you have the choice."

"And what choice is that?" I ask.

"You have the choice to control your thoughts. You can give control to the good I's or to the bad, whichever you choose."

We ride on in silence for a while before I speak again. "I choose to listen to the good I's, but to have a choice, Running Bear, I have to know what constitutes a good I. Eagle Feather and I never spoke of them."

Running Bear holds his arm up. All the braves stop as he tells us to dismount and walk a bit to give the horses a break. We walk along for some time in silence before Running Bear resumes the conversation.

"It is time for you to learn that there are two sides to every human being. This is why we made war on the townspeople. And this is also why the townspeople continue to pursue you. They will not give up control over you. But now you have learned the lessons from Eagle Feather, and you are a warrior. Your fate lies in your own hands. So that you can have the choice that I have spoken of, I will tell you about the good I's. The good I's lie very close to emotion. They do not look for control, nor do they cause confusion. They allow the entire being to feel the moment. They are, in fact, quite interchangeable with your emotions. The thought of the good I will produce that I's corresponding emotion. This also works in reverse, as the emotion may invoke the corresponding I. Either way, they are real and whole."

I think about this for a while. "Running Bear, give me some examples of these good I's so that I can understand your meaning better."

"Very well," he answers as he stops walking and looks into my eyes. "Forgiveness, gratitude, compassion, love, generosity, kindness, all positive thoughts."

He continues walking while I try to digest everything. I do see how these I's, all associated with positive, genuine human emotion, would prevent any confusion in my mind.

"There are many, many more. These are just to name a few. The true I lives among them, and a truly great warrior embraces them all," he says.

Just then, a brave comes up to Running Bear and me, riding extremely fast. He informs Running Bear that the posse has made it out of the swamp. Running Bear gives us the signal to mount up and then tells six braves to ride back and disrupt the posse's progress in any way they can. He then sends another rider ahead of us to find a shallow spot to cross the river.

"We will try to slow the posse down enough so that you will have enough time to do whatever it is you need to do once we reach the clearing."

"But, Running Bear," I protest, "I'm not quite sure what I'm supposed to do when I arrive there, and I don't want any of those braves killed on my account."

"Rest assured, the braves that I sent back are tremendous warriors. They will harass the posse with a hit-and-run style rather than fully engaging them. As I have said, we are here to help you, no matter what."

"I just don't want any fighting," I say.

We ride on in silence. Behind me, I hear gunfire. I take this to mean that the Indians have engaged the posse. After some time, Running Bear turns to me.

"As far as what you are to do when you reach the clearing, I'm sure that you will think of something." I look at him with a bewildered expression. As to what I'm supposed to do in the clearing, I have no idea.

Finally, the rider who was sent upriver returns and points upstream. He tells us that we are close to a crossing point. Running Bear tells him to lead the way. I know that we are getting close, and my apprehension is growing. I am hoping that when we make it to the clearing, I will be magically transported back to my other life.

When we reach the crossing point, we easily make our way to the other bank, the river being much smaller than at any other point downriver. Shortly after crossing, we emerge into the clearing. We ride into the middle and dismount. It looks exactly the same as when I first arrived. I spot the big tree that I climbed, trying to ascertain where I was. And there is the big rock that I slept against.

CHAPTER

71

In no time at all, the six braves sent to badger the posse return. I am relieved to see that they have all made it back safely. One of the braves tells Running Bear that the posse is only a league away. They will be on us shortly.

As I stand there, looking back in the direction from which we came, I see the light from those damn lanterns becoming brighter. The posse will be on us in a matter of minutes. Though I feel the urge to turn and run, I know that I must stay in the clearing. The thought of the impending massacre pulses through my mind. It is not a proper vision like the ones I've recently experienced; it is an indescribable melee of semi-chaos. I know that the Indian braves and I will have no chance against the posse. We are outmanned and, quite frankly, outgunned. It's bad enough that I'll be killed and have to start this journey all over again; it's the thought of all my brave companions being slaughtered that I can't stomach. I begin to think of my time in this crazy place with Eagle Feather and Emma. And all that I have learned about myself. My thoughts then drift to my other life, the life that I came from. I reflect on how different a person I'll be if I ever make it back there. At this point, that return seems anything but imminent.

Somehow, I have to change the scenario. I have to prevent this fight from happening. Perhaps the only way to do so is to stop the conflict that has been raging inside of me. I've succeeded in directing my attention and, in doing so, controlling my mind and my thoughts. I learned this lesson so well from Eagle Feather that I no longer hear the multitude of voices that once jockeyed for control over me. Nevertheless, they are still out there, chasing me through this long, dark night.

I begin to realize that what Eagle Feather said is true: these voices will always be a part of me. The choice that Eagle Feather and now Running Bear spoke of is very real. I know that I must accept my I's, both good and bad, and be master over them. This is the peace that I am seeking.

The lights are almost on top of us now. Our pursuers have crossed the river, and the entire forest around the clearing is illuminated. Running Bear directs the warriors to take up positions to repel the onslaught. My mind frantically searches for a solution. In the middle of all this panic, I hear an extremely calm voice: "You have the power. You have the power to divert this whole thing."

"Yeah, and how do I do that?" I ask.

"Think back to the first day you arrived here in the clearing. What struck you? What drew your attention that day?"

My mind flashes back to my arrival in the clearing. I remember the pure panic that I felt. I remember scaling the tree and trying to find a way out. I remember the anxiety that I felt being swept away from my other life and deposited here, without warning, in the blink of an eye. It was only when my anxiety abates a little that I remember the beauty of the clearing.

"Come on, think!" I beg myself.

Then I remember. I remember the sunlight. The golden sunlight that made its way into the clearing on that first day and animated all the life and beauty of this strange land. I concentrate on that moment, visualizing the sunlight in my mind's eye.

The lights from the posse lanterns are suddenly extinguished, and the clearing and surrounding forest go black. I can hear the men moving around the clearing in a circular fashion, and I know that we are now surrounded. I fully expect the clearing to be filled with a tempest of bullets at any minute. Nevertheless, I stand in the center of the clearing and visualize the sun. I take some small comfort that I will soon reawaken in that clearing, alone again with that beautiful sunshine. "Make a stand," I hear.

CHAPTER

72

Suddenly, light begins to peek through the trees, becoming brighter and brighter. To my astonishment, the sun is rising. As I gaze out into the woods around me, I see the sheriff, the deputies, and all his townspeople staring out at me. Like ghosts, they become transparent before fading away into nothingness. The last of my I's to fade is the wise guy. Our eyes meet, and he lifts his arm, sheepishly waving goodbye before he too vanishes into mist. I'm not entirely sure, but I think I catch a glimpse of a smile on his face as he disappears. I hear the woodpecker once again hammering away on a nearby tree branch.

The sun is up. I've made it through the night and avoided a massacre. The Indian warriors all come out of their positions and circle around me. A sense of relief comes over all of us.

"You truly are a great warrior," Running Bear says with a grin. "Eagle Feather was right about you. You are the one he has waited for, the one sent ahead. And he has shown you the way. Our time here with you in this life has come to an end. We have played our part, and you have played yours."

"Running Bear, why do you have to leave?" I ask sadly.

"We have fulfilled our part in your quest, and now we must return to the source. The source of all that is."

"Yes, yes, I've heard of the source." Emma, Eagle Feather, even the dogs all returned to the source. "Can't you take me with you?"

An astonished look comes over Running Bear's face. He then begins to chuckle. "The source cannot return to itself. Just as a baby cannot return to its mother's womb."

"What exactly is this source that you speak of?"

"The source is the creator. It has created all that you see. The source creates the animals, the trees, the moon, the sun, and even the earth. Without the source, there is nothing. So, we must leave as we are directed."

I want to ask the obvious question: where is this source that he, Emma, and Eagle Feather have spoken of? But the austere look on his face prevents me from asking it.

"A warrior always finds a way," he says. "And a great warrior such as yourself will undoubtedly find a way."

With that, he and all the great warriors circle around me and begin to glow, just as Eagle Feather did before his disappearance.

"Before I go," Running Bear says, "I have one last thing to tell you. It is a message from Eagle Feather. The great war chief Eagle Feather wanted me to tell you that X marks the spot."

"X marks the spot? What am I, a pirate now?"

Running Bear begins to laugh. "This is the message. I have delivered it to you as I promised Eagle Feather."

"Can you tell me anything else?" I plead.

"I can tell you one thing more. After Eagle Feather instructed me to give you this message, he laughed uproariously, much like a woodpecker."

CHAPTER 73

I watch as Running Bear and all the Indian braves slowly fade into nothingness. I am now alone in the clearing, just as I was when I first arrived here. I have come full circle, and yet my intuition is still telling me that it will end here, just as it started. I move over and sit with my back up against the rock. It is a familiar position for me; it's how I slept for my first three days in this strange place. I am exhausted by the events of the long night. While sleep does its best to overtake me, my mind remains restless. Eagle Feather suggested that my thoughts dictated reality. And Running Bear said that the source creates. Am I the source? Did I will the sun to rise? Could I have just created everything and everyone in this strange place? Maybe reality, be it here or even back in my other life, exists only in my mind. The sun is up high in the sky now, and the rock that I'm leaning on—and indeed the whole clearing—is bathed in the warm golden sunlight.

"X marks the spot," I repeat.

Sure, Eagle Feather was a bit of clown the entire time I spent with him. But I know that he often laughed after passing on knowledge; this is definitely a legitimate clue. It now seems quite clear from the time I discovered the backpack to the time I answered the cellphone and up until now, Eagle Feather has been the author of every event, including his getting thrown into jail. If I hadn't spent so much time chopping wood, I'd have never been able to hide behind those woodpiles and escape the cabin. And how did the Indian braves know to find me on the other side of the waterfall after my trip to the water spirit?

I remember the Indian expression that "the spirit goes before you," and I am suddenly terrified by the possibility that the posse will be back here when night falls. Do I really have only one day to find this damn X? And when I first found myself here, I had a backpack full of provisions. Now I don't have crap. And there is that "friend" that Eagle Feather told me would help me end my journey. Where the hell is that friend now, when I need him the most?

The only logical step is to look for this X. But where is it? Is it in the clearing or out in the surrounding woods? Am I completely off base and it's a hundred miles from here? Well, at the very least, if I only have until nightfall, I better get cracking. I stand up and make a loop around the clearing, looking for anything that might be an X. I search the ground of the entire clearing, looking at rocks, trees, the earth, anything that might be the X and might get me back home. I search the perimeter just outside the clearing but find nothing that remotely looks like an X.

It is just like Eagle Feather to be so vague. I decide to widen my search, venturing into the woods and even straying quite a bit from the clearing. Having no luck, I come back closer to the clearing and search around the base of the tree that I climbed that first day. All the while, I repeat what I have been told: "X marks the spot." I search all around the large rock that I slept against, including the rock's flat top. I move over to the stream where I saw the trout and search all along its banks. And here I find … nothing. Absolutely nothing.

Night is coming on quickly. Hunger begins to pain my stomach, and pure exhaustion renders my feet heavier with each step. I don't want to find myself back in the situation I've just left; I've had enough of the posse, and now, when darkness falls, I'll have to deal with them alone, without my Indian brave benefactors. Exasperated, I collapse again against the base of the giant rock. I remember Running Bear telling me that a warrior always finds a way, and while I've remained hopeful throughout my search, frustration has begun to creep in. Where in God's name can that X be?

"On the day you arrived here, where were you standing?" I suddenly hear my one true I say.

I jump up. That's it! I look around the clearing, trying to remember where I was first standing when I found myself in this strange land. Suddenly, a torrential blast of wind whips through the calm day and the clearing, scattering the leaves on the ground as it makes its way back into the forest. This leaves the floor of the clearing exposed. I now remember that I was at the center of the clearing when I first came to my senses after being deposited here. And turning my attention there, lo and behold, I see several rocks on the otherwise bare clearing floor configured in the shape on an X.

"X marks the spot," I say.

I've found it, but now what? Maybe if I stand right in the center of the X, I'll be whisked back to my life? I approach the spot tenuously and put my left foot in the center, followed by my right, so that I'm standing in the dead center of the X. Nothing. I close my eyes and concentrate for five minutes—and still nothing.

"C'mon," I say. "Tell me something." But I hear nothing.

I begin to think of all the pirate movies I've ever seen and back to my childhood playing pirate on Croton Street. X always marks the spot where treasure is *buried*. I look at the dirt around my feet and can see that it's obviously been disturbed. Pulling the tomahawk from my sash and kicking the rocks aside, I begin to work the earth. First, I use the tomahawk as a pick before turning it sideways and scraping the loose dirt away. After I'm three feet down, becoming disheartened and contemplating giving up, I strike something solid. I swing again and quickly realize that it's metal I'm hitting. A few more swings, and I have the item in question dislodged. It is, believe it or not, another can of Boston baked beans!

It is the same kind I had when I arrived here and the same kind Eagle Feather and I dined on ad nauseam. I pick myself up and stagger over to the rock with my buried treasure. Boston baked beans! Delicious! At least I won't starve to death ... not just yet anyway. I strike the top of the can with the tomahawk to open it. And when I look inside ... no beans.

I tip the can upside down, and a piece of paper falls out. I flick my wrist to open it and send some residual dirt flying.

"Call your friend the hawk," says the note, and it is initialed EF.

I have to laugh. Guess Eagle Feather picked up a trick or two from me, and now he's the one writing the notes. I read it again, this time out loud. Now, I've never had to call a hawk before; needless to say, I have no idea how to go about it.

"Hawk! Hawk! Come here, hawk!" I yell, as if I'm calling my dog, Oliver. I look up above the tree line and into the sky. I continue to call the hawk in the same fashion, and it's getting me nowhere. I sit back down against the rock.

"No, no, no," I hear the voice of my one true I tell me. He is laughing at me. "You can't call the hawk verbally. Visualize. See."

So, I begin to visualize the hawk, just as I did with the sun. Off in the distance, I hear a screech, yet I don't let it break me from my meditation. I continue to visualize the hawk, and the screech grows louder and louder. When I finally break from my concentration and open my eyes, I spot the hawk sitting on a branch above me, high up in the canopy of trees. He takes flight, spreading his majestic wings and soaring in circles around me before landing again on a branch off to my left.

"Hello there, Mr. Hawk. Been a while since I've seen you. I suppose you're the friend that's supposed to help me end my journey?"

The hawk swoops down and perches on a rock just a few feet away. I get up slowly and approach him, being cautious not to spook him. But as I get closer, I can see that he seems calm, and I'm very glad to see him.

"Well, Mr. Hawk, I must say it's been quite an adventure. But I can honestly say that I think it's time that I get back now. If you can help me in any way, I'd be much obliged."

He turns and hops over, even closer to me. I look at him, and my eyes meet his steely gaze. I become transfixed, unable to move or speak for some time. Somehow, in this paralysis, I feel whole. I feel whole with myself and with nature. I understand my power; I am a warrior. I am the architect of all around me. The hawk's gaze becomes deeper and deeper until I can perceive nothing else around him.

I feel as though I am being whisked away through a tunnel of sorts. I'm moving faster and faster, the tunnel twirling around me, or me around it; I can't be quite sure which. Off in the distance, I hear a voice saying something, though I can't quite understand what. I am now moving so fast that I doubt I even exist any longer. I seem now to exist only as my awareness. The voice persists, and still I cannot quite hear what it is saying. I travel ever faster, my whole life passing simultaneously in front of me.

And finally, I can hear that voice clearly. And I understand what it is saying.

"Get your racket back. Get your racket back. Good, good."